WITHDRAWN

WITNESS IN HEAVEN

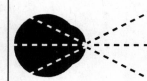

This Large Print Book carries the
Seal of Approval of N.A.V.H.

APPOMATTOX SAGA

WITNESS IN HEAVEN

1863-1864

GILBERT MORRIS

THORNDIKE PRESS
A part of Gale, Cengage Learning

GALE
CENGAGE Learning·

Farmington Hills, Mich • San Francisco • New York • Waterville, Maine
Meriden, Conn • Mason, Ohio • Chicago

GALE
CENGAGE Learning®

LIBRARY OF CONGRESS CATALOGING-IN-PUBLICATION DATA

Morris, Gilbert.
   Witness in heaven / by Gilbert Morris. — Large print edition.
      pages ; cm. — (Appomattox saga, 1863–1864) (Thorndike Press large
   print Christian historical fiction)
      ISBN 978-1-4104-6645-7 (hardcover) — ISBN 1-4104-6645-0 (hardcover)
      1. Virginia—History—Civil War, 1861-1865—Fiction. 2. Young
   women—Fiction. 3. Large type books. I. Title.
   PS3563.O8742W58 2014
   813'.54—dc23   2014026580

Published in 2014 by arrangement with Barbour Publishing, Inc.

Printed in Mexico
1 2 3 4 5 6 7 18 17 16 15 14

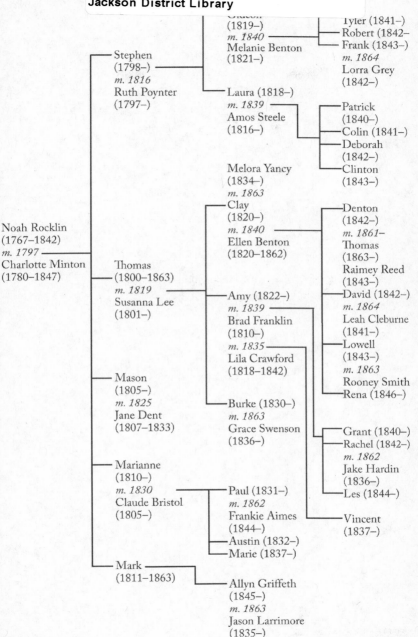

Gideon
(1819–)
m. 1840
Melanie Benton
(1821–)

Tyler (1841–)
Robert (1842–)
Frank (1843–)
m. 1864
Lorra Grey
(1842–)

Stephen
(1798–)
m. 1816
Ruth Poynter
(1797–)

Laura (1818–)
m. 1839
Amos Steele
(1816–)

Patrick
(1840–)
Colin (1841–)
Deborah
(1842–)
Clinton
(1843–)

Melora Yancy
(1834–)
m. 1863

Clay
(1820–)
m. 1840
Ellen Benton
(1820–1862)

Denton
(1842–)
m. 1861–
Thomas
(1863–)
Raimey Reed
(1843–)

Noah Rocklin
(1767–1842)
m. 1797
Charlotte Minton
(1780–1847)

Thomas
(1800–1863)
m. 1819
Susanna Lee
(1801–)

Amy (1822–)
m. 1839
Brad Franklin
(1810–)
m. 1835
Lila Crawford
(1818–1842)

David (1842–)
m. 1864
Leah Cleburne
(1841–)
Lowell
(1843–)
m. 1863
Rooney Smith
Rena (1846–)

Mason
(1805–)
m. 1825
Jane Dent
(1807–1833)

Burke (1830–)
m. 1863
Grace Swenson
(1836–)

Grant (1840–)
Rachel (1842–)
m. 1862
Jake Hardin
(1836–)
Les (1844–)

Marianne
(1810–)
m. 1830
Claude Bristol
(1805–)

Paul (1831–)
m. 1862
Frankie Aimes
(1844–)
Austin (1832–)
Marie (1837–)

Vincent
(1837–)

Mark
(1811–1863)

Allyn Griffeth
(1845–)
m. 1863
Jason Larrimore
(1835–)

GENEALOGY OF THE YANCY FAMILY

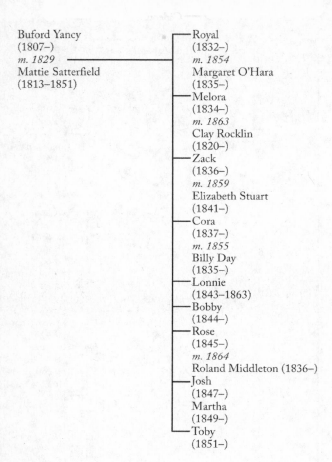

Buford Yancy
(1807–)
m. 1829
Mattie Satterfield
(1813–1851)

Royal
(1832–)
m. 1854
Margaret O'Hara
(1835–)

Melora
(1834–)
m. 1863
Clay Rocklin
(1820–)

Zack
(1836–)
m. 1859
Elizabeth Stuart
(1841–)

Cora
(1837–)
m. 1855
Billy Day
(1835–)

Lonnie
(1843–1863)

Bobby
(1844–)

Rose
(1845–)
m. 1864
Roland Middleton (1836–)

Josh
(1847–)

Martha
(1849–)

Toby
(1851–)

■ ■ ■ ■

PART ONE:
DREAM OF A MAN

■ ■ ■ ■

CHAPTER 1
MEMORIES

As the stars rested in the velvet canopy over the mountains, faint pulses of light from the east began to dilute the cold blackness of the earth, revealing a still figure wrapped in a single blanket. On every side the narrow valley, surrounded by tall, craggy peaks, turned amber and crimson, the light streaming over the tops of the sentinel-like peaks that glittered like icy diamonds. The shadows from the cliff disappeared as the sun stained the earth gray.

As the staccato drumming of a woodpecker broke the silence, Charlie Peace rose from her blanket, throwing it back with a quick gesture, and when she was upright, stamped her feet. Worn buckskin pants were stuffed into knee-high elkskin boots. As she moved to fold up her blanket, the fringe of her soft deerskin hunting shirt swayed gently. Picking up a coonskin cap, she clapped it on her head then stared around her at the dense stand of fir that covered the mountainside. For a moment she considered cooking a hot breakfast, then murmured, "Ain't no time for that if I intend to get me an elk."

She moved to the horse that was staked away from her blanket, patted him on the nose, and asked, "You hungry, Sonny?" She laughed when the horse nickered, and she pulled out a pouch of feed, pouring it on the ground. "You wait here, and I'll be a-comin' back to get you to haul me and my elk back home." She patted the animal on the shoulder then picked up her knife, a pouch, and her rifle that leaned against a tree. Quickly she checked the priming, found it dry, then left her camp.

As Charlie moved through the trees, her feet making no sound on the thick carpet of needles, her eyes were constantly in motion. They were the darkest possible blue, and the short-cropped, curly hair that fell out of her cap was a deep black. She had high cheekbones and olive skin, part of her Crow ancestry, and a wide mouth set in an oval face. At age eighteen, she was a strong-bodied young woman.

At dusk the night before, she had located a watering hole with an abundance of tracks — elk, deer, and mountain lion — so she was confident of making her kill. She took long strides to cover the ground rapidly, her feet avoiding rocks and dry sticks that might snap and alert the game she sought. Now as she approached the stream, she stopped, tested the air, then stepped past a grove of towering blue spruce so as to come in downwind. She moved cautiously, stopping once for more than five minutes, remaining so motionless she might have been one of the trees, or even one of the stones that glittered in an outcropping behind her. Patience was part of her makeup, for her father had taught her that only patience can bring down the game. "You got to learn to set still, Charlie," he had told her when she was but a girl. "Try to turn yourself into one of them stones. Don't move no more, nor even breathe no more'n you can help."

Slowly she worked her way in behind a clump of stunted firs, so crowded they could not attain their full growth. Her eyes narrowed as she settled down, the rifle cradled in her arms, ready to be aimed at once.

At first nothing happened, except a black squirrel ran out along an extended branch over her head. Looking down, he chattered at her angrily to leave his domain. The brisk wind that rustled the pine needles overhead was the only sound then for a time — until

11

a faint rustling reached her. She pulled the hammer back on the rifle and half turned to face the creek. For a time she saw nothing, but she knew how shy these animals were. Finally, a flash of movement caught her eye, and a six-point mule deer stepped out of the shadows of the timber and halted, head high. He seemed frozen for a time as his nostrils flared, testing for scent. Satisfied all was well, he moved forward to the water and lowered his head to drink.

Disappointed it was a deer instead of an elk, Charlie decided to still take the shot. Moving almost imperceptibly with the rifle lowered, she waited until the bead was on the side of the buck by his heart. Then she pulled the trigger. The kick of the rifle jolted her arm and lifted the barrel several inches, but she saw the buck fall sideways to the ground. He kicked wildly, staggered to his feet, then ran toward the woods. He had not gone more than a dozen steps, however, when he fell to the earth, his antlers crashing against the stones that lined the stream.

Charlie smiled with satisfaction. "You ain't no elk, but you'll be prime good eatin'," she said. Speaking aloud to herself was a habit she had formed from being alone so much of the time. Aside from her parents, there was no one for her to talk to

— no brothers or sisters. So she talked to her horse, her dog, and herself.

Reaching into the pouch at her side, she reloaded the rifle. Pouring the powder into the barrel, ramming the ball on top of it, and then adding the powder to the pan to explode the charge took less than thirty seconds; then she rose and walked to the stream. The deer was on the far side. Since she didn't want to get her feet wet, she moved down until she found a narrow spot studded with rocks that could serve as a walkway. Lightly holding the rifle, she skipped across then walked to where the deer lay, his eyes already glazed. Leaning the rifle carefully against the trunk of a dead fir, she pulled a large knife from its sheath and expertly skinned the deer. Rising, she washed her hands in the stream, replaced the knife, then grabbed her rifle and headed back to camp. Throwing the saddle on Sonny, she said, "Got us a good 'un, Sonny. Too bad you cain't bite up on deer meat. It's plumb good, but not for hosses, I guess."

She threw her gear onto the horse behind the saddle, stepped aboard in an easy motion, then drove the big bay at a gallop through the forest. When she reached the deer, she tied Sonny up and again leaned the rifle against the tree. Then she began to put portions of meat into the aged, rank-smelling canvas bags she had brought for this purpose. Her mind was so engrossed with the task that it took Sonny's shrill neighing to catch her attention.

Fear shot through her nerves as she turned, for there, emerging from the thicket, was one of the largest grizzly bears she had ever seen! Lean from hibernation, he still looked monstrous. *It's too early for bears to be out,* she thought wildly, but there was no time. The bear was no more than forty feet away and coming at her with incredible speed.

Charlie Peace had spent her life in the woods and had had her share of close calls. Acting on pure reflex, she leaped for the rifle, glad she always kept her rifle primed. Sonny had broken loose and was running away, but she paid no heed. She threw the rifle to her shoulder, putting the sight right on the bear's mouth. Bears could be hit by half a dozen bullets and not be killed, so she knew it had to be a head shot. If she missed, she would be mauled and probably killed. In the few seconds she had left, she steadied her arms and hands and, as her father had taught her, gently squeezed the trigger. The powder exploded, kicking the barrel up, and Charlie at once turned to run in case she had missed.

But she had not missed. The bullet took the bear right in the open mouth, driving upward through his brain. He took four or five more paces; then his front legs collapsed and he rolled over, awkwardly coming to rest not ten feet from where Charlie stood. Blood stained the back of his head, and his paws made paddling motions for a few moments then grew still.

Staring down at the dead grizzly, Charlie slowly lowered the rifle until the butt of it rested on the ground. Her breath began to come faster then, and she swallowed hard. "Wal now. That was a mite close!" Her voice was somewhat hoarse and sounded overly loud in the stillness of the glade. She smelled the burning powder and heard far off the sound of Sonny as he continued to run through the thickets. But as she looked down, pride swept through her. "Reckon Pa would have been proud of that shot," she whispered. Reaction came then, and her hands began to tremble. *I didn't think nothin' could do that to me,* she thought. *But a full-grown grizzly about to tear your heart out — I calculate even most men would be a little shook up by that.*

She whipped her hat off and wiped her damp forehead. Then she loaded the rifle

15

again before marching off in the direction Sonny had gone. He had not gone far and came back to her call, somewhat skittish. Charlie waited until he was calm. "Reckon you'll have to tote double, because I intend to bring some of that bear meat back to Ma. She always was partial to bear liver. Come on now. I'll skin the critter, and you haul 'em both back."

The cabin that Noah Peace had built for his wife was far better than most found in the rugged mountains. He had built it himself without any help, out of the blue spruce that abounded on the Rockies, and now as he sat in a chair built out of oak that he had hauled from the lowlands, he still felt as he had nineteen years ago when he had first notched the logs and raised them. Noah, a tall, rangy man of fifty with dark blue eyes, a short beard, and a thick growth of auburn hair sprinkled with gray, was not a man who thought deeply. His life in the Colorado mountains had tempered him, and he had lived with the seasons, enduring the frigid blast of winter, often snowed in for weeks at a time. As he glanced over toward the woman who sat across the room, reading by the light that streamed in through the window, his mind went back to the time he had brought her from the western plains to the high mountains. Naomi had been the most beautiful woman he had ever seen, one-half Crow, the other half white — her father a mountain man named Dollar, who had been killed by a hostile tribe. But now whatever disease was attacking her had weakened her and dulled her coppery skin. *She's worse,* he thought, studying her countenance, and sadness flooded through him. *She's gettin' weaker every day. I've got to get her to a doctor or somethin' — though I never had no use for 'em.*

Naomi Peace looked up from the Bible she was reading and caught her husband's glance. She was an astute woman and knew that the sickness she had was more serious than any of them had thought at first. Seeing the concern in Noah's eyes, she smiled faintly. "I'll feel better now that spring is almost here."

"Why, shore you will." Getting up from his chair, he came over, knelt down beside her, and took up her hand, thinking how thin it was and remembering how strong and plump it had been before the sickness had come. Awkwardly he raised it to his lips and kissed it, bringing a look of astonishment into Naomi's eyes. "Well," he said,

17

"I'm gettin' to be quite a Romeo, ain't I now?"

Squeezing the big hand that held hers, Naomi said nothing for a moment. Silence was customary with her, though she often sang as she worked in the cabin and outside in the garden — sometimes the old songs of her people, other times the hymns she had learned at the missionary school where she had been when Noah had come by and seen her. The memory of that day flooded back to her, bringing warmth.

The sun was bright, and the mission school was surrounded by young women working in the garden, some of them washing clothes in a big black pot. Naomi had been hoeing beans, and she had looked up when a shadow had fallen across her. A big man with the bluest eyes she had ever seen and a rash grin looked down at her from a tall buckskin horse. He wore faded blue trousers, a deep blue shirt, and a gaudy yellow neckerchief. For a long time he said nothing; then he slipped off his horse and stood before her, so tall she had to look up. She had waited for him to speak, and when he had, his voice had a softness unusual in the men she knew. He had said, "Howdy, miss. My name's Noah Peace."

The memory remained rich and full in her

heart, making her happy. She put her hand out and brushed back a lock of his auburn hair. "You're getting gray," she said.

"Yep, you're married to an old man."

Naomi smiled and let her hand remain on his cheek. They stayed there for a moment, and then a pain took her. To conceal it from him, she took her hand back and said, "I wish Charlene would come back." Naomi always called her daughter by her given name instead of her nickname, Charlie.

"I 'spect she'll be gettin' on home. I told her not to stay out more'n one night."

Noah straightened and walked toward the window. It was midafternoon, and the blue sky seemed hard enough to strike a match on. The snow was melted, except for the high peaks, and spring would soon be here, although the winds were still numbing. He stood quietly for a while then leaned back against the wall of the cabin. Looking down, he said, "I'm gonna take you down to town to have the doctor take a look at you, Naomi."

"If you say so, but I doubt it will help."

Concern flared in Noah's eyes. He opened his mouth, but one look at her face caused him to cut off the words. Naomi was a firm woman; he had long known that, and he could not break through the Indian part of her. So he walked the floor nervously then stepped outside the cabin and did the afternoon chores. He had just finished them when he heard a shout and looked up to see Charlie riding in from the trail at full gallop. She brought her big bay to a stop and slid off in one fluid motion, her eyes bright with pleasure.

" 'Bout time you was gettin' home, Charlie."

"Pa, I got a six-point buck — and guess what else?"

"Couldn't venture a guess."

"A bear."

"You shot a bear? Didn't know they was out of their winterin' yet."

"This'n was. He's plumb skinny, but I brought some of it home with me."

"How'd you nail him, Charlie?" He stood there proudly as she related the story of her hunt, her face mirroring her excitement, the small dimple appearing at the left side of her mouth. As she spoke, he saw the hint of her will that revealed itself in her eyes and lips — features that showed the swift changes of her mind.

"I brung the head in, Pa," she said, pulling a smaller canvas sack off the horse. "Look, he had his mouth open, and I put the bullet right inside it. Came out the back here, see?"

Taking the head, he studied it then drawled, "I reckon you done good. I couldna done better myself, daughter."

"I'll go show it to Ma."

"Well, she ain't feelin' the best right now, Charlie. Maybe later." Her dark blue eyes, so much like his own, reflected unhappiness whenever Naomi's illness was mentioned. She did not argue but nodded, and he said, "I'll unpack the meat. You go set by her a spell. I reckon she'd like that."

"All right, Pa."

As she turned to go, Noah called her back. "Charlie, I been thinkin' a lot about you and your ma — the way we live out here."

Puzzled, Charlie looked up into her father's eyes. He was, she knew, a man who reasoned things out slowly and could not be rushed into quick talk. It was a way he had of going logically from one fact to another, and now as she waited, she felt a rush of affection for him. She could not remember a time when he was not by her side. When she was barely able to walk, he had taken her into the woods and taught her the language of the forest, the names of the trees, the tracks of the animals, and every bird in the mountains. Now she saw something was troubling him.

21

"I think I made a mistake buryin' us out here in these mountains," Noah said finally.

"Why, Pa, it's a good life."

"Maybe for a mountain man or Indians, but you ain't neither one of 'em."

"I'm part Indian," Charlie said quickly, proud of her Indian heritage. She lifted her head and studied her father carefully, then touched his arm in an unaccustomed gesture. "What's the matter, Pa?"

"Well, this ain't no life for a young woman," Noah said. "You don't never get to go to dances or wear pretty clothes. You don't learn how to sew or do things that young women do. Back when I was a younker growin' up in Virginia, I didn't live in no big mansion, but I worked for Mr. David Radke. Had him a big plantation and a passel of daughters. I'd go by there, Charlie, and there'd be all them girls dressed in pretty white, yellow, and blue dresses. They'd be out on the lawn sometimes havin' a party, their hair all done up, and there'd be young fellers comin' by in carriages and on fine-blooded horses. They'd be dressed real fine, and you shoulda heard 'em laugh and sing and dance, too. I went to one of them dances. Not personal, you understand, but I seen it. The floor was shiny, and Mr. Radke's house had chandeliers overhead with lots of candles, and music with fiddles playin'. It was real nice, Charlie."

"I guess it was, but it's nice out here, too." An impudent light flickered in her eyes. "I bet one of them girls couldna shot that bear like I did with him a-chargin'."

"Likely they couldn't," Noah said, smiling. Then he continued, "I been worried about it. This ain't no life for a young woman."

"I wouldn't want to be nowheres else, Pa." Charlie studied her father's face, not knowing what else to say. He had never talked like this before, although he often talked of his boyhood and young manhood in Virginia. She had asked him once, "Do you wish you'd stayed in Virginia, Pa?" And he had replied slowly, "I don't reckon so, daughter. I always loved the mountains." Now, however, she saw a longing and an unhappiness on his lean face but did not know how to speak to it. Although they were close, this was something she had not learned how to handle. "I'll go in and set with Ma a spell, then fix us a bite of supper." And she walked inside and sat beside her mother, telling her about the hunt, all the while wondering what her father was thinking and why he was so disturbed.

■ ■ ■ ■

Charlie was sitting cross-legged on her narrow bed with a turkey quill in one hand and a large tablet on her knees. She studied the date then nodded in self-approval at the writing. Although Naomi had learned how to write at the mission school, Charlie had not taken well to instruction up to this point, preferring to hunt and trap with her father rather than study with her mother. Now she attacked the job of writing as she did everything else where skill was lacking — with determination. Dipping the turkey quill in the inkwell, which was set on a shelf nailed into the wall beside her bed, she began to write, the quill scratching as it moved across the paper. Her tongue, from time to time, would creep out from between her lips as a particularly hard word had to be written, and her brow would wrinkle.

February 17, 1863

Ma aint doin well atall. I worry bout her somethin awful. She is losin wait, and you can see it in her face and in her neck. She caint eat much and I can tell she hurts real bad — which makes me hurt, too. Pa says he is goin to take her to town to see the doctor, though he dont have much confidense.

Irritation swept through her as she tried to spell through *confidence* in her head several times and then finally shrugged. "It don't make no never mind. I can tell what it is, and ain't nobody else gonna read this here diary anyhow." She steadfastly plowed on through bad spelling and grammar.

Pa has got me worriet. Ever since I kilt the bear last week, he aint said hardly two words together. Its the way he is when he is thinkin bout somethin, and there aint no way to hurry him up. I wisht he would tell me what it is cause its more worry to me not nowin than it would be nowin whatever it is. Maybe he is just worriet about Ma, but then, I am, too.

Pete Ledbetter come by yesterday. He brought a quarter of a deer he had kilt, but I reckon as how that was just an excuse. I been suspectin him for some time of wantin to get his hands on me, and yesterday he done it. We was out at the corn crib, and I was showin him the new shoat. He said he wanted to see it.

Well, theys mighty fine shoats if I do say so my own self, and I raised em all by hand. When we went out there I was just fixin to show him the shoats when he reached out, grabbed me, and hugged me, and would have kissed me right on the mouth, but I just had time to turn my head. I got mad at Pete. I swung on him and hit him smack in the eye as hard as I could. He went a staggerin back and then got mad, askin me what kind of a girl I was that didnt want to be kissed. I told him I would be the one to say when there was a kissin to be did, and if he tried it again I would black his other eye. He went roarin off, and when Pa came out and asked what happened, I told him. He laughed at me, which I didnt like, and said, "You might as well get used to men wantin to sweeten up to you," and I told him it wouldnt be Pete Ledbetter anyway.

Before Charlie could start another sentence her father called from downstairs. "Charlie, come down here, will you?"
She took a little box of fine sand she had gotten from the bed of the river, sprinkled it over the red ink, and then swished it around the paper before blowing it off on

the floor. Then she carefully closed the tablet, put it back on the shelf, wiped the turkey quill off, and capped the bottle of ink. Springing off the bed in bare feet, she started down the ladder, jumping the last six steps and hitting the puncheon floor with a slap.

"You're gonna break your ankles jumpin' out of that attic. I done warned you about it," her father said mildly.

"What you want, Pa?"

"Guess I want to talk to you. Come on over here and sit down. Me and your ma got somethin' to say."

Alarmed, Charlie sat down on a stool before the fireplace. The fire had burned down to glowing coals that radiated heat throughout the cabin. She glanced over at her mother, huddled in a blanket, and saw that her face was stiff and unnatural.

"Charlie, I been doin' a lot of thinkin' all week long, and I done made up my mind about somethin'." Noah glanced over at Naomi and paused, but she said nothing. "Your ma don't quite agree with me on this, but it's somethin' I guess I gotta do." He stood up, back stiff, and went over to the window and looked out. It was an involuntary action, for he was an outdoorsman, and the cabin was confining to him. "It's like this, Charlie. I been considerin' that this kind of life ain't no good for a young girl. I done told you that."

"Pa, I like it here. I don't wanna go nowheres else."

"That's what you say because you never been nowhere else. But you cain't live out here the rest of your life, or you'll have to marry up with somebody like Pete Ledbetter."

"That no-account! I wouldn't have him on a bet!"

"That's all there is around here, trappers and hunters. Some of 'em is mighty fine men, but rough." Noah struggled to put his thoughts into words and finally threw his hands apart in an impulsive gesture that showed his unhappiness. "I been thinkin' 'bout what it was like when I grew up, about them planters back in Virginia around Richmond, and I done decided the best thing to do is to go there."

"You mean — live there? What will we do in Richmond? That's a town, ain't it? It ain't woods like this, and mountains."

"That's right, and that's where you need to be. But the trouble is, I ain't got the money to buy a plantation."

"Then we cain't go," Charlie said swiftly. "I don't keer, Pa. I'm all right here. Me and

Ma like it, don't we, Ma?"

"Your pa has always dreamed of goin' back there." Naomi's voice was low, for this was not one of her good days. She had listened as Noah had explained what he intended to do, and now her Indian blood came to the forefront. She would no more have thought of arguing with him than she would have reached out to strike the sun. "Perhaps he's right. This is a wild place, and you have no hopes here."

"That's what I say," Noah replied. "What I got to do is to make some money."

"You mean trappin'?"

"No, there ain't no money in that. The fur trade is dead." Noah leaned forward, his eyes alight as memories came back. "Before your ma and I married, my friend Lavelle Cole and I went out to Denver huntin' for gold."

"Did you find it?"

"Well, there was lots of gold found all over the West, but it got so bad that the people come floodin' in from everywhere, and I couldn't stand it no more, so I came to the mountains."

"But ain't all the gold took?" Charlie demanded.

"Most of it is, but me and Lavelle went out chasin' some of them creeks back a ways. And, Charlie, we found good color. But Lavelle, he took sick, and I had to bring him back. The poor feller died two months after we got back here to the mountains. I always intended to go back and get that gold."

"You mean we're gonna go gold huntin'?"

"Not *we,* Charlie," Noah said. "Just me. I'm gonna go back and pan enough gold to buy us a plantation in Virginia."

Charlie could not have been more surprised. She shifted her glance to her mother, but Naomi's head was down. Charlie wanted to argue, but she knew her father well. He was indulgent toward her, but from time to time he would speak in a certain tone, and fire would flash from his eyes. When that happened — as it had now — Charlie knew protesting would be foolish.

"All right, Pa. I'll stay here and take care of Ma while you're gone."

Relief flooded Noah Peace, and he expelled his breath with a rush. "That's my girl." He came over and caressed her raven hair with a rough but affectionate hand. "You'll like it back in Virginia when we git on that plantation — wearin' pretty dresses and dancin', and young fellers tyin' their hosses up out at the rail and comin' in to see you. And I'm gonna get me a white suit and a bunch of black cheroots and walk around and be a big plantation owner just like Mr. David Radke."

"How long will you be gone, Pa?" Charlie asked.

"Just long enough to git the gold. I'll send word to you by way of Silas Warmerdam, the fur buyer in town. There's always trappers comin' out this way. He kin ask one of 'em to drop a letter off."

"Kin we write to you, Pa?"

"Well, once I'm at where I'm goin', I'll send word where you kin write. Most likely the post office in Denver."

Charlie *was* worried, although she had better manners than to show it. "All right, Pa," she said. She went to sit down on the floor beside her mother and took her hand. "We'll make out fine until Pa gets back with all that gold, won't we, Ma?"

Naomi Peace knew more than she said. Deep within she knew that unless Noah hurried back, she would not be there to greet him. Her pain was growing much worse, but she stoically refused to reveal it. Now she could do no more than to encourage her daughter as best she could. Although Naomi knew somehow she would probably never live to see Virginia, she managed to smile. "Yes. We'll take keer of each other."

Chapter 2
Two Are Better Than One

Despondent, Noah Peace rode his horse down Black Mountain, leading another packhorse. Up until the time he had said good-bye to Naomi and Charlie, he had been excited about his journey. He had left just after daybreak, embracing Naomi and whispering, "I'll be back, and we'll see all the doctors you need and get you well again."

But as he guided the horses down the old Indian trail, a grayness came over his spirit. He knew Naomi well, and despite her attempts to cover her pain, he knew she felt worse than she would admit.

By noon he had reached the foot of the mountain and crossed the north fork of the Powder River. Turning west, he pushed the horses on until nightfall, where he hit the main body of the river and made camp.

Since the spring grass still had not appeared, he fed his horses the grain he was carrying. Collecting firewood, he made a roaring fire. *I couldna made a fire like this seventeen years ago,* he thought. *I'd have lost my scalp.* As he cooked his bacon and made coffee, then sat back to eat it, he thought of the old days. He wondered if, as men grew older, they lived in the past more than in the present, and certainly not in the future. Overhead the wind whistled through the firs, and the river gurgled beside him, its icy water flowing down from the mountain toward the lowlands. He took a bite of the bacon and chewed it thoughtfully, recalling his youth and strength. He remembered the days he had competed with Crow warriors and when he had first begun to think of Naomi as a woman he might love. She was the most beautiful woman he had ever seen and had turned down many men. A smile creased his tough lips as he gazed into the fire, watching as a log shifted, sending myriad sparks upward like tiny stars to tangle with the larger stars overhead. It reminded him of many campfires of his youth. Finally, he rolled into his blanket and fell asleep.

Arising at dawn, he cooked breakfast, ate it, then saddled his horse and put the load on the packhorse. He continued to follow the path of the river. By late that afternoon he reached Fort Collins and stayed for the night. He had not been in the settlement for years, but now he saw it had changed little. Tying his horses up outside the single hotel that decorated the town's main street, a place he had stayed once before when he passed through, he entered the mirrored lobby. A raw pine desk and a stairway were attached to one of the walls, and through an archway he could see the dining room. He gave his name, made his mark at the register, then went up the creaking stairs and opened the door on the left.

Sealed with rough lumber with cracks between the beams, the room allowed anyone to observe his neighbor. A single window covered by green roller shades discolored by sun and rain opened onto the main street. A lamp was set on a table, and the bed was a mahogany four-poster covered with some lumpy quilts and a pillow without a slip. The floor had once been covered with a lead-colored paint, but now that was mostly faded to a leprous gray and brown.

Back a few years ago, I could have made this trip and still been ready for a night of howling like a wolf. A man gets old. Comes up on him all of a sudden. He still thinks young inside, but when he looks in the mirror, he sees that he's nearer the end of the trails than he is to the beginning, Noah thought, realizing he was tired.

He stripped off his shirt, washed his face, and shaved, grunting as the razor pulled through his whiskers. He had not shaved for some time, and it was a painful chore. Finally, he dried his face, put on a clean shirt, then descended the rickety stairs, turning left into the dining room, directly across from the saloon. Once entering the dining room, he saw a blackboard sign: T-BONES, MASHED POTATOES, AND APPLE PIE — FIFTY CENTS. The notice beneath it made him grin: IF YOU DON'T LIKE OUR GRUB, DON'T EAT HERE.

Sitting down, he waited until a slovenly Indian girl with obviously unwashed hands brought his meal. She gave him a sultry look but, when he did not respond, shrugged wearily. As he ate, he studied his fellow diners, who consisted mostly of roughly dressed miners and a few townspeople, including some farmers and their wives.

After the meal, he filled his pipe and sat smoking it. When it was consumed, he tapped it on his heel, letting the ash fall to the floor. Rising, he threw four bits on the table and made his exit. When he reached the foyer, he hesitated. It was early, and the food had quickened him somewhat. When he heard a tinny piano, he entered the saloon — more out of a desire to escape the leprous floor upstairs than for any other motive. It was a long room with a few battered tables where several games of blackjack and poker were going on, while across the far wall a mirror reflected a long bar. The walls were decorated with elk and deer antlers, and a badly stuffed mountain lion scowled from a table beside the east wall. The smoke was thick, covering the clink of glasses and the murmur of poker players' voices.

Noah became aware of an argument going on over to his left and turned to see the source of it. Three roughly dressed men wearing guns had engaged the few men who stood at the bar. One of the toughs, a large, muscular man wearing a garish yellow shirt and red neckerchief, was belligerently arguing with a tall, elderly man who regarded him steadily. "I ain't lettin' no Yankees tell us what to do! If I want to have slaves, I'll have 'em!"

"That's right, Dud," the slender man on his right said. He was more finely dressed, with charcoal slacks and a pale blue shirt, and wore a .44 pistol on his left hip. "These nigger lovers here need to get back to New York or to Chicago."

The man named Dud was showing off,

Noah realized, for his audience. With a squat neck, curly red hair, and a scarred face, Dud had the look of a professional fighter. Something about his attitude warned Noah that he wanted trouble. *He's the kind that likes it,* he thought, *and he'll have it out of somebody.*

The argument spoiled the saloon for Noah, and he started for the door. But before he could reach it, the man in the pale blue shirt stood up to bar his way. "Which side are you on? Are you a Yankee?"

Noah was not carrying a gun. He had one in his gear upstairs, but it hadn't occurred to him he'd need one. So he just said mildly, "Don't know anything about politics." As he moved to go around the man, Dud joined them. "Well, what is he, Slick?"

"Says he don't know nothin' 'bout politics."

Dud grinned, his teeth large and stained with tobacco. "Don't know 'bout politics. That sounds like some kind of a yellow dog to me. A man that don't know which side to take in this here war ain't worth a lot, is he?"

The third man, tall and gangly, had come to join them. His hazel eyes were rimmed with drink. "If I had my way, we'd rat out all these Yankee nigger lovers and run 'em

37

out of town on a rail!"

Noah suddenly realized these three had located innocent strangers and humiliated them before. Although he was more Southern in view than Federal, he determined he was not going to let hooligans like these force him to give his views. "If you three will just stand aside," he said quickly, "I'll go to my room. I don't want no trouble."

"He don't want no trouble, Devoe. Did you hear that?" Dud said, winking at the hazel-eyed man. "He's one of them Yankees all right. They don't never want no trouble, but they're gonna come down south and tell us how to live and whether we kin own slaves or not." He stepped forward, his eyes hard. "I think I'm gonna make an example out of you, Yankee."

"I wouldna do that."

Dud laughed aloud then, driving his elbow into Devoe's side, and said, "I'm gonna bust you up, Yankee. I'm gonna break your teeth out into stubs and bust your nose so you'll whistle when you breathe. Then I'm gonna kick you until you walk straddle-legged."

Noah knew he had a beating coming. He did not have to look around the room to understand no one would come to his aid. This was a country where a man took care of his own quarrels. Fervently he wished he

38

had brought a gun, for he would have used it if he had. Instead, he tightened his lips in preparation.

The three stood before him, anticipating the fun. Cruelty in his eyes, Dud lashed out, his huge right fist grazing Noah's cheek. Managing to step aside, Noah threw a strong punch that caught Dud in the nose and set him back. As blood immediately spurted over Dud's shirt, he looked down at it with disbelief. Then, seemingly immune to pain, he wiped his nose with his sleeve and grinned even more broadly. "Well, looky here. We got us a live one. Come on, boys. Let's bust him up."

Noah watched as the three separated, Dud in front of him, the other two moving to his left and right. Noah had just doubled his fists and held them up when a voice behind him said, "You boys like good odds, don't you?"

Dud had been poised to attack. The voice set him back on his heels. He lowered his huge fists and stared at the man who had come to stand beside Noah. "You buyin' into this?" he demanded.

"Always like to see even odds."

Noah turned his head to look at the man who had come to his aid. Over six-feet-two, he was about twenty-eight and lean, lithe, and muscular looking. He reminded Noah, somehow, of a mountain lion at rest but ready to spring into action with blinding speed. Deep-set hazel eyes and light brown hair showed beneath the tan hat he was wearing, and he had a scar on his right cheek. Noah noticed that he was smiling. Although most men before violence get tense, there was an ease in his expression. *He's seen the elephants,* Noah thought, relieved. When Noah saw the man had a worn Colt on his left hip, he felt obliged to say, "Don't need to buy into trouble on my account, though I appreciate it."

Dud stared at the tall man. "You'd better butt out of this — or are you a Yankee, too?"

"I'm not givin' my past history today. Why don't you and your two friends go to the bar and have a drink?"

"Easy won't do it," Dud said. He had won many fights, mostly because of the heavy bone that surrounded his brain and his bulky muscles. He needed a fight as most men need food, and now, being deprived of one, he glanced at his two friends and found the odds comforting. "Well, I think you Yankees are gonna get a whippin'. Just like you got at Bull Run." He pulled his fists back and lumbered forward, his eyes glittering with anticipation. His two friends moved around to the side, and Noah stepped back. He had decided to take on the smaller one and try to put him away so that the odds would be two against two. Somehow he felt the tall man would be able, at least, to handle the muscular Dud.

But even as Noah glanced to one side, he was shocked to see that somehow the revolver at the tall man's side had been lifted and then brought down with a crushing blow on Dud's head. It almost drove him down, but the thick cushion of bone kept him from total unconsciousness. He stirred and put his fists up again as blood stained his cheeks, this time from the cut made from the gun barrel. But he had no chance, for once again the gun was lifted and fell on the other side of his head. A hard blow drove him down, where he sprawled loosely on the floor. The muzzle of the gun instantly swiveled to cover the man called Slick. Slick's eyes were blank with shock as he looked into the eyes of the man who had just destroyed his friend. He swallowed hard and said hoarsely, "I ain't joined."

"Better take your friend out. He may need a few stitches."

Noah watched as the eyes of both toughs changed. They were unused to being beaten, but something in the tall man's attitude gave them pause.

"Come on, Devoe. We'd better get 'im to a doctor."

The two men grabbed the unconscious Dud's arms. He was so large they could not carry him, so they dragged him out with his heels bumping across the rough floor of the saloon. They turned to go outside, and the barkeeper yelled, "Look at that blood! Who's gonna get it off the floor?"

Noah turned to the tall man. "I'm obliged." As Noah put out his hand, the tall man's gun seemed to disappear, almost as if by magic; then his hand was met by a firm grip. "Never could stand fellows like that."

"Me neither. My name's Noah Peace."

"Boone Manwaring."

"Got time to sit down?"

"Got nothing but time."

As the two men moved over to a table in the corner of the room, Noah said, "You saved me a beatin', mister."

Boone shrugged. "Glad I was around. This war fever's making men act crazy."

Noah grinned. "Actually, I guess I'm more Southern than I am anythin' else, but I wasn't going to let that hooligan tell me what to believe."

"I feel the same way. Lots of self-constituted committees roaming around

Colorado these days. Most of them never heard a shot fired, but they think they know exactly how to run the country and the railroads."

The two talked of the war for a time. It was going badly for the South, although they had won victories like Bull Run.

"I grew up in California," Boone said mildly. He sat loosely in his chair, relaxed. "I guess if I'd grown up in the South, or even in New York or Chicago, it would be a lot more real to me."

"Your people, they ain't aligned?" Noah inquired.

"Don't have any people, really. My father was a captain on a schooner. My mother died when I was fourteen. I've been at sea most of my life." He hesitated, and an odd expression crossed his face. "We had a shipwreck last year. Only seven of us got off. My father was the captain, but he didn't make it."

"Sorry to hear 'bout that. It must have been hard."

"Most things are hard in this life, I guess."

The remark caught Noah's attention, and he examined Manwaring's face more carefully. Something about this man set him apart. The corners of his lips had a tough, sharp set, as if he had both a sense of humor

43

and a temper that could come out hot as fire behind his quietness.

"That's all the family you had?" he inquired gently.

"Yes. That's all."

The brevity of the reply stirred Noah. "Not good for a man to be alone. That's what the Bible says."

"That's right. In Genesis, talking about Adam."

"You know the Bible?" Noah asked with surprise.

"Know it — don't do it."

Noah smiled at the laconic statement. "That about describes my condition. I got a good wife. She's a fine Christian. So's my girl."

"You got a family? Where are they?"

"Back up in the Rockies."

"Don't know it. Don't know anything about this country."

It was against Noah's inclination and habit to pry into other men's business, but somehow he felt easy enough to ask, "Where are you headed?"

"Guess I lost my compass," Boone said. "I had enough of the sea — for a while at least. Thought I'd see what this country looks like. It came in my mind to go prospecting." He smiled, his teeth white against his tanned skin. "I don't know any more about prospecting than I know about being a lawyer. But it sounds like something a man ought to do once in a lifetime."

Caught by surprise, Noah said, "I kinda got that idea myself."

"Is that right? Have you done any prospecting?"

"Some years ago I did some. Never hit it really big. Me and a partner of mine was in California. But he got sick, and I had to bring him back home."

Boone leveled a gaze on Noah. "What would a fellow need to go prospecting? I'm nothing but a greenhorn. Sometimes I feel like a fool even talking about such a thing." He reached up to scratch his eyebrow with his right forefinger. He looked at the finger and said, "Look." He doubled his fingers under with the forefinger extended. "I can't bend that finger."

"What's wrong with it?"

"Got crushed when I tried to catch a shark when I was at sea. My old man put it back together. I didn't lose it, but it won't bend."

"That's your trigger finger. How do you manage that?"

"I shoot with my left hand. I do most things with my left hand. Didn't use to

45

come natural to me, but it does now. Sometimes I think it would have been easier if it had been lopped off." He gave Noah another look and said, "Where would you figure to go looking for gold?"

Noah Peace was a fair man. "If it wasn't for you, Boone," he said quietly, "I wouldna be doin' any prospectin' at all. Them fellas woulda left me with busted ribs, if I was lucky. I figger I owe you somethin'."

"No need to feel that way."

Although Noah sometimes worried an idea for days or even weeks, he made up his mind instantly. He liked the look of this man. "You saved me a beatin', Boone. That means somethin'. Look, back when me and my partner was prospectin', we found color in a stream that I bet nobody's found to this day. That's been some years ago, but it's the most unlikely lookin' spot I ever seen. It comes out of the mountains and then runs for no more than a few miles before it disappears in a hole in the ground. I always intended to go back and check it out."

"That's where you're headed now?"

"Yep. Be glad to have you go along with me. Fifty-fifty. We'll split what we find."

"You don't know me, Noah."

"I doubt if any man knows another complete, but a man needs a partner in this country. If he's out there, falls down, and breaks a leg, what does he do? Probably dies. The Bible says two are better than one."

Boone leaned forward. "I wouldn't want to be butting in on your find."

Noah laughed. "May not *be* a find, Boone. You've got to understand that. I found some color there, but the creek may have been found and panned out, or it may have been just a flash in the pan — no gold to speak of. But I'd like to have you. There's still a few Indians around there. I'd feel pretty good havin' you by my side."

Boone Manwaring was somewhat taken aback. His life had been hard, and he had found men often to be less than honorable. Now as he looked into Noah's dark blue eyes, he made his own decision. "I'll go along, but I don't know about the fifty-fifty. I don't know the first thing about mining."

Noah flattened his hands on the table. "Not much to learn about it. Once you find it, you dig it out of the ground or get it out of the river. It's a lot of hard work either way. But fifty-fifty is the way it will be. There'll be no more talk, all right?" He stuck out his hand and felt the impact of Boone's gaze. Somehow he knew he had done the right thing.

The two arose before dawn, left the hotel, and began moving south. They did not stop to make camp until dusk. The road was well traveled, so there was little chance of Indians, and for two nights they found a place beside a stream where they could camp and rest the horses. On that second night Boone heard the details of Noah's decision to go prospecting.

Sitting beside the fire, Noah had been thinking about Naomi. "My wife ain't been well," he explained to Boone. "I'm worried about her. That's one reason I'm goin' prospectin' — to git money for good doctors."

Two days on the trail had given the men confidence in one another, so Boone listened as Noah spoke freely about his wife and daughter, Charlie.

"Her real name's Charlene, which is what her ma calls her, but somehow I got used to callin' her Charlie."

"How old is she, Noah?"

"Eighteen years old. She's one-quarter Crow. Naomi is half Crow. Good-lookin' people, the Crows. Best lookin' of all the Indians."

"I don't know much about Indians."

"They're fine people, but they're gettin'

48

pushed aside. That's one reason I went to the mountains, I guess. I lived with the Crows for a while, but I saw their ways was disappearin', so I married Naomi, and we went up to the high country. Charlie was born the next year. We've stayed up there."

"I like that," Boone said. "On a ship you're never alone. Most crowded life on earth, I do believe."

The fire burned cheerfully in the darkness as Noah finally began to speak of his dream. "When I was a boy in Virginia," he said, "I was poor, but I always watched the rich plantation owners. . . ."

As Noah continued to speak of his desire to go back and buy a plantation and make his daughter into a fine lady, Boone felt a gust of compassion. Brought up in a hard school, Boone had decided somewhere along the line that most of life was drudgery and trouble — and that the most fun came only when you worked very hard for it. However, fun came and went too quickly. The emptiness in Boone's soul didn't easily receive good things. Although he was moved by his new friend's dilemma, at the same time he felt there might be trouble ahead.

"It's just a dream I got, but a man's got to fight for his dreams, I guess," Noah concluded.

Boone picked up a stick, stuck the end in the fire till it blazed, and then tossed the whole thing into the flames. "Dreams don't work out — that's been my observation."

Seeing the hardness and doubt in the younger man, Noah said grimly, "This one will, Boone."

Boone didn't move or speak for a time. Then he summoned a grin. "I hope so, Noah. I'd like to see you sitting on a porch in front of a big white house down in Virginia drinking a mint julep and smoking a thin cheroot, and your girl all dressed up. I'd like to see that."

Noah Peace allowed himself to smile. "That costs money, and we're goin' to get that, Boone. Better get some sleep. Once we get to the gold country, there won't be much of that."

Later, as Boone stared up into the sky, spangled with a million points of light, he wondered about what had happened. His father always taught him that a man's life was out of his control — *What's going to happen is going to happen.* Now he had met this man who had a dream he desperately wanted to see come true — if only to refute his own grim philosophy. Finally, the night closed around him with all of its darkness, and he fell asleep.

Chapter 3
The Long Good-Bye

Pale bars of sunlight filtered through the single window in the loft. Charlie blinked and came awake, instantly turning her head to one side to avoid the glare. The cornshuck mattress rustled as she sat up and stretched her arms high, while from outside, as regular as the sun itself, the rooster lifted his clarion call — shrill, clear, and urgent as it announced the beginning of a new day.

"Reckon you think the day couldna start without you servin' notice." Charlie stood and went to the window, loving the mountains and the hills that lay beyond the valley. In some ways, Charlie was a creature of firmly fixed habit — she liked the way things were and was suspicious of change. Now she performed her morning rituals.

Slipping out of her cotton gown, she donned her underwear then poured water from a pitcher into a basin. She took some soft soap on her fingers, spread it on her

51

palms, and lathered her face until it glowed with a rosy tint. She had made this soap herself and added a bit of scent that her father, at some distant time, had brought to her mother. As she rinsed off and dried her face, she thought with some sadness, *But Ma never uses perfume.* As she slipped into her jeans and one of her father's old cotton shirts, she stopped long enough to sit down on her bunk.

Picking up her worn Bible, she opened it at the place marked by a dried wildflower. She sat there, letting the light play over the words of the Psalms for ten minutes, then bowed her head and prayed softly, "Oh Lord, You know Ma's sick, and You know they ain't nothin' we kin do for her. It's plumb out of our hands. I'd be obliged, Lord, if You would see fit to give her a good day. Take away all the hurtin'. And be with Pa. Keep him safe on his travels and bring him back again, for, Lord, You know how bad we need him. And I pray this in Jesus' name."

Placing the Bible back, she picked up her tablet and removed the top from the jar of ink. The ink she had also made herself out of pokeberries and soot from the fireplace. It was not as good as store-bought ink, and she reminded herself to get a supply the next time anyone went into the village. Dipping the turkey quill into the ink, she began to write, as always, haltingly.

July the fifth, 1863

Well, yesterday was Independence Day, but it didnt make no difference to us. Ma had one of her bad spells, and I set by her most of the day tryin to ease her, but it wasnt no good. She never makes no complaint, but I know she is hurtin fierce. I would give anythin to just take it off her, but there aint no way one person can hurt for another, I reckon. I dont like to think about it, but I wonder what it would be like if Ma went to be with Jesus. It would be bedder for her though, I know that, but it shore would be hard for me and Pa. We would miss her so much.

Leaning back, she perused what she'd written, crossed out a word and wrote in a different spelling, then began again.

We had another letter from Pa last Thursday. He claims he was doin good. We got three letters from him, and the writin is the finest you have ever seen.

Its writ by a feller called Boone Manwaring, which is a funny sort of name
for any man. Reckon he was named for
Daniel Boone, but I aint never heered of
no Manwaring in all my born days.
Anyhow, he writes as nice as anything
you ever seed. I wisht I could write like
that, but I caint.

Pa said that him and Mr. Manwaring
was workin hard lookin for gold, but
they aint found much yit. He was plum
worriet about Ma and me. When I writ
him back I told him there wasnt no
sense worryin about me. Ma was doin
poorly. I didnt ask him to come back,
but I sure wisht he would. I dont care
nothin about no gold, and I aint goin to
no Virginia and becomin a lady. These
mountains was good enough for Ma,
and they is good enough for me.

Anyhow, I got to thinkin last night. Ma
is mighty partial to turkey, so I reckon I
will go out this mornin and see if I caint
get one for her. I wisht Pa was here, for
he shore is good on shootin them things,
and I aint as good as him. But if it would
help Ma, I wouldnt keer if I had to stay
out all day.

After finishing the words and sprinkling

sand over the writing, she got out of bed. She slipped her feet into the elkskin boots then descended the ladder to the main living area. Moving quietly, she went to the door of the single bedroom and looked inside to see if her mother was awake. "Are you awake, Ma?"

"Yes. Good mornin', Charlene."

Moving inside, Charlie put her hand on her mother's head and smoothed the hair back. "You ain't never called me Charlie in my whole life. Why is that, Ma?"

"I think Charlene's so pretty. I wish your pa would call you that."

"He won't never do that." Charlie noticed with some shock that some of her mother's hair was white. "I'll fix you up some nice grits and maybe a soft-boiled egg, Ma. Maybe two."

"One will be enough."

"All right, Ma. You lay easy there."

Charlie built up a fire, got the water boiling, then boiled an egg and made grits. She added a cup of fresh milk and took it in to her mother, then went to fix her own breakfast. She fried up a piece of ham and two eggs easy-over, for she liked the yolks runny, and ate them, along with a biscuit left from the day before.

When she went back into her mother's

room, she found the egg only half eaten and the grits hardly touched. "Cain't you eat no more, Ma?"

"I'm not hungry. Maybe later," Naomi said. She reached over and took her daughter's hand. Her face was very pale with strain, and her lips were drawn tight as she whispered, "You have a time takin' care of me. I wish you didn't have to."

"It's okay, Ma." Words came hard for Charlie, for neither of her parents were great talkers. So they sat there saying nothing, both of them aware that the illness that had come the last six months was not going to pass away. Then Naomi looked at her daughter, whom she loved so deeply and strongly, and said, "Charlene, after I'm gone, you must not grieve for me."

"Don't say that, Ma!"

"You're a Christian, Charlene, and so am I. We've talked so much about how hard this life is and how it will be when we are with the Lord." Naomi's eyes were filled with pain, and not all of it was physical. In the smooth face of her daughter she saw the blue eyes, a part of Noah, and the black hair and olive skin that were her own contribution. "I'm glad you're a good girl and know Jesus. It would be hard to go if you wasn't."

Charlie was not a young woman to show emotions, but her eyes began to sting. Despite herself, tears formed. She dashed them away and threw herself on her mother, holding her close. The thinness of her mother's body was a never-ending shock to her, for, like Charlie, Naomi had always been a strong woman. As Charlie's body shook, her mother stroked her back. The two stayed that way for a long moment, and then Naomi said, "Now you go 'bout your business. Sometime this afternoon we'll read the Word a little more. All right?"

"All right, Ma." Charlie straightened up and tried to smile, wiping her tears away with the backs of her hands. "I'm goin' to get you a turkey, Ma. You always liked fresh tom turkey."

"Thank you, Charlene."

Leaving her mother's room, Charlie cleaned the dishes and then picked up the rifle and ammunition pouch. She went to the small, sturdy box where the ammunition was kept and got the shot out, adding it to the pouch she wore slung on a belt around her waist. Moving over to the mantel, she picked up the turkey call her father had made for her. She held the wooden box with paper-thin sides gently in her hand, then picked up a whetstone and drew it across the top edge of one side. The action produced a low, rasping crooning that sounded like a hen turkey; she made it yelp by jerking the stone across. Satisfied, she stowed it in her upper pocket and left the cabin.

Since she had heard turkeys calling not a mile from the cabin, she walked across the yard and through the fields and finally climbed a rise. When she reached the top, she looked down into the valley that glowed in the summer sun like a jewel. It was studded with trees, none very tall. However, long grasses grew there, and the grasshoppers were thick, which drew the turkeys.

It was late to be on the field, and she knew she would have to be patient. She reached a blind made out of deadwood stacked in a rough fence and covered with brush. She and her father had come here often, and now she lay down and checked the priming in her rifle. Carefully she slipped it out through a gap and could almost hear what her father had said the first time he had brought her here. *"Now you cain't move that gun. Don't you even bat an eye, because them turkeys can see better than folks. Just call to him, and if he gobbles as much as twice, that's all you need. You might have to wait an hour, maybe longer, but if you call another time, he'll suspicion somethin'. After he quits gobblin', he'll make out like he's goin' the other way, but don't you fear — he'll slip back."*

For the next thirty minutes the young woman lay still. She had given the turkey call twice, and the last time, after a few seconds, she had heard what seemed to be an echo but was really a turkey responding. Finally, she was rewarded by a flicker to the right. Moving only her eyes, she saw a magnificent tom turkey step out. He nervously stepped forward, making a rapid pecking motion with his head, then uttered a clucking sound again. Charlie did no more, and after nervously making a half circle, the turkey advanced with regular steps. From behind him two female turkeys followed, and Charlie thought, *They'd be more tender than that male. I'll take the second one there.* As it happened, however, as the turkeys marched across the line where her rifle was held, the two hen turkeys were side by side for one instant. Charlie squeezed the trigger, and when the gun went off, the tom charged away into the brush with a thunderous beating of wings. Both of the hen turkeys were knocked to the ground, and as Charlie rose up with an exultant cry, they kicked their last. "Two with one shot! Even if it was bird shot, Pa won't never believe this!" she cried. Running over, she picked up the two turkeys by the feet.

She returned to the house at once, stepped inside, and called, "Ma, I got *two* turkeys. I'm gonna fix you the best turkey you ever had."

"Sounds good, daughter."

After she had dressed the turkey, she rubbed the outside with lard, sprinkled it with salt and pepper, and put it inside the oven, where she baked it for about three hours. When that was done, she combined flour, the cooked chopped liver and gizzards, and water in the saucepan to make gravy.

By two o'clock the meal was ready, and her mother was up watching her as she cooked. She set the table, adding two glasses of sassafras tea, and said, "Ma, yesterday was the fourth, so I guess this is *our* Fourth of July."

"It smells wonderful," Naomi said. She started to get up, but then her face went taut, and she fell back in the chair, gasping for breath.

"Ma, what is it?"

Naomi could not answer. Her eyes were opened wide, and her lips moved as she tried to speak. Charlie reached out and held her hand, crying, "What is it, Ma? Is it bad?"

Naomi Peace struggled with the pain of the white-hot brand in her breast, knowing it was time for her to depart this earth. Struggling to speak, she managed to say in a weak voice, "Tell your . . . pa I always loved him. . . ." She reached out and held Charlie's face between her palms. With loving eyes, she gasped, "You are my faithful daughter, Charlene. I will . . ." She was suddenly taken by another tremendous pain and closed her eyes for a moment. Aware Charlene was holding her hands, she prayed for strength for a moment. Then she said, "I will wait for you in . . . our Father's house."

Then the pain lessened, and she opened her eyes. But she seemed to be drifting away. The outline of the cabin walls, the home that had been hers for so long, faded while her daughter's face grew sharp and clear. Naomi whispered, "I have always treasured you, my daughter," then closed her eyes as strength went out of her. She slumped back, her head turned to one side.

"Ma! Ma!" Charlie cried. She touched her mother's face, but she knew her mother was gone. She began to weep violently, holding her mother's head close as tears rolled down her cheeks and her body shook.

Charlie went to Lyle Gunderson's cabin after she had gotten her mother back into bed and said, "Lyle, Ma has gone to be with the Lord."

Gunderson, at forty-five, was a widower. Having lost his wife two years previously, he stared for a moment with shock at the young woman who stood before him, her back so straight, her lips a white line. "I'm mighty sorry to hear that, Charlie," he said finally. "I wish your daddy was here. There ain't no way to get him, I don't reckon."

"No. Will you help me, Lyle?"

"Why, shore. I'll go right now to get the preacher, and then I'll get the word out to everyone that your ma's passed." He hesitated and said, "Can you watch the kids while I go?" He had three children, all under the age of ten.

"I'll take keer of them, Lyle. I'd like to have the funeral as soon as we kin."

"I won't waste no time, Charlie."

The funeral was over, and the neighbors had left. Several of them had urged Charlie to come and stay with them, but she had shaken her head, saying, "I'll wait here for Pa."

There had been more than twenty-five people at the funeral, and the preacher had come from the village. It had been a good funeral, for Rev. Smith had known Naomi Peace well. She had attended his meetings, and he had preached a fine sermon. Later he had expressed his condolences, saying, "Child, she's with the Lord, but I know it's still hard." When Charlie had not answered, he said, "What will you do until your pa gets back?"

"I'll be all right, Reverend."

The preacher had looked at her then said quietly, "I believe you will, Charlene. Let me know as soon as your pa gets back. I'll be wantin' to talk to him."

Now only Lyle Gunderson remained after the grave had been filled, and he came to stand quietly beside Charlie. He was a red-faced man who was habitually silent, and the task of raising three lively children had put lines in his face. He hesitated until she finally said, "Come in, and we'll eat some of this here food, Lyle. I'm beholden to you."

" 'Twern't nothin', Charlie. I wish I could have did more."

The two moved inside the cabin, and Charlie, glad to have something to do, heated some of the turkey, thinking it had been years, rather than little more than a day, since she had brought the turkeys home.

"Fresh kilt, ain't it, this turkey?" Gunderson asked. He was wearing his only suit, which was small for him. Before eating, he took off his coat and hung it on a peg on the wall. He listened as Charlie told how she had killed two with one shot.

"Don't reckon I ever heered of a shot like that." Admiration shaded Gunderson's eyes as he ate quickly and hungrily. Outside, his children were playing, their voices keen in the air.

Charlie thought, *Death means so little unless it's one of your own.* Inside, however, there was a dull, empty ache. "Would you keer for some more turkey, Lyle?"

"Reckon I've had aplenty." As he sat up, Charlie noticed he was nervous. Not fathoming why, she began to clean the table off.

"Charlie, I thought I might say somethin' to you. I hope you take it right."

Surprised by his tone, the young woman asked, "Why, what is it, Lyle?"

Gunderson shifted uneasily and ran his big hand over his taupe-colored hair. "This ain't no time to speak of it, but I figured I ought to say it now. What it is, Charlie — well, I got three kids and don't know how to raise 'em. Now you're a growed woman, and I been thinkin' on it for some time. You got no man, and if you ain't spoken for, it appears to me like we need each other."

Charlie's olive skin flushed, and she dropped her eyes for a moment. Gunderson's announcement did not come as any great surprise to her, for she and her parents had often talked of how he needed a wife to share his life. She also had been aware of his eyes on her from time to time, but to her he was an old man. It was not, however, uncommon for young girls to marry older men in the mountains. They needed husbands, and the older men, after they lost their wives, needed a companion.

She liked Lyle Gunderson. He was always polite, a slow, soft-spoken man she had always admired for his kindness to his neighbors, his willingness to help. He also was a good father. But there was nothing that moved inside her toward him, so she said gently, "I thank you for your offer, Lyle, but I reckon I'll just go on like I am for a time."

"It's your say, Charlie," Gunderson said, disappointed. "But if you ever change your mind, I reckon I'll be ready."

Gunderson left soon after that, and Charlie, unable to bear the cabin with the many reminders of her mother, picked up her rifle out of pure habit and walked the woods until dark fell. It was hot and sultry, but she did not heed the weather. Her mind was full of her mother, and she knew that for days, or weeks, she would not be able to stop the rush of fond memories.

Finally, going back to the cabin, she stood irresolutely for a moment then put the gun over the mantelpiece and climbed the stairs. Lighting the candle beside her bed, she got out her writing material. With an unsteady hand, she began to write, *Dear Pa, I got reel bad news for you. Ma went to be with the Lord just yesterday. . . .*

CHAPTER 4
YELLOW DUST

March 1863

By the time Noah and Boone reached Denver, the mountain peaks to the west of the fledgling city still glittered with snow, but a lush smell of fresh earth and vegetation pervaded the air.

"Not much of a town, is it, Noah?" Boone observed as the two entered by the north of the city. He took in the treeless, dusty streets lined with false-fronted buildings and dotted by an occasional brick edifice. Boone had seen many cities in his travels, and here the brick buildings were strangely incongruous in the incivility of their surroundings. The two rode on through the population of miners, merchants, Indians, town boomers, drifters and drovers, lawyers and gamblers, and it was Noah who said, "The town's a lot bigger than it was the last time I was here. Weren't no brick buildings here then."

"Are we going to stay in Denver?"

"Just for tonight. I reckon we'll get a room if we can and see if we can't get some wind of what's goin' on."

The two pulled up in front of a three-story yellow building with white-framed windows that bore the sign HAMILTON HOUSE. "This ought to be good enough for us," Noah said, grinning.

They dismounted, tied up their horses, then stepped inside. The lobby was busy with men talking loudly of the war. "I guess there's no way to get away from this war," Boone said.

"I reckon not." Noah waited his turn in line then asked the pimple-faced young clerk, "Got a room?"

"If you got ten dollars, we do."

"Ten dollars for one room?"

"That's the price, mister." The clerk's hair was slicked back with grease, and there was a nervous tic in his right eye. "Do you want the room or not?"

"Reckon so." After Noah made his mark on the register, Boone wrote "Noah Peace" after it then signed his own name.

"Number 208," the fledgling clerk said. "Next!"

Carrying their gear upstairs, the two men entered the room and saw one sad-looking bed with a sagging mattress.

"Reckon I'll take the floor," Boone observed.

"We'll cut the cards for it. Come on, let's wash up and go downstairs. I need to find out what's happenin'."

The two men washed, changed shirts, and went downstairs, walking leisurely down the dusty street. As they moved along, they heard many accents — sharp-clipped voices of New England, Irish brogue, and the soft tones of Virginia and the South.

"It looks like there are people here from all over the country," Boone observed. "Gold draws people like honey draws flies — and most of it ends up in places like that." He pointed at the Golden Horseshoe, a saloon with a man out in front begging customers, "Come on! Give us a bet! Step inside, sports! Pretty ladies and win your fortune at the wheel of fortune!"

"That's where most of it winds up," Noah agreed.

"Does a meal occur to you?"

"Reckon so. I'm hungry enough to eat a buffalo, hide and all."

Ten minutes later the two were seated in a large restaurant filled with men determined to speak as loudly as possible. The din was tremendous. "I wonder why they all talk so loud," Boone said.

"They don't get to talk much when they're out workin'. I guess they try to make up for it here."

"Are most of these miners?"

"Shore. That's what Denver's here for. If it wasn't for the mines, this wouldn't be nothin' but a dusty spot at the foot of the mountains."

After the meal, they made their way to the Golden Horseshoe and sat at the bar, each nursing a beer. The talk was either of the war or of mines and claims and strikes. Boone Manwaring knew the talk of the sea, but all of this was like a foreign language to him, so he kept quiet until finally they were outside, stepping along the boardwalk. "Did you find out anything about where to prospect, Noah?"

"Why, I wasn't figgerin' to find that out." Noah gave Boone a surprised look. "I thought I explained that. We could stay here for ten years and never hit a strike. Our only hope is that one spot I found last time I was here with my partner. Reckon we'll pull out in the mornin'. We'll stock up on supplies today. Load our packhorses down."

"Will it take a lot of equipment?"

"Not as much as you might imagine," Noah said. "Come on. Let's go buy our supplies; then we'll rest up today. Get a good night's rest and start out in the mornin'."

Boone looked at the creek that meandered between large outcroppings of rock down the slope of a ridge. Somehow he'd been expecting something different, and he lifted his eyebrows as he turned to his partner.

"That's it, Noah?"

"What did you expect, the Mississippi?" Noah grinned at Boone. "Greenhorns come out here expectin' gold to come poppin' out of the ground, maybe like popcorn. It ain't like that!" He reached over to his packhorse, opened a canvas bag, and pulled out a tin pan twelve inches in diameter and several inches deep.

"Guess you're due fer a little education, Boone. Come on. Let's set up the tent and cook us up some supper. This trip's done wore me out."

The two had left Denver at dawn that morning, covering thirty miles that day. Weary and dusty, they set up the tent and installed the cots with mattresses, for Noah had said, "I've done slept on the ground enough. We're liable to be out here for weeks."

When the tent was up, they had a quick meal of flapjacks, which Noah made expertly. "Reckon you'll get sick o' these

71

before long."

"I don't know. They're mighty good. We didn't have these on board ship."

Noah speared a fragment of flapjack, mopped it in the molasses he'd poured in beside it, and then stuck it in his mouth. When he had chewed it thoroughly, he washed it down with a cup of scalding coffee and then waved his cup toward Boone. "It's time fer a little education," he said.

Boone finished his meal and took a swallow of coffee, making a face. "That's strong enough to raise the dead!"

"You'll get used to it. Now if we was comin' out here to *mine* gold, that'd be a different story," Noah explained. "We'd have to have shovels, and picks, and dynamite, and saws to make timber — all kinds of stuff. Why, in the winter when the ground freezes, you have to build a fire over the ground to soften it up. Then you dig down a couple of feet to where you hit frozen ground again, then build another fire. A foot or two a day is mighty good goin'."

"Sounds like a lot of work."

"Work? That's the name of gold huntin', Boone. Tenderfeet come out here, and bank clerks, and ribbon clerks, and lawyers. Ain't never done a hard day's manual work in their life. They don't last long as a rule.

Farmers make good miners. They're used to hard work. And cowboys, they don't last long. All they want to do is ride a horse, although they're tough enough."

"So we're not really miners, then?"

"No. That takes a long time and a lot of capital. And time's the one thing I ain't got — or capital either." He picked up the pan. "We'll be lookin' for 'placer gold' — means gold in a creek or a river."

"How did it get there? What's it look like?"

"Well, I'll show you what it looks like tomorrow. Maybe, maybe not. But it gets there from being washed down from the high country. See those hills over there, where this creek comes from? It winds all around almost from the top, and if there's gold there, over a lot of years, it picks up a flake here and there, washes it along the bottom of the stream, and finally sometimes it bangs up against a rock. I've found pockets of gold as yellow as a hound's belly, but usually that ain't the way. I'm tired, Boone. I'll give you your first lesson tomorrow."

The two slept soundly, and after breakfast — pancakes again — Noah picked up a pan and handed it to Boone. "You're gonna get them fancy boots wet. You'd better put on the ones you bought in the store."

He waited until Boone had put on the rough brogans, then went down to the edge of the creek. "Here's all there is to it," he said, squatting down. Dipping the pan into the water, he dug at it until it was half full of pebbles and sand. "The trick," he said, staring down inside the pan, "is to get everythin' out of this pan except the gold — if there be any."

Boone watched as Noah rocked the pan back and forth, letting a little of the sediment at the bottom clear the edge. It looked simple enough, just a twist of the wrist, and finally when the pan was almost empty, he asked, "Any gold?"

"Not a particle."

Somehow, despite the warnings from Noah, Boone was disappointed. "Does that mean there's no gold here?"

"It means there wasn't no gold in that pan I just did. I'll move here and try again. Sometimes you get nothin' and move six inches and find that yellow dust. Have a try at it."

Boone imitated Noah's actions. "How do I know what I'm looking for?"

"Anythin' that glitters is suspect. May not be gold, but it might. Here, I'll just watch you fer a spell."

Boone eagerly tried several experiments,

feeling awkward, but Noah encouraged him. "Ain't no great art in it," he said. "You're doin' fine." Then he stopped abruptly and said, "Look! Right there!"

Peering down into the pan, Boone saw a flicker of light as the sun shone into the pan. With excitement, he asked, "Is that gold?"

"Let me see." Noah peered at it. "That's gold all right."

"How much is it worth?"

"Probably about ten cents."

"You mean only a dime?"

"That's right." Noah was enjoying the look on his partner's face. "Now if you did that about a thousand times today, you'd make a day's wages." He laughed at Boone's astonished face. "But the next pan might be worth fifty dollars. Who knows?"

That was the beginning. The two men worked the creek slowly, but Boone's legs soon ached from the unnatural squatting position. Noah spotted this and said, "You'll git toughened up soon. I guess I'd have some kind of problem if you had me on your boat haulin' sails up."

Boone soon discovered there was nothing really difficult about panning for gold. It was just tiring and enormously hard work. Hour after hour, he worked doggedly on. They paused at noon long enough to cook a quick meal, then went back to work. All afternoon under the glittering sun they kept at it until finally, at three o'clock, Boone said, "Well, I reckon that's enough for us today."

As Boone arose, his legs protested, pain shooting through the backs of them. "My legs are killing me!" he groaned. He looked over at the older man, who was peering at the bag where they carefully kept the gold they had panned. "How much did we make, Noah?"

"Maybe ten dollars. Maybe a little less." When he saw the expression on Boone's face, he continued, "But wait till tomorrow. We'll probably strike it rich."

"I think I'll have to lie down tomorrow. That squatting is killing me!"

"You'll get used to it. A man can get used to anythin'. Come on. I'll fix you some more pancakes."

"None of that. Let's have some steak tonight before it spoils."

As the weeks wore on into April and then became May, Boone's legs grew stronger. He was able to match Noah hour for hour as they moved slowly upward toward the mountains. It was dull, boring work, but no more so than some of the duty he had put in on board ship. He did not complain and thus won Noah's approval.

"I reckon you're doin' good, Boone," Noah said as they roasted the jackrabbits he'd caught. The odor of the cooking meat made both men ravenous. "You ain't afraid of work, and you got a strong back. That's about all you have to have to be a prospector."

Pulling the stick back, Boone tested the flesh with his knife and found it to be done. He began tearing strips off and, careful not to burn himself, chewed on the tough meat. From time to time he took a spoon and dipped into the can of beans he'd opened.

The two men ate quietly and then, as usual, opened up a can of peaches to share for dessert. They drank the bitter coffee and listened to the sounds of a night bird. Looking up into the sky, over toward the timber, Boone said, "Mighty quiet life."

"Like bein' at sea?"

"No, not like that. A ship's a noisy place. Usually crammed with more men than there's room for, and not beds enough for the hands."

"Where'd they sleep?"

"They have watches at different times when they're on duty. They get to sleep in a bed when somebody's gone on watch."

"Don't think I'd keer for it. Too crowded."

Boone nodded but said nothing. The two sat there in warm companionship. Boone had learned over the past weeks that Noah was a single-minded man. He worked like a machine and never seemed to grow discouraged, where Boone himself was not so motivated. But Boone knew that sooner or later, as he did every night, Noah would begin to speak of Virginia and then of his family.

"Back when I was a younker, I remember the planters used to go huntin' foxes. Somethin' to see."

"Never saw anything like that," Boone remarked.

"Well, I don't know what they do it fer. Don't reckon a feller could eat a fox. Probably taste about like a hawk."

"You've tasted hawk?"

"Oh, shore. Once I got lost for a day or two and had to eat somethin'. Hawk was all I could git."

"What did it taste like, Noah?"

Noah laughed aloud. "About like fox, I guess. Tough as saddle leather and wild. I guess Naomi could have made it better, but she weren't there." His rough face softened as he began to speak of his days back in Virginia. They were very real to him, Boone discovered, though many years had passed. Noah had a fixation about the gentry in Virginia. Finally, Noah said, "I'm gonna git me one of them plantations. Maybe not a big one, but Charlie, she'll like it, I bet."

"Might be different with the war on. It's bad enough out here," Boone commented.

"Oh, I reckon there's fightin' all right, but that'll be over soon. Them Yankees, they'll give up and go home soon enough."

Boone had doubts about this, for he had studied the political situation more than his companion. He knew Abraham Lincoln was not a man to quit, and the North had the edge in manpower and munitions. However, he did not attempt to persuade Noah, for he had discovered there was a blind spot in the man's thinking. He had his dream, and he was going to achieve it — war or not.

"I thought we'd hit good color before this," Noah said after a long silence. "I found another little spur of this here creek. Ain't more'n three or four feet acrost, but sometimes you find color there. Maybe we'll move over and try it tomorrow."

They did try the creek, which was barren, and finally in early June had to go back into town for supplies. When they got there, they were astonished, for they found that most of the town had burned down. They stared at the blackened skeletons of buildings and on an inquiry found out that flames had burst out in the night on the roof of the Cherokee House on Blake Street in the middle of town. The wind had pushed the flame around, and the fire had leaped from false front to false front. Men had tumbled out of their beds to form ragged bucket brigades from the South Platte River, but their efforts were useless.

"Looks like Denver's about gone," Boone murmured, looking at the wreckage.

"Guess it is, but they'll build it back. Where there's gold, men'll build. Let's go see if there's any supplies to be had. I'll bet they're pretty short."

The two managed to get what supplies were available, paying a high price for them, and then returned to their camp. They worked hard for three days. It was on the third day that Boone said, as they pulled their blankets up, "I don't think we'll ever find it, Noah."

Noah lay silently for a while. Then he asked, "Do you want to give up?"

"Just about."

"You go on, then. Me, I ain't leavin'."

"What about your family?" Boone had written several letters to Noah's family and had read the two letters that had come from Charlie. He had picked them up in Denver on his trips in for supplies. The spelling was abominable and the writing only passable. He had a picture in his mind of the young woman from Noah's description, and now he thought of the last letter that had spoken of Naomi Peace and her illness. He did not feel qualified, however, to remind Noah of this. He knew Noah was worried, but the fixation in his mind of finding gold and getting his family out of the high country and back in Virginia was too strong.

"I'll try awhile longer, Noah," he said finally.

It was two days after this conversation that Noah came crashing across the creek where Boone was panning. "We got it, Boone — we got it!"

Boone stood up, his face alive with excitement. "What is it, Noah?"

"Over there!" Noah grabbed Boone's arm and shook him, then began to dance around like a wild man. "I found it for shore! Look!" He opened his bag with trembling hands and poured out a stream of yellow nuggets and dust. "That's one pan, Boone! Just one pan, and it's all collected right there in a little bend smashed up against a

rock ledge. All we gotta do is git it out!"
Then he stopped dancing, and tears ran
down his face as he stared at the yellow
dust. "I reckon the good Lord led us to this
place."

"I'm glad, Noah. Now you can take care
of your family."

"Come on. We gotta move camp."

The two moved hurriedly, Noah frantic
with urgency. The creek that Noah led
Boone to was inconsequential. "Probably
dries up in the summer," Noah said, "but
right now it's here. Come on — I'll show
you."

He led Boone to a bend in the creek that
dead-ended into a solid sheet of rock. Noah
waded out into the middle then drove his
pan up against the rock. "Try it, Boone!" he
yelled.

Boone followed him out and scooped up
half a pan of rock. As he lifted it, his breath
grew short, for he saw at least half a dozen
nuggets, some no bigger than a pinhead,
but two at least as large as a pea. His hands
began to tremble, and he looked up wildly
at Noah. "I never saw anything like it," he
whispered.

"I did when I was here before, but I was
afeered somebody would git to it. Come on,
Boone, we got work to do."

■ ■ ■ ■

Boone Manwaring had known hard labor at sea, but never had he worked as hard as he did for the next several months. Every day he rose before first light, ate a hurried breakfast, then went at once to the creek, which they named "Mogo." He worked steadily throughout the day until nearly dark; then the two staggered to camp for a meal. Supplies ran low over time, so one of the two would go hunting. For if they went to town, Noah warned, there was always a chance that somebody would follow them back to their strike.

"It's happened plenty a times, Boone," Noah told him. "Man finds gold, he goes into town, shows a nugget — then everybody in the whole creation is out diggin' elbow to elbow with him."

"But we got to get grub, and we're out of salt, Noah," Boone finally protested. His bones were aching with the unaccustomed work, toughened as he had become. He had watched the yellow dust grow in the bag Noah had brought as an act of faith, and every day he waited for Noah to say they had enough. Now it was almost September.

At last Noah relented. "You go on to

town, Boone, and git some supplies. Take both pack animals. Bring enough back to last another month. I'll stay here and pan out some more dust."

Boone left the next morning for Denver. He got the supplies then moved to the brand-new post office, built out of raw timber and smelling of rosin. As he stepped inside, he nodded to the postmaster, who remembered him. "Hello, got a letter for your friend. His name's Peace, ain't it?"

"That's right. Noah Peace."

"Right here."

"Thanks. Get this one off, will you?" Boone asked.

Boone took the letter with the familiar writing he knew to be Charlie Peace's. He stuck it in his inside pocket then went out, mounted, and led the packhorses out of town. He made the trip back quickly and arrived at dusk.

"You made good time, Boone."

"I was afraid I might go into a saloon and get drunk and tell about the Mogo out here, but I didn't. Letter from Charlie."

"Let's unload them supplies and cook up some of this grub. Then you can read it to me."

They unloaded the supplies and turned the animals loose to graze before Boone

84

said, "I'm the cook tonight. I brought a bunch of canned stuff."

"I could eat shoe leather," Noah said eagerly. "You do the cookin', and I'll do the cleanin' up."

The meal was different, for it included canned oysters, canned corn, beef, and for dessert a pineapple that had somehow found its way to Denver. After the meal was over, Noah leaned back and patted his stomach. "Reckon that'll keep me fer a spell. Now read me Charlie's letter."

"All right." Reaching into his pocket, Boone used his knife to slit the envelope. He pulled out a single sheet of paper and started to read. " 'Dear Pa, I got reel bad news for you. Ma —' "

Boone broke off abruptly, and Noah Peace grew very still. "What's it say, Boone?"

Boone bit his lip and couldn't answer for a moment. "It's bad news, Noah."

"Is it — Naomi?"

"Yes," Boone said.

"Read it."

I got reel bad news for you. Ma went to be with the Lord yesterday. She went easy, and the last thing she said, almost, was to tell you how much she keered fer you. I am rite sorry that I have to tell you this. I know how it will hurt. I will wait here til you get back, or if you will write to me maybe I can come and be with you. I am sorry, Pa. I miss her a lot.

Your loving daughter,
Charlene Peace

Noah held out his hand, and Boone put the letter in it. As the older man ran his fingers over the writing, the fire crackled, and from somewhere far off a wolf sang his lonely song to the night sky.

"She was a good woman, Boone."

"I'm sure she was, from what you tell me."

Noah said quietly, "I got to git back, Boone. We've got enough gold here to buy that place in Virginia. I'm gonna take Charlie and go there."

Although Boone still had his doubts about Noah's plan, he saw the sorrow in the big man's dark blue eyes. "I'm right sorry, Noah." He tried to say something comforting, but there was nothing except, "You need to get back with your daughter."

"I'll start first thing in the morning."

"That'll be best."

"What you figure to do, Boone, with all this gold we dug out?"

"No plans, Noah. I'm like a ship without

a rudder." Boone sat there looking into the fire.

Abruptly Noah said, "Wisht you'd trail along with us, Boone."

"You mean back to the mountains?"

"No, I mean go with us back to Virginia. You ain't ever seed that part of the world, have you?"

"No. Never been to the South."

"You'd like it there, Boone. It's mighty good country. They ain't got big mountains like these, but they's got the Shenandoah Valley. Ain't nothin' prettier than the Smoky Mountains. Not even the Rockies, to my judgment."

Boone's curiosity was stirred. He had heard much of the fighting, and he knew that Noah Peace was doomed for some disappointment. "I guess I'll go along just for a while," he said. "I'd like to see those Smoky Mountains, and I'd like to meet that girl of yours, too."

"She's like her ma in a lot of ways."

They were silent for a while; then Noah finally said, "I feel like I been shot right in the middle, somehow. A man stays with a woman long enough, she gits to be part of him, and when she's gone it's like losin' an arm or a leg. But with me it's more like I done lost a heart."

There was nothing Boone could say, so he made no attempt. *I'll go with him,* he thought as the two went to bed. *He doesn't need to be alone. Maybe I'll like it in Virginia.*

The next morning they got up, packed their gear, and left. As they took one look back at the creek, Noah said, "We didn't get it all. Someday you might git a notion to come back and take the rest."

"Don't think I'll do that," Boone said softly. He let his eyes run over the creek and felt the solid weight of the gold in the canvas sacks slung over his pommel. "I don't think a man should go back too much. If you look too much at what's behind you, you can't know what's going on now, or what may come tomorrow."

Noah nodded. "That's true, but it's hard fer a man not to look back. Come on. Let's get to where Charlie is. . . ."

CHAPTER 5
PROMISE TO A FRIEND

The late-afternoon sun had dropped behind the barricade formed by the Rocky Mountains by the time Noah and Boone reached Denver. Casting a critical glance at the long shadows that were beginning to fall, Noah murmured, "Let's treat ourselves to a little celebration, Boone. We can put up in a hotel, have a good meal, and start out by first light."

Stretching high in the saddle, Boone arched his back and nodded. "That might be all right, as long as we don't get into a poker game and show some of this color we're packing."

"You're right 'bout that. We'll put our dust in the stage office for safekeeping." Noah laid his hand on the bulky canvas bag tied on behind his saddle. Looking thoughtful, he said softly, "More money here than I've ever seed in my life. It'll be plenty to buy that plantation for Charlie." He turned his attention toward the saloons that were already belting out their tunes. "I'm not gonna throw any away on things like that. I might have, though, when I was a young feller like you."

Sensing the unspoken question, Boone returned Noah's gaze. "Don't worry about me, Noah. A good meal and a bed is celebration enough. There's the stage office down there."

The two men wound their way through the traffic that lined the streets, for though it was only approaching dusk, Denver was winding up for its nightly spree. When they reached the false front of the stage office, they slid off their horses and removed the canvas bags from behind the pommels of their saddles.

When they entered the stage office, an elderly man with blue eyes asked pleasantly, "May I help you with something?"

"Like to keep this in your safe overnight," Noah said, dropping the bag on the counter. Boone followed suit. The agent studied the bags for a moment then picked one up, his eyes widening at the weight of it. "Where'd you dig this out?" he asked, not expecting an answer.

"Over that away," Boone said, waving irresolutely toward the east.

"Don't blame you for keepin' a tight lip," the agent replied. He was an old hand and knew that prospectors went to any lengths to avoid telling their secrets. He started to speak again, but two men came in and stood waiting. Glancing at the two who had fastened their eyes on the canvas bags, he murmured, "I'll just put these in the safe for you gentlemen." He turned and opened the safe at the back of the building to his left. Then, grasping one bag in each hand, he put them in, shut the door, and twirled the combination wheel.

"It'll be here for you," he said when he returned.

"Appreciate it. We'll be back in the mornin'. What time do you open?" Noah asked.

"Eight o'clock."

As the two turned to leave, one of the men who had entered smiled. Wearing an ornate, colorful vest and a long, fashionable black coat, he was certainly no miner. "Struck it rich, I take it," he commented.

"Just fair," Noah said then left the building.

"Sometimes I think folks can *smell* gold," he remarked to Boone as they mounted their horses.

"It's only yellow gravel," Boone replied as

he turned his horse's head and the two started down the dusty street. "Butter's yellow, too, and you can spread it on bread. You ever try that with gold?"

Grinning slightly, Noah asked, "That may be right, but did you ever try to buy a mansion with butter?" The two laughed, for there was a lightness, a release of tension as they rode to the hotel and entered the lobby. After signing in, they carried their gear to their second-floor room then washed up.

Leaving the hotel, they ambled in a leisurely fashion down Denver's main street. Some of the saloons were already in full roar. As they moved down the street, the spielers were crying, "Come on over and give us a bet!" Lights beamed through the yellow windows, glittering against the dusk, and bedlam hammered out of the joints. A man stood on one corner as the two passed, lifted his gun and shot into the air, then gave a high-pitched yelp and walked away. Overhead a woman stuck her head through a window and screamed but drew no attention from the passersby, except for Noah and Boone.

"A rough place," Boone observed.

"All towns are bad," Noah said sarcastically.

"Well, you're going to Richmond. That's a town."

"It's different in the South. And anyway, we won't be inside Richmond. I want a place at least ten miles away with cotton fields, corn, and a garden."

Later the two stopped at Franklin House, where they ate a leisurely meal of the usual beefsteak. But there were also fresh vegetables. Curious, Boone asked the waitress, "Where do you get the fresh vegetables?"

"A Chink grows them just outside town." Although the short, heavyset waitress had a harried look on her face, she stopped long enough to give Boone a speculative look. When his eyes rose to meet her gaze, she waited, expecting him to say something. When he did not, she was surprised. "Ain't you gonna ask me what time I get off?"

"What time do you get off?" Boone asked, returning her smile.

"Nine o'clock."

"Too late for me, I guess. I'll be pounding the air by that time. I never have any luck," he said to soften his remark, then shook his head regretfully.

The waitress snorted. "A grown man like you goin' to bed at nine! What's wrong with you?"

"A lot of things, but nothing you could

fix, I guess."

Noah had taken in this encounter with interest. "Right pretty. You ain't interested?"

"I'm just interested in getting to bed and getting to your place, Noah. I'm anxious to meet Charlie."

"You'll like her," Noah said, his thoughts on home and the mountain cabin. "She won't like leavin' the mountains," he admitted. "A time or two Naomi and me tried to get her to put on dresses and go to dances and things in town. She tried it out a few times, but she always came back and said she liked huntin', fishin', and bein' away from people."

As Noah spoke, Boone thought, *If she hates towns, people, dances, and dresses, how in the world does Noah think she's going to fit into Richmond society? From what I hear, they're a pretty snooty bunch. Almost like royalty, those planters are, with everybody else a serf.* But since Boone himself felt much the way Charlie did, he simply said, "It'll be interesting seeing the South. I've heard a lot about it, but what you hear isn't always the way things are."

"I been gone a long time, but I remember enough to know I liked it. Good country, Boone, and good people, too. A might high-tempered, but generous and hospitable."

The two men lingered at the table, and when they rose, Boone put the price of their meal on the table then added a silver dollar for the waitress. "If I'm going to be rich, I might as well start tipping like a rich man," he said. Then he moved out of the restaurant, aware of the gaze the waitress fixed on him, but he did not return it.

The two men went back to their room and went to bed at once. They were more exhausted than they knew from the long months of panning gold, for there had been almost no time when they had gotten good rest. Now they dropped off to sleep at once and were not awakened by the noise on the street below or by their sometimes noisy neighbors.

The next morning, as Noah and Boone visited the agent to reclaim their gold, a thought struck Noah. "Boone, it just occurred to me it might not be so easy to get gold dust broke up into spendin' money."

"I can do that for you," the agent said, his eyes alert.

"Be a good idea," Boone said.

The agent weighed up their gold, figured the worth, and then asked, "How will you have it? Gold coins or greenbacks?"

"Gold coins," Noah said instantly.

But Boone shook his head. "They'd be too hard to carry, Noah. Greenbacks will spend anywhere."

"Even in the South?"

The agent answered at once. "They'll spend better there. Confederate money's gone down to nothin'. If you're headed that way, you can live like a king on U.S. greenbacks."

Noah hesitated. "All right, mostly greenbacks, but I want some gold coins, too." He stood there while the agent counted out the fresh greenbacks, all brand-new notes, and then made up the rest in gold coins, which he put in small canvas bags.

"You leavin' town now?" he asked after the two had counted their money.

"Reckon so."

"Wouldn't travel after dark — that's a lot of cash you're carryin'."

"Thanks for your interest," Noah said as they left the office. The two had already had breakfast and loaded their pack animals, so they swung into the saddle. "Let's be on the way," Noah exclaimed. "I'm hungry for home."

They left Denver, and when the sounds of the city faded, Noah took a deep breath and expelled it excitedly. "I'm always glad to be out of towns," he said, picking up their earlier conversation. He looked over and asked curiously, "Do you like towns, Boone?"

"They're interesting. I went to China once. Now *there* were some towns for you."

"You went all the way to Chiney?"

"Sure. Once."

Noah pondered this amazing fact and finally asked cautiously, "That's on the other side o' the earth, ain't it?"

"Just about, Noah."

"Hard to figure why they don't fall off." He laughed at his own foolishness. He felt lighter, as if the darkness that had dwelled in him since the news of Naomi's death had lifted. "Let's make time," he said and kicked his horse into a fast trot.

The September air was cool and fresh. The mountains glittered over to their left, and to the right were the beginnings of the flatlands, the plain country of Colorado. They followed the road that curved between two groves of evergreens as it lifted in a steep incline. The horses, laboring, slowed to a steady walk. Noah and Boone had almost reached the top of the grade when, without warning, three men dashed out of the thick woods to their right. They had been hidden behind a massive outgrowth of rock, and their intent was obvious, for all were masked.

"Stand where you are! Don't move!" one of the men shouted.

Although both Noah and Boone were wearing guns, they had been taken unaware and were helpless. Two men, with guns out and loaded, flanked a fancily dressed man — a man wearing a colorful vest. With a flash, they realized it was the man they'd seen in the stage office when they had deposited their dust.

"Stand easy and you won't get hurt! We know you got money. If you want to live, toss it down, along with your guns."

With a bitter taste in his mouth, Boone realized they had no chance. He reached into his inner pocket slowly to pull out the thick wallet containing the bills that constituted his share of the money. But while his hand was still inside, he was startled, for Noah had let out a sharp cry and pulled his gun. Boone wanted to shout, "Don't do it! It's suicide!" but it was too late. Noah got off one shot, and it knocked one of the men out of the saddle. He threw his hands up, uttered a short cry, hit the ground, and did not move.

But the other two men opened fire at once, and Boone, who reached to pull his

.44, heard one of the slugs hit Noah, who grunted in the saddle but continued to fire.

As Boone lifted his Colt at the chest of the man with the fancy vest, a slug raked along his ribs, throwing his aim off. Other bullets hissed beside his ear. Noah slumped to the ground, still firing blindly.

Pulling down on the hammer again, Boone could not get a steady bead, for the horses were plunging wildly. Another shot took his hat from his head. When he said, "Steady boy," and his horse steadied, he stretched his arm out, drew a bead, and got off one shot. It struck the vested man so that he slumped, but it didn't kill him. Boone then turned his fire on the other man, who apparently had exhausted his ammunition. Boone's next shot grazed the man's neck, and he dropped his gun and reached up to grab the wound. Then Boone heard him yell, "Let's get out of here!" Boone shot twice more, but the men's horses were plunging, so he missed both times. He pulled the trigger again, but the hammer fell on an empty chamber.

As soon as the men were gone, Boone swung off his horse and ran to where Noah was writhing in the dust on his face. Rolling him over, he demanded, "Are you hurt bad, Noah?" Then he saw that he was. Blood seeping out of his chest had stained his shirt, and his right thigh was also crimson.

Boone whipped out his and Noah's neckerchiefs and made a tourniquet to stop the bleeding of the leg. Pulling the shirt back, he saw that the bullet had entered high and to the right. *If it got a lung, he won't make it,* Boone thought.

"Take it easy, Noah. Don't move."

"Did you — git 'em, Boone?" Noah gasped.

"They're gone. You lie still. I've got to work on this leg."

As he cut away the pant leg and studied the wound, Boone's mind raced. *This is bad. I've got to get him back to a doctor, but I don't know how he'll stand the ride.* His face and mouth grim, Boone considered the options. He was a man of quick decision and action and now said, "Noah, you lie here. I'll make you a travois. You can't sit in the saddle."

"They didn't git — the cash, did they?"

"No, they didn't get the cash." Boone was thinking, *I wish he had let them have it. We could have gone back and dug more gold.*

Edward Fitzgerald was a man of culture, immaculately dressed, hardly fitting into Denver's schemes. But he was the best doctor in Denver. He stood looking down at

100

the still form of Noah Peace, his eyes speculative. He was accustomed to dealing with bullet wounds — indeed, they were his chief stock-in-trade. And now as he looked at the wounded man, he was clinically weighing his chances. Finally, he seemed to have made a decision. "We got the bullets out, but you lost a lot of blood, Mr. Peace."

"Am I gonna make it, Doc?" Noah asked. His voice was thready and weak, and his face pale as paper. But his dark-blue eyes were alive, and he studied Fitzgerald's face as a man might study a book.

"I can't say. I've done the best I can. If you don't get an infection, I think you might make it." Fitzgerald turned to Boone and said, "You'll have to keep him here until he recovers."

"I thought that," Boone said.

"No, I got to git home."

"Don't be a fool, man," Fitzgerald said with irritation. "You're not going anywhere! Come along, Mr. Manwaring!"

Leading Boone out of the room, which was adjacent to his main office, Fitzgerald said, "It's pretty bad."

"What are his chances?"

"I'm not a gambler. I don't deal in chances."

"You've got a pretty good idea, Doctor.

You've seen a lot of men shot."

"Too many." Fitzgerald's reply was glum and his eyes bleak. "The leg will be all right, but he's lost so much blood. It's a wonder he didn't die on the way in. You did a good job getting him here," he admitted grudgingly. "But infection's the problem. When a bullet goes into a man, it carries some of the clothing in. I can't get it out. If it gets an infection . . ." He hesitated then said, "If you're a praying man, I'd suggest you start praying. Are his family close?"

"Up north. Almost at the border."

"I wish they were here."

"Is it that bad?" Boone asked soberly. He searched the doctor's face but found no hope there. "Do all you can for him, Doctor. Money's no problem."

"I'll do the best I can."

Boone walked back into the room where Noah lay, pulled up a chair, and sat down beside him. "Well," he said cheerfully, "it looks like we've got a little change in plans."

"Boone, you reckon you might go git Charlie? I got a feelin' I might not see her if you don't."

Boone had considered this, but he knew it was a hard trip, and he hated to leave Noah alone. "Let's wait a day or two and see how you make out," he said finally. But as he leaned forward and looked at Noah, he knew there was no way he could fool this man. "You've got a good chance, Noah. The doctor said so."

Noah kept his eyes locked on Boone's and smiled faintly. "I don't kid myself 'bout things like this. Somehow it don't seem I'll make it."

Boone tried to think of a cheerful rejoinder but could not. Finally, he said, "I've seen men hurt worse than you make it. I'll be right here, Noah."

"I still think it's a fool thing to do."

Noah looked up from the wagon bed where he was lying. Boone had gotten some help and brought him there, but the pain had been worse than he had thought. "If I'm gonna die, Boone, I want to die on my own place, and I want to be buried beside Naomi."

"You don't know you're going to die," Boone said with some irritation. He had been shocked when Noah had told him the previous day that he wanted to go home. He had argued and pleaded and brought in Dr. Fitzgerald, who had told him it was next to suicide, but Noah had been adamant. "If I'm gonna die, I'd like to see my girl one more time," he had said and finally demanded Boone take him there.

As Boone squatted beside him, arranging the pillows and blankets, he remembered Fitzgerald's comment. *"You may as well take him, Mr. Manwaring. He's got an infection. I don't think he'll make it here, and there's a chance he might get to see his family."*

"Are you comfortable?"

"Yes. Just go."

Boone stepped over the wagon seat, sat down, and took up the lines. He had traded in the two packhorses on a wagon and team, and now he slapped the reins on the backs of the bays. "Get up!"

As they left Denver, depression settled over Boone. He was totally aware that Noah was likely not going to make it. Barring a miracle, he could not live, but it was Boone's avowed purpose to get him home before he died.

He drove slowly all morning, avoiding the potholes as best he could. He passed by freighters and solitary riders and once a stagecoach, but paid them no heed. At noon he pulled up, made a fire, and heated the broth that he had brought in sealed glass jars put up by the hotel cook. He did not attempt to take Noah out of the wagon and could get him to take only a few swallows. Finally, he gave up, and when Noah asked for water, he poured him a cupful out of the canteen and held his head up while he drank thirstily.

"I guess we'll go on if you feel up to it, Noah."

"Yes," was the single monosyllable Noah was able to manage.

Stepping back into the seat, Boone started the team again and drove steadily all afternoon. He paused at dusk to camp beside a swift mountain stream. He took care of Noah's needs, built a fire, and cooked up supper, but once again Noah refused to eat. He seemed to have lost his appetite completely, and nothing Boone could say could cause him to put down more than a few swallows.

After Boone had eaten, he moved back to the wagon and sat beside Noah. He seemed to have drifted off into a coma, and his fever was up, which Dr. Fitzgerald had warned about. Never had Boone Manwaring felt so helpless as when Noah tossed and threw his arms around.

The next morning he rose at sunup, ate a quick breakfast, then changed the bandages on Noah's chest and leg. Noah was more alert, was able to eat some breakfast, and drank a great deal of water. His fever, however, had not gone down. He said softly,

"Go as fast as you kin make it, Boone."

"All right, Noah. I'll do my best."

Noah died two days away from his home.
Both men recognized it was coming. The
fever grew worse, so that Noah passed into
unconsciousness, tossing and turning, his
skin dry and burning. Boone was helpless.
He tried to bring the fever down by bathing
the parched body with cold water from the
mountain streams, but it did no good.

The end came at dusk where Boone had
just made camp. He heard his name called
and at once sprang into the wagon. "What
is it, Noah? Can I get you something?"

"Ain't gonna . . . make it, Boone." The
voice was such a dry whisper that Boone
had to lean forward to hear it.

For two days Noah's eyes had been cloudy
with the fever, but now when he opened
them, they were clear. His mind, too, was
clear for the first time, and he reached up a
tentative hand to touch Boone's chest.
Boone took the hand and held it tightly. It
was hot and dry, and fear swept through
him. "What can I do, Noah — anything?"

"I hate to lay a chore on you, Boone, but
I got no one else to ask."

"Ask it, Noah."

Noah studied the bronzed face that

loomed over him. "I got to ask you to . . . take keer of Charlie. She's a woman growed in body, but she's just a child inside."

"I'll help her all I can, Noah. I promise."

"It's more'n that." Noah closed his eyes. He tried to swallow, and it seemed hard. Boone thought he had passed out again, but then he opened his eyes and whispered, "Take her . . . to Virginia."

"You want me to do that, Noah?"

"I'm askin' you to do so."

Boone desperately wanted to refuse. He could already guess the problems that would ensue, but the dying man's eyes were on him, so he cast aside his reservations. "All right. I will, Noah. I'll take her to Virginia."

"See she's treated right. Find her a place. Stay with her, Boone."

"I promise, Noah."

"And . . ." The chest heaved as he fought for breath. There was a rattle in his throat as he said, "Find her . . . a good man. I'm askin' it."

"I'll — I'll do my best, Noah. I promise."

The eyes looked at him then with something like startled surprise, and the voice was suddenly clear. "I . . . thank you, Boone." Noah was quiet for a while, and he only spoke once more — this time in a faint whisper that came out twenty minutes later.

As Boone held his hand in despair, he saw the lips move. Leaning over, he asked, "What is it? What did you say, Noah?"

"Reckon . . . I'll see Naomi . . . !"

The end was easy, for Noah simply ceased breathing. The chest grew still, and the hand that was in Boone's relaxed.

Boone sat there in the darkness, holding the limp hand with great sadness. He had learned to love and respect this man in a manner that was unusual for him. He was basically a loner, and Noah's friendship had become a vibrant and living thing in his life. He had looked forward to going to Virginia with Noah, and now the man was gone, blotted out in a moment of senseless violence.

Boone looked up into the dark sky and saw only clouds and a few scattered stars. Doubt and almost anger washed over him. He had wondered for a long time about God, for he had seen the savage side of life, and nothing seemed fair. Now as he held his friend's hand, he wondered, *Why did You have to take him, God? He had a dream that was good, and he's got a daughter. I don't feel equal to doing it, but I gave my word.* He looked up, shooting his mind's questions to the velvet canopy overhead, but received no answers. The clouds rolled on, and the earth's silence enveloped him, yet still he sat there, wondering why a man like Noah had to die when others less worthy lived.

Lowering his eyes, Boone realized that he had no alternative plan. He had nothing better to do with his life than to fulfill this promise to Noah. Boone may not have been a cultured, rich man, but he considered a man's word to be his bond. And he felt responsible, at least partly, for Noah's death. Boone looked to the sky again and knew what he must do.

CHAPTER 6
"I DON'T NEED NO MAN!"

The wind in the trees around the cabin had a soothing effect on Charlie, bringing restful, easy sleep. Since her mother's death she had slept poorly, and her appetite had dropped off. With every day that passed, she realized more and more how great her loss was. But tonight she had gone to bed early and fallen asleep at once.

Then, through the curtain of her subconscious mind, she heard a sound, and at once her eyelids opened. She lay in the bed listening, not frightened but alert, like an animal that has scented danger.

Again the sound came, and she slipped out of bed, pulled on the buckskin trousers she had started wearing when fall had come and a wool jacket, then thrust her feet into the deerskin moccasins beside her bed. Moving quietly, she descended the ladder and crossed the room, lit only by moonlight. She reached up over the fireplace mantel for her rifle and checked the priming. Since the sound had come from the front, she slipped out the side door, standing still in the murky darkness.

Charlie was aware of the source of most sounds at night. The cry of a night bird or the howl of the wolf were familiar enough, but this sound was different. She had not been able to identify the source of the sound, but then she picked up on movement coming down the trail. Slipping out from the shadows of the cabin, she crept to the stand of pines that her father had left growing to create shade for the cabin. The sounds were clearly coming to her now, the sounds of footsteps. Living alone had made her more conscious, for there were rough men in these mountains. Lifting the rifle, she waited, and a shadowy figure emerged. He seemed bulky, and she saw he was tall. He also was carrying a gun, but she could not see the face, for his hat shaded his features.

The figure walked slowly forward, almost as if he were uncertain. He came so close to Charlie she almost could have reached out and touched him. At first she thought it might be her father, but he was bulkier than that, and the moonlight had revealed just a glimpse of his features — a face she had never seen. Moving out behind him, she stepped on a dry stick that snapped, and the man whirled, throwing the rifle up. Instantly Charlie brought her rifle down over his head. The hat cushioned some of the blow, but she heard the solid clunk as the metal hit his skull, and he collapsed bonelessly at her feet.

Breathing hard, Charlie bit her lip. *I'm glad I didn't have to shoot him,* she thought. *But I may have to yet.* Carefully she rolled him over, and the hat fell off. She saw a lean face, rather handsome, and as she studied it she wondered what had brought him to the recesses of the mountains. If he'd come in daytime, she might have welcomed him. But he had come like a thief, and now she reached down and pulled the revolver from the holster at his side. It was a heavy gun, and she stood up and checked the load as best she could by the silvery moonlight. She waited patiently, studying his face, her lips drawn in a tight line.

Consciousness came back to Boone with a rush — and a splitting pain that made him shut his eyes and groan. He felt the dry grass under him and knew he was lying full length, but for a moment he couldn't even remember where he was or what he was doing there. Startled, he opened his eyes and sat up, which made the pain worse. Something moist ran down his forehead, and, reaching up, he touched a raw wound on his scalp. Then a voice said, "Set right still!"

Looking up, Boone saw a young woman whose face was illuminated by the faint starlight. The moon came out from behind a cloud, throwing its silver beams across her, and he took in the high cheekbones, the oval face, and the wide mouth.

Boone sat still but explored the bump that was already beginning to rise. The gash was bleeding freely.

"Do you always greet people by knocking their brains out?" he said angrily. As he slowly got to his feet, he saw she was standing clear but was holding his revolver leveled steadily at his stomach.

"I'm keerful when strange men come bustin' onto our place in the middle of the night totin' a gun." The voice was cool and steady, rich with mountain dialect, but he couldn't see her eyes.

"Are you Charlie Peace?"

"That's my name. How come you know it?"

It was an awkward moment for Boone Manwaring. He stood there for a moment, unable to think of a reply. She watched him carefully, and then he said, "I —" He could not finish the sentence, for to tell her that her father was dead was a hard thing. Finally, he said, "My name is Boone Manwaring. I came — to tell you about your father."

The gun wavered slightly, and the light from the moon made a silver line along the barrel. "My pa?" she asked quietly. "You know my pa?"

"You been getting letters from him. I'm the one who wrote them."

And then suddenly Charlie remembered. This was the man who had written with such beautiful handwriting. "You're Boone Manwaring?" she said. She looked past him. "Where's Pa?"

The howl of a wolf from the neighboring ridge floated over the still air as Boone tried to think of some way to break his terrible news. At last he cleared his throat. "I've got bad news for you, Charlie."

Instantly the young woman grew still, and she lowered the revolver. "Is it about Pa? Is he hurt bad?"

There was no way out, and Boone would rather have been any place on earth than facing her dark eyes. "He's dead, Charlie. I'm sorry."

The words hit the young woman like a

blow. She dropped the revolver and walked blindly away toward the cabin. Not knowing what else to do, Boone reached over, picked up the revolver, and stuck it back in his holster. He picked up the rifle that she had leaned against the base of a tree and stepped forward until he was only a few feet away. As he stood there silently, he noticed that her shoulders were shaking. He wanted to go forward to put his arm around her, but he was a stranger.

Finally, the young woman seemed to recover. Without turning, she said, "Come on in. I'll fix your head."

"You don't have to do that."

She did not answer but went inside and lit a lamp. Boone followed her and stood helplessly, but she did not speak. She moved stiffly toward a shelf nailed to the cabin wall, and he saw that her face was pale. "Set here," she said, and when he obeyed, she filled a basin with water and tore a strip from a piece of cloth. "It will hurt a mite," she said then began to cleanse the wound. After she had washed the blood away, she said, "This here will sting," then applied some sort of salve that smelled like balsam. Boone gasped at the fiery bite of the ointment then asked, "Does it need sewing up?"

"Reckon not. Have to be washed out fer a

few days."

Turning abruptly, she emptied the basin, replaced it on the shelf, then said, "I'll fix you up a bit to eat." Going to the fireplace, she raked up the coals and threw some sticks on. Almost at once a fire began to crackle, sending tendrils of smoke up the chimney. Boone took a chair over by the rough-hewn table, feeling more uncomfortable than ever before in his life. He thought of leaving but knew that wouldn't do. He watched as she made coffee, fried ham, then threw some eggs into the skillet. She took a plate off the shelf and laid it in front of him, along with a knife and fork.

"Reckon this'll have to do you, Mr. Manwaring."

"Boone will do." Boone began to eat. He was not really hungry, or if he was, he was so disturbed he could not think of it. She poured a cup of coffee and sat down across from him. When he had eaten, he murmured, "That's mighty good, Charlie."

"Tell me 'bout it. What happened to Pa?"

Boone began, "I met your pa in Denver. We got on very well. . . ."

Charlie listened with hungry eyes, as if the words had sustenance for her. When Boone finally talked about Noah's last words, he did not face her but looked down at his hands that were folded on the table. "He asked me to make him a promise, Charlie. He had it in his mind to take you to Virginia. You and your mother at first, but when the word came that she died, the dream was even stronger in him."

"I know. He always figured he'd missed somethin' there. I don't know if he did or not." She held her coffee cup with nervous hands, turning the cup. When she looked up at him, her pale face made her dark blue eyes look almost black. "I told him the mountains was good enough fer me, but he wanted me to go there. He wanted me to put on purty dresses and learn how to dance."

"That was his dream," Boone said. "And I promised him I'd take you there, Charlie, and I will if you want me to."

Neither of them spoke for a time. Finally, Charlie said, "I'll think on it."

"It's your say, but I'll do my best because I promised your father." He hesitated and said, "He was a fine man. Maybe the finest I ever knew."

She looked up at him then, and he knew her heart was empty and at the same time filled with grief. She rose suddenly and motioned toward the bedroom. "You kin sleep in there — Boone."

"All right."

She banked the fire then picked up the rifle and headed for the door. "I'm goin' out fer a spell." As she began to disappear into the darkness, he remembered the wagon. He ran outside and caught up with her. "I stopped the wagon about a quarter of a mile down. I couldn't get it up the trail in the darkness. I've — I've got your father there."

"You brought Pa with you?"

"He wanted to be buried beside your mother. . . . Charlie, he wanted more than anything else to see you before he died. I did my best to get him here, but he just couldn't make it. He said he loved you then asked to be buried beside your mother."

"I'm thankin' you, Boone," Charlie whispered. "Reckon we'll go git him now."

Charlie carefully penned *October 5, 1863* at the top of the sheet then wrote:

We buried Pa today right beside Ma like he always said he wanted. I am proud they are together now. In a way its funny. It makes me feel better bout Ma that she aint lyin out there alone. It seems like I been walkin around without much sense ever since Boone brought Pa back, but now that they are side-by-side I feel considerable better.

Reaching over, she dipped the turkey quill into the ink. It was late afternoon, when the sun was going down over the peaks, spreading its rosy rays over the valley. She admired it then began to write again.

Boone aint said much, but from what I kin make out Pa wanted me to go to Virginia and become a lady. I aint got no hankerin fer that, but if its what Pa wanted, I reckon I will have to do it. It will plum tear my heart out to leave this place. I reckon I will sell it to Jed Tompkins. He made an offer to buy it just after the funeral, in case I wanted to sell. I guess I will be glad to go. Every place I look now I would be thinkin about Pa on the outside of the cabin, just like I been thinkin about Ma on the inside. Maybe the best thing is to git away, and thats what Pa wanted. So I have made up my mind that I am goin.

She finished writing then went downstairs. Boone was not there, but she heard the sound of an ax splitting wood. Stepping outside, she saw him wield the ax and called out, "Boone!"

Boone turned toward her. The paleness had gone somewhat, and he admired the smoothness of her olive skin. She was, he thought, the most beautiful woman he had ever seen. "What is it, Charlie?"

"I reckon I'll go to Virginia."

"You sure that's what you want?"

"It's what Pa wanted, the last thing he asked, so I got to do it."

"I think it might be the best," Boone said thoughtfully. "When would you want to go?"

"As soon as we kin. It makes me sad to be around here."

"It's not easy to lose someone."

"What 'bout your folks?"

"Don't have any."

"They're both dead?"

"Both of them. I guess I'm all alone in the world."

Charlie regarded him carefully. She had done so since he came, for he was different than the other men in the mountains. There was a fineness about Boone Manwaring that interested her. But the fact that he had widely traveled and was educated made her feel somewhat awkward around him. Once, she had put in her diary, "I wonder if he thinks I'm nothin' but a country bumpkin', which I guess I am." Now she said quietly, "I got to do it, Boone."

"Whenever you're ready, we'll go."

"Pa wanted to buy a big mansion and make a lady out of me."

Alarmed, Boone felt constrained to say, "I tried to talk to your father about this, Charlie. It was his dream, but dreams sometimes don't turn out well when we get them."

"What do you mean by that?"

"I don't know how to say it, but sometimes a man or a woman will think, *If I just had this, I'd be happy.* Then they get it and find out that it wasn't what was lacking in them." Seeing she was puzzled by his words, he continued, "But I think it's right to go to Virginia. From what I hear, the people there are hospitable. They're brave, too, taking on the whole United States army and navy."

"I reckon they are. You don't have to go with me," she said abruptly.

"I promised your father."

"But I'm releasin' you if you want it that way."

"No. I did promise your father, but I always wanted to see the South. We'll go when you're ready."

"We're ready for sunup tomorrow," Charlie said. The two were standing on the path outside the cabin. They had stepped outside after supper into the night, and now long shadows reached out over the hills. Quietness had fallen in the cool fall air.

"Are you glad to be going, Charlie?"

"I reckon I am. I won't be comin' back here, not fer a long time anyhow." She looked around and whispered, "I'll miss this place."

"Always hard to move on, I guess." He was standing close enough so that his shoulder almost brushed hers. "Care to walk and take one more look around?"

"All right."

The cows lowed as they passed, and she spoke fondly, saying, "I'll miss you, Betsy." Then she added, "I'm glad Jed Tompkins wanted all the critters. I'd hate to just turn them loose."

The two walked under the whispering trees until finally they stopped at the edge of the forest. "I — I ain't thanked you proper fer what you did fer Pa. Ain't many men woulda did it."

She seemed very vulnerable at that moment, and Boone felt a rush of pity. "It's been hard on you, Charlie — losing your mother and then your father. I'm sorry."

She looked up at him, tears in her eyes. She had not wept, at least in his sight, since her father's funeral. But now he saw that the thought of leaving was oppressive to her, and her lips trembled.

"Charlie, it'll be all right," he said softly. Impulsively reaching forward, he drew her close and held her against his chest. For a moment she pressed against him, then suddenly struck him in the chest and stepped back. She dashed the tears from her eyes and flared out, "Don't you ever tetch me!"

"I meant nothing by it, Charlie."

"You heered me, Boone! I don't ever want to be tetched! I know right well what men say — and what they do! They've been around here often enough! But I don't need nothin' like that!"

"Your father asked me to get you settled, to help you find a good man for a husband."

Charlie Peace straightened her back, a fierce glint in her eye. She said almost vehemently, "I don't need none of your help to get a man, Boone!"

Boone stepped back, not willing to argue. "I'm sorry," he said again. "I won't interfere."

"Best that way!" Charlie said. As she walked back toward the cabin, she threw these words over her shoulder: "We'll leave first light in the morning."

Ever since Boone Manwaring had made his vow to Noah Peace, he'd been apprehensive. Now, watching Charlie's disappearing form, he felt almost angry at him-self. *Why'd you have to get into this?* he thought. *Why didn't you just leave things alone?* But he knew why: When a man has a friend, he stands by him. Now he stood in the falling daylight and wondered, *How am I going to keep my promise to Noah? She needs a father, and she doesn't have one.* Finally, he went back to the porch and sat there for a long time, watching as the sun finished going down. Then he went to bed, dreading what was to come.

■ ■ ■ ■

PART TWO:
THE MISFITS

■ ■ ■ ■

CHAPTER 7
YOUNG LOVE —
AND NOT SO YOUNG

In November 1863, winter came to Virginia almost with a single bound. One day the air was mild with fall's gentle breezes and the land bathed in sunshine. Then the beast of winter arrived, shriveling the grass to a deadly gray.

Clay Rocklin sat in the parlor with his wife, Melora, who was sewing the new symbol of his authority onto the sleeves of his gray Confederate army uniform. Outside, low-lying clouds formed. "I think there's snow coming."

Looking up from her needlework, Melora said, "It will be a bad winter, I think. Paul said the pecans had extra-thick shells."

"And the caterpillars were more woolly than usual. He said that, too, didn't he?"

Melora Yancy Rocklin's green eyes crinkled as she smiled. "Paul always knows what the weather's going to do."

"I expect he does," Clay answered, shrugging. "Are you about through with that uniform?"

"Almost." Melora took a few more stitches. As she did, Clay watched her. She was only twenty-nine to his forty-three, and sometimes he wondered if he had done the right thing in marrying such a young woman. She had waited for him, however, since she was a young girl. Quickly he thought of his first wife, Ellen, who had made life such a misery to him and everyone around her — and to herself most of all. He recalled her death with sorrow, for she had not had a happy life, and Clay had never reconciled himself completely to the fact that he had not made her any happier. He had married her on the rebound after being rejected by Melanie Benton, who had married his cousin Gideon.

As Clay studied Melora, taking in her black hair and smooth cheeks, he was grateful. Although it had been difficult, for he had loved Melora for years, he had been faithful to Ellen even though their marriage had been a travesty. And now it seemed that the Lord was rewarding them. Melora was nearly two months pregnant and due in June. "How are you doing today?" he asked, smiling at her.

"We're fine. Both of us."

"Take good care of that new son of mine."

Melora stood up, holding the coat out for him. "I'll take good care of our *daughter*," she said. It was a long-standing, teasing argument between the two of them. Although neither actually had strong preferences for either a boy or a girl, it was one of those little games they had played since their marriage. When she had discovered she was pregnant, Melora had been ecstatic. But Clay had looked solemn, worried about Melora and the baby because of his dangerous line of work. When he voiced his concerns that he might die in battle, she had touched his cheek, saying, "God didn't let me wait for you all these years to lose you, Clay. We're going to grow old together. You can shout into my hearing trumpet, and I'll keep up with your false teeth."

Slipping into the coat, Clay looked down at the sleeves of his uniform where the curling insignia of a lieutenant colonel wound in a serpentine fashion. "I think they made a mistake making me a colonel."

"They don't make mistakes like that."

"Well, it's only a brevet rank, you understand. You know what that means?"

"Not quite," Melora said.

"It means I'm not really a colonel and that when they get a real one, I'll go back to being a major. You'll have to pick out all those stitches." He grinned, tenderly putting his arms around her and drawing her close. "I love you, Melora."

Melora pulled his head down and kissed him. One of the things she loved about him was the fact that he wasn't embarrassed to tell her of his love. She kept her arms around his neck, pleased just to hold him. Knowing that time was short, that soon he would ride out with the regiment, she put aside her apprehension and instead looked up into his eyes. He was the handsomest man she knew. His raven hair had only a few gray hairs, mostly along the long sideburns, and his olive skin was smooth and clear. Known as one of the "Black Rocklins," he was still muscular and trim.

"Your coat's a little too large," Melora chided. "You've lost weight."

"Well, you've gained it," he teased her.

"There's that much more of me for you to love!"

"Right! Now let's sit down, and you can tell me what a beautiful *son* I'm going to have."

He led her over to the horsehide couch in front of the window. It was a favorite place for both of them, for they could look out on Gracefield's sprawling lawn and circular drive. Over to the east, the hills formed a cup that held the valley; to the west the land leveled out to the cotton fields, filled only with stalks, and after that the second-growth timber that lay between them and Richmond.

Clay listened as she talked about the child who was about to come. But Clay could tell, even in their brief time of marriage, that she was worried, because the right side of her lips tightened. It was unconscious with her, he knew, so he finally said, "Are you concerned about something?"

She murmured, "You know me too well, Clay."

"Is it about the baby?"

"No, it's about the war." She ran her fingers down the back of his hand then asked, "What's going to happen?"

"We're going to lose."

Startled, Melora looked up. She had known Clay was filled with doubts about the war. He had not wanted the South to secede in the first place, and he had joined only out of a desire to help Lowell, his youngest son, who was going through a difficult time. He had enlisted and risen rapidly through the ranks, becoming an officer very quickly, but all the time, through the hard-fought battles of Bull Run, Antietam, and Gettysburg, she had seen that his hope for victory had been quietly put away. He served now out of duty, she understood, to his state and because he could not lift his hand against his family or his people. She suspected there were many in the South who were in the same position, for most men in the Confederate army owned no slaves.

"Do you think there's no hope at all?"

"Look at it this way, Melora. Every time we have to keep a line of battle, every time one of our men gets wounded or killed, that leaves a hole in that line. There's no one else to put in that hole, Melora. We've taken every young boy of fifteen to man of fifty, and they're all gone now. If the North loses twenty thousand men, all they have to do is reach back into their reserves and bring up another twenty thousand. Their factories are turning out munitions at an unbelievable rate. We have hardly a factory left in the South we can count on. If Atlanta falls, or Richmond, it's all over."

"Why doesn't President Davis simply surrender?"

"He'll never do that," Clay said sorrowfully. "He's too proud. We'll go on as long as we have an army. That's all that keeps them out — the Army of Northern Virginia here in Richmond, and Joe Johnston's Army of the Tennessee."

"Things didn't go well in Tennessee, did they?"

"No, we took a terrible beating at Lookout Mountain. We won Chickamauga, perhaps, but it didn't help. Now Sherman is gathering a huge army, and he'll begin to push Johnston back toward Atlanta."

"Can General Johnston hold him off?"

"No. All he can do is retreat. There's only one end to that."

Melora listened as Clay spoke, and she saw the air of fatality that gripped him. He would never quit, she knew; he loved his men too much for that. Fiercely she wished the war were over, but she knew women in the South — and North — were wishing for the same thing.

Finally, sensing she was depressing Clay, Melora said, "Well, it's as God wills. Whether we win or lose, we'll have our family."

"That's my girl. You always had more faith than any woman I ever saw."

"Not more than your mother."

"I think you're a close tie," Clay said. Then he frowned. "I'm worried about Marianne and Claude."

He spoke of his aunt Marianne, his father's sister, who had married a stranger named Claude Bristol. It had been a very romantic courtship, but Clay knew they did not have a happy marriage. Claude did not fit into the Rocklin family as well as Marianne had hoped. From a French background, he had a volatile temperament and a store of good looks, but bad luck. The family was kind enough to call it "bad luck," although Marianne's brothers knew it was more than that. Claude Bristol was a sportsman, a gambler, and he drank too much. Although his charm and wit had carried him along in the society, and one could not help liking him, Clay wished he had more sense and less charm.

"What's wrong with them?"

"I'm afraid they're in financial difficulties."

"Why, aren't we all?"

"I know, but I think it's worse for them. If something doesn't happen, I think they're going to lose Hartsworth."

"Why, that can't be true, Clay! It isn't that bad, surely!"

"I think it's worse than anybody knows. Marianne doesn't talk to me much about things like that, but I picked up the idea from Paul and Austin."

Paul Bristol, the older son, had married a

woman named Frankie Ames. He had become a fine photographer and had moved to Birmingham, Alabama, where he continued his profession.

"Paul told me the finances were in an absolute mess, and Austin said the same thing."

"I talked to Marie last week," Melora said thoughtfully. "She didn't say anything about trouble." Marie was Marianne and Claude's only daughter, a beautiful young woman. "She usually says whatever's on her mind."

Clay shook his head. "I don't think she would — not in a case like this. I'm going by there and see. Maybe I can talk to Claude. Not that we have any money to help anybody with." He reached over and hugged her. "We're pretty well broke ourselves." Then, anxious to get away from the talk of finance, he said, "I'm more concerned about Rena than I am about our finances."

"She's all right," Melora said quickly. She had always been fond of Clay's daughter, now seventeen. The two were close friends, and Melora was proud she had become a mother, indeed, to someone who had had great difficulties earlier in life. Rena had been ashamed of her mother, Ellen, and ashamed of being ashamed. Melora looked up at Clay and asked, "Are you worried about Josh?"

"I guess I am a little bit," he admitted, "although he's a fine young man."

Josh was Melora's seventeen-year-old brother. They came from a large family, and Josh was, perhaps, her favorite among the boys. "Why are you worried, Clay?" she queried.

"Rena keeps talking about wanting to get married, and I think it's a bad idea right now."

"That's what people said about us."

"I know, but it's different with us. We're older."

"Young love — and not so young," Melora said. "What's the difference?"

"I guess young love may be more impulsive. I'm afraid they'll get married, and sooner or later Josh is going to be in the army. He's already begged me to take him into the brigade."

"I know. He's talked to me about it. He wants me to influence you. I hate to see him go. We've already lost Lonnie."

"He'll go; there's no question about that. I just wish they'd wait until the war is over."

"That's easy to say, Clay," Melora mused. "But when you're seventeen and in love, it's hard to think logically."

The two talked for a while, and finally

Clay arose. "I've got to get back to camp," he said.

"When will you be able to get back again?"

"I'm not sure. It depends on Ulysses S. Grant. When spring comes he'll move his army down from Washington. And from what I hear of that fella, he won't stop until he gets to Richmond or dies trying."

"Come back as soon as you can, Clay. I want every second with you."

"You can believe I'll do that." He put his arms around her and kissed her cheek, then her neck. "You're so beautiful, Melora," he whispered. "When I leave here it's like tearing part of myself away. Sometimes I want to just let everything slide and stay with you."

"I feel that way, too, Clay, but we can't," she said, her eyes tender. "Come back, Clay. Come back soon!"

"Do you know what this arbor's for?" Rena asked, her eyes twinkling with mischief as she regarded Josh Yancy, who sat beside her on the cold bench. They had come to the arbor covered with scuppernong vines shortly after Josh had arrived at Richmond. Josh was tall, lean, and muscular like his father, and Rena was convinced she'd been in love with Josh forever. Now she waited for his answer. It was slow in coming, for he was not a quick-speaking young man. In moments of distress he often exhibited the slight stutter that had plagued him most of his life.

"I reckon it's to raise grapes," he said, admiring Rena shyly.

"No, that's just an excuse. This arbor's where all the Rocklin men bring their girls to court them. Look, no one in the house can see a thing because of the vines." She pulled the vines back and pointed toward the house. "See, no one can see what we're doing. Does that give you any ideas?"

Josh's lean face flushed, for he knew she was teasing him. "I reckon I do," he said. He leaned forward and kissed her on the cheek, then hesitated and said huskily, "You're mighty sweet, Rena, and the prettiest girl I know."

Rena waited for him to kiss her again and to pull her into his arms as he had done on a few occasions. Josh had a reserve that sometimes pleased her — and other times, such as now, got on her nerves.

"I declare, Josh Yancy, you have no more romance in you than a — than a doorknob!"

"A doorknob!" Josh blinked with surprise. "Why, I don't know what you're talking about!"

"Why, I mean here we are all alone, and all you can do is give me a peck on the cheek! I bet if Henry Watson were here, he'd do better than that!"

"Well, I'm not Henry Watson!" Josh's eyes kindled slightly as he mentioned the name, for this wealthy planter's son was not a pleasant thought to him. It seemed that every time Josh went to Gracefield, Henry Watson was parked there in the parlor with Rena. "If you want Henry Watson to paw you out in this arbor . . . !"

"Oh, I didn't mean that!" the vivacious Rena said quickly. She touched Josh's cheek. "I was just teasing you. Don't take things so seriously."

Josh knew he was not as lively as some of the young men who came to court Rena, but he was held back by the knowledge that they were the sons of wealthy planters or merchants in Richmond, while he was the son of a small farmer who had nothing but a few acres back in the deep woods. It troubled him, and he wished he could express himself better to Rena. He remembered when he had first met Rena — how he had stuttered so horribly that he would not say a word in her presence. But over a period of time, as they grew up, she had won his confidence and encouraged him so that, during the war, he had learned to love her as he had never thought he could love anyone else.

Rena leaned back on the bench. "You don't seem very happy today."

Josh shot her a glance. "I guess you know me pretty well. . . . I came over to talk to your father."

Rena's eyes flew open, and words involuntarily leaped to her lips. "You're going to ask him if we can get married?"

"Why — no! Not that, Rena!" Josh stuttered somewhat, for he knew that they had talked about this before. As the excitement in her eyes died down, he took her hand. "I came to ask him to let me join the Stonewall Brigade."

All the joy went out of the morning for Rena Rocklin. "I knew you were going to do it."

"I've got to do it, Rena. You can see that, can't you?"

"I suppose so."

Her bleak reply did not encourage Josh, so he went on to defend his actions. "I'm seventeen," he said. "All the other fellows my age are already in the army."

Rena listened with a sense of gloom as he spoke. She had known it was coming. Her father and Melora had warned her, and Josh himself had insisted that sooner or later he would have to go. Now that the moment had come, however, she said despairingly, "Let's get married before you go to the army. We can take a few weeks."

"Why, it wouldn't be fair, Rena. What if something happened to me?"

Rena had thought of that also. The country was filled with eighteen- and nineteen-year-old widows. The toll of the war had been harsh, but Rena put all that out of her mind. "I love you, Josh," she said simply.

"Why, I love you, too." Josh Yancy threw his arms around Rena, and she nestled close to him. He lost himself in the pleasure of the moment as her soft lips found his, and her hands clasped his neck.

Rena drew back and whispered, "Please, Josh, let's get married!"

"I can't do it, Rena. It wouldn't be fair."

That was the beginning of the quarrel. Rena argued gently at first, and then when Josh was stubborn she grew more demanding. Finally, she said stiffly, "You don't love me at all!" Rising to her feet, she started for the house.

Josh hurried after her, saying, "Oh, Rena, don't say that! I do love you, but it wouldn't be fair!"

"Well, go on and join the old army, then!"

Tears now blinded Rena's face, and she did not want him to see her crying. He caught her, however, turned her around, and when he saw the tears, exclaimed, "Don't cry — please don't cry!"

So the quarrel was made up as it is by young lovers — with a sweet kiss. Later Rena watched Josh as he swung aboard his strawberry mare with the natural grace of a born horseman. He waved at her and smiled as he galloped out of the yard, shouting, "I'll stop back and see you after I get signed up!"

Rena called back, "I'll wait for you!" and then went at once to the kitchen, where Melora was making a pie. Taking a tall stool, she set it by her stepmother and asked, "Are men always so stubborn, Melora?"

Startled, Melora's eyes flew open, and then she laughed quietly. "What do you mean?"

"Josh always has to have his own way. He's going to join the army."

"You knew it was coming, didn't you? He's talked to you about it."

"Oh yes, but I thought we'd get married before that happened."

"You won't?"

"I asked him to marry me. He said it wouldn't be fair."

"Josh is very levelheaded. He's always been that way," Melora remarked, beginning to speak of how Josh, even as a young boy, had been steady and reliable. Melora noticed that although the talk pleased Rena, she still seemed dissatisfied and unhappy. Finally, Melora said, "You'll have to wait a little, I guess."

"Melora, what's it like being married?"

"Why, what in the world do you mean, Rena?"

"Well, I don't know anything about — well, about marriage." Rena's cheeks were tinged with pink. "Most girls had a mother, I guess, to teach them what a woman's supposed to do, but Mother never talked about those things with me. So if I get married, I won't know anything."

"There are worse things than that," Melora said quietly. "Some girls know everything. They bring their husbands nothing fresh. Be thankful you can come to your husband with a sweetness that hasn't been touched."

"But shouldn't I know something?"

For the next half hour the two women talked quietly of the physical intimacies of marriage and then of what a marriage really meant even beyond that. Rena listened intently as Melora concluded, "God gave us

143

two sides of marriage, Rena. The physical side and the spiritual side. Both are important, and no one can tread the way for you. But if you love Josh, and he loves you, you will discover the joy of marriage."

"I can tell you and Pa are so happy," Rena said. "I hope Josh and I will be like that."

Melora opened her arms, held Rena for a long moment, then whispered, "You will, daughter — you will!"

A general air of dilapidation hung over the city of Richmond. There was nothing shining or polished about the streets as Clay threaded his way between the wagons, horses, mules, and throngs of people.

"Colonel — Colonel Rocklin!"

Clay, at first, was shocked, for he was not accustomed to his new office title yet. Turning, he saw Sam Birdwell, the tall, thin owner of the Crescent Saloon, coming across the street. Stopping his horse, Clay called, "Hello, Sam." Then, seeing the agitation in Birdwell's blue eyes, he asked, "What's wrong?"

"Well, I hate to bother you with it, Colonel," Birdwell said, "but I got to." Birdwell ran his hand through his salt-and-pepper hair. "It's your uncle, Mr. Bristol."

Alarmed, Clay asked, "What is it, Sam? Is

he drunk again?"

"Dead drunk this time, Colonel. I tried to make him leave, but you know how he gets sometimes. He threatened to shoot me if I didn't leave him alone and serve him whiskey."

"Where is he now?"

"He passed out, and I took him into my office. Got him on the couch. I won't mind if you want to leave him there."

"No, Sam. That's good of you, but I'll have to get him home. I'll have someone come by as soon as I can."

"Sorry to bother you about this, Colonel."

Clay offered his hand. "I appreciate your concern, Sam. It was good of you."

"Nothing a'tall. Nothing a'tall, Colonel."

Clay nodded then moved on down the street. Spurring his horse into a fast gallop, he headed for the camp, which lay just north of Richmond. His mind worked quickly, trying to think of a way to handle the situation, but he could not. "I can't go back now. I've got to get to my duties. Austin will have to handle it."

Five minutes later he pulled up in front of the large white building that housed several of the government agencies, one of them being the War Department. He stepped out of his saddle, tied the horse, then saluted

145

the young sergeant who stood guard at the door. Once inside, he mounted the stairs two at a time until he came to the second floor. He entered the third door on his right and saw Austin Bristol sitting at his desk.

"Hello, Austin."

"Why, Clay —" Austin jumped up, his blue-green eyes shining with pleasure. "I mean, Colonel! Sorry about that, sir!"

At the age of thirty-one, black-haired Austin Bristol was one of the neatest young men Clay had ever seen. He always looked freshly barbered and shaved, and his clothes were meticulously right, as if whatever Austin Bristol put on achieved a sort of grace. He came forward limping slightly, for he had been wounded in an earlier skirmish and had complications. Now he served as one of General Lee's liaison officers in the War Department. "How does it feel to be a colonel?"

Clay shook his head. "Somebody made a mistake somewhere. If they have to have me for a colonel, we're in real trouble."

"I don't think so, sir."

Clay shifted his feet nervously. Usually he was a straightforward man, able to handle most things by "setting them on the front porch." Now, however, as he looked at Austin, he hated to bring him more trouble. He already knew that Austin and his sister, Marie, were very concerned about what was happening on their plantation. But it had to be done.

"I hate to bother you with this, Austin, but Sam Birdwell down at the Crescent stopped me."

Instantly Austin's eyes hardened. "Is it Father?"

"I'm afraid so. He drank a little too much and passed out."

"Where is he?"

"Sam put him to bed in his office. I'd like to take care of him, but I'm just getting back."

Austin settled back on his heels, his jaw hard. "I'll take care of him, sir. Would you give me permission to be absent from my desk?"

"I'll see to that. Take him home. Come back in the morning, Austin."

"Yes, sir."

"I'm sorry about this."

"We're all sorry about it." It was unusual to hear bitterness in Austin's voice, since he was normally a cheerful, easygoing man. But Austin was ashamed of his father, so now he simply said, "I'll be going."

"Austin, don't be too hard on him," Clay said quickly. "He's not a happy man."

Austin gave Clay Rocklin a look that was almost harsh. "He's made his life, Clay," he said, forgetting to use the title.

There was nothing Clay could say, so he watched as Austin left the room hurriedly, then moved out to find the officer of the day to get belated permission for Austin to be gone. As he walked down the busy hallway, he thought with a twinge of anger toward his uncle, *He doesn't have to be like this! He could do better if he wanted to!*

Chapter 8
The Wrong Man

"How old are you, Ketura?"

The black woman who walked alongside
Marie Bristol did not answer until the pair
of them reached the end of the section set
off for the slave quarters. The cabins the
Bristol slaves inhabited were neat, though
small, and carefully whitewashed. They
reflected the sun that spread itself over the
earth and warmed the November breeze
that came in from the north.

"How old I be? Why, laws, Miss Marie, I
ain't got no ideer!" The idea intrigued the
black woman, for she stopped in front of a
three-foot-high wooden structure and rested
her hand on it as she considered. A fine
network of wrinkles crisscrossed her face;
even her lips appeared shriveled. Finally,
she said, her old dark eyes glowing with
humor, "As far as I can calculate, I must be
somewhere between eighty-five and ninety."

Marie, who had been partially raised by

Ketura and loved her, smiled and took the woman's hand. It was bony now, not strong and hard like Marie remembered it as a child. But even then Ketura had seemed old to her. "Do you remember much about when you were a girl?" she asked gently.

"First I remember I belonged to Mr. Tom Hadley in Louisiana. My ma, she worked in the rice fields there, and my pa, he cut timber for Mr. Hadley. He was a fine man, my pa," she said, struggling to bring the memories into focus. "Once, the men tried their strength to see who could throw an anvil the farthest, and my pa threw it a full ten feet past what them other men did. He was a powerful strong man, my pappy!"

Twenty-six-year-old Marie Bristol hesitated for a moment, thinking. The breeze caught her rich brown hair, ruffling it slightly, and the sun added a slight reddish tinge. Her deep eyes were full of intelligence — and also known for the hint of deviltry that would leap into them at times. Her plain woolen work dress, which had been dark red, was now faded after innumerable washings. "I don't remember him," Marie finally said.

"Oh no, child! He was sold downriver. We heard he went to a man in Georgia, and my ma, she was sold to Mr. James Clifford when I was fifteen."

Such sadness filled Marie that she asked what she probably would not have asked another slave woman. "Did it hurt you a lot to be separated from your ma and pa?"

"Of course it hurts, child. Why you reckon it wouldn't hurt? Think how you would feel if you was separated from your ma and pa."

"I know. It was a stupid question."

Ketura patted Marie's arm, a fondness in her eyes. She shifted the sweet-gum stick that protruded from her mouth as she answered, "I guess people hurt whether they're black or white." Then, seeing Marie's depressed mood, Ketura said more cheerfully, "But 'bout that time I married up with my first husband. His name was Roscoe, and whooee — he was a scutter!"

Loving to hear the tales of Ketura's youth, Marie grinned broadly. "Was he good looking, Ketura?"

"Good lookin'? I speculate he was! He was tall and strong, and every gal that ever got close to him couldn't keep her eyes off him!"

"Did you have trouble keeping him honest?" Marie teased.

"No, ain't had no trouble with nothin' like that!" Ketura said. "Woman's got to know how to keep a man happy if she wants to keep him close to home. 'Specially if he's good lookin'."

"Maybe you'd better tell me how you did it in case I ever stop being an old maid and get a husband of my own someday."

"You get you a man; then I'll tell you how to keep him!" Ketura said. "Now let's get started on this here soap. We done run nearly plumb out, and Mr. Austin say they ain't none to be had much in Richmond. I don't like that soap he buys nohow! I can make better than that!"

It was not unusual for Marie Bristol to spend time with Ketura. She had learned a great deal about the myriad details involved with plantation life, and early in the morning she had asked Ketura to let her help with the soap making. Now the two stood there before the V-shaped affair that was wide at the top and came to a point at the bottom. It was nailed together with boards and lifted up on poles. Out of the bottom ran a spout, and under the spout was a large tin bucket.

"We make the lye first of all," Ketura announced. "This here is ashes from the hickory you done burned already. Hickory ashes make the best lye for soap. Sometimes you have to use oak or somethin' else, but hickory's the best. You just start pourin' water in over these ashes."

Marie watched as Ketura's grandson Isley brought bucket after bucket of water from the nearby well. As he poured the liquid in, it soaked into the ashes at once.

"I don't see how this makes lye, Ketura," Marie said when the black woman finally cautioned Isley to stop.

"I don't know neither, but it do! And soon as that bucket under that spout fills up, we're ready to get to our soap makin'."

The two women went back to the house, where Marie sat back, listening to more of Ketura's tales of her youth and drinking sassafras tea. Sometime later Ketura said, "Appears to me like that lye ought to be about done. Let's go get that bacon fat we been savin'. . . . If you want this soap to smell sweet, go get some rosewater or some of that perfume you got."

"All right, Ketura." Marie ran at once to her room to look through the bottles of perfume that she had collected from time to time. Finding one bottle her father had given her three years earlier, she snatched it up and went back downstairs and then outside. She found Ketura speaking strictly to her grandson, Isley. "You better get that fire built! You're as slow as molasses! And get some more buckets of water, too!"

"Yes, Granny. I'm doin' it fast as I can."

Soon a hot fire was going under the black pot, and Ketura shooed Isley away. "You get on 'bout your other business now!"

As soon as Isley disappeared, she said, "You put about two pints and a half of water; then put your lye in there."

Following Ketura's instructions, Marie filled the pot then went over to get the bucket full of lye. "How much do I put in?" she asked.

"I don't never measure nothin'. Just pour it in till I says stop." She watched critically; then finally as the brownish fluid poured out of the bucket, she said, "That's 'bout enough! Now you stir it until it dissolves good."

As Marie began to stir the mixture with a paddle whittled out for that purpose, she suddenly thought, *We might lose this place.* That idea disturbed her more than she liked to admit. Hartsworth had been home all of her life. She knew every inch of the house and practically every foot of the fields. She had ridden over it from the time she was a girl and could sit a horse. But she knew that being forced to leave was a real possibility, for she did part of the bookkeeping work and knew exactly how heavily mortgaged Hartsworth was.

Unaware of Marie's disturbance, Ketura

154

continued her instructions. "Now it looks 'bout like chicken gravy, don't it, beginnin' to thicken up. Pour that perfume in there, child." She watched carefully as Marie uncapped the bottle and poured the cologne into the thick mixture. "Now pour that bacon grease in." Marie again followed her instructions. "Now there ain't much else to it. We just keep on a-stirrin' and a-cookin' until finally it's all right."

Thirty minutes later Marie's arm was tired, for she had agitated the liquid steadily. "Now we're gonna dip some of that out in these pans."

Marie carefully spooned the thick white mixture into flat pans, then asked, "Is that all there is to it?"

"That's all. We let it cool then cut it up into blocks. You done good, honey."

Sometime later, after the mixture had cooled, Ketura cut the soap up into blocks about three inches square. Marie took one of the blocks and said, "I'm going to try it out right now." Turning, she made her way back toward the house. As soon as she cleared the large hedge that blocked the house from the slave quarters, she stopped with surprise. There, coming down the road, was her brother Austin driving a wagon. *Austin never drives a wagon,* she thought. *I wonder where his horse is.*

Glad to see him in any case, she waited until he pulled up. "Hello, brother! It's good to see you!" She stopped then, for she saw that Austin's face was set with an emotion she could not identify. "What's wrong?" she asked, still holding the soap with both hands.

"This is what's wrong!" he said, motioning toward the bed of the wagon. He stepped down, looking down at the ground.

Puzzled, Marie peeked into the wagon and saw her father lying on a blanket. His face was pale, he was snoring heavily, and his clothes were filthy, for he had evidently thrown up on himself. Her heart turned sick within her, and she moved away from the sight. "Where was he?" she asked.

"In the Crescent Saloon. Birdwell put him back in his office. I suppose everybody in town had a look at him, though. Why can't he do his drinking in private, and why does he have to do so much of it?" Not waiting for an answer, Austin said, "I'll get some of the slaves to help me carry him to his bed."

As he strode toward the slave quarters, Marie heard him calling out, "Solomon — Solomon!"

She looked down at her father again, although she hated the sight of him. It was not the first time this had happened. For Claude Bristol, getting drunk was common enough, but to get "helpless drunk" in Richmond with all the world to see was something else again. She stood aside when Austin came back, followed by Solomon and Alexander, two husky slaves who said nothing as they carried him inside the house. With a flash, Marie thought, *This is going to hurt Mother.* The only thing Marie could do was comfort her.

In midafternoon Marie stood at the kitchen table polishing the silver. It was something one of the slaves normally did, but she was restless. She had come in to find her mother alone and had tried to find some way to open the conversation but found none. Finally, she looked across the table and said, "I had hoped this would never happen again, Mother."

Marianne Rocklin Bristol, at the age of fifty-three, was still an attractive woman. Although her black hair showed traces of silver, her blue eyes were clear and she was still shapely and attractive. She looked up now and shook her head. "It's happened before," she said briefly.

Marie could not meet her mother's eyes. "Why does he do it?" she murmured.

Marie expected no answer, for her mother never spoke of her marriage to Claude Bristol. But something had broken within the older woman this time, and she looked out the window, her hands idle. "I wish you could have seen him when he was a young man, Marie. I met him at a ball in Charlotte. He was the most handsome man I ever saw — and the most charming. You can't believe how witty he was. All the young women were after him, although he was not wealthy." She continued to speak of that time, her voice soft but tinged with bitterness. Finally, she looked up with pain in her fine eyes and said, "I knew he was a gambler, but I wouldn't listen to my parents. I thought I could reform him. But I couldn't. . . . I knew that before we'd been married a year. It's like a disease with him, gambling, and then he drinks to forget."

Marie felt helpless, for her mother had never spoken like this before. She moved to put an arm around her. "I'm sorry. Maybe this will be the last."

"I doubt it." Marianne's eyes were sober. "Never marry a man on your emotions, Marie."

"Why, you have to love a man, don't you?"

"Yes, but love is more than a palpitation of the heart. I had that, for Claude could

158

make a girl feel like the most beautiful, wonderful woman in the world. He still can, or could the last time he tried. . . . But he hasn't tried in a long time, since he's ashamed." She continued, "Be wise, daughter. It's easy for a woman to be swayed by a handsome face and a trim figure — by a man who knows how to use words. But marriage is more than that. I want you to find a man who's solid, who doesn't have the — the faults your father has." Marianne broke off her words then finally said, "I shouldn't be speaking like this. We have to love him no matter what he does."

"I do love him, and I know you do, too, Mother."

Marianne Bristol gave her daughter one more searching look then said in a terse voice, "Make sure your man has something besides romance. It's a thin diet for a marriage." She turned and left the kitchen, leaving Marie to stare after her.

A little later, when Marianne called Marie and Austin in for supper, Austin said briefly, "I'll stay over tonight. I've got to talk to Father about this business."

"No, let me do it," Marianne answered.

"Are you sure, Mother?"

"Yes, I'm sure."

"You'll have to be firm. I don't even know

where he got the money that he lost. It was considerable. I think he gave an IOU. I don't know how in the world we'll pay it."

None of them enjoyed the meal — all were glad when it was over. Austin went to the study and closed the door. Marie helped her mother and Ketura with the dishes then went to speak with Austin. Going to the door, she knocked and called out softly, "Austin, can I come in?"

When he answered in the affirmative, she entered and found him sitting behind the rosewood desk. "Sit down, Marie. We've got to talk." He waited until she was seated, then said, "What can he be thinking of?"

"He's not happy. That's when he gambles."

"Well, if he has to gamble every time he gets dissatisfied, he's going to spend the rest of his life at a poker table!"

Although Marie and Austin had always been close, even with the five years in age separating them, Marie found herself unable to meet her brother's eyes. Marie knew he had joined the army full of high expectations. But after being wounded and spending weary months in the hospital, then at home, he seemed to have become discouraged. She also knew he was bored with his duties at the War Department. But in spite of herself she blurted out, "What's going to happen to us, Austin?"

"We're going to be thrown off this place! That's what's going to happen!"

"Oh, Austin, we can't let that happen!"

"It's not going to be our choice! Father's run up so many bills, and he's gambled away what little profits we made. Now with cotton not worth a dime a bale, what else can we do? I'd be in favor of selling out, but nobody's buying land these days."

"There's got to be another way!"

Seeing the distress in her eyes, Austin rose and walked over to put his hand on her shoulder. She covered his hand with one of her own.

"I guess," he said with a flash of his usual humor, "one of us will have to marry well."

"You mean you'll have to get a rich wife?"

"Or you'll have to get a rich husband."

Marie disagreed almost violently. "Don't be foolish!"

"Not as foolish as it sounds. People do it all the time. Look at Frank Burrows. That place of theirs was down to nothing until he married Mary Delchamp. It seems to have worked all right."

"He didn't love her! Everybody knew it! Even Mary knew it!"

"Well, she thought he was her best bet. At

least she's got a husband now and a baby on the way. And Frank's got what he wants — a fine plantation. They'll survive whoever wins the war."

"You can't be serious, Austin!" Marie said. She couldn't believe he really meant what he was saying. Then she relaxed. Austin often was guilty of teasing her like this. "You'd never think of doing such a thing!"

"Not in normal times, but these aren't normal times, Marie. The name of the game is going to be survival." His shoulders slumped as he said, "The North's going to win this war. We might as well make up our mind to that, and when they do, they're going to be hard on the South. Anybody whose land isn't paid for will lose it! You watch what I tell you!"

Marie did not like to hear her brother talk like this, but she saw that he was serious. "Well," she said quietly, "I guess we'd better do some shopping."

"Might be a good time for you to think about Malcolm Leighton." He saw her face darken. "I know he's a little flashy, but he's got those two ships, and he seems to have success running the blockade. He's making money hand over fist."

"He's bringing in perfume and patent leather when he ought to be bringing in bandages, gunpowder, and muskets."

"Not much money in those. There is in perfume, though, for those who have the cash. Malcolm's not a bad fellow." He saw her shake her head firmly. "You're too romantic. That's what your trouble is. Now, me, I'm practical." He stood up straight, put his hand over his heart, and announced, "Here I am, ladies! For sale, one slightly cynical, prospective husband! Bathes often, no bad habits to speak of, would make an excellent flatterer! Come make your bids!"

Marie stood up and laughed. "You fool! You could never do it!"

Austin's foolishness left him then. "I'll tell you the truth, Marie. I'd do anything to keep this place. I love it just like you do! Don't be too sure that I wouldn't marry any woman, providing she's got enough cash."

The two went to bed shortly after that, and the next morning at breakfast they were already eating with their mother when their father came in.

"Good morning, Claude," Marianne said quietly, ignoring the wan, harried look in Claude Bristol's eyes.

"Good morning," he said, including them all in his greeting. He was, at fifty-eight, still a fine-looking man, despite his heavy drinking. He was an inveterate rider, and the exercise kept him trim and strong. He removed a biscuit from the plate and looked down at the eggs that Marianne spooned onto it for him along with two pieces of bacon. Taking a bite of the eggs, he chewed them slowly then swallowed and reached out for the coffee. He tasted it and made a face. "What is this?"

"It's not coffee," Marianne said. "It's impossible to get that, Claude. It's a recipe Sally Tompkins gave me, making coffee out of burned acorns."

"I'll just take water," Claude mumbled. He could not meet any of their eyes, and none of them said anything about the condition he had come home in. Finally, Austin stood and dabbed at his lips with a napkin. "I've got to get back to the War Department," he said. He gave his a father a hard look, as if he appeared ready to say more. But with a glance at his mother, who shook her head slightly, he said only, "I'll be going, then." He went over and kissed his mother on the cheek then said quietly, "Good-bye, Father."

Marie got up soon afterward and left the room, leaving Claude and Marianne alone. When their eyes met for a moment, Claude dropped his to the table. Picking up a fork, he traced an intricate design on the white tablecloth until the silence grew unbearable. Then, without looking up, he said, "Doesn't do any good to say I'm sorry. I've said it too many times." When she didn't answer, he looked up and saw a strange expression on her face. "Why are you looking at me like that?" he demanded, his head beating painfully from a raging headache.

"How long is this going to go on, Claude?"

"Time for a sermon, Marianne?"

Usually this would be enough to stop Marianne, but now she was desperate. "I think you *need* a sermon, Claude. You set out to destroy yourself some years ago, despite all I could do." Her voice was cool, and there was a steady light of anger in her eyes. "Now you're going to destroy Hartsworth, your children, and your wife! Is that what you want?"

"No, it's not what I want!"

"Then why do you act as you do? What's *wrong* with you, Claude?"

Claude Bristol wanted desperately to answer her. He wanted to say, *What's wrong with me? I'm no good! That's what's wrong with me! I never have been, and I never will be! You're used to the Rocklin clan — strong, noble men. And instead you got me — a gambler and a drunk!*

Not being able to read Claude's thoughts, Marianne finally said firmly, "Claude, there's no more money. Do you understand that? I don't see how we can save Hartsworth, but I've talked to the banker, and you won't be able to draw any more funds." She saw his eyes fill with shame. "I hate to do this to you. It's not the way a marriage should be, but I must try to save something for the children." She hesitated then said, "You're not the man I thought I was marrying, Claude."

Claude Bristol sat quietly for a moment then tossed his napkin down. He got up and headed for the door. But he had to grope for the doorknob before he could find it and leave.

CHAPTER 9
A SHOPPING TRIP

Stepping off to the platform, Boone automatically turned to help Charlie Peace down from the train, but she ignored his hand and leaped to stand beside him. "So this here is Richmond, is it?"

"Guess so. That's what the conductor said." Manwaring was very much aware of the curious glances the two were drawing from the crowd that had apparently come to meet the train. To their right was a line of soldiers, corralled by a short, muscular sergeant with a full beard. They were not watching him, Boone realized, but Charlie. *I should have made her buy a dress. Those buckskins stick out like a sore thumb on a young woman around here — or anywhere for that matter.* "Come on, Charlie," he said quickly. "Let's get out of here."

"Shore is a busy place," Charlie said. She was carrying a plaid carpetbag in her right hand and had pushed the coonskin cap back on her head so that her black hair hung down in curly masses around her forehead. "What are them fellers starin' at?" she demanded, glaring over at the grinning soldiers. Before Boone could speak, she stepped over closer to the sergeant and asked, "What's the matter with you fellers? You act like you ain't never seen nobody from Colorado before."

The sergeant and soldiers laughed loudly.

"Well, guess I ain't seen nobody like you, missy. You're from Colorado, you say?"

"Shore! Where you from?"

"Arkansas."

"Well, you ought to teach them fellers of yours to keep some manners! They shore ain't got any!"

"That'd be a pretty big job," the sergeant said. "They're a rough bunch, but I don't reckon they see a sight like you every day of the week."

Charlie was about to answer when Boone grabbed her arm and pulled her away, shouldering his way through the crowd. He was exhausted after the long trip from Colorado, which had involved more than he had thought. The train service had not been bad traveling through the North, for their lines were intact. But the Southern railroad system had been so ravaged by the war that the trip had involved many detours, including once taking a coach ride around a section of line that the Northern troops had captured. Now Boone just wanted a bath, a shave, and a bed.

When they reached the outer perimeters of the station, Boone saw a carriage with a FOR HIRE sign on it. He hailed the driver, who was leaning against the wheel eating an apple. "Can you take us to a hotel?"

"Shore. Which one you want?" The speaker was a hollow-cheeked individual with a patch over his left eye.

"What's the best hotel in Richmond?"

"That'd be the Spotswood."

"All right. Take us there." He moved to help Charlie with her baggage, but she simply tossed it in the back and leaped agilely up and seated herself beside the driver. She looked around and repeated the same words she'd said at every city of more than five hundred they'd passed through: "Shore is a big place." As the driver climbed up beside her and picked up the lines, he lifted the eyebrow over his remaining eye but said nothing except to the horses. "Get up there, Babe! Come on, Dixie!" The horses started up, and as the hooves clattered over the cobblestones, he finally asked, "Just got in, I see?"

"Yes," Boone responded. "Came in from Colorado."

Charlie sat upright between the two men, her eyes alert as she studied the milling crowds that filled the streets of Richmond. "Where are all these people goin'?" she asked the driver.

"Well, I reckon they're goin' to work, some of 'em. Lots of soldiers here. They're gettin' ready for the next battle. Some just come out to see what's goin' on. You never been in Richmond afore, I take it?"

"Nope. Never been in Virginia," Boone answered.

"Well, you come at a bad time. Was a nice town before the war. It's gone to perdition in a bucket now!"

They wound their way through the heavy traffic, passing by several factories that belted out black smoke. Finally, they pulled up in front of a four-story building with a sign saying SPOTSWOOD HOTEL over the front. "How much?" Boone asked.

"Confederate or U.S.?"

"U.S.," Boone said.

"Well, that'll just be a dollar. It'd been fifteen Confederate." He took the coin Boone handed him and shook his head ruefully. "Don't see much of this kind of money around these days."

170

Boone grabbed his two valises and watched as Charlie jumped to the ground and retrieved hers. She looked up and said, "It looks pretty fancy, Boone."

"Well, that's good. I'm ready for a fancy hotel." Boone strolled inside, Charlie keeping step with him. The lobby was expansive and humming with the sound of people coming and going. Moving over to the desk, Boone waited until the clerk, a man with alert gray eyes and red hair, asked, "What can I do for you?"

"Two rooms, please."

"Yes, sir. Just happen to have two. You're lucky. Got a cancellation. They won't be together."

"That doesn't matter."

Boone signed the register for himself, hesitated, then signed "Charlene Peace" beneath his own.

"You need help with the luggage?"

"No, we can take it, but we're pretty tired. Do you suppose we could get some hot water hauled up for a bath?"

"Yes, sir! Mackey!" The clerk waved his hand to a young man who stood nearby. "We need two baths, Mackey. One for this gentlemen and one for this — lady." Charlie didn't notice he hesitated over her status.

"Take 'em to rooms 204 and 221, Mac-key."

"Yes, sir! This way, please!"

Mackey reached over to get Charlie's suitcase, which surprised her. She jerked it away from him, saying, "What do you want? What are you doin' tryin' to get my things?"

Boone laughed aloud. "He's not going to steal it, Charlie. He just wants to carry it for you."

"I guess I carried it from Colorado; reckon I can make it upstairs."

Boone sighed. "Here, you can take mine, Mackey."

"Yes, sir. This way." Mackey smiled at Boone then led the way up to the second floor. He stopped at the first room and said, "Will you take this one, sir?"

"Are they just alike?"

"Yes, sir. Both pretty much alike."

"Doesn't matter, then. Charlie, you take this one. This young fellow will bring you a tub and some hot water. Guess you could use a bath."

"A bath? You mean all over?"

Mackey stifled a laugh and then looked away, trying to keep his face straight.

Boone gave Charlie a disgusted look. "You do what you want to! Usually a bath is all over, but that's up to you. I'll come back in about an hour, and we'll talk."

Mackey then led the way to Boone's room. Opening the door, he stepped inside and deposited the suitcases on the floor beside the bed. "Anythin' else besides the bath?"

"Where's a good place to eat, Mackey?"

"Well, our restaurant's about the best, I guess." As he saw the coin Boone handed him, his eyes opened wide. "We don't see much of this hard U.S. money, sir."

"Things are pretty bad, are they, with the cash situation?"

"Just terrible! Have to practically take a wheelbarrow to the store to get a little load of groceries. They keep printin' the stuff, but it don't mean nothin'." He flipped the coin up in the air, caught it adeptly, then nodded. "I'll be right back with those tubs and have plenty of hot water for you. I didn't catch your name, sir."

"Manwaring."

"Right, Mr. Manwaring. Glad to have you stayin' at the hotel."

When the door shut, Boone sat down on the bed and pulled his boots off. He examined his socks, stiff with sweat, and ripped them off, too. He tossed his coat on the bed then sat down in the chair to rest and let the weariness flow out of his body. Watching the crowd outside his window, he noticed that clothes were worn and patched and that even the men's uniforms were in a sorry condition. Then, thinking of Charlie, he muttered aloud, "We may have made a big mistake, Noah. I don't think that girl of yours is ever going to fit into this place!"

Meanwhile, Charlie was looking over her room, saying aloud to herself, "This is the best room I ever saw! Better than any of them places we stayed on the way." They had stayed in several hotels on their journey, most of them very rough — especially when they had reached the South. More often they had slept on the train, which had been difficult for Charlie. She was used to privacy and quiet, and there had been little of that on this trip. Now she walked around and touched the wallpaper, which was a design of strange beasts she had never seen. She looked at them in wonder, especially an exotic-looking animal with a tremendously long neck and long legs. "Don't know what you are, but I wonder if you'd be good to eat."

Taking off her coat, then her moccasins and socks, Charlie walked around in her bare feet, enjoying the somewhat chilly sensation of the carpeted floor. Then she moved over to the window to watch the activity in the streets below. She was fascinated by the traffic, for it included cannons drawn by horses that were driven by soldiers. Wagons passed in a steady stream. The women's dresses particularly interested her, for she knew Boone would insist on her becoming more feminine. Some of them wore skirts that stuck out in the shape of a bell. "They can't be that big under them dresses!" she said, puzzled. "I wonder why they do a thing like that? It looks plumb silly!"

More exhausted than she knew, she went to sleep in the chair. Awhile later a knock at the door startled her. She leaped out of the chair and opened the door. The young man, Mackey, was there with some black servants. "Got your tub and some hot water, miss," he said.

"Well, I guess you kin come in." They brought the tub in and set it in the middle of the floor, filling it from huge kettles. The steam rose in the air. "Brought some fresh towels for you, ma'am," Mackey said. "Anythin' else?"

"I reckon I can handle it from here," Charlie said, giving him a level glance. She had thought he was making fun of her, but he only smiled and said, "Let me know if you need anythin', miss," then left.

As soon as the door closed, Charlie looked warily at the copper tub. She had never had a bath, except in the creek during suitable weather, so she approached it cautiously. Reaching down, she touched the water and found it was very hot.

"Why, I kinnot get in that! It'd cook me like a boiled squirrel!" she exclaimed. But as she set about to simply wash her face and hands as she ordinarily did, curiosity got the better of her. She picked up the bar of soap and said, surprised, "Why, it smells like roses!" The two towels were large and thick, and there was a smaller one for a washcloth.

Finally, she made up her mind. "You don't know till you try!" she said aloud then stripped out of her buckskins and underwear. Throwing them onto the floor, she felt strange, so she put a chair underneath the door handle then hastily looked out the window to make sure no one could see in. She waited until the water was bearable, stepped in, and then sat down, gasping as the hot water splashed over her. Gingerly she took the soap, dipped it in the water, and worked up a lather for her face. She soaped her upper body then held one foot up. "I reckon you need washin'!" She began to scrub. "Didn't know takin' a bath was this much fun! It's a little bit different from them cold creeks up in the mountains." She scrubbed every inch of her body then decided to wash her hair. After rinsing it, she lay back in the now-tepid water and relaxed. Her eyes drooped, and without volition she went to sleep.

When someone outside the window fired off a gun, Charlie started and splashed wildly for a moment, unable to recognize where she was. "What in the cat hair — ! Reckon I musta gone to sleep!" She got up and shivered, for the room was cold. She took the towels and rubbed herself down fiercely. Stepping to the carpetbag, she pulled out her clothes — long underwear, a pair of men's wool trousers, and a plaid wool shirt — and quickly slipped into them, then pulled on a pair of thick socks. Refreshed by the brief sleep, she plunged again into the carpetbag and pulled out her tablet, ink, and quill. Putting them on the table beside the bed, she sat down and began to write.

November 12, 1863

Well, here we are in Richmond. Caint say as I would like to make that trip again. It shore was a humdinger! We rode trains till I got plum sick of em. Sorry way to get from one place to another, but Boone said it was the only way.

We took a long time to make this last leg of the trip. Boone said it was because of the war. Trains was all messed up. I kept lookin out the windows to see if there was any fightin, but we didnt see none. We did see lots of soldiers, and Richmond has got more soldiers than dogs got fleas. I got to say though I dont see why Pa liked it so much. It dont look no better than no other town to me, but then I dont like no town no ways. I git lonesome sometimes for the cabin, but they aint no way I kin go back there, I dont reckon.

She paused, dipped her quill into the ink bottle, and sat musing for a few minutes before she continued:

I can tell Boone is ashamed of the way I look and dress. Well, I caint help that, but he has been tellin me the whole trip that when I got to Richmond I would have to put on dresses and learn how to fix my hair and be a lady. Peers to me like thats too much of a job, but he says it kin be did. He has been real nice to me on this trip. I kept expectin him to take liberties, but he never done such. As a matter of fact, there was a feller that came up and tried to make up to me on the train when Boone was gone to the bathroom. The feller just set down in Boones seat and started talkin to me, and when I ignored him, he put his hand on me. I was gettin ready to bust him one when suddenly there was Boone. He had his pistol stuck in his belt, and when the feller saw it he kinda swallowed hard, got up, and said, "Guess I must have got the wrong seat." When Boone set down, I said, "He didnt get no wrong seat! He was tryin to put his hands on me! If you hadnt come, I was fixin to hit him in the mouth!" Boone laughed and said, "I guess thats another thing you will have to learn, Charlie. How to get rid of unwelcome attention." I asked him what unwelcome attention meant, and he said it was men comin around me that I didnt want around me, and I told him I didnt want none of em. He laughed at that too.

I guess I will have to say that Boone is a nice feller. I dont spect he would be as good a man in the woods as Pa, but he shore knows how to get from one place to another, how to find hotels, and how to eat right. Got more good manners than any ten men I ever see.

Just then a knock sounded at her door. Charlie went to answer it. "Hello, Boone," she said.

"Hello, Charlie." He glanced at the bathtub. "Did you enjoy your bath?"

Charlie flushed, for there seemed something wrong with the question, but she could not figure out what. "It was all right."

"I guess it's about time to go down and eat, unless you want to sleep first."

"No, I slept on the train, and I'm hungry as a bear!"

Manwaring looked at her clothes. They looked terrible, but there was nothing he could do about it. He had cleaned up his own clothing as best he could, but it, too, was wrinkled.

"They say the restaurant's got good food. Why don't we eat and then try to find something to wear?"

"All right with me."

The two made their way down the stairs. As they entered the lobby and then the door that led to the restaurant, Boone was uncomfortably aware of how much attention

Charlie was drawing. *No help for it, I suppose, but I'll be glad to get her some decent clothes. Feels like we're a traveling circus!*

A waiter came over and, deliberately not looking at Charlie, asked respectfully, "Yes, sir?"

"Table for two."

"Yes, of course. Right this way, sir."

As they walked toward their table, whispers and eyes followed them. Most of the patronage was composed of army officers and the upper strata of Richmond society, Boone realized. *Well, let them look!* he thought. When the waiter reached the table, he pulled out a chair for Charlie, who just stared at it. "What's wrong with the cheer?" she asked.

Boone grinned. "Just sit down on it, Charlie." He winked at the waiter, whose face broke into a slight smile. He pushed the chair under Charlie, put two menus down, and said, "I'll be back for your order, sir."

"Does he think I'm crippled?" Charlie demanded. "Cain't sit down by myself?"

"He was just being polite. Waiters do that."

"Oh!" Charlie realized she had made another mistake, and her face reddened. In the woods she was steady and never had a moment's doubt about what to do, but this new world was alien to her — frightening.

Now she looked covertly around the room and noticed that many were watching her. A woman in a bright green dress a few tables down was staring at her with hard eyes. She leaned over and said something to the man with her; then both of them laughed.

Charlie turned to the menu with an absurd temptation to weep. *I'm just tard,* she thought. *What do I care what them people think 'bout me!*

"See anything you like, Charlie?"

"Whatever you get will be good enough for me."

"Well, the selection's kind of limited. But it'll be better than what we've had."

Boone ordered fried chicken and mashed potatoes and asked if there were any vegetables. Upon finding that there were none, he said, "I sure would like some fresh milk and bread."

As the waiter left with their order, Charlie was strangely silent, so Boone asked her what was wrong.

"I'm right tard," Charlie admitted. "Travelin' on them trains is worse than walkin' through the mountains."

"I think you're right there," Boone agreed, studying her and her clothing.

Charlie had steadfastly refused to buy any

clothes on the journey, saying, "What I've got is good enough for these old trains. If I have to have a dress, I'll buy it when I get to Richmond."

"What are we gonna do, Boone?" she asked abruptly, lifting her dark blue eyes to his.

Under the light that streamed in from the window, he was almost startled to see how beautiful her eyes were. And she had washed her lustrous black hair so that it was shiny and soft, lying in curls around her head. "I guess we'll go buy some clothes if you're up to it after we eat."

"I mean after that. We gonna buy us a place somewhere?" As she spoke the words, Charlie suddenly realized she spoke of them as if they were somehow married. The thought gave her a jolt, and she wondered if Boone had noticed it. However, he leaned back and shook his head.

"Well, that's a big item. You don't just run out and buy a plantation like you buy a new dress or a pair of shoes. We'll have to ask around, find out how much places cost, and where would be a good location. Unfortunately, I'm the wrong man for this. We'll have to find somebody here who knows property."

"You think we kin do it? I don't know anythin' 'bout farmin' really. 'Cept how to raise a garden. I don't guess you do either?"

"No. All I know is how to run a ship, Charlie." As he smiled at her, she was aware of how fine looking he was. She had not missed how other women had let their eyes linger on his tall figure. *Reckon he could have any woman he wanted,* she realized.

After the waiter came with the food and left, Charlie said, "Do you want to ask the blessin', or do you want me to do it?"

Boone had run into this before. He himself was not a person of faith, but Charlie was. "I told you, Charlie, the Lord wouldn't hear anything I had to say. You'd better do it."

Charlie lowered her head, but she did not lower her voice. She spoke the prayer so loudly that several people in their vicinity listened carefully, looking surprised.

Charlie said, "Amen," then picked up a chicken leg and bit into it. "Hey, Boone, this is good chicken!"

"I always heard people in the South knew how to cook. I had a first mate from Mississippi who was always talking about the fried chicken, how he missed it." He bit into a piece of the breast. "I reckon Motley was telling the truth!"

The two ate hungrily, for it was the best meal they had had since leaving Colorado.

They cleared their plates then had apple pie and coffee. Afterward Boone lit up a cigar he had bought.

"I didn't know you smoked," Charlie said.

"I don't. Just saw one of these and thought I'd try it. Charlie, you have to give up chewing that tobacco."

"Why would I do that?"

"Well, it's not ladylike." Boone had been appalled the first time Charlie had pulled out a plug of tobacco. She did not chew it often, but from time to time she would, and he was both amused and repelled by the sight. "Young women don't do that in Richmond society."

"How do you know? You ain't never been here!"

"I just know, that's all. Now I'll tell you what — I'll quit smoking cigars, and you quit chewing tobacco."

Charlie stared at him. "You talk like you're my daddy! I'll chew what tobacco I please!"

"I guess I am your daddy," Boone said with a grin, imagining what it would be like if Charlie pulled out a plug of tobacco and chewed it at a fancy ball in Richmond. "That's what your pa wanted me to be."

"Well, you ain't my pa! You're too young for one thing, and you just ain't for another!"

"All right. I'm your manager, then. If you're through, let's go shopping."

Finding shops in Richmond was not difficult, and soon after their meal Boone led Charlie down along the street that was lined with dressmakers and general stores.

"I guess this one's a good place to start." Boone waved his hand toward a sign that said ANDERSON'S DRESS SHOP. "Let's see what they've got to get you dressed up like a queen."

"Don't reckon I hanker to be no queen."

"Just a manner of speaking. Come on."

The spacious shop smelled like cloth as they walked inside. Several dressmakers' dummies were spotted around, and Charlie, who had never seen one of these before, was fascinated. "Ain't that somethin'! Just like a real person!"

"May I help you?"

Boone removed his hat and nodded to the matronly woman who approached with a genteel air. "My name's Manwaring, and this is my — uh, ward," he said, finally settling on a word, "Miss Peace. We've just come in from the mountains and couldn't bring any luggage with us."

"Oh, so you need complete outfits, Miss Peace?"

Charlie stared at the woman and nodded curtly. "I reckon that's the way it is."

"Well, we don't have as good a selection as we have had in days gone by — the war, you know — but we'll do the best we can."

What followed next was rather a nightmare for Boone. He had not grasped how uncertain Charlie was, nor how she covered this uncertainty with a brash, loud manner. As Charlie began to speak loudly, he noticed that a young woman to his right was trying not to show curiosity. However, he met her gaze, and she flushed delicately then turned away from him. *She probably thinks we're both crazy,* he thought. *Sure is a fine-looking woman, though.* Then his attention turned to the argument Charlie was having with the clerk, Mrs. Jones, over a dress.

"All I want's one dress! A woman can't wear but one dress at a time no matter how fancy she is!"

Mrs. Jones gave Boone a startled look. "I understood you wanted a complete wardrobe!"

"That's right. We do. Charlie, will you listen to Mrs. Jones?"

"I guess I kin have a say in what kind of clothes I'm gonna wear! You're not gonna wear 'em, and neither is she!"

Embarrassed, Charlie did not know how

to act. She wished heartily she were back in Colorado. She was also angry at Boone, somehow, for putting her in this situation, although she knew he was trying to help her. Stubbornly she thought, *I'll do what I please, even if this is a fancy shop in Richmond!* She reached into her pants pocket and pulled out a plug of tobacco. She glared at Boone, daring him to say something, then bit off a piece. Stuffing the plug back in her pocket, she tucked the bite of tobacco inside her cheek and said, "Now let's get on with our rat killin' here."

This time Boone heard a distinct giggle from the young woman and turned toward her, admiring her trim figure, but was embarrassed to meet her gaze.

For some thirty minutes Mrs. Jones struggled violently to help Charlie, and finally after considerable argument in which Boone could say nothing that pleased Charlie, several items were selected.

"I guess that'll be all for today," Boone said, anxious to get out of the place. He had felt like a fool, for the young woman across the aisle from him had remained to see the show — or so he thought.

Charlie stared at the collection of clothes, which included two dresses, two skirts, and two blouses, then said loudly, "Well, what 'bout underwear? I cain't go neked under these things, kin I?"

Mrs. Jones gasped, and Boone, if he had not been so irritated with Charlie, would have laughed. Instead, he turned to the young woman who was concealing her smile well. "Hello, I'm Boone Manwaring. This is my friend, Miss Charlene Peace."

"How are you, Mr. Manwaring? I'm Marie Bristol. You're just in from the West, I take it?"

"Yes, just in from Colorado."

Charlie took in Boone and Marie's conversation with interest. She was more impressed by the woman's bearing and good looks than she wanted to admit. *That's the way he wants me to look,* she thought. For some reason she was irritated — and she grew more so as Boone and Marie Bristol continued to talk. Finally, Marie put out her hand and said, "I'm glad to know you, Miss Peace. Welcome to Richmond."

The woman's smile was so winsome and her air so generous that Charlie could not help but be impressed. She took Marie's hand and found it to be soft but not weak. "Thank you," she said. She looked around the store and said, "I ain't never been in a big store like this, and I don't know how to buy clothes, neither."

"Perhaps you would let me help you, if you wouldn't mind. I love to shop, but I can never afford to buy what I want."

"That's most kind of you, Miss Bristol. Why don't I give you ladies a chance to finish up? I'll wait outside." Boone found the cold outside a welcome relief. "Blast that girl! Why can't she act like a woman instead of some kind of wild mountain man!" he growled. He thought then of Marie Bristol with pleasure. "Now *that's* what a woman should look like. Maybe she could give Charlie some pointers."

Pleased that Marie Bristol had offered to help, Charlie had to admit that the woman was kind. She did not insist on anything but just recommended certain items of clothes. But after Marie had helped her select some underthings and another outfit, Charlie began to grow restless. "I reckon this is enough to wear for a year."

Marie Bristol laughed and nodded toward the purchases. "You have some nice things here. I hope we haven't spent too much."

"No, I got enough money to burn a wet mule," Charlie responded.

"Really?" Marie said, startled by that evaluation.

"Yep, my pa and Boone found gold out in Colorado."

"I see! Well, in that case this won't be too expensive."

Marie Bristol went to the door and waved Boone inside. "I think we're all finished."

"I appreciate your help, Miss Bristol."

"Since you're strangers in town, perhaps you'd like to come to the Charity Ball tomorrow night."

"Why, that's very nice of you to ask us. What do you say, Charlie?"

"I don't keer."

"We'd be glad to come," Boone said, sensing Charlie's uncertainty but not understanding why. "Where is it to be held?"

"Down at the Fenway Hall. Anyone can tell you where that is."

"We'll see you there tomorrow. Perhaps you'd save a dance for me?"

"Certainly. Maybe I can introduce you to some of Richmond's finest."

"That would be most kind."

After Marie left, Mrs. Jones packaged the purchases and then said breathlessly, "That will be four hundred and fifty dollars, sir."

"Is that Confederate?"

"Why, yes, of course!"

"How much in U.S. notes?"

"Oh my! Let me see!" Mrs. Jones figured rapidly with a pen. "Forty-eight dollars and fifty cents."

Boone reached into his pocket for some gold coins and counted them out. "Mrs. Jones, you've been very nice to us. Keep the change. We'll probably be back for more later."

Leaving the shop, they made their way back to the hotel. Entering Charlie's room, Boone put the packages down. That's when Charlie said, "I don't like it here, Boone."

Shocked, Boone looked up to see her face set stubbornly in displeasure. "What do you mean you don't like it? We just got here! And already we're meeting people. That Miss Bristol, she can help you."

"I don't like her!"

"Don't like her? What do you mean you don't like her?" Boone demanded.

"She's stuck up!"

"That's foolish talk, Charlie. She was very helpful."

"I don't keer! Let's go back to Colorado, Boone."

For the first time Boone saw beneath Charlie's brash exterior. She was a strong young woman, mannish in her ways, but how could she be anything else? As she lifted her eyes, he saw her fear. *How would I feel if I were thrown into a new life as she's been?* he thought, leading him to speak gently to her. "I know it'll be hard, Charlie, but we'll make it. You and I, we've come here to do something that your pa wanted. I promised him, and in a way, you did, too."

Thinking of how Boone had used "we" made Charlie feel better. "All right, Boone," she said finally, "if you say so. But I don't think we kin ever make a lady out of me!"

"I think the good Lord already did that, Charlie," Boone said, smiling. He reached out and grasped her hand, holding it warmly in both of his. "We just need to polish up your manners a bit. After all, a diamond is only a rough piece of rock until a jeweler polishes it until it sparkles. That's what we'll do with you."

Charlie could not speak for a moment, but then she whispered, "All right, Boone, if you say so."

CHAPTER 10
A MATTER OF FAMILY

Josh Yancy took a deep breath and approached the corporal who had his left arm in a sling. "I'm Josh Yancy," he murmured. "I'd like to see the colonel."

The corporal looked up at the young man with a critical light in his eye. "The colonel's busy," he said.

"I'll be glad to wait."

The corporal shrugged. "Okay. Sit over there. What's your name again?"

"Josh Yancy."

"I'll tell the colonel you're out here when I get time."

"Thank you, Corporal."

Josh moved away from the tent. The Stonewall Brigade was only a small part of the Army of Northern Virginia, but it was not an unimportant part. It had become famous under the leadership of the famous Stonewall Jackson, and after Jackson was killed in the Battle of Chancellorsville, the unit had remained intact. All around soldiers were being drilled by sergeants, and over to his left an artillery crew was going through gun drills without actually firing.

With the hint of bitter weather in the air, Josh pulled his wool coat up close to his ears, thinking mostly of Rena, whom he loved. Josh Yancy was an imaginative young man who dreamed vividly, so he had no difficulties summoning up her face, scenes, or events. He remembered how, the previous summer, her eyes had sparkled as they were fishing on the creek — how, when he had pretended to throw her in the creek, she had screamed and thrown her arms around him, begging him not to. That was a good memory, and Josh's face softened. So he was startled when the corporal said, "All right. You can go in now, Yancy."

Josh stepped into the interior of the Sibley tent, a canvas structure that rose to a high peak, and stopped before Clay Rocklin's portable desk, waiting until Clay lifted his eyes.

"Why, Josh!" Clay set down his goose quill and put out his hand. "I can guess why you're here."

"Yes, sir. I think I've got to join the army, and I'd rather be in your outfit than any other, if you'll have me."

Clay sighed heavily. "Of course I'll have you. You'll be as good a soldier as Lonnie was." He spoke sadly of Josh's brother who had died in action. He had looked much like Josh, with the same lean look and slightly freckled face. Brushing the memory aside, Clay continued, "We'll get you signed up. You've told Rena about this?"

"Yes, sir, I have. She wanted us to get married, but I told her it wouldn't be fitting with me leaving right away."

A warm feeling came to Clay Rocklin then. This young man had character like an iron bar, and although he had no wealth and did not come from aristocracy, still Clay was not displeased with Rena's choice. He could remember several marriages among his kinfolk that had turned out badly when young women married simply for those reasons.

"I appreciate that, Josh. I'm not much of an example, because Melora and I married knowing I'd have to leave and go into action. But you're younger than I was. Come along. We'll get you signed up."

Clay made the arrangements with the corporal then said, "I've got to make a trip to see my aunt, Corporal. I'll be back before dark. Tell Major Evans he's in charge until I get back."

"Yes, sir."

Moving to where the horses were kept, Clay said to the private who saluted him, "Bring my horse out and saddle him for me, Private."

"Yes, sir!"

Ten minutes later Clay was on the road out of Richmond. It was a relief to him to be away from the camp for a while. Since his return he had worked almost night and day, and his mind was exhausted with the myriad details. Finding enough food and proper uniforms for his men was difficult enough. Since the Confederacy had been encircled by the blockade by sea and the armies of Grant and Sherman by land, the South could only count on what they could manufacture themselves. Many of the men were armed with muskets and bayonets taken from the Yankees after battles, and as for new arms, so few were smuggled through the blockade that they were almost non-existent.

The sun was a pale disk overhead as Clay made his way toward Hartsworth. He arrived there shortly before noon and handed the lines of his horse to Solomon, who greeted him with, "Hello, General."

"Not a general yet. Probably never will be, Solomon. How are you doing?"

"Oh, fine, suh! You go right on to the house. I'll take care of this fine hoss of yours."

Clay approached the steps of the large, two-story brick home that was painted white with dark green shutters. But he had no chance to knock on the door, for he was met by Marianne, who opened it. "Come in, Clay."

"Hello, Marianne." He gave her a hug and kissed her cheek. "You're still the second-best-looking woman in Virginia."

"Melora will be glad to know she's still number one. Come into the parlor. I've got a fire there."

Clay followed Marianne into the parlor, and the two sat down in front of the fireplace. Clay relaxed and stretched out his legs, holding the soles of his boots toward the fire. "It's cold outside," he said. "I wouldn't be surprised if we have snow for Christmas."

"A white Christmas. We haven't had one of those for a long time."

"No, about three years, I think."

As Clay sat loosely in the chair, Marianne called for tea then asked, "Can you stay for supper, Clay?"

"No, I've got to get back. Mainly I just wanted to get out of camp. But I can stay

198

for lunch."

"Are you going by Gracefield?"

"I sure am. I wouldn't pass this close without going to see Melora. I'm still a new bridegroom, you know."

"And about to be a father again! Are you happy about that, Clay?"

"Yes, I am! For my own sake, but also because Melora's so happy," he said simply. "It's good for her, I think." He sat up straighter as Ketura brought tea, and they went through the business of putting in sugar and cream. He sipped the hot liquid gratefully. "I'm concerned, though, that something might happen to me."

"Melora would manage. She's the strongest woman I know. I've always admired her."

"So have I," Clay said, grinning. Then he frowned slightly. "Josh came in and enlisted this morning. I knew it was coming, but I hate to see it."

"Are he and Rena talking about getting married?"

"Rena wants to, but Josh said it wouldn't be fair. That was fine of him, wasn't it?"

"Yes, it was. I worry about him, though, Clay, and all the young men. So many of them are gone now."

"The best rushed out and joined up when

the war started. Too many of them are buried in shallow graves out by Antietam and Gettysburg."

Fond of each other, Clay and Marianne found solace in one another's company. When Marianne mentioned the Charity Ball, Clay said, "I guess I'll take Melora. Are you and Claude going?"

"I'm not sure, Clay," Marianne said. You know what it's like. There's no money, and we've got mortgages on this place."

"Who hasn't?"

"I suppose that's true." But Marianne didn't want to talk about Claude, so she said quickly, "Malcolm Leighton is taking Marie."

Clay lifted an eyebrow. "Is she serious about him?"

"I don't think so, but who knows these days? I hardly ever see Austin. You probably see him more than I do."

"No, I don't go near the War Department any more than necessary. They're liable to make me a general. Then where will I be?" he said comically.

"In any case, I asked Marie about Leighton, and she just laughed and said, 'He's working his way through all the young women in Richmond alphabetically. He's on the *B*s now.' She wasn't serious, of course, but I don't know. It's a bad time for young women. So many young men are gone now."

After a while the two went in to the lunch that Ketura had prepared. They were eating chicken salad and pork ribs when Claude came in. He took one look at Clay and nodded. "I'm glad to see you, Clay."

"Hello, Claude. I'm eating your food up. Sit down before I devour it all."

Claude Bristol sat down. He wore a tan double-breasted jacket with a narrow collar, a red tie, a white shirt, and baggy white trousers. As usual he looked neat, but his face was rather drawn, and he could not meet Marianne's eyes. After the meal Marianne said, "Why don't you two go into the study? I'll join you later."

Claude rose with alacrity and led the way into the large study, carpeted with multicolored pastels. Its walls were covered with light tan and floral paper and pictures in thick gilt frames. One wall held many books on dark wooden shelves. Between two long windows was a comfortably padded sofa and two brown and ivory armchairs. "Claude, this is a beautiful room, but then, Hartsworth's the most beautiful place I know."

Claude stared at Clay nervously, trying to

find some meaning in his words.

Knowing Claude Bristol well, Clay was aware something was on the man's mind. He waited for Claude to bring it up.

After some light conversation, Claude suddenly stood up and said, "Clay, I want to join the army."

For a moment Clay Rocklin thought he had misunderstood Claude. His mind raced as he tried to find an answer. "I don't think that's the best idea you've ever had, Claude."

"You think I'm useless! Well, you're probably right." Claude pulled out a cigar and lit it, watching the smoke rise in the air. "I haven't been any help to Marianne or to the children. In fact, I've dragged them down." He made a hopeless gesture with his hands. "It would have been better if Marianne had never met me, Clay."

Clay shifted uneasily in his chair, since he'd often thought that himself. But he had never said one word about Claude to Marianne or anyone else. "If you want to help Marianne and the children, the best thing you can do is straighten up. Be some help around the plantation here."

"I'm no good at that. Marianne does a better job running this place. And she's the real heart of Hartsworth. Always has been.

All I've done is throw money away with both hands, but that's over, Clay."

"Why the army?"

"It's the only thing I can think of where I might be of some use. I thought of just leaving Marianne, going off and getting out of the way, but — I love her, Clay, and miracle of miracles, somehow she still cares for me. Even after all I've been."

"Yes, she does, Claude."

"I saw Austin the morning after he hauled me back drunk. There was disgust in his face, and I don't blame him. Marie covers it up better, but she has no respect for me either. Why should she?" Claude paced the floor nervously. He came to stand over Clay, looked down at him, and said, "I know I'm not a soldier, but there must be *something* I can do rather than be deadweight around here. At least I'd like a chance."

For a few minutes Clay argued with Claude then saw the man was adamant. "I still don't understand why you want to do this, Claude," he said finally.

"It's a matter of family, Clay. You're a Rocklin, and I know your pride in being a Rocklin. Marianne's the same way. But I take no pride in being a Bristol! If I could do one thing right, I think I might be a part of the Rocklin family, even if it's second-hand." His eyes caught Clay's, his lips tense. "I don't know how to beg, Clay, but I wish you'd give me a chance to do something."

"The Stonewall Brigade is a fighting outfit. We'll be leaving Richmond soon because Grant's coming down. If you go with us, you could get killed."

"That's all right with me," Claude said bitterly. "Better to die than to go on like I've been going. Will you do it, Clay?"

As Bristol waited, the pleading in his eyes was more than Clay could stand.

"If you're serious, Claude, I'll do what I can. No combat, of course, at your age, but you can be my clerk until you're ready to be made adjutant. You'll come in as a second lieutenant, but you'll be in for some trouble. This is a fighting outfit, and they'll scream that I'm showing you special treatment."

"I can stand it if you can, Clay. Will you do it, then?"

Clay nodded. "Come when you get ready. I'll enlist you, and we'll find you a uniform. You'd better hurry if you're going, because when Grant strikes, we'll be pulling out overnight."

"I'll come the first thing in the morning."

"Have you told Marianne any of this?"

"No."

"You'd better have a talk with her. It's a big thing. I don't know what she'll think about it. She may blame me."

"She won't do that." Claude put out his hand. "I know this is charity on your part, and I'm thanking you. If I die, that's all right. . . . I'm hoping that I can do this one thing, and that my wife and children won't think so badly of me."

As Clay shook the man's hand, he thought, *Claude Bristol has never done anything unselfish in his life, so I'm probably making a big mistake. But he's right about one thing — it is better to die than to live as he has been.*

"I'll be leaving in the morning, Marianne."

Marianne was preparing for bed. She had on her nightgown and had paused long enough to take the combs out of her hair. As it fell down, she turned to her husband with surprise. "Leaving for where, Claude?"

"I'm joining the army," Claude said nervously and seriously. "Clay has agreed to take me as his clerk. I'll be a second lieutenant."

Marianne stared at her husband, her mind swirling. "Why are you doing this, Claude? You've never shown any interest in the Confederacy."

"I still don't have much, but I'm interested in —"

Bristol broke off, embarrassed. He stood before Marianne and put his hands on her shoulders. "I'm interested," he said slowly, "in doing one thing that you admire before I die."

"Why, Claude!" Marianne said, still in shock. "Why do you think this would please me? You might get killed!"

"So I might. That's what Clay said. But I've not been a man you could admire, Marianne. When we first met, and when we married, I thought I might be, but it hasn't happened. Maybe it never will, but if there's any chance at all you could see something in me that's good, I've got to take it."

Marianne was aware Claude was asking her for something. It had been so long since he had asked her for anything, she could not believe it nor understand it. She knew he was an unhappy man, that under the gaiety he often showed outwardly, there was a sadness, for he recognized the failure of his life. Slowly she reached up and touched his cheek, then said softly, "Be very careful, my dear."

"I still love you, Marianne, and one day I hope you'll think better of me." His face working with emotion, he walked out of the room. When he did not return, Marianne lay in bed wondering what had happened. A faint hope began to grow in her, and she prayed then for this husband of hers who had been such a trial. Finally, she whispered to herself, "Nothing's too hard for God. . . ."

CHAPTER 11
A DISASTER AT THE BALL

Charlie stepped out of the copper tub and stretched luxuriously. The water dripped down her arms as she reached to pick up a towel. *A body could get used to this here bathin'. It ain't as bad as I figured it'd be.* She had learned, almost at once, to love the feel of cleanliness, both in body and in clothes, and now as she dried off and slipped into the undergarments that seemed very soft after the rough underwear she was accustomed to, it made her feel odd. Actually, it made her feel feminine, but she would not have thought of it like that. After she had donned her underthings, she stared at the apparatus Mrs. Jones, the store clerk, had called a bustle. Marie Bristol had mentioned that many women were wearing them, so Charlie put it on, tying the strings in front. She looked back and found herself grinning. "I guess they figure women didn't have enough behinds, but you sure do with one of these things." Then she turned to the fashionable blue silk dress, both fearful and admiring of it. The bodice was edged with a delicate white frill, and the overskirt was looped up at the sides and accented with black lace. A black ribbon tied around her neck would complete the outfit.

Carefully she pulled the dress over her head. It was tight enough that she had to work at it. Finally, it slipped over, and she turned to the mirror fastened over the washstand and gasped.

"Why, I can't wear a thing like this!" Even though she was alone, her cheeks flushed as she saw how much of her neck the dress revealed.

But it was too late now, for she had no choice. She tried first pulling it up, but it slipped right down again. Finally, she stripped the dress off. Going through the underwear she had bought, she found what the woman had called a vest. At least *it* buttoned all the way and covered up her front. She slipped it on, nodded with satisfaction, then pulled the dress on again. Staring at herself in the mirror, she said, "Now that's more like it! Can't imagine a female runnin' around not wearin' no more clothes than this! That woman must've forgot part of it!"

Moving over, she picked up the pair of shoes and slipped them on her feet. Taking several experimental steps, she found that they pinched her more than she remembered at the shop, and she teetered back and forth in them. "Don't know why women have to try to be tall. It's like standin' on your toes — and they hurt."

For a while she moved around irresolutely, stopping to look at her hair. She had seen some ornate hairdos, but there was nothing she could do. In the first place, she didn't know how, and in the second place, she was rebellious enough to say, "If my hair don't suit 'em, let 'em look at somebody else." Defiantly she ran a comb through her black curls. Picking up a small box marked RICE POWDER, she opened it carefully and stuck her finger down in it. "It looks like flour you can make flapjacks with," she murmured. Gingerly she spread some on her face, leaving streaks. "That looks plumb silly! I just ain't gonna wear it!"

When she got up and walked around, she liked the crinkling noise the dress made, but the shoes still hurt. Finally, she reached down, removed them, and slipped her feet into her moccasins. "Don't see what difference it makes. Ain't nobody gonna see my feet as long as this here dress is." A knock sounded at the door, and she marched over and pulled it open. Boone stood there, as she expected, and she saw his eyes widen. "Well, that's a pretty dress!" he said.

"Come on in, Boone." The two examined each other. What Boone saw was a very attractive young woman who had something strange on underneath her dress. "What is this thing, Charlie?" he said, pointing to the garment that covered her from neck to below the front of her dress.

"I think they forgot part of this here dress, Boone. Why, I was plumb scandalized when I put it on! It hardly covered me up a'tall!"

Boone restrained a smile, since it was no time for a lesson. But he thought, *She'll have to talk to Marie Bristol about some of these things.* "You look fine," he said.

"So do you, Boone. Well, you look as good as a lawyer or an undertaker."

Boone laughed aloud. "I suppose I should say thank you, but I don't care for either breed." He was wearing a dark gray jacket, a white shirt, a black waistcoat, and black-and-gray-checked trousers. A red tie was knotted around his neck.

"You look powerful good," Charlie said; then a worried look passed across her features. "I still think I'd rather not go to this here dance. Do you suppose they'll do any hoedowns?"

"I don't know," Boone said. "Never been to a dance in Richmond."

"That's the only kind of dancin' I know, and I don't know much 'bout that." Her eyes narrowed. "I bet you're a good dancer, ain't you, now?"

"Well, just fair."

But Charlie knew better, for she had learned that Boone was a quality man. During the brief time they had been together, her attitude had changed. Back in the cabin when he had tried to touch her, she had grown angry. All during the trip she kept waiting for him to make some kind of move again, but he never had. Somehow this had irritated her. Now as he picked up her coat, a pearl gray wool coat with a fox collar she loved, and slipped it over her shoulders, she thought, *He knows women.*

"All right," Boone said. "I hope Richmond's ready for us."

"Boone, don't let me get into no trouble."

"Trouble? How could you get into trouble?"

"I don't know. I feel funny goin' out dressed like this. You know how to do things like this. I ain't never been out of the woods, Boone." Her eyes were so large and vulnerable that he wanted to run his hand across

212

her hair. But he knew better than that, so he smiled instead, saying, "Why, you'll do fine, Charlie. A month from now you'll have Richmond at your feet."

"You really think so?"

"I know it! Come on. Let's go to the ball."

Malcolm Leighton leaned back in the carriage and allowed his shoulder to touch Marie Bristol's. She instantly removed her own a fraction of an inch, amusing him. "You don't exactly make a fellow feel good, Marie. Every time I try to touch you, you run like I was a copperhead or something."

"Sorry you feel like that, Malcolm," she replied, "but a girl has to be careful with young men. Especially young men with your reputation."

"Who's been giving me a bad word?" Leighton asked, affecting surprise. "I'm only a poor country boy trying to get along."

"I know all about that," Marie said. Malcolm Leighton *was* a country boy. He had grown up poor, as he had told her once, and determined to be one thing — rich. He had gone to sea as a cabin boy, had risen rapidly in his profession, and now at the age of twenty-eight owned two ships, both excellent blockade runners. He was also sought after by half the eligible unmarried ladies in Richmond and in the surrounding countryside. "You know what I told my mother about you, Malcolm?"

"I'm not sure I want to hear."

"You've heard worse, I'm sure." Turning to stare at his handsome features, which consisted of a straight nose, high cheekbones, and glossy brown hair, Marie said, "I told her you were looking for a wife but that you had started at the As and were working through alphabetically."

"Oh, that's foolish!"

"Is it? What about Betty Ashland? You chased her for two months, and after that was Charlotte Allison. You worked your way through the As and now you're down to the Bs."

"I don't know what to make of you, Marie," Leighton said lightly. He had known women perhaps more beautiful, but none with a wit sometimes so sharp it hurt a little bit. To tell the truth, he was tired of being successful with women. With his good looks and money, he could take his choice, and it seemed all he had to do was smile and the victory was won. With Marie Bristol, however, it was different. He had known that from the beginning. And now as he smiled at her through the growing darkness, he thought, *Why is it I always want something I can't have? Marie doesn't have a dime. Her folks won't have a pin after the war's over. . . . But I guess as long as one of us has money, that's enough, and she is a handsome girl!*

The carriage clattered over the brick streets and stopped in front of the large building where the Charity Ball was to be held. The door opened almost at once, and a tall black man offered her a hand down. She looked up in surprise to see that it was Solomon, one of the slaves from her own plantation. "Why, Solomon, what are you doing here?"

"I'm the doorman, Miss Marie." Solomon's white teeth flashed in the reflection of the lanterns that lit up the street and the front of the building. "They payin' me ten dollar just to help folks out. I do it for nothin' all the time. Ain't that somethin'?" Then he nodded toward Malcolm. "Good evenin', Mr. Leighton."

"Hello, Solomon." Reaching into his pocket, Malcolm pulled out a coin and passed it over. "Buy yourself a new necktie."

"I shore will! A red 'un! Thank you, suh!"

Marie took Leighton's arm, and the two entered. As they stepped inside, Leighton whispered, "It looks like everybody in Richmond is here. I never saw such a crowd."

"It's for a good cause."

The cause she spoke of was to help pay for medicines and supplies for Chimborazo, the large Confederate hospital outside Richmond. Marie was a fervent supporter of that and spent much of her time there. Now as they made their way through the packed room and across the white marble floor, she said, "There aren't many places this large, and they fixed it up for the ball so nicely." Chandeliers glittered from the high domed ceiling, and a fire blazed in the two large fireplaces on each side of the room. Long tables clothed in white linen were heaped high with silver plates, bowls, and platters of delicious-smelling food. At the far end of the room, double French doors led to a large porch, then a beautiful garden.

Over at one end of the ballroom, ten musicians were playing. The brilliant reds, greens, and yellows of women's dresses swirled around the room, counterpointed by the brass buttons and epaulets of the many officers.

Marie heard her name called and turned to see Austin exiting the floor with Ida Campbell. Austin was wearing his uniform, and Ida was wearing a new red silk dress with layers of flounces pinned up at the back with a fabric bow. She could well afford it, Marie knew, for she was the daughter of Clara Campbell, a wealthy widow. Her father had owned an immense plantation, but now Mrs. Campbell stayed most of the time inside Richmond mingling with the affluent. Ida came at once to Marie, and the two women hugged each other. Ida, at twenty-seven, was a year older than Marie. She was not exceptionally pretty, but Marie liked her honesty and openness. They exchanged compliments on their dresses while the two men talked.

Suddenly Ida said, "Who in the world is that, Austin?"

Austin squinted through the yellow light from the candles, lanterns, and chandeliers. "I never saw them before."

"I have," Marie said. "The man's name is Boone Manwaring."

"How do you know that?" Malcolm asked with surprise. "Is he a friend of yours?"

"No, not really, although I invited them to the ball." She felt their questioning eyes upon her. "I was in Mrs. Anderson's dress shop when they came in. They're from Colorado."

"His wife's a pretty woman," Ida said.

"Oh, she's not his wife," Marie replied.

"Not his wife? You mean she's his mistress?"

"I don't think so. I don't know the whole story, but he introduced her as his ward."

"Well," Leighton said with a grin, "that's one way of saying it. She's a pretty thing, isn't she?"

"There's something strange about her. Look how she walks," Austin said, watching the two cross the floor. He could not put his finger on it for a minute; then he said, "Look how long her steps are. She keeps up with that tall fellow with her. Manwaring is his name?"

"Yes, and her name is Charlene Peace, but she prefers to be called Charlie."

"She sure walks like a clodhopping farmer," Leighton said, studying the pair. "And what's that she's got on? I can't make it out."

Ida said, "Introduce us, Marie. It looks like they might be interesting. He's a fine-looking fellow!"

"Remember, I'm the fellow who brought you to this ball, Ida," Austin said quickly. "He may be taller than I am, but surely he's not better looking."

Ida laughed. "I like to make you jealous, Austin. . . . Look, they're coming this way!"

Boone Manwaring had seen Marie Bristol

218

and her party. He had leaned down to whisper, "Come on, Charlie. Here's a way to get introduced."

As they moved across the floor, Charlie's heart was thumping. She was stunned with all the activity, the colorful dresses, the loud music, the couples whirling around the floor, and now she wanted desperately to leave. But there was no hope for it. Boone's hand was on her arm, and he guided her through the crowd until they stood before Marie Bristol and her friends.

"How do you do, Miss Bristol? I took you up on your invitation," Manwaring said, smiling.

"I'm glad you did, Mr. Manwaring. This is Boone Manwaring. May I introduce my brother Austin. This is Mr. Malcolm Leighton, and this is Miss Ida Campbell."

"I'm happy to know you all, and may I introduce Miss Charlene Peace."

Charlie could do no more than swallow and nod as the others returned her greeting. Aware they were all looking at her peculiarly, Charlie clung desperately to Boone's arm, far more frightened than she had been when attacked by a grizzly bear. Finally, Boone said, "I think this is our dance, Miss Charlene, but if I may put in my bid, Miss Bristol and Miss Campbell, I would like the honor of a dance with you later on in the evening." He received assurances from both women and then pulled Charlie away.

"Boone," she said in a horrified whisper, "I cain't dance!"

"Sure you can. You said you could do a hoedown."

"Well, this ain't no hoedown!"

Noticing that people were staring, Boone said almost roughly, "Look, Charlie, there's nothing to it! Here, give me your hand! Now put your other hand up on my arm! Try not to fall over my feet!"

Charlie swallowed hard. "I don't know how to do this, Boone, but I'll try."

He was careful not to do anything complicated and was pleased to discover she had a natural rhythm. "That's fine, Charlie — you're doing real good!"

"Am I really?"

"Sure you are! Why, you'll be bragging someday that you had the best teacher in Richmond. Here we go now; we're going to try a little turn."

The four they had left were watching them. "What was that thing she had on under her dress? It looked like undergarments," Ida said.

"I think it was," Marie said. She hesitated,

then feeling it might be kinder to give a little detail of her meeting, explained how the two had just come from Colorado. She ended by saying, "The girl just lost her parents, and somehow Mr. Manwaring is taking care of her. I don't know the details, but in the dress shop it became obvious she had never had a dress on before. She was wearing buckskins with fringes and a coonskin cap."

"You're joking!" Leighton said. "You made that up!"

"No, I didn't. Can't you see how frightened she is? I feel sorry for her."

Ida turned toward the couple and smiled. "Well, she seems to be learning quickly. Come on, Austin; let's dance."

Austin agreed at once, and when they were out on the floor halfway through the dance, he said, "I'll tell you what, Ida. I'm going to give you a chance to dance with that fellow, Manwaring, that you think is so handsome."

Suspicious, Ida asked, "You're going to dance with that girl, aren't you?"

"I'm curious about her. Maybe I'd like to find some sweet, unspoiled young girl, totally innocent. Sort of a noble savage."

Ida liked Austin tremendously and considered marrying him often. She had turned down more than one offer, for she was a quick-witted girl and could read men rather easily. They had been after her money and little else. In all honesty she did not think this of Austin, but now as she glanced at Manwaring, she said with humor, "All right. Let's trade partners."

Austin maneuvered Ida out until they were even with Boone and Charlie, then tapped Manwaring on the shoulder. "I don't know about out west, but here we always cut in on strangers. Would you exchange partners with me?"

Boone saw the terror in Charlie's eyes but smiled encouragingly. "Why, of course! You'll dance with Mr. Bristol, won't you, Charlie?"

He gave her no chance to say no. Instantly he bowed to Ida; then the two moved off. As Charlie stood there almost paralyzed, Austin astutely realized she was frightened. "There's no need to be afraid," he said quietly.

"I ain't scared!" Charlie fired back. But then she bit her lip. "I ain't a good dancer, Mr. Bristol."

"Well, I'm an excellent dancer, so we'll average out. You step on my feet, and I'll step on yours in revenge." When he smiled at her, Charlie felt much better. This was an honest young man, she saw, and when he put his arm around her and took her hand, she did her best to follow. As they moved around the floor, he questioned her cautiously. "You've just come to Richmond, then, Miss Peace?"

"Yes. Me and Boone, we come in three days ago from Colorado."

"And how do you like Richmond?"

"Don't like it! Wisht I was back in the mountains!"

Amused by this blatant honesty, Austin smiled broadly. "I don't blame you a bit! I don't like it myself, but I live here, so I can't leave. Are you here for long?"

"My pa wanted me to come here. He grew up in Virginia. He wanted to buy a place and bring me and Ma here, but she died. So did he."

"Sorry to hear that." The dance moved on and he asked, "So you still intend to buy a place, a house?"

"Not a house. Pa wanted to get a plantation." By this time Charlie did not have to give all her attention to her feet. She had found that all she had to do was follow Austin on the floor, which to her surprise she did rather easily. She explained her father's dream, and Austin listened carefully then said quietly, "I'm sorry he didn't live to see his dream come true. It's a shame."

Charlie looked up to see the genuine concern in the young man's eyes. "That's neighborly of you to say so, Mr. Bristol."

"Look, why don't you just call me Austin, and perhaps you'd let me call you by your first name."

Shyly Charlie said, "Everybody calls me Charlie. My real name's Charlene, but only my ma ever called me that."

"I think I like Charlene, if you don't mind."

"I reckon it'd be all right." Charlie was pleased, for she did like the name Charlene, but her nickname had stuck so firmly that she did not know how to reverse it. As they continued to dance, she found herself enjoying his conversation and little knew how his tact made things easier for her.

Across the room Boone Manwaring kept an eye on the two. "Your escort is a very good dancer," he said. "I was worried about Charlie."

"Everyone's curious about her, of course, and about you."

"I understand why they would be," Boone said. "She lost her parents recently, and she's not over the shock of it yet."

"Do you intend to stay in Richmond?"

He started to tell Ida the story, then

224

decided it was too complicated. "I hope to find a place somewhere and get Charlie set up. She needs a home, a place of her own," he said simply.

"There's some fine old homes in Richmond. I could find out which ones are for sale."

"That's very gracious of you. I'll take you up on that, but we'd rather have something outside town. Something with some land."

"How much land?"

"I'm not sure." Again he almost told the story but said instead, "I'm a sailor, Miss Campbell. I don't know farming or plantations, but I guess I'll have to learn since I have to look out for Charlie."

Ida Campbell burned with curiosity to find out the relationship between the two, but she knew this was the wrong place and time to ask.

As the two danced, Ida found herself intrigued by Boone Manwaring. Boone himself, as he looked down into her face, was entranced by her smooth complexion, sparkling brown eyes, and gracious manners. *If all Southern women were like this, it'd be a heaven for bachelors,* he thought.

When the dance ended, Boone escorted her over to the refreshment table, where Charlie and Austin stood beside Malcolm

Leighton. "I think I'll have to claim this dance, Miss Peace," Leighton said at once.

Charlie glanced at Boone for reassurance. He nodded, and she moved out to the dance floor. Boone asked Marie Bristol to dance and was amused at how she tried to find out more about him and his ward. "Are you and Miss Peace related, Mr. Manwaring?"

"Not at all. I was a good friend of her father."

"I see," Marie said, but she did not at all. "And her parents are both deceased?"

"Yes. She doesn't have any family."

"And what about you? Excuse my curiosity," she responded, "but my mother says I have the curiosity of ten cats."

Boone liked the woman instinctively, so he sketched his background, his experiences on the sea, and finally said, "Not a very exciting biography. It was really more exciting looking for gold with Charlie's father."

"And you found the gold?"

"We found some of it," Boone said cautiously, not wanting to reveal the extent of his wealth. After the dance, they went back to the table, where he found Charlie fielding questions from Malcolm Leighton.

"Ah, I was just asking Miss Peace about you, Mr. Manwaring. I understand you're a seafaring man?"

"All my life," Boone said.

"So am I. If you're interested in a place, I can find room for you on one of my ships."

"That's very obliging of you, Mr. Leighton. I don't anticipate going back to sea anytime soon."

"Sooner or later someone will ask you about your politics, Mr. Manwaring," Leighton said. "We can't ask what time it is without asking that in this part of the world."

"I noticed that," Boone said, grinning. "My politics are to get rich, I guess."

His answer pleased Malcolm Leighton, and he laughed aloud. "I think we belong to the same party, sir. We'll have a drink on that." He proposed a toast. "To making money!" But it was Marie who said immediately, "And to the Confederacy!"

"To the Confederacy!" Malcolm said. "I stand rebuked!"

Staring at Boone, Marie said, "I'm afraid you'll have to be a little more specific. Making money is nice, but how do you stand on the war?"

She was, Boone saw, very serious, and the others were also listening carefully. *I've got to say this right, or I'll get off on the wrong foot,* he thought almost grimly. Speaking deliberately, he said, "Out in the West, you

227

wouldn't believe how little the war matters. I know that sounds odd to you, for it's your whole life here. But when you're in the middle of the mountains, or when you're out at sea, it's another thing. As for my politics, I really don't have any. I've spent much of my life at sea, and all I know about the war is what I read."

"Are you saying you don't care one way or another about the war?" Leighton asked sharply.

"If I had cared about it," Boone said, shrugging, "I would have joined either the Union or the Confederacy. I suppose right now you'll just have to put me down as undecided."

"End of questioning!" Austin said quickly. "A very fair answer, Mr. Manwaring. I hope that when you do decide, it will be for the Confederacy."

At that moment they were interrupted by a civilian, a bulky man almost as tall as Boone, who wore a fine suit of clothes. Without preamble he said, "Excuse me, Austin. I see we have some visitors. Could I ask that you introduce me?"

"Certainly," Austin said with reserve. "This is Miss Charlene Peace and Mr. Boone Manwaring, and this is Mr. Jack Cowling."

"We're glad to welcome you to Richmond, sir," he said, bowing slightly to Manwaring. Then he turned to Charlie. "Miss Peace, may I have this dance?"

Once again Charlie was frightened, but she had gained enough confidence to murmur, "I reckon so."

As she moved out on the dance floor with Cowling, Austin said, "He's one of the most influential men in Richmond, but nobody knows exactly where his money comes from."

"Part of it comes from making rotten uniforms that fall apart the first time they're worn!" Ida Campbell said, looking with distaste at Cowling.

Coming on the heels of Leighton's questions about Boone's politics, it was an uncomfortable moment — as if someone had exposed a secret that had been better off unmentioned. Boone understood at once that there were people in the Confederacy who weren't particularly admirable. He asked, "May I have this dance, Miss Bristol?"

"Of course."

The two moved out on the floor, and Boone said little. When the dance was half over, he stopped abruptly, causing Marie to miss a step. They both had heard a voice that could only be Charlie Peace's because it was loud enough to be heard over half the ballroom: "Keep your slimy hands to yourself!"

Instantly sensing trouble, Boone said, "Pardon me," and pushed his way through the crowd. He came upon Charlie, who was glaring at Cowling. Cowling's face had a red mark on it.

"What's the trouble, Charlie?"

"Why, he put his hand on —" Charlie stopped short then said, "He put his hands on me in a place he shouldn't, and I punched him fer it!"

"I'll have to ask you to excuse Miss Peace, Mr. Cowling," Boone said.

Cowling was unaccustomed to being slighted. Certainly no one had ever struck him in public in a ballroom, and his rage was evident. He had been drinking, for his eyes were slightly bloodshot. "If you want to make more of this, you can have your man call on me! I'll be glad to oblige you!"

For a moment Boone was tempted to take up the challenge. Instead, he said, "I try to delegate all the fighting to my dog."

Cowling's face turned pale and he opened his mouth, but a friend came quickly to his side and said, "Come on, Jack. You're drunk."

"I want to go home, Boone! Let's get out of here!"

"All right, Charlie."

Boone threw one look at Marie Bristol and shrugged helplessly; then he and Charlie left the room. When they were outside, Charlie said emphatically, "If that's your fine society, I don't keer much fer it!"

"I don't think Jack Cowling was a good sample."

"I don't like any of this, Boone!" Charlie whispered almost plaintively. "Cain't we go away from here?"

Feeling sorry for the girl, Boone stood there silently as the music floated out of the building toward them. "I'll tell you what, Charlie," he said, "let's try it for a while. If it doesn't work out, I'll take you back to Colorado. Is that fair enough?"

Charlie knew she had behaved badly, and she was humiliated. After all, she had only done what she would have at a dance back in the mountains. She had expected Boone to take up the challenge and was surprised when he did not. Looking up now, she saw the concern in his hazel eyes and suddenly realized how much she had come to depend upon this man since her father had died. He was, in one respect, the only friend she had.

"I reckon that's fair enough, Boone."

Chapter 12
A Favor for Boone

Marianne was sitting in the parlor working on a new quilt. She would have the women in for a quilting later that afternoon, so she was gathering the material together. Ketura came to the door and said, "They's a gentleman here to see Miss Marie."

"Who is it, Ketura?"

"I can't say his name. It's funny."

Wondering who it could be, Marianne rose and went to the foyer, where she saw a tall man dressed in a new suit. "I'm Mrs. Bristol, sir."

"Mrs. Bristol, my name is Boone Manwaring. I don't know if your daughter has spoken of me or not."

"Why, as a matter of fact, she has! She mentioned she met you at a dress shop."

"Yes, and then again at the Charity Ball three days ago. I would like to see her if she's home, Mrs. Bristol."

"I believe she's up in her room. If you'd

care to wait, I'll go get her."

"Thank you, Mrs. Bristol."

Marianne showed Boone to the study and then went upstairs. She found Marie reading a book before the fireplace. She was wearing a simple gray dress with white buttons.

"You have a visitor, Marie."

"A visitor?" Marie put the book down. "Who's out in this kind of weather?"

"It's Mr. Manwaring. The one you told me about. You didn't say he was so good looking, though."

"Boone Manwaring?" Marie cocked her head in puzzled surprise.

"Didn't you invite him here?"

"Well, in a general way, but it looks like he took it specifically."

Marianne smiled, saying, "He didn't bring his young woman with him. I was hoping to see her after what you told me about the incident at the ball."

"I'd better go down," Marie responded. "I'll tell you about it later, Mother."

"Very well. I'll be anxious to hear."

When Marie reached the parlor, Boone was standing in front of the fire. He came forward at once. "I'm sorry to impose on you, but I hope you'll forgive me."

"Certainly! I'm glad you came in. Let me

have some tea brought in."

Happy to be warmly received, Boone said, "That would be nice."

Marie went to the door and called to Ketura. They spoke of unimportant things until the tea came. Then when it was served, she sat back and waited for the reason he had come to see her.

Boone went over again in his mind what he intended to say. Since the ball, he had spent some time investigating land prices but had been too concerned about Charlie to do much more. He had taken her out to meals, and they had walked around to see the sights, but she was obviously unhappy with life in Richmond.

"A man hates to ask favors," Boone said abruptly, "but that's what I've come here to do."

"What is it, Mr. Manwaring?"

"Do you suppose you could call me Boone?"

"Oh, I suppose so, and if I'm going to do you a favor, perhaps Marie would be better than Miss Bristol."

"Thank you. That's very charitable of you." Now that the moment had come, Boone was at a loss for words. He stared down at his boots for a moment then looked up, a serious expression on his face. "It's complicated. Do you mind if I tell you how I met Charlie?"

"I'd be interested to hear it." A dimple appeared in Marie's right cheek. "You have no idea how curious I am."

"Not just you. Everybody's curious. I'd call it nosy, at sea, but I suppose it's natural enough. An unmarried man and woman ride in, and with Charlie dressing like she does and acting like she does, I suppose it's inevitable."

"How *did* you meet her?" Marie asked quietly. She sat very still while Boone went back over the story of how he and Noah Peace had met then worked together to find the gold. She knew he was taking special pains to prepare the way for the favor he wanted to ask, but she still couldn't imagine what it was. Finally, when Boone got to the part where Noah had died and had made his last request, Marie began to understand. She leaned forward. "I suppose that's why you're here, then, to fulfill her father's last request."

"That's it, Marie," Boone said, "but it hasn't been easy." Marie refilled his tea, which had grown cold, and he held the cup in his hands. "You see what she is. She's a good girl, but a disaster at a ball. She doesn't know what to wear. She doesn't know how to act. I don't know how in the world I'm going to handle it. That's why I came here."

"I'm afraid I'm a little dense. Why exactly did you come here?"

Boone took a deep breath, for the dreaded moment had come. He appeared ill at ease, but he was a determined man. "I've got to have help, Marie, with Charlie. I've got to buy a place and see that she's not cheated, and I don't know anything about land prices. I can learn a thing like that, but I can't help her with the other things — like what to wear, how to talk, and what not to say. Did you know she chews tobacco?"

"I remember she had a plug at the dress shop!"

"I think she does it to irritate me." He paused then and shook his head despairingly. "I've got to have some help! So that's the favor. Will you help me make a lady out of Charlie?"

"Why, I'd be happy to do anything I could."

"Would you really? That would be so much help. Why, I could tell in the store you knew what to do with her."

"I didn't think she liked me much."

"She's afraid of you, Marie. When she sees somebody like you, so beautiful and poised, why, it scares her. I guess it would scare anybody."

Inwardly pleased at his evaluation, Marie asked, "What does she say about all this? Would she be willing to learn from me?"

"Oh, I haven't said a word to Charlie," Boone responded. "I wanted to ask you first. It wouldn't do to disappoint her."

"Exactly what did you have in mind?" Marie queried.

"Well, this is the hard part to say. I wish there was a school of some kind where I could send her. I guess there are schools like that, aren't there?"

"Yes, there are. Several, but Charlie's a special case. For instance, the school I went to wouldn't know what to make of her."

"That's exactly right, but you do. I could see that right away." Boone floundered for a minute then hurried on. "Could I hire you to teach Charlie? I know you don't need the money, but it would make me feel better to put it on that basis."

Marie almost said, *Need money? Why, bless your heart, we need all the money we can get.* But somehow she could not bring herself to say these things. Times were not that hard yet!

"I'll be glad to do what I can, Boone, but there's no question of money." She leaned back in her chair. "As a matter of fact, I've always wanted to create a new person. Maybe I could practice on Charlie."

Boone was immeasurably relieved. "That's what I came to ask, and I have to say I expected to get thrown out. I'll have to make this up to you some way, Marie."

Marie's quick mind came to a decision. "It would be hard to train her for just an hour or two a week. What would you think about having Charlie come and stay here at Hartsworth? Say, for a week? Then we could see how we get on."

"Why, that's more than I would ever dare to ask. Are you sure it would be all right?"

"Oh, of course. There's just me and my mother here, besides the servants. My father is leaving with the army soon. He's in camp already. We just rattle around this big old house. It would be a pleasure to have her."

Boone expelled his breath. "Sometimes I think we spend so much time worrying about things that never happen that we never have time to worry about the things that do happen."

"I've thought the same thing. Do you think she'll come?"

"I think she might. She's sick of that hotel room. She might be a little afraid of you,

239

but you've got a way that puts people at ease."

He rose and squeezed her hand, saying fervently, "You don't know how much I appreciate this, Marie."

"Well, let's wait and see if I'm able to help. But somehow I think it can be done."

"Charlie learns fast. She's stubborn as a mule, but then, so am I."

Marie smiled, pulling her hand back. Apparently he'd forgotten to turn it loose. "Bring her anytime."

"Would today be too soon?"

"Not at all. I'll have her room ready."

"I thank you very much, Marie. And Charlie will, too, when she's had a chance to think about it."

After he left, Marie went at once to find her mother, who was in the kitchen. Marianne listened to the story until Marie concluded, "He wants me to make a fine lady out of her — and I think I might be able to do it."

Marianne was more doubtful. "It's not safe to play with people's lives, Marie."

"You don't mean that. You're always 'playing with people's lives.' Only you call it trying to help them."

Marianne laughed then. "I suppose you're right. The poor girl needs help. Do you really think it can be done?"

"I think it's a dangerous thing — you're right about that. Not because it's about learning better manners and how to dress, but because it's a dream her father had. I'm not sure that same dream will work for Charlie."

Marianne was silent for a while. "No," she said sorrowfully, "dreams usually don't come true."

Marie knew her mother was thinking of her father and their life together. She rose, saying, "Well, I'll go get her room ready." As she moved upstairs, calling Ketura to come with her, she thought, *Boone Manwaring is some man. Most men I know wouldn't have taken a promise this seriously, especially a promise to a dead man.* "Well, I'll see what I can do, but I can't promise Charlie will like what we make of her."

■ ■ ■ ■ ■

Part Three:
Confederate
Christmas

■ ■ ■ ■ ■

CHAPTER 13
LOVE IS MORE THAN A KISS!

"Rex, you'll have to get down — how can I write with you perched in my lap like this?" The big yellow tabby cat who had plopped himself on top of Charlie's journal did not find her statement particularly impressive. He closed his eyes and began to purr deep in his throat, the tip of his tail switching wildly. The big tom had taken up with Charlie as soon as she had arrived at Hartsworth and now felt it was his prerogative to interrupt any of her activities. Desiring Charlie's full attention, he put his claws out and began flexing them, digging them vigorously into her thighs.

"Stop that, Rex — it hurts!" Charlie exclaimed, then put down the quill and began to stroke Rex under the throat. He raised his head, eyes closed in ecstasy, and rumbled noisily.

Rubbing the thick fur, Charlie smiled faintly. "I wish I didn't have any more problems than you do, Rex. All you have to do is eat and catch a mouse once in a while, then come and get tickled. That's some life you've got there."

Outside, the sky was gray, but there was a hint of snow in the lowering clouds. Charlie missed the snow from the mountains and wished sometimes she were back there, forging her way on snowshoes through the deep drifts with a rifle, looking for an elk. No matter how easy things were at Hartsworth, she felt out of place — and lonely.

Charlie picked Rex up and dropped him gently over the edge of the bed. "Go catch a varmint, you worthless critter!" She smiled as Rex yawned hugely then lay down with his head on his paws to sleep. Then she opened the tablet again and intently began to write.

Boone come over here twice this week. He said he was lookin round for a place, but he did not seem too eager bout it. I did not complain, although I shore wanted to. Its been a hard thing tryin to learn all that stuff Marie wants me to know. Theys a million things to learn just bout dresses. Seem like these women in the South dont do nothin but put on clothes and take off clothes. Got to have a different dress every time you spit! I told Marie there wasnt no sense in so much clothes changin and she just smiled and said that is the way ladies done in the South. And I told her it wasnt the way you done in Colorado. A pair of buckskins was all you needed cept for goin to meetin. She laughed at that and said sometimes she wished she could just wear pants and a shirt like a man.

Outside, the wind began to moan like a wounded creature, causing Charlie to look up. The limbs of the walnut tree outside her window began to scrape the side of the house. Charlie remembered how, back in Colorado, the aspens had whispered overhead and brushed against the side of the loft where her bed was. She sat still for a time then began to write again.

Seems like I been here forever, and they aint no end to it. I told Boone again it would suit me to go back home again, but he said this was gonna be home. I know he gets put out with me, and I caint help it. Seems like he is the only one I got left now. I been thinkin bout him a lot lately. I was thinkin about the time before we left home — well, the old place, anyhow — and he put his hands on me and I yelled at him. As I think on it, there werent no sense in that. He was just tryin to be nice, and I acted like he was a bear tryin to claw me or somethin. I told him never to touch me again. Well, I hate to admit it, but theys been times when I wish he would touch me!

Charlie looked back at the sentence she had just written, mesmerized by her thoughts. *What in the cat hair am I thinkin' 'bout? I was the one to tell him to keep his hands to his self, and now I'm wantin' him to put 'em on me again? Reckon I've gone crazy since I come to this place, but it would be nice if he would put his arm 'round me a little bit and tell me he liked me. I don't know how to tell him to do that. He'd think I was makin' up to him, for sure, and he ain't thinkin' 'bout me like a woman. To him I'm a wild colt he's got to break to halter.*

The tree again brushed the house, interrupting Charlie's thoughts. She flushed slightly at what was in her mind, then began writing again.

I cant help but see why Boone wouldnt

want to be foolin with me. I dont know much about courtin and all that, but it sure is plain Boone likes Marie. Caint blame him fer that. She is bout the prettiest woman I ever seen, and when he looks at her I kin tell there is somethin in his eyes. He somehow acts different round her. I dont know how to word it, but he is stuck on her, that is fer sure. Well, who cares? Let him like her! Dont make no never mind to me! I will git me a big house like Pa wanted, and I will git me a man bigger, finer lookin, and smarter than any old Boone Manwaring!

Dissatisfaction and longing swelled in Charlie Peace as she sat on the bed. She had been happy back in the mountains, hunting and fishing and taking care of her mother. Now, however, that world had passed away, and she was lost and confused in a new one. What it was she wanted she could not say. It had something to do with Boone Manwaring, she knew that much, and now as she balanced the tablet with her pen held loosely in her hand, she wondered if this was only a part of growing up — of becoming a woman. "I've got to have me a man someday," she muttered. "Every woman's got to have a man, but I ain't never worried about it. Not till now, anyways."

Closing the tablet abruptly, she put it away then cleaned the quill and laid it down on the shelf. Swinging her feet over the side of the bed, she stared down at the red carpet that covered the pine floor. *Maybe it would be better to git away from Hartsworth,* she thought sadly. But she had grown very fond of the people here, especially of Marianne Bristol, and knew she would miss them — that she would be even lonelier. Then Charlie said aloud, "Me and Boone can get us a place somewhere and git away from all this. I ain't never gonna learn to be the kind of lady he likes anyway!"

It had not taken Boone Manwaring very long after the Charity Ball to learn that when one lived in Richmond, it was necessary to think about the war. When he had been at sea, he had lived in a microcosm with the captain as the monarch, the officers as the aristocracy, and the sailors as the serfs. The captain's word was law, right or wrong, and it could be death to disobey him. The land world had been far away, and things such as politics were alien to his thoughts.

But Richmond was no ship. It was a

beehive of activity, and the thoughts of every man and woman were intertwined inextricably with the struggle for survival in which they found themselves. Everyone avidly watched for news from the fronts. The battles that had taken place in the west around Lookout Mountain had been something everyone talked about. Boone was amazed to discover that even the very young knew the names of the commanders. Sherman and Grant and Thomas, for the Union, and the Confederate generals — Cleburne, Hardee, and Breckinridge — were as familiar to them, almost, as their own names. The story of the fierce battles of Lookout Mountain and Missionary Ridge had been brought back by some of the wounded, and the whole city listened as they told of the fighting above the clouds.

As Boone finished shaving and put on a clean shirt, then tied his cravat carefully, he was baffled over the whole matter. "I don't see why they keep on fighting," he murmured as he slipped into his frock coat and put on his wide-brimmed black hat, settling it firmly on his head. "They must all be fools to think they could win. Almost every day they get news about losing a battle — and everybody, even the kids, knows that Grant's got an army of a hundred thousand men. He'll be knocking at Richmond's door before spring, but they keep on acting like they're going to win. I don't understand."

Transferring his wallet from the table to his inner pocket, he eyed the .44 and considered carrying it, but then left the room without it. Going downstairs, he entered the restaurant and was surprised to see Malcolm Leighton sitting alone at a table. When Leighton saw him, he waved him over. "Come and keep me company. Always did hate to eat alone."

"Thanks, don't mind if I do." Boone took the chair and ordered bacon and eggs, then picked up the cup of coffee that the waiter poured. He tasted it then made a face. "I thought this was coffee! It's tea!"

"Coffee's mostly gone. I meant to tell that waiter." He hailed the waiter when he went by and said, "Bring Mr. Manwaring a cup of that coffee you keep back for me."

"Yes, sir!"

"Well, how's the experiment going?"

"Experiment?" Boone asked, slightly puzzled. "You mean coming to settle in the South?"

"Yes, we don't have many folks coming this way. Most of them are leaving Richmond if they've got enough money to get away." Leighton, who wore black wool

252

trousers, a green jacket, a crisp white shirt, and a green and black tie, toyed with the eggs on his plate while his sharp eyes probed Boone carefully. "How is it going with your ward, Miss Peace?"

"Very well. She's been a guest of the Bristols for the last few weeks."

"So Marie tells me. Sort of a finishing school, I take it?"

It angered Boone to hear Leighton put it this way. Boone had a quick temper that he had learned, after hard examples, to keep under control, so now he let nothing show in his face. Instead, he said smoothly, "Charlie hasn't had many advantages. It was very generous of Miss Bristol to offer to help."

"Yes, it was." The coffee came then, and the waiter poured it from a silver pot into Boone's cup. As he left, Leighton asked, "What about yourself? Are you going to settle here around Richmond? You'll have to forgive me, but strangers are fair game for speculation. As a matter of fact, quite a few people are wondering about you two."

"I suppose the gossip system is effective wherever you go," Boone said, smiling slightly. "No great mystery about it." He sipped the coffee then continued, "Charlie's father was a good friend of mine. When he

253

passed on, he asked me to look after her until she married. He was from Virginia himself, although he hadn't been here for many years, and he wanted to come back and let her have a life here. So after he died, I decided to try to do what he wanted."

Leighton pursed his lips. "A pretty big order, Boone."

"Well, Noah Peace was a good man. He would have done the same for me."

"Fine thing, loyalty." But the statement fell flatly from Leighton's lips. "Have you had a committee yet, investigating your politics?"

"Not formally, but I get a lot of odd looks. I guess any man my age who isn't wearing a uniform is suspect."

"You're right about that. The South is scraping the bottom of the barrel now. You may get a few insults, since some of our firebrands here get pretty blunt when it comes to the Cause. It'll probably get worse. That is, if you decide to stay."

"I'll stay until I do what I came to do. You can depend on that."

"I figured that might be the way of it. Well, I don't know much about plantations. I guess you and I know about ships and not much else."

The truth of the remark struck at Boone.

"That's about the story." He would have said more, but the waiter came back with his breakfast. He plunged into it hungrily as the two men spoke of the war and the prospects of the South. Boone found it difficult to read Leighton, who was certainly not a firebrand. In fact, he seemed almost indifferent to the war news. *I guess he's mostly interested in making money,* Boone thought, *which I suppose is not uncommon, even in the Confederacy.*

As they finished breakfast, Leighton said, "I'm going out to the Bristol place this afternoon. Can I take any word to Miss Peace?"

"Tell her I'll be out later, if you would."

"Be glad to." As Leighton rose, he said idly, "You might go see Colonel Clay Rocklin. He's Marie Bristol's relation. Knows pretty much everything about land and plantations. He might have some ideas on a place that would suit you."

"Thanks, Malcolm. I'll do that."

When the two men separated, Boone decided he did need advice. Moving down to the livery stable, he rented a horse, a rather undersized bay, but all that was available. "Do you think he'll make it to the camp?" he asked the hostler with humor.

"If he dies, you get your money back."

"Good enough." Boone swung into the saddle and rode through the town. He had been anxious to see the camp, in any case. Even in Colorado he had heard of the legendary Army of Northern Virginia and its equally famous commander, Robert E. Lee. He was not sure Lee was in Richmond now, but he suspected so. When he reached the camp, he asked for directions, and twenty minutes later he was stepping down before what was apparently a commander's tent. A flag with a military insignia he did not recognize flew over it, and as he tied his horse to a sapling, he turned to see an officer approaching. The man wore the uniform of a second lieutenant and looked oddly familiar.

"May I help you, Mr. . . . ?" the lieutenant asked. He was not a young man, Boone observed.

"Manwaring."

"Manwaring? Boone Manwaring?"

Boone was astonished. How far had his and Charlie's "fame" spread?

The lieutenant laughed, and again Boone wondered if they'd met before. "My daughter has told me of you and your friend. I am Claude Bristol of Hartsworth!"

The truth dawned. *Marie's* father. Austin's father. No wonder the resemblance. "Well, hello, Mr. Bristol. I didn't expect to see you here."

Claude Bristol smiled wryly. "You're echoing the sentiments of most people. Ever since I joined the army, people have been in a state of shock."

"Why should they be surprised?"

"Because I've never done anything before that was unselfish or right. I think they're all waiting to see if I'm not a spy for Lincoln."

Boone was surprised at the frankness of the older man. He had picked up a little bit of the Bristol family's problems from Charlie, and other information he had gleaned from things other members of the family had said. Now as he looked Bristol over carefully, he noted marks of dissipation from years of self-indulgence, but found no viciousness. Bristol had a lean, aristocratic face, and his uniform fit perfectly. Although there was a cynical air about the man, he was cheerful enough as he asked, "I don't suppose you came to join up?"

Boone grinned. "Not quite, sir."

"I thought not. Well, what can I do for you?"

"I came to talk to Colonel Rocklin. You probably know I'm trying to find a plantation that would be suitable for Charlie.

Malcolm Leighton said the colonel knows land and values as well as anybody around. And also that he's honest."

"That's a good evaluation, I think. I wish I could help you, but I was never a businessman. I think the colonel's free if you'll wait here."

Boone waited as Bristol disappeared into the tent then reappeared almost at once. "Go right in, Mr. Manwaring."

"Thank you, Lieutenant." Stepping inside, Boone saw that Colonel Rocklin was wearing a heavy coat and there was no fire inside the tent. But he stood up from his desk at once and put out his hand.

"How do you do, sir? Mr. Manwaring, isn't it?"

"Boone Manwaring. I'm glad to meet you, Colonel. I've heard a great deal about you from Mrs. Bristol. She thinks a lot of you, of course."

"Well, I think a lot of her. Won't you sit down? Wish I had some coffee, but I'm afraid we're all out, unless you can drink acorn coffee."

"No, thanks. I only need a few minutes of your time." As Boone explained his mission, he grew more and more impressed with Clay Rocklin. No wonder men and women alike spoke so well of him — there was a strength and kind power in the man. Boone finished his story by saying, "I wouldn't want to make a bad buy, Colonel."

Clay had listened carefully. "I can't tell you whether it's a good time or a bad time to be buying land. If you have greenbacks from the United States government, you can get a good price. There are some good places for sale, but what will happen in the future nobody knows."

"I understand that. It was Miss Peace's father who wanted to come here. I tried to tell him things would be different than when he was growing up as a boy, but he wouldn't listen."

"Those days are gone," Clay said at once. "We'll have to start over again after this war is over, and it'll be hard. In all honesty, Mr. Manwaring, it would be better to invest your money in land elsewhere. If you want to stay in the South, even a border state like Kentucky would be safer."

"If it were my choice, I would do that at once, Colonel. But I'm bound by my promise to Charlie's father."

"Let me think on it. Plenty of places for sale, but you'll want to do the best you can for the young woman."

Boone said, "Thank you very much for your time. I'm staying at the Spotswood if you get word of anything good."

"I'll put out some feelers right away. In the meantime, I hope to see you again." Colonel Rocklin cocked his head. "Don't suppose you'd be interested in joining a good outfit?"

"No, I think not. Thanks for your offer."

"Never hurts to ask. Good day, sir."

"Good day, Colonel."

Boone stepped outside and waited until Lieutenant Bristol finished speaking to a sergeant. Then he said, "I'm on my way to your home. Can I take any message?"

"Why, I don't believe so, except to tell them I'm healthy."

"I'll do that, sir."

Boone left the camp and made his way toward Richmond, taking the side road that led to Hartsworth. It was a cold day, and by the time he reached there, his face stung from the bitter weather. When he stepped off his horse, he could not feel his feet. Solomon came running up to take his horse, and he murmured his thanks then climbed the steps to the front door carefully lest he turn an ankle. When the door opened, Charlie stood there, her eyes bright. "Boone, I'm glad to see you. Come in out of the cold."

"How are you, Charlie?" Boone asked as he took off his coat and hat. He watched as she put them on a coat tree and then turned to him. She was wearing a dress he hadn't seen before. "That's a pretty dress."

"Miss Marie helped me pick it out. Do you really like it, Boone?"

Boone looked at the dress more closely. Simply made of brown wool with tan stripes, the dress was modestly cut with white lace around the edge of the neckline and around the bottom of the full skirt. "I sure do. It goes well with your hair." Then he remarked, "Your hair is getting longer. Are you going to let it grow?"

"I don't know. What do you think?"

Boone laughed. "I'm no expert in ladies' fashions. Is there a fire around here?"

"Yes. Come on in. Are you hungry?"

"I'm starved."

"Let's go to the kitchen. I'll fix you somethin' to eat."

The two went to the kitchen, where Charlie bustled around, fixing a meal. "Dinner ain't ready yet, but we got some biscuits left over from breakfast, and I'll fry you up some bacon. That ought to do you till dinnertime."

"That's fine, Charlie. Tell me what you've been doing."

Charlie chattered on, and Boone was amazed at how lively she seemed. When she brought the meal and sat down across from him, she folded her hands and asked, "Did you find us a place yet?"

"Not yet, Charlie. It's a pretty big job, and I don't have a head for things like this. Now if it was buying a ship, I could do something."

He continued to tell Charlie about his goings, for she was always interested, and as he spoke, Austin Bristol came in, accompanied by Marie. Boone stood up at once. "Hello, Austin — Marie. How are you?"

"When did you get in?" Austin asked, shaking his hand. He seemed genuinely pleased to see Boone.

"I went out to the camp and met Colonel Rocklin this morning. Your father was there, too. He said to tell you he was well. Marie, please pass that along to your mother."

"Thank you, Boone. Now don't eat any more! We'll fix a proper meal." Marie was glad to see Boone, for she'd been thinking about him a great deal. Now she began instructing the cook about the meal, then said, "I want to hear all about what you've been doing, Boone. Come along."

Austin happened to be watching Charlie's face as his sister spoke. He saw the change in it and knew Charlie was disappointed. *Why, she's jealous of Marie!* he realized with astonishment and said, "Charlene, I want to show you my new horse."

For a moment he thought Charlie would decline, but then she said quietly, "All right, Mr. Austin."

"Not *Mr.* — just Austin."

They put on coats and walked to the barn, where Austin exhibited his new horse, a rangy bay, with pride. "Maybe you'd like to ride him? He's a bit of a handful, though."

"Let me git my britches on, and I'll show you I kin ride him! I cain't ride nothin' in this here dress!"

Austin laughed. "You ever ride sidesaddle like Marie?"

"No, that's a foolish way to git on an animal, with your leg all crooked 'round the horn."

"I guess it is. I don't think I could stay on. Tell you what, you go put on some 'britches,' as you call them, and I'll saddle another horse." As he saddled the horse, he puzzled about the relationship between the two who had come to Richmond. The girl was beautiful, though rough around the edges, but that wouldn't stop a man. Marie had told him Charlie was learning quickly, and though it would take time, one day she'd be able to take her place in the ballrooms and tea parties of Richmond society.

Charlie came back wearing a pair of jeans, a wool shirt, and a black coat. She mounted the horse expertly, asking, "What's his name?"

"Thunder."

"Well, I'll race you, then!"

Caught off guard, Austin grinned. "All right. We'll race to the tree down by the creek. You ready?"

"When I count three, we'll go. One — two — three!"

They had their race, and Charlie was delighted when she won. "This is a good hoss!" she said. "If an Indian had him, he could git him a good squaw fer just this one hoss."

"Is that right? I never thought of a horse in terms of how many brides it would buy."

"Indians do it all the time. Hosses are money fer 'em."

After a cold ride, they started back, and Charlie grew quiet.

"You're very fond of Boone, aren't you?"

Charlie's cheeks reddened. "He's been good to me," she said simply.

"You ever think of marrying him?"

The tinge of red grew deeper. "I don't think 'bout things like that, Austin."

"Oh, I guess I was mistaken, then. I thought —"

"I don't want to talk 'bout it."

"All right, Charlene."

He thought the conversation was over, but when they were inside the house, she asked, "Why ain't your sister, Marie, ever got married?"

"Never found a man she loved, I guess."

"Was she ever spoken fer?"

"Two or three wanted to marry her, but she didn't feel anything for them."

"You reckon she'll marry someday?"

"Oh yes, I'm sure she will." Glancing at Charlie, Austin saw she was deep in thought. "You'll have a man of your own one day, Charlene."

"I don't think 'bout it much."

"Well, you're probably the only girl in Virginia who doesn't."

"What 'bout you, Austin? Why ain't you ever got a woman?"

"Just looking around."

"You're pretty old not to be married."

Austin laughed with delight at her bluntness. "You come right out with the thing, don't you, Charlene? You don't know how refreshing that is after listening to women hint and scheme."

"Why should I do a thing like that? And

what did I say? 'Bout you being old?"

"Most women wouldn't put it that way."

"How old are you?"

"Thirty-one."

"That ain't old," Charlie said, smiling. Her hair, black as night, curled out, rich and lustrous, from beneath the soft gray hat she wore, making her eyes look even darker.

Austin leaned forward. "Why, you have blue eyes, dark blue! I thought they were black."

Charlie stared at Austin and said, "I guess so. You think you ever will git a woman?"

Austin hesitated. His weeks-old conversation with Marie about marrying for money brought a jolt of shame to him. "Maybe someday."

"Be sure you git a good one. You deserve a good woman."

Boone had been asked to stay over, which he did. Charlie was extremely quiet, but when he had tried to find out why, she simply said she didn't feel like talking.

Before supper, Marie and Boone took a walk on the grounds of Hartsworth. It was almost dark when they again approached the house, and she stopped, looking around. "I'd hate to think of living anywhere but here."

Boone said quietly, "It must be nice to be in one place all your life. I never had anything like that."

"You never had a home?"

"We had a house, but I was mostly at sea. Some say they liked to call the ship a home, but it's not like this."

"That must be lonely, not having a place," Marie said. This was the first time they had been alone, and he was suddenly aware of the curve of her mouth, her lovely throat, and the way her face mirrored her change of feelings. As she spoke of Hartsworth, he sensed her love for the land and felt a stirring inside. He couldn't decide whether it was Marie's beauty or the loneliness that had been with him for a long time.

As the darkening light played over her form, her soft fragrance slid through the armor of his self-sufficiency.

Marie stopped speaking and looked up with surprise, seeing in his eyes that Boone was thinking of her as a woman.

As for Boone, he could not have told what he was feeling. But as the last glow of the sun touched her face, he strained against the leash of his reserve and put his arms around her. As he kissed her, he felt her relax and thought, *This is what I've been looking for.*

As for Marie, she was in shock that she had allowed Boone to take her in his arms and kiss her. She was not a woman who gave caresses easily. Although she had been kissed, it had not always been her choice, and now she knew as she lay in his arms, with the pressure of his lips against hers, that this was something she had chosen. But she was also troubled by the emotion she felt when his arms pulled her closer. Perhaps it was then she realized how she needed a man's strength, so she surrendered, allowing the kiss to go on longer than she had intended. Then she drew away.

"When a man's alone," Boone said quietly, "he's what he is. But when he sees a woman and gives something to her, he never gets it back. If he wants to be whole again, he's got to go to that woman."

Marie stared at him, taken by his words. "Do you think things like this often, Boone?"

"When I think of you, I do."

"Have you thought of me often?"

"Yes." He would have pulled her forward again, but she put her hand on his chest. He stepped back, put his hands behind his back, and clamped them together. "I never met a woman like you before."

"You've known women, Boone."

"Every man, maybe, knows something about women, but it doesn't amount to much. And then one day, maybe at dusk like this, he kisses a woman and sees what he really is — what's been driving him all his life."

Impulsively Marie wanted to step forward, throw her arms around his neck, and feel the touch of his lips on hers again. But she fought against it and said instead, "I think we'd better go inside."

"All right."

"What do you think about Boone?"

Marie had been sitting beside Austin at the desk, going over the figures of the plantation. The question surprised her, and she blushed. "What do you mean by that?"

"I mean about him and Charlene."

"I don't understand you, Austin."

"Why, the girl's foolish about him. Surely she's told you that."

"No, she hasn't. What makes you think so?"

"Why, she practically told me — and she's jealous of you, Marie. You didn't notice?"

Marie remembered how reticent Charlie was whenever Marie spoke of Boone and how strangely silent Charlie had been during Boone's most recent visit. "I suppose you're right. It would be only natural. She doesn't have anybody else."

"I don't know how he feels, but she's in poor condition, ripe for the wrong man to come along. I hope it doesn't happen."

The two turned back to their figuring. Austin finally said, "We've got to do something, Marie. I don't see how we can last another month. The bank's screaming for money and talking foreclosure."

"They've done that before."

"They mean it this time. I know this sounds odd, but have you thought of Boone as a man you might marry?"

Marie rose abruptly, eyes flashing anger. "Because he has money? What about you? All you have to do is ask Ida. She has more money than Boone, I'd say."

Austin dropped his head. "I'm a fool," he said, "but it's driving me crazy, Marie. I don't know what to do. I can't stand the thought of losing this place."

Marie loved Austin deeply. She got up and stood behind him, putting one hand on his shoulder and brushing his hair back from his forehead with the other. "I know," she whispered. "I've thought of it, too. But wouldn't it be wrong?"

"I don't know anymore what's right and what's wrong."

"Neither do I." She thought of the kiss, knowing she would not forget it for weeks. But then her mind spoke rebelliously, *Love is more than a kiss!*

CHAPTER 14
A MATTER OF COURAGE

Major Olan Ferguson was too old to be an officer, but Robert E. Lee was scraping the bottom of the barrel. Ferguson had graduated from West Point and, like Lee and many others, had resigned from the United States Army at the beginning of hostilities. He was a martinet, and the sight of a missing button on an enlisted man's uniform was, to him, the sign of complete degradation, militarily speaking.

Clay Rocklin had inherited the major and was not certain that the brigade was better for having him. He remarked once to Melora, "He's about ready for a rocking chair somewhere, and I wish he'd go there. He's driving me crazy, and I don't know what to do about him."

Claude Bristol was the current catalyst that stirred Major Ferguson's ire. He had, upon hearing of Bristol's recent acceptance as Clay's adjutant and clerk, sputtered angrily, saying loudly in an open meeting of the officers, "What good will he do? Has he ever been to the Point?"

"The Point doesn't converse saintship on men, Major," one of the officers suggested, which did no good to the major's state of mind.

"He'll not be worth a pin to us! Watch my words!" Ferguson had snapped. He had almost welcomed Bristol's coming then, eagerly awaiting with a vulturelike attitude the first mistake that Claude Bristol would make.

And the mistake was not long in coming. It was on his second day that Major Ferguson publicly rebuked him over failing to return a salute.

"I will not put up with this sort of behavior among our officers! Things have gotten too slack, and I intend to see that it stops!" he had ended by saying.

Clay, later that afternoon, heard a private report and took time out from his busy schedule to say, "Lieutenant Bristol, let's take a walk around and see what the brigade looks like."

The two strolled along the line of tents where men sat outside, gathered around fires. Snow was in the air, but there was a general air of contentment among the men that Clay noticed and approved of. When he spoke to a sergeant, commending him for his work on getting his men into good condition, the sergeant's eyes lit up.

"I don't think I'll ever be able to please the major," Bristol said sadly.

"You mustn't pay too much attention to Major Ferguson," Clay said encouragingly. "He's a relic from the old army. He should have been retired and probably will be very soon. You're my adjutant and my clerk, and you're going to be very helpful to me." Clay grinned ruefully. "I'm not the best record keeper in the world."

"Neither am I, Colonel, but I'm going to do the best I can."

For the next week Claude Bristol threw himself into his quest to become a soldier with more energy than he had ever used on anything — even gambling and horse racing. He stayed up late at night by the light of a candle going over the manual of arms and the various regulations that are necessary for any army. At dawn he was up early studying again. Soon it became familiar around camp to see him walking with his nose in a book. Len Baylor, a grizzled sergeant, took him under his wing. He also had been doubtful of Bristol, knowing he was related to the colonel. But Bristol had admitted cheerfully, "Sergeant, I don't know the first thing about the army. I'd appreciate it if you would be patient with me and give me some of the basics."

The sergeant had nodded approvingly then reported this to Clay. *Maybe it'll be all right,* Clay thought to himself, satisfied by the sergeant's report. Perhaps it would have been, but Claude could not avoid the blistering criticism of Ferguson. It grew so bad that he dreaded to see the old man coming, and finally Clay noted that Bristol was growing tense and nervous.

"Lieutenant, I think you've put in some good time, and you've learned a great deal. Sometimes, if you're like me, you soak up all you can and then you have to wait for it to settle down." Clay had looked up over his desk, speaking to Claude, who was reading *Cooke's Cavalry Tactics,* his brow furrowed. "I think it might be good for you to take a few days off."

"You don't have to make exceptions for me!" Bristol protested. "That might look like favoritism!"

"No, it won't, because I'm sending you on detached duty. We're desperate for horses to pull our artillery. I want you to make a swing through the countryside and see if you can come up with some." Grimacing, he added, "We don't have much money, and only Confederate, so I don't think you'll have much success. All I ask is that you don't steal any. But maybe if you can come up with even two or three, that will be a help. And go by and touch base at Hartsworth. Stay there for a couple of days. It'll be good for you, and you'll be fresher when you get back."

"Yes, sir. If that's what you want," Bristol responded. He half suspected Clay was getting him out of Ferguson's way and was grateful for it. Leaving Clay's tent, he went to his own quarters, which he shared with First Lieutenant Maylin Meyers, a short, muscular twenty-five-year-old who had been amused at Bristol's eagerness to learn, but pleased by it.

"So you're on detached duty. Bring me back some fresh ham or maybe even a chicken if you can find it."

"I'll do that, Lieutenant," Bristol said. "You can depend on it."

Claude drew an ancient horse from the quartermaster. "I have to respect my elders," Bristol said, smiling. "What's his name, Sergeant?"

"Methuselah, I reckon, sir," the sergeant replied, grinning back at him.

"An apt name indeed. Come along,

Methuselah. I'll try to get him back to you alive, Sergeant."

Claude took his orders seriously and before going to Hartsworth did make a sweep of the country. He was actually successful in buying three horses, none of them prizes, but at least they were able to walk around and could pull the weight of a cannon. Claude well knew the terrific toll the war had taken on horseflesh, and it had saddened him, for he loved horses best of all animals on the earth. He took turns riding them, sparing Methuselah, and finally, on the morning of December 20, rode up to Hartsworth, where he was met by Solomon, who greeted him ecstatically.

"Why, Marse Claude, look at you now! Ain't you fine in that pretty uniform!"

"A uniform doesn't make a soldier, Solomon." Bristol slipped off Methuselah and handed the lines of all four horses to Solomon. "Take these fellows out to the pasture and see if you can't find them something to eat."

"Yes, suh! You gonna stay for a while, Lieutenant?"

"No, I'll be leaving tomorrow or the next day."

Claude was surprised at the eagerness with which he approached the house. Although he had been gone only a short while, he had felt the separation keenly. Almost every day it had entered his mind that he might never see it again. Although he wasn't on the front line of battle, he well knew that the location of the "front line" was sometimes flexible. Now he paused for a moment, looking at the familiar structure. Shocked at his happiness, he murmured, "I didn't know I was such a homebody. But this place means more to me than I ever understood." Bristol was not a sentimental man, and yet, under the cynical exterior he had covered himself with over the years, he suddenly realized that life was a precious thing — and that this house was more than wood and glass and carpet. He had spent many years here, and now he felt a thread of disgust at how he had wasted his life. *If a man could go back again and do it all over, I wonder if he would do it any better. When I came here, I had all sorts of dreams, and yet I haven't fulfilled one of them. I've wasted my money betting on horses and cards, and it's hurt Marianne and the children. Why did I do it? Why does a man allow himself to fail like that?*

"Claude, come into the house!"

Claude glanced up to see Marianne holding the door open. He moved forward quickly, putting his morbid thoughts behind him. When he got to the door, he saw that Marianne had a smile and an embrace for him. *She's still as beautiful as ever,* he thought. He kissed her and then, when he lifted his head, whispered huskily, "If I had known I'd get such a welcome, I would have joined the army a long time ago."

"Claude, what are you doing here? We didn't expect you."

Thirty minutes later the two were sitting in the kitchen, and Claude was ravenously attacking the fried ham, hominy, and fresh bread Marianne heated for him. He washed it down with two glasses of sweet, fresh milk and then, when he had finished, said, "It's the best meal I've had since I've been in the army."

"You look thinner," Marianne said. "Isn't the food good?"

"Not like this," Claude said. He looked around the kitchen, taking it all in. "It seems like I've been gone for a long time. I've discovered how much I miss Hartsworth."

"Do you, Claude?"

"Yes. It surprised me. When I rode up and saw the house — well, it got to me, Marianne. I realized how much I love this place."

Marianne Bristol felt a surge of hope. She'd been praying that Claude would develop the same kind of love for the land, house, and tradition that went with it that she herself held.

Claude reached over the table and captured her hand. "I was standing out in front of the house, looking at it and thinking how glad I was to be back," he said thoughtfully. "And I thought how different it should have been. I haven't been the kind of husband I should have, Marianne. And just in case, I want to tell you now. You've been the best wife a man could ever have, and I've been a failure."

For years Marianne had longed to hear this simple statement from Claude, and now it had come! She squeezed his hand tightly. Somewhere along the way, she had lost the first love she had had for this trim, handsome man. He'd had such great gifts, and he'd squandered them like a prodigal. But now as he sat there, his hair still brown without a touch of gray, and pain in his fine eyes, she found herself thinking of their first meeting, their courtship and marriage. It had been a time of wonder and pure joy. Only afterward had it grown bad. Finally, she whispered, "It's never too late for love, Claude."

Claude Bristol blinked with surprise. "I think it may be for us, but I want you to know that whatever happens, you have never failed me, Marianne. You're the pride of my life."

That evening Marianne listened for two hours in the parlor as he told her of life in the camp. He was excited, she saw, and pleased with being able to do something. Finally, they rose and went to bed. When he lay beside her in the darkness, her arms went around him. She kissed him softly at first, then with a hunger she had thought was buried deep within her.

The next day Charlie was sitting alone in the study, laboring over her handwriting exercises. Marie had given her several lessons, but she still found herself grasping the delicate pen as if it were a plow handle or a musket. Her tongue appeared at the edge of her lips as she moved the quill across the paper, trying to make the same smooth, graceful strokes that Marie made so easily. Finally, she gave it up in disgust. "Rats! I won't never learn how to write pretty!"

"Oh, I wouldn't give up!" Claude Bristol had been passing by the library door as Charlie uttered her cry of despair. Now he stepped inside and went to stand beside her. "You're doing very well, Charlene."

"Do you really think so, Mr. Bristol?"

"Why, you can write better than I can write now, but of course that's not saying a lot," he said, smiling. As he sat down in the chair beside her, admiring her freshness and innocence, he noticed how the blue dress she was wearing matched her dark blue eyes. Claude Bristol was a perceptive man, and Charlene Peace's story had attracted him. He felt a great interest and even compassion for this young girl so alone in the world, and being a witty man, he was soon able to make her smile.

Charlie liked Claude Bristol. During the time he had been at Hartsworth, he had gone out of his way to speak to her, and the previous afternoon he had asked her to join him for a ride around the place. She accepted at once, always eager to get on a horse, and when he saw how well she rode, he praised her highly.

Now, however, she was in one of those moods that had occupied her lately. Boone had not been back for several days, and she was beginning to feel that she could not stay at Hartsworth much longer. She grew so quiet that Claude asked quickly, "Is something wrong, Charlene?"

"I reckon I just got the mullygrubs."

"Mullygrubs?" Claude said, grinning. "I don't think I've ever heard of that particular ailment."

"Just down in the mouth, Mr. Bristol. Don't you ever git that way?"

"Frequently, but then, I'm an old man and you're a beautiful young lady."

"No, I ain't! I may be young, but I ain't no lady, and I ain't beautiful! I cain't talk right neither!"

"Why, Marie tells me you're making wonderful progress. My wife has seen it, too. And surely Boone has noticed it."

"No, he ain't noticed it," she said. And then before she could think, the words slipped out. "He's too busy spendin' time with Marie to pay any attention to the way I talk!" Looking shocked, she clamped her hand over her mouth. "I didn't mean to say that. Ain't none of my business if he wants to come courtin' Marie."

Claude Bristol instantly realized, *Why, she's in love with the man — or thinks she is.* He said quietly, "It's not easy being young, Charlene. You ever see a magnifying glass?"

"Yes, I seen one of them things."

"Well, when you're young, you see everything through a magnifying glass. When something goes wrong, you hold that glass up and the trouble looks about five times as big as it really is. So right now you're having a hard time, but the troubles aren't as

283

bad as you think."

Charlie listened gratefully as Claude Bristol spoke. Somehow just being able to talk with this easygoing, friendly man relieved her. When he began to tell her stories of his foolish mistakes as a soldier in camp, she found herself laughing. Finally, she said, "I feel a lot better, Mr. Bristol. Maybe I *kin* learn to be a lady."

"I'm sure you can, Charlene," Claude said fondly. "I'll be going tomorrow, but I'll be expecting to hear good things. Maybe you'd write me from time to time and tell me how things are going. Soldiers like to get letters — at least I do, although I don't call myself much of a soldier."

"Oh, you wouldn't want to read stuff I might write."

"That's where you're wrong. We're friends, aren't we, Charlene?"

"Yes, if you say so, Mr. Bristol."

"Austin will be coming out to the place from time to time. Any letters you might write, you could give to him."

On his way back to camp the next day, Bristol thought of Charlene Peace and Boone Manwaring. *I wonder if he knows the girl's in love with him. If he's not a fool, he must.* He had met Boone only once, but he determined the next time he saw him to find out how the man felt about this young girl. "She's very vulnerable," he mused quietly. "I hope she doesn't get hurt."

The closest thing to a gentlemen's club in Richmond was the billiard room of the Spotswood Hotel. There was a ladies' parlor adjacent, which could have been half a world away, so different were the activities of the two rooms. The ladies' parlor was designed much like a parlor in a fine home, but the billiard room was far different.

Austin Bristol leaned back in his chair, taking in the two billiard tables, neither of them occupied at the moment. The billiard room itself was spacious, being twenty feet wide and thirty-five feet long. Sofas, chairs, lamps, and tables were arranged so that a man could come and read or meet friends. The two bigger tables, imported from New Orleans, were the pride of the owner even though the green felt was worn. At one end of the room, four tables were set up for card games; however, only two of them were occupied, for the day's crowd was rather thin.

Austin was tired, for the paperwork at the War Department bored him out of his mind. He had applied for active duty on numerous occasions, but each time his superior officer, Brigadier General Thad

Cornwallis, had briskly denied him with the words, "Can't do without you here, Austin. Too much work for me. You'll just have to fight your war from your desk as I do. All of us would like to go, but we're doing important work here."

Now Austin moved over to the poker table and sat in an empty chair. He received a greeting from the players, which included Malcolm Leighton and Boone Manwaring. "Deal you a hand, Austin?" Leighton asked. As always he was dressed immaculately and expensively, this time in a black suit, white frilled shirt, and string tie. "I'd like to get some of that army money," he said, grinning.

Austin returned the smile but shook his head. "Too rich for my blood," he said then turned to Boone. "How's it going, Manwaring?"

"Very well," Boone said, nodding. He motioned toward a large stack of chips in front of him. "I've had a lucky streak."

Across the table Earl Dillon, a sleek man with cold eyes, spoke his challenge. "A bit too lucky, I think."

Earl Dillon, Austin knew, was one of the shady characters who floated around wartime Richmond. He always appeared to have money, although to Austin's knowledge he never worked. Most had decided that he made his living with the cards since he was a good gambler. Now, however, the stack in front of him was small, and Austin sensed he was angry. He also knew Dillon was quick tempered and that he had already fought three duels, killing two of his opponents and badly wounding the other.

Silence fell around the table, with every eye on Boone, waiting for him to respond to Dillon's remark. It had not exactly been an insult, but there was a bold sneer on Dillon's lips.

But Boone well understood men like Earl Dillon from his career on the sea; he knew that Dillon was a bad loser and that it wasn't worth taking up the challenge. So he simply shrugged and said, "Sometimes I'm lucky; sometimes I'm not, Dillon."

Seeing that Boone was not going to respond to Dillon's challenge, Leighton picked up the cards. "Another hand, then. Maybe you'll be luckier this time, Earl. I never saw such a run of bad luck."

Austin sat back. He was not much of a cardplayer himself, but as the game went on, he sensed that Dillon had lost heavily and was now trying to restore his fortunes with a single big win. As the time droned on, everyone in the room came to stand around the tables, for Richmond loved drama.

As Dillon's complexion turned ruddier and ruddier and the tension in the room grew, Boone was very much aware of the situation. He would like to have pulled out, but it was against the code of cardplayers to quit while a big winner, and he knew he would have to tough it out. He also had heard stories of Dillon's prowess with a dueling pistol, and even with his own skill he had no desire to fight the man.

The stack in front of Boone continued to grow as Dillon's diminished. The climax was coming. Boone had just dealt himself three eights, which he thought would be enough to win the hand. "I'll stand on these," he said, making his voice as pleasant as possible. Dillon stared at him, dislike evident on his face. "I'll meet that and raise you," he said, counting his chips and shoving them into the center of the table, "two hundred dollars."

For a moment Boone was tempted to fold, but he assumed Dillon had a good hand to bet that much. "I'll see that," he said and shoved out chips. He turned his hand over. "Three eights is all I've got."

Dillon's face paled, and his lips tightened. Then he threw down his hand. "You're a cheat, Manwaring!"

Boone narrowed his attention on the gambler. "I'd be careful about names like that," he said softly. He was not sure whether Dillon was wearing a gun. He himself was not, so he put his hands carefully on the table, waiting to see what would happen.

Dillon stood up, his voice tense. "I'm saying you're a cheat, and a coward, too!"

In that moment Boone Manwaring knew that his future in Richmond was hanging in the balance. He had just been called a name no one would take, and as he glanced around, he saw every man was expecting him to take up the challenge. He was not afraid, for he was of more than average skill with a gun, although he had never fought a formal duel. Now he knew that if he walked out of this room without challenging Dillon, he would be a marked man. Yet why should he kill a man over a few dollars? Boone wished he could just shove the money back and walk away, but he knew the situation had gone far beyond that easy solution. "I won't fight you, Dillon," he said, getting up. He gathered the chips into his hands and left the room.

Austin felt sick. His eyes met Leighton's, who shook his head. Both men were thinking the same thing: Boone Manwaring was a coward.

Dillon began to curse. "He's a no-good Yankee! A coward and a cheat! Wouldn't take my challenge!"

Austin rose slowly and left without another word. Somehow the scene of a man breaking under pressure was nauseating to him. He had grown up in a culture where physical courage was necessary. No man could exist in his world without it. Austin himself would have answered Dillon's challenge, even though he would die the next moment for it.

Leaving the hotel, he went about his duties for the rest of the day. Later that afternoon he saw Marie coming into his office. "Why, Marie," he said. "Didn't expect to see you."

"Have you got time for a woman with nothing but time on her hands?"

"Of course. Let's go down the street. We'll maybe find some ice cream."

"Ice cream in Richmond?"

"Well, that's optimistic." Soon the two were seated inside a restaurant where there was no ice cream, but they both had slices of fresh raisin pie.

Marie spoke of the plantation then said, "I brought a list into town of things that we need, but I don't have the money to pay for it. Our credit's stretched pretty thin. What do you think, Austin?"

"We'll get it somehow, if those are things we have to have," Austin responded, somewhat preoccupied. Then he continued, "Pretty bad thing happened in the billiard room at the Spotswood this afternoon." He went on to relate the incident and watched Marie's face as he ended. "It was a sorry sight. I thought better of Boone. He just turned and walked out."

Marie had listened to her brother carefully, and now she sat silently, saying nothing for a time. She had no doubt about Austin's reaction, for she knew, like all the men in her acquaintance, to prove oneself to be a coward was the worst possible thing that could happen. Finally, she said, "Maybe he just doesn't like to kill a man over cards."

"It wasn't over cards, Marie. It was a matter of honor. No man can let himself be called a name like that."

"I suppose not." But Marie was not altogether sure what she thought. She knew men who fought over things that to her were utterly ridiculous — and to her it was a tragedy. Although she wasn't sure of her feelings for Boone Manwaring, she knew they weren't mild. He had stirred her with a single kiss.

"I may be wrong," Austin said, "but I thought I saw something in you for this man." When she did not speak, he continued, "Don't mean to pry, but I'd hate to see you involved with a man who had no spine."

Marie saw the concern in Austin's eyes. "I don't think you have to worry about that, Austin."

Austin sighed with relief. "I guess I was mistaken, then."

Marie kept up the thread of their conversation then left Austin to go on her errands. As she moved along the cold streets, however, she drew her coat closer around her. She could not reconcile what had happened at the Spotswood with what she had seen in Boone. *But I know so little about him,* she thought. *And there are men who are not courageous.* Turning into the hardware store, she tried to put him out of her mind. However, she knew she wouldn't be able to, for Boone Manwaring had gained a larger place in her thoughts than she had imagined.

CHAPTER 15
AT THE CHESNUTS

By December 1863, it was not, perhaps, apparent to either the North or the South, but a turning point had come. It was like a small leak in a large dike, unnoticed for a time and allowed to become more and more damaging until finally the entire structure was threatened. So it was with the Confederacy. The year of 1863 had produced some great victories for the South, and some may have argued that the South still held the advantage. They were defending their home grounds, and Robert E. Lee had proven himself to be a fine general.

But by this point in the war, the North had transformed itself into an industrial giant, pouring out arms, ammunitions, uniforms, wagons, buttons, canteens, and the myriad pieces needed to put an army in motion. The South, on the other hand, was producing barely enough to keep the thin lines of the Confederacy together. The men were often hungry, and heaven help Union prisoners who were in Confederate prison camps, for, unable to feed themselves, the Confederacy could do little for its prisoners.

What Jefferson Davis needed was a miracle, for it would take that to save the South. The government was bankrupt. Paper money was not worth the paper it was printed on, and a larger burden would have to be borne by fewer people if the Confederacy were to stand. Yet Jefferson Davis refused to listen to proposals for peace.

Several weeks earlier, across the brief distance that separated Richmond from Washington, D.C., another president, Abraham Lincoln, had been invited to the little town of Gettysburg to dedicate the new National Soldiers' Cemetery.

When November 19, 1863, arrived, parade marshals wore mourning rosettes. Abraham Lincoln stood up to make a few appropriate remarks. His words were brief, and he spoke of peace — words that have been repeated more than any other words from any other speech by any other president in history. Americans have never forgotten them and never will. When he sat down, there was long applause. Then the crowd broke up, and people began their long journeys home. Soon Gettysburg grew quiet again.

"I don't want to go to no old party, Marie!"

Marie Bristol was patient but adamant as she helped Charlie pull the dress down over her head. "You've got to go. We've already accepted the invitations, and I promise you'll like it. There'll be a lot of young people there." Stepping back, she admired Charlie's rose-colored dress trimmed in black lace. "You look so nice!"

"I feel like a big dressed-up doll!" Charlie complained, shaking her curls in front of the mirror. "All we ever do at them parties is talk."

"Not *them* parties. *Those* parties."

"*Those* parties, then! But all we do is talk!"

"What else would you want to do?" Marie demanded. "It's what people do at this sort of thing. And besides, I want you to meet the Chesnuts."

"I can't remember the names of half the people I done already met!" Charlie exclaimed. "I mean that I already met!" she corrected herself, seeing Marie's lips framing a rebuke.

"You're doing much better with your

grammar, Charlie." Marie smiled then said, "I mean, Charlene. I'm so used to calling you Charlie, I don't know if I'll ever change."

Charlie ran her hands over her hoop skirt. Secretly she liked to dress up but would die before admitting it. Indeed, Charlie had made almost every step of her education more difficult. She could not have explained to herself why she did this, for she knew Marie Bristol and her mother worked hard to smooth out her rough edges. But Charlie was basically an independent, stubborn young woman and hated to be pushed in a direction that was foreign to her. For weeks now she had practiced for hours every day on her writing and her grammar, and she had even been taught how to dance by Austin, who had come often to the house. Still, she had the feeling she was living in a world not her own, and she longed for her simple life back in the mountains.

"I guess we'll have to go," she said resignedly, then commented to Marie, "You sure look pretty." Marie's baby blue taffeta dress had a full skirt with layers of flounces at the bottom, all edged with white lace. "I bet Malcolm Leighton will think so."

Marie shrugged. "He's seen this dress before."

"Does he aim to marry up with you?"

"He hasn't asked me."

"I expect he will, though. He looks at you funny all the time."

"What do you mean *funny*, Charlie?" Marie demanded.

"I mean he cuts his eyes 'round when he thinks you're not lookin'. It's like he was sizin' up a horse he was aimin' to buy."

Marie Bristol burst into laughter. "I expect that's pretty close to the truth," she admitted, her eyes sparkling with amusement from Charlie's directness. "After he's looked over all the other young ladies and evaluated our worth, I expect he'll make an offer on the one who will bring him the most value for his money."

Struck by Marie's offhanded reply, Charlie asked, "You don't mean that, do you? It's not really like he's going to buy you."

Marie, suddenly serious, bit her lip and wondered what Charlie would think if she spoke the exact truth. *Yes, he's going to buy me, and I'm going to have him because he has money.* She could not bring herself to say such a thing and struggled as she attempted to explain. "It's rather complicated — this matter of marriage."

"Wasn't where I come from. Feller just came by and courted a girl, and if she liked him, she'd marry him."

"I wish it were that simple here," Marie said fervently.

"Well, why ain't it?"

"You mean, why *isn't* it? Why, I don't know, Charlie. It's more complicated than it should be, I think." Disturbed by the conversation, Marie said, "I think you're all ready now. Let's go to the Chesnuts'."

The two left the house wearing heavy coats and wrapped up in blankets, for the weather was turning steadily colder. The horses moved along rapidly toward the Chesnuts' house until they arrived. Solomon helped Marie out, but before he could turn, Charlie had already leaped to the ground. "I don't reckon I'm old enough to be helped out of a carriage, Solomon."

"I reckon that's right, Miss Charlene," Solomon said, grinning. He was quite taken with the young woman, as were all the slaves. She had free and easy manners with them and thought nothing of going into their quarters and eating corn pone and ham with them for supper. "You be careful now, Miss Charlene," Solomon said. He winked at Miss Marie. "There's some of them mens that ain't the gentlemens they should be. Young ladies has to be careful about 'em."

"Austin will protect you," Marie said.

Austin had ridden up and was just getting off his horse. He tied him up and came over, saying, "Well, just in time for the festivities."

"Don't you ever do any soldierin', Austin?" Charlie asked.

"Not very often." This was a sore spot with Austin, for he was sensitive about his lack of frontline duty, so he turned quickly and said, "Let's get inside. It's getting cold. I think it's going to snow."

"I wish it would," Charlie said, taking his arm. It felt strange to do this, but it was something Marie had taught her to do. "I wish it would snow two feet deep, or three, or four! I always liked it when we got snowed in on the mountains. Once, we got snowed in for a month! Good thing we had plenty to eat, or we'd have starved to death."

"What did you do all that time?" Austin asked. "I think I'd go crazy if I was shut in a cabin for a month."

"Oh, Ma read a lot from the Bible, and me and Pa listened. We made moccasins and a pair of buckskins fer Pa. It wasn't so bad." Almost wistfully, she continued, "I wisht I could do it again. I shore miss Ma and Pa."

Marie and Austin exchanged glances; then Marie changed the subject. "It looks like

everyone in Richmond has come tonight."
As they stepped inside, a man took their
coats. They moved down the hall and, turning to the left, entered the large parlor used
by the Chesnuts for entertainment. At once
Mary Chesnut spotted them and came over.
"There you are, Marie and Austin. I'm glad
you could come in this bad weather."

As she took their greeting, Mary Chesnut
smiled at Charlie. "And who is this delight-
ful young woman? I don't believe we've
met."

"This is Miss Charlene Peace," Austin
said. "She's a visitor to Richmond, hoping
to settle here."

"Oh yes! I believe I have heard your name.
You're here with Mr. Manwaring."

"You know everyone in Richmond and
what they do, Mrs. Chesnut!" Austin exclaimed with surprise.

Mary Chesnut, indeed, knew most people
in the upper regions of society. Her home
was often visited by President Davis, for he
was an intimate friend of the Chesnuts. She
was not a beautiful woman, but nobody ever
noticed this. Her eyes were lively and
expressive, her complexion lovely, and she
had a wit and charm that attracted others
to her.

"Yes, ma'am. Me and Boone come down

from Colorado — came down from Colorado. Do you know Boone?"

"I met him yesterday in town. He spoke with my husband about a piece of property that we once owned. I'm glad to think you're considering settling here."

Charlie nodded, feeling awkward yet charmed by the woman. Mary Chesnut loved young people and was especially fond of beautiful young ladies. She took great pride in pairing couples together. Now she took Charlie's arm, saying, "Come along. I want you to meet some of our guests."

Charlie did not remember the names of all of the guests, but she did remember one. She was introduced to General Robert E. Lee, a fine-looking older man. He bowed when they were introduced and welcomed her to Richmond.

Nearly half an hour later, Charlie looked up in the crowded parlor and saw Boone entering. He spotted her at once and came over, smiling. "That's a pretty dress. I haven't seen that one."

"Marie helped me pick it out. I feel silly wearing this here bird cage." She patted the hoop that held the skirt out. "Thing's big enough to keep a flock of chickens under."

A laugh arose from those close enough to hear. Charlie flushed then noticed there was good humor in all the faces.

"Have you found any property that looks good, Boone?" Marie asked, not really thinking of the property, but of Boone's encounter with Earl Dillon.

Boone was not easily fooled. He was aware of the tenseness of the situation. He knew that word of his encounter with Earl Dillon was all over Richmond. Although he himself had said nothing to either Austin or Marie and they hadn't mentioned it to him, there was a stiffness and restraint in their manner that hadn't been there before. So he began to speak of the property and finally ended by saying, "I don't know if it's a good buy or not."

Mary Chesnut had listened to this with some interest. "I know that property. It's close to our old home place. The Dillons had it for a while."

At the name Dillon, a hush fell over the group. Mary Chesnut added, "The Dillons both passed away a few years ago. Their son, Earl, had it for a while, but I believe he has sold the property to the Thompsons."

Boone had never felt more vulnerable in his life. Looking directly at Marie, he saw an odd expression on her face. *She thinks I'm a coward,* he thought, and then his eyes shifted to meet Austin's, seeing regret and dislike there. Quietly he said, "I expect that's the same property."

Mary Chesnut, an astute woman, knew she had said something to create the silence. Later she found her way to Austin and asked, "What did I say?"

"You haven't heard about the quarrel between Boone and Earl Dillon?"

"No, I haven't." She listened as Austin briefly explained, then said, "What a shame! Such a fine-looking man!"

Austin looked at the floor for a moment. "I guess fine looks don't mean much. It's what's inside a man that counts."

CHAPTER 16
CHRISTMAS AT HARTSWORTH

Snow began to fall on December 24. As Boone stood in his room at the Spotswood, looking out at the tiny flakes drifting down, laying a white glaze on the dirty streets of Richmond, his mind went back to the mountains of Colorado. He thought of how he had first met Charlie and felt a loss he couldn't explain. Somehow Noah's plan had not worked out as he had expected — but then again, he wondered what it was that he had expected. Despite his reservations concerning Noah's plan to bring a new life to Charlie, Boone had summoned up a hope that it would all work out. As they had traveled south, he had let this hope grow in him until finally, despite his normally cynical way of looking at the world, he had come to expect better things. But those things had not happened, and now he wondered what would come next.

Turning from the window, he picked up a

week-old newspaper that almost fell apart in his hands. Even worse than the quality of the paper were the editorials that threw all the blame for Confederate hardships onto President Jefferson Davis's shoulders. The editor of the *Mercury* wrote in such a shrill tone that finally Boone threw down the paper in disgust. "He sounds like a whining kid!" he muttered. "Why doesn't he toughen up and do what he can to encourage people!" It surprised him that he thought like this, for he had settled the matter in his mind that this cause for the South was lost. He knew in his heart that the Confederacy could not stand, although he was careful not to speak of this when others were around.

A knock interrupted his thoughts, and he opened the door to find Charlie and Marie Bristol there. Surprise washed over him, but he recovered quickly, saying, "What a nice surprise! Won't you come in?"

"Oh, Boone, we cain't stay!" Charlie said hurriedly. She was smiling vivaciously as she added, "You've got to come to Hartsworth for Christmas Eve and Christmas!"

Shooting a glance at Marie, Boone said, "I wouldn't want to impose. That's a family time."

Marie had come to town with Charlie to buy a few last-minute gifts, and in her forthright fashion, Charlie had asked if Boone could come to spend Christmas Day at Hartsworth. With some reluctance Marie had agreed, but now she covered this, saying, "Don't be silly! We'll be glad to have you, Boone. As a matter of fact, we have plenty of room. You could go back and stay the night there."

"Come on, Boone!" Charlie urged, her eyes shining. "There's no point staying in this old room by yourself!"

For an instant Boone hesitated, not sure a "coward" would be welcome at the Bristols', but not wanting to spend the evening alone with his thoughts. "All right," he said. "Let me throw a few things together, and I'll meet you in the lobby in ten minutes."

As Marie and Charlie moved down the stairway, Charlie said with satisfaction, "Now he won't have to be by himself."

"He seems like a man who can bear solitude," Marie answered. They reached the landing and stepped toward the brocade sofa on one side of the lobby. "I wonder if he has any family."

"No, he doesn't. I guess that's why I feel close to Boone. . . . I didn't really like Boone at first, but I just didn't understand him then."

"You like him very much now, don't you, Charlie?"

"I guess so," she replied cautiously, then asked, "Do you like him, Marie?"

Marie Bristol was a woman who usually spoke straight out, but at this moment she was uncertain. She *had* liked Boone Manwaring very much, but the thought that he might be less a man than she had at first thought troubled her deeply. Yet determined not to hurt Charlie's feelings, she answered diplomatically, "Why, I expect I do. We haven't known each other long, of course." As they waited, Charlie spoke volubly about the celebration to come. But when Boone came downstairs looking handsome in a brown suit, white shirt, and shiny black boots, Marie thought, *It's a shame he's not what he ought to be on the inside.*

That evening, talk ran cheerfully around the large white-clothed table. Set with china, crystal goblets, fine silverware, silver candlesticks, and sprigs of holly, it was a sight to behold. A large turkey, cooked slowly in the cast-iron cookstove, was placed at the head of the table, and silver bowls were filled with cabbage-and-apple salad, corn pudding, green beans, corn bread stuffing, sliced potatoes with onions in a cream sauce, and fresh bread and butter.

As Boone sat at the table, he felt strangely out of place, despite their hospitality. Claude Bristol, who'd been allowed to come home for the holiday, sat happily at the head of the table, wearing his spotless gray uniform. To his left was Marianne Bristol, her mulberry-colored dress setting off her patrician beauty. Across from her sat Austin, wearing a light blue coat and dark blue trousers. Occasionally his eyes rested on Boone with a silent displeasure. Next to Austin sat Marie, wearing an emerald dress and jade earrings that caught the light from the candelabras.

As Boone sipped the elderberry wine, he half wished he had not come. Turning, he studied Charlie, who was wearing a pale orchid dress. She looked at him often, as if she wanted to say something, but there was little privacy at the table.

Austin watched carefully, for he was concerned about Marie's feelings for Boone. He had liked Manwaring very well at first, but being a son of the South, he could countenance nothing like cowardice in a man. It troubled him to think Marie might be seriously interested in the tall man who sat down the table from him. As he swirled the dark red liquid in his glass, he thought, *Surely Marie knows better than to be interested in the fellow. But he does have money, and I think either of us would do anything to save Hartsworth. Still, it would be a bad match.* Involuntarily his eyes went to his father, who seemed to have lost the depression that had settled on him before he had joined the army. *He looks well,* Austin thought, *but he still has been a failure, and I think he knows it.* Then Austin looked fondly over toward his mother. He admired her more than any other woman, and now he saw, despite her youthful appearance for her age, that the years had laid their hand on her. Most of it, he thought resentfully, was due to his father's behavior.

Claude Bristol tasted the blackberry cobbler that had been brought to each member of the table. "Why, this is fine, Blossom! You always made better blackberry cobbler than anyone!"

"You always say that, Mr. Claude," Blossom said, smiling ear to ear. She was a short, heavyset woman with enormous brown eyes and had been the cook at Hartsworth for many years. "You just hopin' to git a second helpin', ain't you, now?"

"And maybe a third," Claude said.

"You'll be too fat for your uniform, Father," Marie said, smiling. She was pleased that her father looked better and also that he seemed to be more at peace with himself. He was not a man, she knew, to worry greatly about the future, while she, Austin, and their mother thought about it a great deal. Now, however, it was Christmas, and she wanted to take this moment and shut out the rest of the world. Wistfully she said, "It's nice being here, not having to think about Grant or Lincoln or what to plant instead of cotton."

Austin shifted uncomfortably. "Yes, it is," he admitted, "but that world's still out there."

"But we don't have to think of it tonight," Marianne said quickly. She looked down the table and smiled at Charlie. "What did you do for Christmas back in the mountains, Charlene?"

"Oh, Pa would always go out and chop down a tree. Ma and I would string red berries for decorations and pop popcorn and make strings of it. I'd go out and shoot a turkey, and we'd have roasted turkey and sweet potato pie." Her eyes grew nostalgic as she spoke. "It was fun! Pa always made a big thing out of Christmas. He'd go into town and git Ma and me some nice presents and bring them back, callin' himself

Santa Claus. Last Christmas it snowed us in pretty bad, but Pa put on some snowshoes and hiked all the way to town. He came back near frostbit, but he loved Christmas."

All were silent around the table, for they were aware of Charlie Peace's aloneness in the world. As Austin saw once again her vulnerability, he noticed again what an attractive woman she was, with her beautifully textured olive skin, black hair, and dark blue eyes. "I'm glad you could be here with us, Charlene," he said quietly, smiling at her when she looked up with some surprise.

Marie saw this interchange. She was very fond of her brother and worried sometimes about what the world would bring to him. He was a young man of superior qualities — she felt sure of that; and his position in the War Department had kept him out of the fierce battles that had laid so many young men in unmarked graves throughout the South. But hard times were coming, and her heart caught suddenly as she thought what would happen if this vibrant brother of hers were to die.

Down the table, Boone Manwaring caught Marie's look. *She loves her brother a lot,* he thought, *and he cares for her. Nice to see a family close like this one.* Once again, feeling like an outsider, he kept quiet until Marie, sensing his awkwardness, finally said, "Tell us about some of your voyages, Boone. I've never been on an ocean trip. What's it like?"

Boone leaned back in his chair, masking what he was feeling. He ran his hand through his thick brown hair, touching the scar on his right cheek with the index finger of his right hand. He held it up for a moment and said, "Every time I think of the sea, I think of that finger."

"How did it happen, Boone?" Marianne asked.

"I threw a line overboard to catch a shark. Got one all right, but the line got snarled, and my finger got caught in it. The shark weighed probably eight hundred or a thousand pounds. I thought I'd lose the finger. It was crushed, but my old man put a splint on it and I kept it. Never could bend it, though." He pointed at Charlie and smiled. "It's good for pointing but not for much else."

"Do you like the sea? Will you go back there?" Marie asked.

"I doubt it. I went to sea a lot with my father as a young boy. It was a hard life. Exciting for a boy, but it's not a good life for a man — especially a married man."

"Do wives often go with their husbands on board ship?" Marie asked.

"Only the captain's wife from time to time."

"Did your mother go?" Marianne asked curiously. Drawn to Boone because she sensed his longing for something better, she sensed that Boone didn't give his trust easily.

"No, my mother never liked the sea. She stayed home, and sometimes my father and I were gone for a year or even more. I think she grew very lonely at times and wished my father had followed some other trade."

"Tell us about some of your adventures, Boone," Charlie said. "Tell about the time you nearly got shipwrecked down in the South Seas. The one you told me about."

Boone related the story of the terrible typhoon and how the ship had been tossed about like a poker chip. When he finished the story, they pressured him to tell more about life at sea until he finally said, "Strange things come to the minds of sailors. They are very superstitious."

"Do they have a girl in every port?" Charlie asked impudently.

"I don't know about that," Boone said, smiling at her. "I didn't." His thoughts went back to his days at sea. "I think sailors develop some kind of sixth sense about life."

"What do you mean by that?" Claude

asked, puzzled.

"Sometimes you feel almost prophetic. You know something's going to happen, but there's no evidence for it. Do you know what lee shore is?"

"No, what's that?" Marie asked.

"It's a shore you don't want to get too close to because the wind will carry you into it, not away from it. And when you get caught off a lee shore, you're almost lost. The funny thing is," he mused, his voice dropping, "sometimes even when I couldn't see a lee shore, like in the middle of the night when there were no stars out and it was absolutely black, I would know somehow that lee shore was there."

"How could you know that?" Austin demanded. "If you couldn't see anything, I mean."

"That's what I mean about superstition. It came sometimes when there was not a sight of the sun or an observed shoreline for days. You don't have any idea where you are within a hundred or two hundred miles, but at night you feel the loom of that shore under your keel. You can see nothing, but you can almost hear the rocks grinding out the bottom of your ship." He paused then continued, "And it's not just at sea. Sometimes I've felt bad things were about to hap-

314

pen and had no reason for supposing it to be."

"Do you feel that way now, Boone?" Marie asked, intently listening, aware he had revealed part of himself. Now he was tense, she saw, and his hazel eyes looked disturbed as he lifted them to her, considering her question.

"Yes, I do feel like that." When he saw the effect of his words on the group, he gave a short laugh. "Why am I talking like that? Don't pay any attention to a superstitious sailor!"

"I know how you feel," Claude said soberly. "I've never been at sea, but I've had feelings like that."

After the meal was over, they moved into the parlor. Marie entertained them by playing the pianoforte and singing with her fine contralto voice the hymns of Christmas, insisting they join in with her. Charlie sat beside Boone, her shoulder touching his, and once she whispered, "This is nice, isn't it, Boone?"

"Yes, it is. I haven't been in a home like this for many years." What he really meant was never, but he did not say so.

Finally, it grew late, and Claude and Marianne excused themselves, going to bed. "We'll get up early and have a good breakfast, then open a few presents."

Austin, sitting beside Charlie, turned to ask, "Are you sleepy, Charlene?"

"No. I hate to go to bed at night."

"What are you afraid of?"

"Nothing. I'm just afraid I'll miss something." She smiled at him.

"I'm the same way," he admitted. "Maybe we'll sit up all night and watch the dawn."

"Not me," Marie said. "I'm sleepy."

Boone rose and nodded to her, saying, "Good night, Marie."

"Good night. Good night, Charlie and Austin."

After she left, depression settled over Boone. Finally, Austin, sensing the silence, said, "I guess I'll go to bed. I'll see you all in the morning. Good night."

When he had left the room, Charlie came over and sat down beside Boone. "That was fun, wasn't it?" she said, slipping her shoes off and holding her feet out to the fire. "You know, I miss my moccasins more than anythin' else. I don't see why women around here love shoes that hurt their feet." She wiggled her toes. "Did you have a good time, Boone?"

"Yes," Boone said, not quite truthfully. He turned to her and saw the reflection of the fire blossom in her eyes. "You know," he said, "you've got the most beautiful eyes I've ever seen in a woman."

Charlie was stunned. It was the first remark Boone had ever made like that, and she could not think how to answer him. She dropped her eyes, unable to meet his, very much aware of the pressure of his shoulder on hers. "Thank you," she said. "That's the nicest thing you ever said to me."

"I guess it is, isn't it? Now you say something nice to me. Tell me how pretty my eyes are."

Knowing he was teasing her, Charlie met his eyes again. "You have funny eyes. They're hazel. I never seen a man with hazel eyes like that." She reached up and touched the scar that traced its way down his right cheek. "How did you get that? In a fight?"

"Yes. Back when I was young and foolish."

"Young? You're still young, Boone!" she protested.

"I'm twenty-eight. Not a boy any longer." He was very conscious of the touch of her finger on his cheek and also of the sheen of her hair. He had always admired black hair, and he barely refrained from running his hand over the curls as they cascaded around her face and down the back of her neck. "You like Marie very much, don't you?"

"Yes. She's been very nice to me. You do, too, don't you?"

"Yes, I do."

Troubled by his brief answer, Charlie was quiet for a while then said, "I like Austin, too."

"Fine man."

They sat there speaking from time to time, and there was a comfort about it. Finally, Boone turned to her. "You know what I like about you, Charlie? A man doesn't feel he has to keep up a line of chatter. I can be quiet with you and not feel like I'm letting you down."

"Why, I feel the same way, Boone," Charlie said. "People do talk a lot in the South, don't they?"

"No more than elsewhere, I wouldn't think."

"Yes, they do, too!" Charlie argued, waving her hand for emphasis. "Pa and Ma would go, seem like, four or five hours without saying a word."

Boone laughed at this and reached out to catch her hand.

The next day Austin was sitting in the study when Charlie burst in. "Austin, where's Boone? I can't find him."

"Why, Marie invited him for a ride around

the place. I think they left about half an hour ago."

"Oh, I see!"

Seeing the happiness in Charlie's eyes fade, Austin said, "I don't see why they should be the only ones to go outside. Let's you and I join them."

"No. I wouldn't want to do that," Charlie said flatly.

"Well, we don't have to, but I would like a ride. We need some exercise."

Charlie hesitated, but she loved to ride, so she finally nodded. "All right."

Twenty minutes later the two were riding knee-to-knee across the hills west of Hartsworth. As the horses' hooves moved silently, cushioned by the freshly fallen blanket of snow on the low-lying ridges, Austin said, "We don't get much snow down here. I suppose you've missed it."

"Yes, I have."

Austin tried to keep the conversation going, but Charlie was silent. Then she blurted out, "Do you aim to marry up with Ida Campbell?"

Caught off guard, Austin stammered, "Why — what makes you ask that, Charlene?"

"That's what everybody says."

"Who's everybody?" Austin demanded.

"Oh, I don't know." Actually, she had heard Blossom say to another of the house servants, "Ain't no doubt in my mind but that Mr. Austin is gonna marry up with that Ida Campbell." Now Charlie turned in the saddle to ask, "You ain't gonna marry her, then?"

Although Austin liked Ida's wit and warmth, he knew, however, that these were not the qualities that had made him consider marrying her. At a loss for words, he finally said, "It would be a good marriage for both of us."

Charlie looked puzzled. "A good marriage? I thought all marriages were supposed to be good."

"I mean — well, it would have advantages."

"What does that mean?"

Again set back by Charlie's directness, Austin fiddled with the lines of his horse. "It means that you have to think about what comes after marriage."

"I reckon you have kids. Is that what you mean?"

"Of course there's that. What I mean is — Ida needs a husband, and she's a fine woman." Then honesty compelled him to say, "And if you must know, Charlie, it's likely that our family will lose this place."

"Lose Hartsworth?" Charlie was shocked. She had thought the Bristols were immensely wealthy. With the large house, the servants, the spacious fields and timber, she could not imagine money being any kind of a problem. "How could that be?" she demanded.

"Well, things are pretty bad right now in the South. And some unwise decisions were made. As a matter of fact, Hartsworth is mortgaged to the hilt. If we don't come up with some money, we'll lose it."

Charlie leaned over and patted the sleek side of the chestnut mare, letting this information sink in. Then she straightened up to look at Austin. "Is that the 'advantage' you're talkin' 'bout? That she's got money, and you'd marry her to keep from losin' your place?"

Her directness made Austin feel foolish. Then he realized she was merely showing the same response he himself had felt. He had despised himself at times for even thinking about marrying for money, and now he could not answer except to say, "I guess that's about it, Charlene."

A heavy silence lay over the land as the two made their way along. Heavy drifts came up to the horses' fetlocks, and overhead the sky was unmarked by even a single cloud. Finally, Charlie asked quietly, "Ain't there more to a marriage than that, Austin?"

Austin lost his temper. "If you had more experience, Charlene, you'd know it's not that simple." He clamped his lips together, sorry he had been provoked into such a reply, and moved his horse closer. He grabbed her arm and pulled her toward him so he could read her eyes. "I guess you think that's terrible — a man marrying a woman because she has money."

Very much aware of Austin's hard grip on her arm, Charlie answered quickly, "I heard of women marryin' men for money, but I never knowed it to be the other way 'round."

"Happens all the time," Austin said briefly and released her arm. Then he wheeled his horse around. "Let's head back to the house." He waited until she had turned her mare around, and then the two trotted through the drifts of snow. When they dismounted and handed the lines to one of the slaves, Austin said, "Pretty cold. We'd better get inside." He glanced down at her face as they waded through the snow, and before they reached the house, he stopped to face her. "It may sound pretty bad to you, Charlie, but I really like Ida and I think we'd get along. She needs a husband, and

I'd try to make her a good one. Can't you see that?"

Far away a dog barked frantically. Although Charlie noticed it, she paid no heed. She was trying to find a way to put Austin at ease since she had embarrassed him. "It ain't any of my business, Austin. If you like Miss Ida and she likes you, there ain't no reason you shouldn't git married up."

Feeling he'd explained the matter badly, Austin said, "Marie hates to lose this place as bad as I do. It's not impossible that she would marry. A rich husband could come up with enough to save Hartsworth."

"You mean she might marry that Malcolm Leighton?"

"Him or somebody else." Then he said almost involuntarily, "She might even marry Boone."

Eyes wide with shock, Charlie could not speak for a moment. Finally, she said, "You don't reckon she'd do that, do you?"

"I hope not."

"So do I," Charlie said. "You reckon he cares for her?"

Hearing an uncertainty in Charlie's tone, Austin said, "I'm not sure, but I am sure of one thing. After the way he's run away from Earl Dillon, she wouldn't be happy with him."

"He ain't no coward!"

"He's given a mighty good imitation of one, Charlie. I know he's your friend, but he can't stay in this country. A man can't live down a reputation like that. Men will be laughing at him behind his back." When he saw the hurt in Charlie's face, he said gently, "I'm sorry to speak so plainly, but I know it's something you've probably already heard."

As a matter of fact, Charlie had been aware of this, but now she replied fiercely, "I don't care what they say! Boone ain't no coward!"

Almost at the exact moment Austin and Charlie were standing outside the house, Boone and Marie had stopped their horses by a grove of towering pine trees. Marie had pulled up first, and when Boone had stopped his mount beside her, she said, "Boone, I've got to talk to you, and it's not going to be easy."

Boone was aware of Marie's intensity. From the first time he had seen her, he had guessed at her depth. She showed a great deal of pride, and he was aware of the powerful emotions that lay beneath the surface. Now he noticed that she was attempting to control her eyes and lips, as though she feared to reveal herself.

"Before you tell me what you've got on your mind, Marie," he said, "I want to say one thing." The saddle creaked as he shifted his weight, and the metal of the bridle made a musical jingle as his gelding tossed his head. "Every man, I guess, goes through this world looking for some kind of beauty." Seeing the guard in her eyes, he almost didn't go on. But then he said softly, "Tough on me, but you're the kind of beauty I see nowhere else. No other woman possesses it for me."

Marie Bristol dropped her eyes, breathing rapidly, for his words had come as a shock to her. Finally, she lifted her eyes and met his. "That makes what I have to say a little harder, Boone."

"I can guess what it is."

"Can you?"

"Not too hard to know what people are saying. You want to know why I'm running away from Earl Dillon."

"Yes." Other women might have dodged, but Marie Bristol was not that sort. And she knew she could not let the matter rest. "You know what's being said about you, I suppose."

"That I'm a coward? That I'm afraid of Earl Dillon? That I'm no part of a man. Is that it?"

"Some people don't say that out loud, but if you'd been in the South long enough, you would have known what people think of a man who won't defend his honor."

Boone wanted to answer rashly, but he managed to control himself. "Would you have me kill a man over a card game, Marie?"

Marie shot back, "It's more than that, and you know it!"

"Marie," Boone said slowly, "a man comes out of nothing and heads toward something. He can't turn and go back through nothing. I know what's behind me, but I don't know what's ahead. All a man's got at the end of his life is a set of memories — things done well, things done poorly. I can't kill a man because of words he spoke over a card table. A man's life has got to mean more than that."

Marie knew there was wisdom in what he was saying. In fact, for a brief second she thought, *Perhaps the whole war is like this. Men can't put up with an insult, so hundreds of thousands of men are dying because of it.* But Marie was still a daughter of the South, where the code of honor was strong, so she said aloud, "But there are certain things a man must do."

"That's right, Marie. A man is full of things meant to be used or given away — or maybe destroyed. The more he spends, the more he gets back." He suddenly wanted Marie Bristol to understand him. "I can't speak for others, but I know there's something more to life than what I've seen in the past. . . . And whatever it is I'm searching for, I've seen part of it in you, Marie."

"Don't — don't say that to me!"

"You would turn down a man because other men called him a coward?"

"I wouldn't marry a man I couldn't respect. I've seen too much of that in —" She almost said "in my father" but bit the words off. She saw, however, by the expression in Boone's eyes that he understood her. "You can't live like that, Boone. When you live among people, you have to live up to their expectations."

At that moment Boone knew that Marie Bristol cared for him because of the pain in her eyes. But he responded, "I can't kill a man because of some rules somebody made up. If it were on board a ship, I could fight him with my fists. We'd get our heads bloodied, but then we'd heal up and get on with life. But that's not the way the code is around here, is it? Somebody's got to die for a rude remark. I don't see it, Marie."

Marie held her hands over the saddle horn firmly so that Boone would not see their trembling. Her emotions ragged, she examined his face and saw the tough set of his lips. She knew he had a temper and that sometimes he was moody, hot as a flame. As he considered her steadfastly, she felt he was weighing in the balances what kind of woman she was. Finally, she could bear his gaze no longer. "I need to get back to the house."

As they moved rapidly through the snow, Marie wondered why the scene had been so disturbing. *Do I care about this man? What has shaken me so much? If a woman loved a man, she would love him even if he wasn't perfect, right? And he may be right. Is killing a man for an insult, or maybe dying yourself, worth it?* However, she could not answer these questions, and when they dismounted she went into the house without saying another word. He followed, knowing that they'd both lost something precious during their encounter under the pines.

CHAPTER 17
AUSTIN AND IDA

The large blue-and-gold-wallpapered room in which Ida Campbell and her mother, Clara, sat was most pleasant. Light blue draperies edged with gold fringe delicately framed the windows and the looking glass over the fireplace. Brightly colored oil paintings adorned the walls, accenting the burgundy, light blue, and dark green design in the carpet. A corner bookcase contained hundreds of books. "I've always liked this room," Ida murmured. "It's my favorite. It seems so livable."

Clara Campbell sat on the blue sofa in the center of the room, sewing on a delicate piece of material. "It should be," she told Ida, glancing around. "I spent more time decorating this room than on the rest of the house put together." Clara paid careful attention to her stitching for a moment then put the cloth down, carefully plunging the needle into a crimson pincushion. Rubbing her eyes for a moment, she murmured, "My eyes aren't as good as they used to be." Leaning back in the walnut rocking chair covered with emerald plush, she asked, "Austin hasn't been here in a few days. Did you two have a spat?"

"No," Ida said quietly, smiling at her mother. "You think a lot about Austin, don't you?"

"I think about you."

"About my getting married." Ida's smile left her face. "Maybe I'm destined to be single."

"That's foolishness!" Clara Campbell snapped. "You could have had half a dozen men. Why, there's that nice Bobby MacIntyre. He was very serious about you a few months ago. What happened? I thought you might make it a match."

"I can't say. I suppose he would be a good husband. I could get him back, I think." It was unusual for Ida to speak like this, and she got up and walked to the fireplace. Standing over it, she looked into the flames, soaking up the heat from the bed of coals. "I like Bobby a great deal, but he's not very exciting."

"Exciting!" Clara exclaimed. "You're not talking about going to a play! Some of the most *exciting* men I know turned out to be terrible husbands."

"I know," Ida said. "I'm being foolish. I really do like Bobby. Maybe I've always wanted more romance than I found."

Just then a tiny bird emerged from the door of the room's clock, uttered three shrill cuckoos, and then went back into hiding. Staring at the clock for a moment, Ida mused, "I never did like that clock."

"It came all the way from Germany. It cost a great deal of money."

"I know, but it seems silly."

"You're not in a good mood today. I take it you and Austin must have had some sort of problem."

"No, Mother, really we didn't. He said he'd be by this afternoon. I expected him before now, but he's never sure when he can get off."

"He's a fine man, and good looking, too." Hope was scarcely hidden in Clara Campbell's voice. She herself had been married at the age of nineteen, and now here was her only daughter at the age of twenty-seven, still unmarried. Since her husband had died, Clara had been even more anxious to see Ida marry and perhaps have a family. Now for the first time she said with a trace of regret, "I'd thought by this time I'd have grandchildren, Ida."

The words hurt Ida, and she dropped her head for a moment. She had no answer for her mother, realizing the only thing she could do to help her was to do as she requested — marry and have children. It was true enough that she could have married. She had been asked three times, but one suitor was nearly sixty; the other two were young, but both were obviously after the Campbell treasury.

"Now that I think on it," she said finally, "I cared more for Bobby than for any man I've ever known."

"Not Austin? I thought you were very attracted to him."

"He's not really attracted to me, Mother. For a while I thought he was, but he's not really." She went over and patted her mother on the shoulder. "I think we'll have Bobby over for dinner Sunday."

Clara Campbell had always favored Robert MacIntyre, the son of a local banker who was rising in his profession. He had served in the army, then was wounded, and now walked with a slight limp. He was a cheerful young man, full of energy, and not at all bad looking, though a trifle thin. "That will be fine," she said. "I'll fix his favorite dishes."

■ ■ ■ ■

Austin stared down at his books. As often before, he had come to the conclusion that the work he did had almost no effect on the war itself. Now as he critiqued the fine handwriting he had used to fill up sheet after sheet, he grew disgusted, rose, and pulled on his coat, then settled his hat firmly. Leaving the office, he murmured to Corporal Jenkins, "I'll be out for the rest of the day."

"Yes, sir. See you in the morning, sir."

Leaving the War Department, Austin spoke briefly to the men he knew, but his mind was elsewhere. He had not slept well over the past several nights, and now he was at loose ends. Remembering he had promised to visit Ida Campbell, he mounted a horse at the quartermaster stables and rode out of Richmond. The Campbell plantation was only four miles outside Richmond. He enjoyed the bite of winter air and the azure sky with patches of clouds sailing along in a stately fashion. Austin took a deep breath. "This is what a man ought to do. What good is it being stuck in a stuffy office?" As he thought this, again the impulse came to transfer out of the War Department and get in some branch of the service that offered some action. He had seen action before and knew there was no glamour in it, as many had thought at the beginning of the hostilities. He remembered how young men had flocked into Richmond, fresh-faced, eager-eyed to be in battle. But after the massacres at Shiloh and Antietam, everyone realized the war was going to be a grim business with little romance about it. Yet in spite of knowing this, Austin still felt useless, as if life were passing him by. More and more he thought about after the war. He had settled it in his mind that the South had no chance and the only hope he had was to make Hartsworth a good plantation. Now even that hope was slipping from his grasp.

When he pulled up in front of the Campbell mansion and stepped down out of the saddle, a short, muscular black man took his horse. "Good afternoon, Lieutenant."

"Hello, Bill. Are the folks at home?"

"Yes, suh. You go right on in."

Austin moved up the steps, his eyes taking in the elaborate three-story redbrick home with black-shingled roof. Six enormous Corinthian columns set off the front of the house, and two colonnades connected the main house to its two wings, one housing the kitchen, the other now a spare room that had once been used as a schoolroom by Ida. Surrounding the mansion was a carriage house, cotton gin, sugar mill, guest houses, dovecotes, and slave quarters. *This certainly isn't a poor man's home,* Austin thought as he stepped into the rich polished-pine foyer furnished with antiques brought from Holland. Ida came at once to him. "I saw you ride up, Austin. I'm glad you could come."

The two moved to the cozy parlor, the fire sparking a note of cheer that reflected in Ida's eyes. But Austin was in a complaining mood, so she listened as he sipped tea and talked about his useless existence. Finally, he said, "I guess I'm not very good company today."

"I know it must be discouraging. Actually, you weren't made for that kind of job. Seems someone made a mistake putting you there."

"Well, after I got wounded, I couldn't move around too much, so it was the best I could do. But I've been thinking about transferring out."

"To what branch?"

"The artillery. I've always been interested in that branch of the service."

"It's pretty dangerous, isn't it? Doesn't the other side always try to put the artillery out of action?"

"Oh, I don't know. I suppose they do, but it's what I'd like to do."

As they talked, Austin grew more restless. When he began shifting uneasily in his chair, Ida knew he was struggling with something he wanted to say.

Finally, Austin, who had pondered this moment for many weeks, gave up on subtlety. Without warning, he looked straight at Ida. "Ida," he said in a restrained tone, "have you ever thought about me as a man you might marry?"

Ida Campbell had a great inclination to say yes. She was not a girl any longer, and she needed a husband. She also longed for children. Austin Bristol was one of the most attractive men who had ever come calling on her. But she had never expected him to ask, for deep down she knew he did not love her. She was well aware of his family's financial problems, yet out of kindness did not resent the fact that this was a factor in the question he had just asked her.

"Yes, I have thought of it, Austin," Ida said, her voice low. "But I don't anymore. You don't really love me, Austin, any more than I love you. We've always been such good friends, but that's not what a marriage is based on."

Austin was taken by surprise. He had

expected Ida to accept his offer at once, or at least to give him encouragement. But she was firm, and he knew that a further move would be useless. "I thought husbands and wives should be good friends," he said. "Some of the couples I know can't stand each other."

"I can't argue that. I know some couples like that. I've been waiting a long time to marry, and you're one of the finest men I know, Austin — but we simply don't have the love that should exist between two people. I haven't hurt you, have I?"

"You have in a way," Austin answered, "but I suppose I'll get over it. I'm not romantic enough to go out and shoot myself because you turned me down."

"Austin," Ida said, reaching to hold his hand, "I don't have many good friends. I can't afford to lose you. Let's not destroy that."

Austin had always liked Ida Campbell, but now he felt a tremendous admiration for her. He knew her honesty had cost her, so he said, "Good friends always." He leaned forward and kissed her on the cheek. "I suppose I should go out and get drunk, as a rejected suitor."

"Don't do that," Ida said, laughing. "There's a young woman somewhere waiting for you. Go and find her."

"You may be right about that. In any case, I'll be going now." When she escorted him to the door, he said, "The best of luck to you, Ida. Some man will find a good woman when he finds you."

"Good-bye, Austin. Come often."

When Ida closed the door, she realized with a sudden pang what she had done. But she was a straightforward young woman, and she murmured, "All right, Bobby. You're going to get your chance, but you're going to have to be more romantic than you have been in the past." Then she turned away from the door, putting the idea of Austin Bristol out of her mind forever, except as a friend.

When Austin returned to his room, he found a note from his father:

Let's have dinner together if you've nothing else to do. I'll be at the Spotswood at seven if you can come.

Austin did not want to be alone. The break with Ida Campbell had put a closure on something that had been a great deal in his thoughts. In truth, he was ashamed of himself, for looking back he realized he had come very close to bringing tragedy into both of their lives. *I'm glad she spoke up,* he thought as he made his way toward the Spotswood. *We would have been one of those couples who get along very well but are bored with each other. Ida deserves better than that.*

Entering the dining room, he saw his father over at a table at the far side and went at once to greet him. "Hello, Father."

"Glad you could come, Austin. Have a seat."

The two put in their order, and after the waiter disappeared, Austin said, "How's everything going? Are they still giving you a hard time?"

"Oh, a little bit, but that's to be expected. The old-line army officers resent being saddled with a greenhorn like me. I get along with the men," he said with a slight smile, "better than I do with the staff, except for Clay, of course."

The meal, which consisted of roast beef, potatoes, and carrots, came after a time. "I wonder where they got these carrots? They must be tinned," Claude said. "They taste like it anyway. We grow better than this at Hartsworth, don't we, son?"

"A lot better." The mention of Hartsworth stirred Austin's thinking. He hesitated for a moment then decided it would do no harm to talk about the situation. "I've been wondering how we're going to make it. It looks pretty grim financially."

A shadow came into Claude Bristol's eyes, and he put down his fork. "My fault," he said briefly.

"Not entirely," Austin countered. "A lot of plantations are in trouble over this embargo."

"The great regret of my life is that I didn't look to a time like this. If I hadn't been such a wastrel, we could have been out of debt. A man thinks about things like that when he finally comes to himself." Bitterly he continued, "All the years I was out racing horses and gambling, I could have put that time and money into our home. Your mother deserved it, and so did you, Paul, and Marie. I've let you all down, Austin, and in case I haven't said it, I'm sorry for being that kind of father."

Austin was taken aback. One glance at his father's face told him Claude was more serious than he'd ever seen him before. Austin finally said, "We all make mistakes."

"Well, I made a bad one. God gave me a wonderful woman and fine children, better than anything I ever expected when I was a young man. I haven't told you much about my life before I married, but my father was a gambler. I don't remember much about my mother." The din of the tables made a pleasant hum as Bristol spoke in a low tone, regret etched on his features. "I grew up thinking I'd get rich, then I'd quit gambling. Well, that's a fool's paradise. All gamblers have it, I suppose, but now that I've grown old, it's hard to realize what a fool I was."

Suddenly Austin felt again the affection for his father that he thought he'd lost long ago. "We're not lost," Austin said. "It'll be tough, but we can survive."

Claude Bristol straightened and blinked rapidly. Then in an unsteady voice he said, "It's generous of you to say that, Austin. I don't deserve it, and I know that better than anyone."

"I wish we could take a day or two off and go home. Maybe we could make some plans and get to know each other better. Maybe go hunting."

"Would you really do that, Austin?"

"Why, sure. It would be good for both of us. Can you get a couple of days' leave?"

"I think the regiment will somehow survive my absence," Claude said, a light of amusement in his eyes. "What about you?"

"I don't think they'll even know I'm gone. Tell you what. Let's go in February, for a couple of days anyway."

"Good. I'd like nothing better."

Grasping the quill firmly, Charlie drove it across the page of the tablet, paying careful attention to the instructions Marie had given her. Now her writing was even and rather beautiful, and she took pleasure in the act. It was one of the things she could point to and claim as an improvement in her life. Steadily she wrote:

January the fourth, 1864

I aint seen Boone — I mean I havent seen Boone — since Christmas, and that is over a week ago. He sent word out by Austin that he would come, but he hasnt.

What I think is that he has got his mind on Marie, and since nobody will ever see this I guess I can put it down. It makes me feel bad because I like Marie so much. She has done a lot for me and so has Boone. To tell the truth, I guess I am in love with Boone, but I am afraid he will never think of me as a woman. All he can think of, I guess, is me runnin round in buckskins and shootin a bear. No matter how many silk dresses I put on, he can only think of that.

I been thinkin bout what Austin said bout him marryin Ida, or Boone maybe marryin Marie. It bothers me a whole lot. Of course, Marie Bristol is probably the prettiest woman I ever saw and any man would be lucky to get her, but somehow I hope it wont be Boone. I am gonna write Boone a note and have Solomon take it in. I am gonna ask him to come out here so we can talk about what we are goin to do.

Charlie ceased writing. Somehow the writing had not pleased her. She was more unhappy than she had been at Christmas, and she knew somehow that it had to do with the artificial life she seemed to be living. More than once she had said, "I can't stay here forever. I've got to get on with things." Now as she stood in the center of the room, a determination came to her, and she said, "I'm goin' to see Boone! I cain't stay here no longer!"

She changed clothes, went at once to the stable, and had Solomon hitch up the buggy. When she got in it, she said, "I'll take good care of this horse, Solomon."

"Yes, ma'am. He's a good hoss. He'll get you there and back."

All the way into Richmond, Charlie's

mind was tumultuous. "If I love Boone," she said, "I reckon he likes me some. He just don't know it yet. But if we git away from here, just him and me, on a farm of our own, why then maybe he'll see that I'll make him a good wife."

This thought, in one form or another, stayed with her until she drew up in front of the Spotswood. She stepped down and handed the lines to a servant.

She went directly to Boone's room, knocked on the door, and was relieved when he opened it. "Hello, Boone."

"Why, hello, Charlie," Boone said with some surprise. "Is something wrong?"

"No — well, maybe a little bit. I got to talk to you, Boone."

"Let's go down to the restaurant."

Charlie knew his words were to avoid compromising her, so she waited until he slipped into his coat and stepped outside. On the way down he questioned her about what was going on at Hartsworth. Finally when they entered the restaurant, were seated, and had been served, she said, "Boone, I cain't live the rest of my life out at Hartsworth."

"Don't you like it there? The idea was that you would — well, learn things from Marie."

"I know, but it would take me forever, and I never would be as fine a lady as she is."

"You don't know that, Charlie," Boone said. "You're very quick. You need to give it a chance."

"No, Boone, I don't want to do that! We come to Virginia to buy a place. That's what Pa wanted. Well, fur as I kin see, we ain't gettin' nowhere!" She looked at him so fiery with independence that he knew an easy answer would not do.

"I've been looking around and mostly trying to learn what places are worth. It's hard, Charlie, because all I've ever really done is operate a ship. Here I'm lost."

"You got to try, Boone. Will you?" she asked, her dark eyes intense.

He stared at her for a moment. "All right," he said. "I'll see what I can do."

Relief washed over Charlie, and she somehow felt that a load had been lifted from her. Impulsively she clasped his hand and said rather shyly, "I know I'm a pest, Boone, but I gotta git a place of my own."

Conscious of her hand on his, Boone smiled. "I guess I know the feeling. I've felt the same. We'll get at it right away. Now maybe you and I can ride around and look at the countryside today. It's pretty cold, but —"

"That's all right, Boone," Charlie said quickly. "Let's do it."

A month later, Austin found out that his father could not get leave as he had hoped. "It's that Major Ferguson," Claude had said. "His chief occupation in life is to stop people from having fun. Some other time."

Austin had been disappointed but had still gone to Hartsworth. He had stayed for two days, spending most of that time with Charlie. During the days, they loved to ride. In the evenings, he, Marie, his mother, and Charlie would sit around the fire. On the last night of his stay, Charlie and Austin found themselves up late, almost midnight, in the kitchen. It had been a good evening: They had played cards and Marie had sung. Finally, Marie and his mother had gone to bed, and now Austin had said something about being hungry. Charlie at once had said, "Come on. I'll fix up a bite."

They had gone to the kitchen, where she had made a huge omelet, something Blossom had taught her. When she had divided it onto plates, Austin bit into it. "Why, this is better than anything I've had in weeks! I didn't know you could cook like this, Charlene."

"Oh, Blossom's teachin' me to cook."

346

"Well, she's done a good job." He ate heartily, and they also enjoyed coffee, for he had brought a half pound with him. "Drinking coffee these days is like drinking gold. When this is gone, I doubt if we'll have any more."

As they talked, they began to laugh so loudly that once Austin had to say, "We'd better keep it down. They'll be getting up to send us both to bed." They stood before the large fireplace sipping the last of the coffee, and when it was gone, they put their cups on the mantel. "The last of the coffee," he said. "There's always the last of everything, isn't there, Charlene?"

She looked at him, puzzled. "What do you mean?"

Austin looked at her, thinking how much she had changed. Rather than her buckskins, she was wearing a gray dress with a pink sash. "Let's draw up some chairs and toast our feet. I'm still not sleepy."

"All right, Austin."

They drew up a deacon's bench, and he said, "Here, there's room enough for both of us." She sat beside him, conscious of his nearness when he continued. "I was thinking about church last Sunday, when the preacher preached on the brevity of life. It was a good sermon. It made me feel kind of little."

"Me, too."

"Well, I guess I couldn't get away from that text. What was it? Man's life is like a flower — here today, and then it's gone. So I got to thinking. Sometime I'll see my mother for the last time, I'll have the last sip of coffee, the last kiss from a woman." He grew serious. "Do you ever think of things like that, Charlene?"

"Not much. I guess I'm not much of a thinker."

Laughing, he grabbed her hand. "Don't say that. You're quick. I've always said that. Look how much you've learned."

"Do you think I've changed, Austin?"

"Why, of course you have! When you first rode to town in man's clothes and packing a musket, I thought you were a mighty attractive young woman. But now, why, you can stand up in any drawing room in Virginia."

Charlie swallowed hard. "I'm mighty proud you think that."

As the fire cast its warmth on them both, Austin did something he had always wanted to do. Her black, curly hair had always intrigued him, so he whispered, "Charlene, your hair is the most beautiful thing I've ever seen." He stroked her curls with his hand. "It's lovely. No other woman has hair as pretty as yours."

Charlie Peace, although she did not know it, was hungry for this kind of attention. She wanted to be told she was pretty, and the touch of Austin's hand on her hair released something in her. She sat there not protesting, lips parted slightly, her eyes large.

As for Austin, the feel of her soft hair released something in him, too. He suddenly saw her not as a rough, boyish figure but as a beautiful and enticing young woman. As he looked at her sweet, wondering face and generous mouth, he put his arm around her and drew her close. As he bent his head, her lips came up, quick and eager, and for Austin it was like falling into softness. Prolonging the moment, he did not release her.

The strength of his arms and the pressure of his lips on hers were like nothing Charlie Peace had ever felt. She drew back finally, the light in her eyes glowing warmly.

For Austin, Charlene had become a fragrance, a melody. Despite what she had been, Charlene Peace had grown into a beautiful and desirable woman.

Afterward, neither of them could speak,

and finally Austin said, "I suppose I ought to apologize for that, Charlene — but I won't."

If he had apologized, Charlie would have been hurt deeply. Now she saw something in his face that pleased her. She rose and whispered, "Good night, Austin." She made her way out of the kitchen, went upstairs, and went to bed. But she could not sleep. Austin's kiss had confused her even more. She could not help thinking, *If Boone had kissed me like that . . .*

CHAPTER 18
DEATH AT SUNRISE

Charlie was standing in the kitchen looking out the window as she peeled potatoes when Boone drove a buggy up the driveway. At once she dropped a half-peeled potato along with the knife and ran out of the kitchen. "Boone!" she called out. "Boone! Here I am!"

Pulling up the pair of matched bays, Boone grinned then laughed as Charlie took a leap and cleared the front wheel of the buggy, landing beside him. "Don't be bashful," he said. "Just climb right in."

It was now March, a month since Austin had kissed her, and she had been unable to put the incident out of her mind. She had finally recorded in her journal, "I guess I'm just a country girl, but he is a good-lookin' man, and I don't reckon he meant anythin' by it." Now as she looked at Boone, she said eagerly, "I'm glad you're here. Come on in, and I'll fix you somethin' to eat."

"No. Go get changed. We're going to look at a plantation; then we'll go into Richmond and have supper together. I reckon it'll be too late to bring you home."

"Boone, you found a place?"

"Well, I found a place for us to look at."

"Let's go now."

"All right, but you'll have to stay in the hotel tonight. Go pack a suitcase with whatever you need overnight. Hurry along with you now!"

Jumping back out of the wagon, Charlie stormed back into the house. She nearly ran into Marianne in the hall. "Oh, excuse me! I'm goin' with Boone to look at a farm. I won't be back tonight. He says it'd be too late."

Racing upstairs, she rapidly changed into a pale blue dress, pulled on calf-high shoes, then yanked a dark blue wool coat from the chifforobe. Running down the stairs, she yelled, "Good-bye, Miss Marianne! I'll see you tomorrow, probably, unless we buy the place — then I might just stay."

Marianne watched the pair leave. "That young woman is certainly impulsive," she murmured.

The day had been exciting for Charlie. Boone had taken her to a small plantation that was not more than five miles outside Richmond and less than six from Hartsworth. He had warned her, "It's not fancy like Hartsworth or Clay's place. Don't be expecting too much."

Charlie had not expected too much and had been delighted with the property. She knew little enough about farming, and Boone knew not much more, but the owner, a tall man with gray hair and mild blue eyes, informed them, "It's an easy place to farm. Don't take many hands to do it." His name was Stafford, and he told them within five minutes that his wife had passed away a year ago and he wanted to move to his daughter's home in North Carolina. "Nothing around here for me now," he said, "except memories. I'll make you a good price on the place."

Charlie was fascinated by the house, which was, indeed, not so large as Hartsworth. It had four bedrooms, however, plus a sitting room and a huge kitchen with a magnificent fireplace. She moved from room to room, followed by Boone. "Look, Boone! These ceilings are high as our old cabin back in Colorado." She marveled at this and at the wallpaper that evidently Mrs. Stafford had taken a special interest in. "Shore is pretty, ain't it? I mean, *isn't* it,

Boone?"

"It's a nice house," Boone agreed. They investigated every nook and corner inside and then went outside so Stafford could drive them around the perimeter of the place.

Finally, Stafford said, "You and your wife will want to talk about this. Come back and see me when you make up your mind. Reckon we can handle the financing between us."

At the words "you and your wife," Charlie had flushed and shot a look at Boone. He had winked at her and shaken his head, as if to say, *He'll find out soon enough.*

They left for Richmond, arriving about dark to obtain a room for Charlie. But she turned to Boone, saying, "It's too early to go to bed."

"Sure is," Boone said. "Let's get something to eat, but not here. I've eaten here until I know every biscuit that's coming."

The two went to a restaurant called the Pioneer, a place Boone had found on one of his nightly excursions. It was frequented mostly by officers of the army stationed outside of town, bachelors who were looking for a meal to break the monotony of the army diet. The room also held several civilian families.

When the meal came, Charlie said, "This is good cookin'! I could do this good, though."

Boone sipped his coffee, or what passed for coffee. "Maybe you can get a job here," he suggested. Then he frowned, "I wonder what they put in this cup."

A waiter overheard him and asked, "Something wrong, sir?"

Boone winked at Charlie. "If this is coffee, bring me tea. If it's tea, bring me some coffee." Charlie giggled.

The waiter, rather disgruntled, said, "If you don't like it, sir, I can get you some sassafras tea."

"No, I'll muddle along with this." Boone waited until the waiter left, then said, "I guess it doesn't do to complain about the food here. That fellow is downright sensitive!" He sipped from the cup again and shook his head. "Too much for me. What did you think about the place, Charlie?" He sat there listening as she, with a glowing face, spoke about how much she liked it. Finally, he said, "Not fancy like Hartsworth."

"Well, I'm not very fancy myself," Charlie said happily.

"We'd be a pair trying to farm, wouldn't we? Probably plant crops under the trees so we wouldn't have to work in the sun."

"Oh, I know better than that!" Charlie said indignantly. "Did you ever farm at all?"

"Not even a garden. It's hard to farm when you're out on the sea in a schooner. Might be fun to learn, though."

The two talked until a crowd came in and the waiter looked at them with impatience. "I guess we'd better leave. The waiter's liable to throw us out if we try to hang on to this table any longer," Boone remarked.

He picked up Charlie's coat, which was draped over the back of her chair, and held it for her. When she slipped her arms into it, he smelled the freshness of her hair. "You've been sneaking around washing your hair again, Charlie. It smells good."

Charlie turned and said, "That's not very polite, Boone, to talk about a girl's washin'."

Boone only grinned at her and stepped aside to let her walk toward the door. They had almost reached the entrance that led from the main dining room into the large foyer when Earl Dillon appeared with three men. He stopped to stare at Boone. "Well, look what we got here! Fighting Boone Manwaring!"

An alarm as clear as a bell rang inside Boone. He saw Dillon had been drinking and, indeed, was weaving slightly. His eyes were red-rimmed, and his speech was loose, slack with drunkenness. Stepping forward, Boone took Charlie by the arm and pulled her slightly to one side without speaking, hoping Dillon would pass on, but keeping his eyes steadily on the man.

"This here's the famous mankiller. You may not have heard of him." Dillon raised his voice so everyone in the restaurant turned to watch the scene. Only the clattering of dishes in the kitchen could be heard.

Boone felt something begin to burn inside and recognized it. When he had become angry, a few times in his life, it had built up like a volcano and then burst with such violence that when the fight was over, it had sobered him. He knew he was capable of killing when he fell into such a mood, and now, in order to still the rising violence that troubled him, he said quietly, "Come on, Charlie."

"Wait a minute!" Dillon stepped forward and grabbed Charlie's other arm. He leered down at her. "What's a pretty thing like you doing with a yellow-belly like this? You deserve a real man!"

The fiery anger boiling inside Boone turned into a coldness, for he knew it was hopeless to try to pacify Dillon — indeed, he did not want to. Now he stepped forward and with one blow struck Dillon in the chest, driving him backward. Dillon cartwheeled into his friends and would have fallen if two of them had not caught him.

"Step over there, Charlie," Boone said then turned to face what he knew was coming. Dillon had caught his balance now, and his face had turned white. He pulled his coat together then said, "I don't take a push from any man! If you're too much of a coward to face me like a man, then I'll whip you like a dog!" His hand flashed out and would have struck Boone on the cheek, but Boone easily blocked it by grasping Dillon's wrist in a vise and squeezing it.

As he heard a slight gasp come from Dillon's lips, Boone said, "I'm tired of you, Dillon! You've been pushing this. You're the kind of man who has to be seen. I have some things to do first, but I'll see you the day after tomorrow at dawn. My man will call on you. If you need an excuse, here it is." Boone swung his free arm in an arch, short and powerful, and threw his body into it. His open hand caught Dillon squarely on the left cheek and drove him backward so that he fell into a table. Two women sitting there screamed as the table fell over beneath the careening body. Dillon got to his feet slowly, the mark of Boone's hand on his face.

"Enjoy your meal, Dillon," he said. "Come along, Miss Peace." He took Charlie's arm and guided her outside.

The violence had shaken Charlie, since it had seemed to explode from nowhere. As they walked down the street toward the Spotswood, she finally took a deep breath. "Does this mean you're goin' to fight him, Boone?"

"No choice. I'll have to."

Looking up, Charlie saw that his lips were set in a tight line and thought, *What will I do if Boone dies?* The idea struck her like a physical blow. She found it difficult to imagine where she would turn. Since Boone had come into her life, she had unconsciously learned to look to him, and now she felt it was more than that. When he stopped at the door of her room, she awkwardly laid her hand on his chest. "Boone, don't do it! I've heard 'bout him. He's already killed two men and shot another."

"There's no way out, Charlie. Go to bed now. I have things to do."

Charlie watched, unable to move, as Boone walked down the hall then disappeared down the stairway. She entered her room and sat down on the bed, feeling empty and almost paralyzed by the fear that Boone might die and leave her.

"You haven't heard about Boone, Marie?" Austin Bristol had looked up the next morning when his sister entered his office. As he saw her smile fade, he knew instantly she had not heard the news. "He came to me last night. Seems that Earl Dillon insulted Charlene down at the Pioneer."

"What happened, Austin?"

"Well, I guess I've been wrong about Boone," Austin admitted. He stroked his cheek thoughtfully. "I wasn't there, but I heard about it later. From what Boone told me, Dillon put his hands on Charlene, and Boone knocked him across the room."

Marie could not think for a moment. Duels were not uncommon in Richmond and in the countryside, although they were illegal. She had always taken them for granted as a part of the Southern way of life, but now she looked at Austin in consternation. "I don't know what to say."

"I don't think anyone else does either. We've all put Boone down, but I guess he had other reasons than cowardice for not wanting to fight. I'll have to help him with this."

"Isn't there some way to avoid it?" Marie

asked, her lips dry.

"You know what Dillon is. It's what he's been screaming for." Austin shifted nervously, running his hand over his hair. "I don't like it, though. He's a dead shot and quick as a snake. I talked to a man who saw him when he killed Jerry Fowler. He said Fowler never even had a chance. It was like a murder."

"We've got to stop him, Austin."

"I've talked to him, but it's too late for talk. I think we're responsible for this, and that's what worries me. Boone's a pretty sensitive man, and he knows the talk that's been going around about his being afraid of Dillon. His eyes used to be sort of laughing, but now they're cold as ice."

"I'm going to talk to him! Do you know where he is?"

"It'll do you no good."

"I have to try anyway!"

"You can probably find him in his room."

Marie went at once to the Spotswood and knocked at Boone's door. When he opened it, she saw exactly what Austin had meant. Boone's eyes were not the same. "I just talked to Austin. He told me about Dillon."

"Pretty common knowledge. We ought to fight in public and charge admission. We could make a fortune." Bitterness, some-

361

thing Marie hadn't heard from Boone before, tinged his speech.

"Boone, you don't have to do this. Everyone knows what kind of a man Dillon is."

"That wasn't the way you felt before."

Boone's words hit Marie hard. She dropped her eyes, feeling ashamed, and worked to regain her composure. When she looked up at him, there was a vulnerability in her mouth and eyes. "I deserve that," she said quietly. "It's the way we've lived around here, but I've never been this close to the thing before. It was always a story about two men I didn't know, but it's real enough now." When he did not answer, she said, "I'm sorry I misjudged you, Boone, and Austin is, too."

"I suppose it had to come. Dillon would never have given it a rest. I'm just sorry Charlie had to get involved in it."

"Where is she? That's why I came to town. She didn't come home."

"She's got a room down the hall — 202. It might be good if you'd go be with her. She's pretty upset."

"I should imagine. So am I."

Boone cocked his head to one side. "I don't want to be impolite, Marie, but I'd appreciate it if you would leave me alone. Go down and see Charlie."

Desperately Marie wished she had never let Boone suspect her feelings about his courage, or lack of it. Now she saw it was hopeless, but still she had to try. "I remember once you said that a game of cards wasn't worth killing a man for. It sounds odd coming from me, but let me ask you this. The man didn't hurt Charlie. Is it worth killing him because he insulted her?"

"I don't know the rules. I didn't make them up. I only know that sometimes a man has to fight, and this is one of them." A serious light touched his hazel eyes, and he paused to gather his thoughts together. "I expect there's many a man in the army who doesn't feel anything about slavery in particular, or states' rights either. He's there because of pressure, what his people would think of him, and what his friends would think. So finally, regardless of what he thinks about the political situation, he goes into the army, and sooner or later he has to kill — or be killed. It seems like it's something that's built into men. I don't like it, and I wish it didn't exist, but it does."

"But, Boone, what if you're killed?"

"Then I'll be dead."

"Don't be foolish. I know this is no time to preach, but I've sensed that you don't know God personally. That's what frightens me the most, although I —" She started to say, "I've come to care for you," but cut her words off. It would sound false and hollow now. In truth, anything she said sounded foolish to her own ears. If she really cared for him, why hadn't she spoken to him about things like God and eternity before? "Boone, please put it off for a while. Give it time."

"I can't do that, Marie. Go to Charlie." He hesitated then said, "If all goes well, I'll see you tomorrow."

Marie had no choice. She wanted to hold him, beg him not to go, but her pride would not let her do that. And now that this moment had come, she realized how much her feelings for Boone had grown since he had kissed her.

"Good day, Marie," he said then closed his door. It sounded like a death knell to her as she stood outside numbly, unable to think, devastated by fear. Then she moved down the hall to the room Boone had mentioned and knocked on the door. When it opened, she saw Charlie's pale face and eyes red with weeping. "Oh, Marie!" she said. "He's gonna git killed!" She threw herself into Marie's arms. Marie held the trembling young woman close and heard her desperate words. "He's goin' to die, and

I love him, Marie! I love him!"

Marie could only stand there, her hand patting the back of the sobbing girl ineffectually. Although she had suspected Charlie loved Boone, now it had come from Charlie herself. Without a doubt, Marie now knew that this young woman's life was tied up with the tall man who, down the hall, was preparing himself for death.

That night Boone went to bed. After lying there for a long time, he finally went to sleep. He awakened, however, after an interminable period, not knowing how much time had passed. Looking out the window, he sensed dawn was not far off. He rose and shaved, using cold water, and then dressed as carefully as if he were going to a formal wedding. He had finished brushing his hair when a tiny knock sounded, and his eyes narrowed. He moved to the door and asked, "Who is it?"

"It's me — Charlie."

Opening the door, Boone said, "You shouldn't be here, Charlie. Go back to your room."

"Boone, I couldn't help it." Charlie looked exhausted. "You don't have to fight that feller. Let's get away from here. We've got enough money to go anywhere. Please,

365

Boone, let's go!"

Astonished by her emotion and the tremor in her lower lip, Boone grasped her cold hand. "Charlie, I've got to do this thing. Then if you don't want to stay in Richmond, we'll go someplace else."

When she started to speak, he said, "There's no point talking, Charlie. I wrote a letter and delivered it to the bank yesterday. If I don't make it through this, it's all yours. So you won't have to worry about anything."

"I don't keer 'bout the money! I just keer 'bout you!"

Charlie threw herself against Boone, holding him tightly. He felt her trembling. "I've got to go, Charlie. It's time. I'll be all right. I'm a tough old bird."

Charlie lifted her head and locked her hands behind his neck, pulling his head down for a kiss. Boone tasted the saltiness of her tears and her soft lips. As she clung to him desperately, Boone was astonished at his own feelings for her.

"You cain't go," Charlie said, releasing him at last. "It don't mean nothin'. He didn't hurt me."

"A man has to live with other men, Charlie. I couldn't stay in this place unless I faced up to Dillon. Most duels," he said,

366

grasping at straws for the most part, "don't get anybody killed. Shot in the arm or the leg, maybe, but if I don't make it, I'll say this: I've become very fond of you."

"I love you, Boone," Charlie said simply.

"Why — you're just a child, Charlie. You see me as a father." He saw her shake her head and knew then he had to get away. He carefully pushed her away then picked up his coat. "Stay here at the hotel. I'll be back."

And then he was gone. Charlie stared after him then took a ragged breath and went back to her room. She sat down on the edge of the bed to begin her long vigil, her thoughts on the encounter that would take place outside Richmond at sunrise.

"Are you all right, Boone?" Austin asked nervously. He shifted his feet and looked over the slight rise where three men were waiting. "Maybe he'll apologize; then we can all go home and forget it."

"You can forget about that, Austin. You know Dillon better than that."

"I guess that's right." Austin saw the grim determination in Boone's face. "You've got to be fast and get in the first shot. From everything I hear, that's what Dillon does."

"I doubt if I can beat him; he's had more

practice than I have. But he'd better hit me in the brain, or he's a dead man."

They were approaching rapidly now, and Boone saw that Dillon had already taken off his heavy coat. He was wearing a white shirt, and it occurred to Boone, *You'll get that shirt bloody if things don't go your way.*

Austin said at once, "Gentlemen. I think, Masters, we would be ready to consider an apology."

Masters, a bulky man with cold eyes, said, "My principal will make no apologies. Is your man ready?"

Austin said in a thin voice, "Yes."

The third individual now produced a case and opened it. "You may have first choice of the weapon, Mr. Manwaring."

Carelessly Boone picked up one of the pistols and glanced at it. It was a fine dueling pistol, but he would have preferred a Colt .44. However, he made no complaint. Dillon sneered but said nothing as he took the other pistol.

Boone watched as Austin and Masters carefully charged the pistols. When Austin handed him the weapon, he held it loosely at his side and listened as the third man gave the instructions. "I will count to ten as you march away from each other. On the count of ten you will turn and fire. Is that understood?"

"Yes," Dillon said and turned his back. Boone merely nodded and took his place. He heard the count begin almost at once. "One — two — three —" His mind seemed to be working more rapidly than usual. He was not thinking of his own death, although that might be only seconds away. His thoughts were of Charlie and what would happen to her. If he had fear, it was that she would not be able to make her way in the world, and then he thought, *Marie will help her.*

"Eight — nine — ten!"

Boone turned quickly, holding his body at a right angle, presenting the least possible target. As his own weapon swung up, he saw he was not going to be fast enough, for Dillon had already whirled and leveled his weapon.

He's going to get me, Boone thought, but his arm continued its upward sweep. It was as if he moved underwater, so slow did he seem, and then as his finger tightened on the trigger of the pistol, he was aware a great blow had struck him. As his own pistol discharged, the earth began to grow quiet; the rising sun darkened. Then, as if he were struck with a powerful fist, he fell over backward, not feeling his body as it hit the ground.

■ ■ ■ ■

PART FOUR:
SHADOW
OF THE END

■ ■ ■ ■

CHAPTER 19
A TIME TO LIVE

Charlie Peace had never spent such a bad day in her life. Dawn came, rosy and bright, but she had no eyes to see the beauty of the sunrise. Slowly the crimson disk turned to a harvest yellow and rose over the city as Charlie sat mutely at the window. From time to time she would get up and pace the floor, her face tense, agitation spreading throughout her as she thought about the outcome of the duel.

"I shouldn't have let him go!" she murmured. "I could've found *some* way. We could've left this place and gone someplace else. What do I keer 'bout this place if Boone dies?"

She moved over to the washstand, filled the basin with fresh water, and, soaking a washcloth, pressed it against her face. Then she assumed her lonely vigil, sitting in the chair and staring down at the street. Her reverie was broken by a sharp rap on the door. Leaping to her feet, she sprang across the room and, seizing the doorknob, jerked it open. "Austin!" she cried, and then could say no more. The words "Is he dead?" had almost passed her lips, but somehow it seemed unlucky to even let the words be spoken, although they were in her heart.

Austin exhaled what was almost a gasp. "He's alive, Charlie!"

"Thank God!" Charlie said. As her face paled, the room swayed around her, and Austin leaped forward to put his arm around her.

"Here," he murmured, "sit down awhile." He guided her to the bed and sat down beside her, keeping his arm around her. "It takes you like that sometimes. I don't know why. Good news can hit you as hard as bad news."

"Is he bad hurt, Austin?"

"Well, he's not going to die." His mind went back to the scene of the duel. A vivid image of Boone's face and hair covered with blood filled his mind. He had thought at that moment that Boone was killed instantly. "He took a slug along the side of the head. He's down at Dr. Malone's office now."

"I got to go to him, Austin."

"That's why I came." Rising, Austin watched carefully to make sure she wasn't still dizzy. But she had regathered herself. Taking her arm, he said, "Better put on a coat."

Charlie grabbed her coat from the armoire then said hurriedly, "Come on! Let's go, Austin!" Her unbrushed hair framed her face with curls.

"He was unconscious," Austin said, "but I wouldn't want him to wake up alone."

The two hurried out of the hotel, and Austin led her to Dr. Malone's office, which was upstairs over the general store. They ascended a rickety stairway and went in to find Malone. He was a burly man of fifty, thick-fingered, broad-shouldered, and with the beginnings of gray in his brown hair and beard. His eyes sharpened as he took in the young woman, but he said nothing.

"How is he, Doctor?" Austin asked quickly.

"Same as when you left. Unconscious." Malone had a New England way of speaking, for he had been born in Massachusetts and studied medicine there. He had married a Southern girl and had come to take up his home in Virginia. Even though his heart was not in the Confederate cause, he stayed, like many others, because of family ties. Now his blue-gray eyes caught the agitation in the young woman. "You can sit beside him if you wish," Malone said.

Charlie followed Dr. Malone through the door that led off to the right and at once saw Boone lying stretched out on a cot. The sunlight threw golden bars across his face, and the white bandage he wore around his head made him look odd and out of proportion. Quickly moving across the room, she knelt down beside him and took his hand. Oblivious to the stares of the two men, she searched Boone's pale face for signs of hope. Finally, she turned and met the doctor's eyes. "How is he, Doctor?"

"I think he's going to be all right. If that bullet had been a half inch to the left, he'd be dead. As it is, it's given him a pretty bad concussion. The wound itself isn't so bad. I cleaned that out, and it shouldn't get any infection, but the concussion is what I'm worried about."

"Anything else we can do?" Austin asked.

"Just wait."

"Kin I stay with him?" Charlie asked.

"Don't see why not. May be a little noisy when patients start coming in, but they won't bother him." Questioning in his mind, *Sweetheart? Wife? Sister?* Dr. Malone finally said, "I don't know your name."

"Charlie Peace."

"Well, Miss Peace, this may go on for

several days. I hope not, but I hate to give false hopes."

"I won't be in your way, Dr. Malone."

Malone nodded brusquely then walked out. Austin followed him. "I've got to get back to my office, Doctor. Send for me if anything develops, will you?"

"Nothing likely to happen," Malone answered. "That girl, is she his intended?"

Austin always had difficulty explaining the relationship between Boone and Charlie. Now it came again, and finally he gave it up as a bad job. "They're just good friends," he stated flatly. "Let me know if he wakes up."

Malone's eyes narrowed as Austin left. "Just good friends," he muttered. "What the devil does that mean?" He went over to a table and began rolling pills and stuffing them into glass bottles. In spite of the many illnesses and injuries he'd treated over the years and especially during the war, Dr. Malone had somehow retained the gentleness and goodwill he'd had as a young man just leaving medical school. "Just good friends," he said, rubbing the side of his nose with a thick forefinger. "Now they'll get married and live happily ever after." He continued with his task for ten minutes when the door opened. "Why, hello, Marie," Malone said. "You just missed your brother."

"I know. I was at his office waiting for him." Marie's face was drawn and her clothes wrinkled. In truth, she had not slept at all but, like Charlie, had waited for news. When Austin had not returned to his office, she had heard from one of his officers that there had been a duel and that one of the survivors, a Mr. Manwaring, was in Dr. Malone's office. She asked quickly, "How is he?"

"Not bad, considering he nearly took a bullet in the brain." Malone hesitated then nodded. "Miss Peace is in with him." He had delivered Marie into the world as a young doctor, and now his eyes took in his handiwork. She was, and always had been, an attractive young woman, but now he noted that her hands were unsteady. "You can go in and join Miss Peace."

"Thank you, Doctor." When Marie entered the room, Charlie looked up. "Has he awakened yet?"

"No," Charlie whispered. She was still holding Boone's hand. She had drawn up a straight chair and was sitting beside him. "He looks so weak and helpless. I'm scared, Marie."

Marie touched Charlie's shoulder then looked down at Boone's still face. "Dr.

Malone says he'll be all right. It'll just take a little time." She said this more to comfort herself than Charlie, for she, too, was accustomed to a healthy, bronzed Boone Manwaring. Now he was weak, and his helplessness stirred her instincts, maternal and otherwise. She put her hand on his brow. "No fever," she said.

"Dr. Malone said it wasn't a bad wound as far as a cut's concerned, but he said something else. A con-something."

"Concussion, I expect," Marie said, finding another chair and sitting quietly beside Charlie. Finally, Marie asked, "What about Dillon?"

"I didn't hear."

"Austin didn't tell you?"

"I guess he was too set on takin' care of Boone, and I was too troubled to ask." She patted Boone's limp hand then stroked it gently. "He don't look good to me, Marie."

If Marie had been alone, she would have done exactly what Charlie Peace was doing, taken Boone's hand and held it. But somehow that office was taken — and by a person hopelessly in love with Boone Manwaring. As Marie mutely watched the two, she wondered what was going on in the young girl's heart. She knew Charlie was innocent as far as men were concerned, that she had not known a man. And there was something almost pathetic about the way she held on to Boone. *He's all the family she has. I can't begrudge her that,* Marie thought.

Finally, Marie arose and said briefly, "I'll be back in a moment, Charlie."

Stepping inside the office, she found Dr. Malone dismissing a patient with, "Take this home and give it to your wife. I'll be by early tomorrow."

"Thank you, Doc."

Marie waited until the man had left and then said, "Dr. Malone, just how bad is Boone?"

"I think he'll be all right." Then, studying Marie, he asked, "You got an interest in this young fella?"

Flustered by the doctor's question and the curious look in his eyes, she blushed. "I . . . He's a good friend."

"That's what Austin said he is to that young woman in there. He's got a lot of good-looking lady friends," Malone observed. Then, enjoying teasing Marie, he said, "A Yankee of some sort, ain't he?"

"No, he's from the West."

"Some talk around town about him, even before the duel." Malone clasped his hands behind his back. "I don't guess there'll be any more talk about his courage. From what

Austin told me, he was as cool as a cucumber."

"What about Earl Dillon?"

"The devil looks after his own," Malone said wryly. "He didn't get a scratch."

"That's good."

Malone's eyebrows lifted. "How do you figure that?"

"Boone didn't want to kill a man — not over something like a card game or an insult. He wouldn't have fought this duel if Dillon hadn't insulted Miss Peace."

"Well, be that as it may, I think it's going to be all right."

"Dr. Malone, would it be all right if we took him to Hartsworth?" She saw a greater interest spark in the doctor's eyes. "We can take better care of him there. There will be three of us. My mother, Charlie, and me."

"I don't see why not. He ought to wake up soon, but I've got my rounds to make and nobody to stay with him." He pondered for a moment then nodded. "Get a wagon and fix a bed in it; then we'll get someone to carry him down. Drive slow and easy, and put him in bed the same way. I don't want that head shaken any more than it's already been."

"Thank you, Doctor." When Marie was back at Charlie's side, she said, "We're going to take him to Hartsworth, Charlie."

"Oh, that'll be good, Marie!" Charlie's eyes brightened. "We kin take real good keer of him there, cain't we?"

"Yes, Charlie. We can take care of him real good."

"Do you think he's looking better, Marianne?"

Charlie and Marianne had been changing the dressing on Boone's head while he lay still as a statue. They had made the trip very slowly, having to hold the horses back to their slowest possible walk. Finally when they had reached Hartsworth, the two women had dismounted, and soon Marie had gathered up enough strong men to put Boone in a blanket. They had each taken a corner and, as Charlie held the door open, had gone into the house.

Marianne had been caught off guard but at once said, "We'll put him in the green room at the end of the hall."

"That'll be good, Mother," Marie said. "It's bright and sunny there. When he wakes up, it won't be so gloomy."

They had installed Boone in the room, putting him into bed, and it had been Marianne who had removed his clothing with some help from Ketura — and had gotten him into a clean cotton nightshirt. She had been ready to bathe Boone's face when Charlie had come in and said, "Let me do that."

So Marianne watched as Charlie bathed Boone's face. "His breathing is steady," Marianne said reassuringly. "We had a man who fell out of the loft three years ago and got a bump on the head. He was out of it for two days. When he came back, he was good as ever. Still here as a matter of fact. That's Solomon, who works with the horses."

"He's just got to be all right," Charlie whispered.

Marianne Bristol studied Charlie for a moment then left the room. Once in the kitchen, she found Marie staring out the window. "Marie, are you all right?"

"Oh, Mother, I didn't hear you." As Marie turned around, Marianne could tell she was tense. "It could have been much worse," Marianne said.

"I know it could, and it would have been my fault if he had been killed!"

Surprised by her daughter's vehemence, Marianne asked, "Why would you think that?"

"Oh, not my fault alone!" Marie struggled to find the words to express the tumult within her breast. "I egged him into this! We all did it!" Angry, she said, "I get so sick of this *honor* business! How many young men do we know who are in their graves because of it — and older men, too! Remember Roy Jacobson? He had a wife and four children. He went out and fought a duel with shotguns, no less, with Henry Rodgers. Now does that give his wife any satisfaction? She's trying to raise those children alone. Her husband should have thought of that!"

Marianne had had the same sort of thoughts that Marie had just expressed, so she said, "Unfortunately, if men have courage, we think they're fools. But if they're cowards, we despise them."

"I know — and I was the biggest fool of all!" she said, her eyes narrowed. "I'll never make that mistake again, God willing."

Wanting to turn the conversation, Marianne asked, "What about Dillon?"

"Alive and well. Dr. Malone said the devil takes care of his own. But I'll tell you one thing, Mother. If he pursues this, I'll shoot him myself!"

"That's strong talk, Marie," Marianne said, staring into her daughter's determined eyes. "Do you feel that strongly about Boone?"

"I don't know. It bothered me, this dueling business, and it bothered Charlie worse." She paced the floor energetically then faced her mother. "Charlie's in love with him."

"I don't know about that. She's very attached to him, but that's only natural. With her family dead, he's the only friend she had who could come to her rescue."

"I expect they'll marry."

Marianne knew this fiery daughter of hers well. She noticed that, besides her typical determined spirit, something new had been added to her daughter's character — a tenderness and softness due to the near death of Boone Manwaring. It showed in the relaxed set of her shoulders and the gentleness that came when she spoke his name. Marianne wanted to pursue the matter but knew that it was not yet time. "Well," she said firmly, "we've got to get him well first."

"That's right. We'll do that, won't we, Mother?"

"Of course. Now I think *you* need to get a little rest. You don't look like you've slept in a week."

"All right. I'll lie down for a while." Once in her bedroom, Marie removed her dress, washed her face, and stretched out on her bed. She closed her eyes, but her mind was like wild birds in a cage. Thoughts fluttered and came like ghosts, whispering to her until she drifted off into a troubled sleep.

Darkness was all there was, except for tiny spots of light that would flicker on like candles far off in the distance. He could not see them clearly, and somehow his arms and legs would not move, and this frightened him. Sounds then came, but he could not understand them. They were voices — he knew that much — different voices. From time to time, as he struggled to free himself of the darkness, hands touched him and his brow and face would grow cool.

Although a week had passed, time had lost all meaning. The same troubled dream came to him again and again, and he tried to drive it away. Someone was standing close, but he could not see a face, for it was too dark.

Then one day light crept under his closed eyes. Cautiously he opened them, but the light was so strong he quickly shut them again. He stirred and found he could move. He reached his hand up and touched something around his head. He could not understand where he was or what was on his head. His thoughts swirled, confused and formless, until he heard a voice calling his name.

"Boone — Boone, are you awake?"

Carefully he lifted his eyelids and turned slightly away from the light. He was lying flat on his back; he knew that much. Someone bent over him as he opened his eyes. He saw Marie's face then grew dizzy. As he shook his head to clear it, agony shot through him.

"Don't move, Boone! Keep your head still!"

Marie's voice was gentle but insistent. "Do you know me, Boone?"

"Sure, but —" He opened his eyes again and once again grew dizzy. "I can see — two of you!" he exclaimed.

His words frightened Marie. She had never heard of such a thing, and she said quickly, "Just keep your eyes shut, then. You're just dizzy, I suppose."

Boone lay there, and memory flooded back. The scene flashed through him of Dillon turning, the muzzle of his pistol looming like a giant tunnel. "I got shot in the head, didn't I?"

"A crease along your temple, but you're going to be all right."

"What about Dillon?"

"He's all right."

Boone relaxed. "That's good," he said, aware of the faint scent of violets that Marie used. Weakly he asked, "Where am I?"

"At Hartsworth."

"How long have I been here?"

"About a week. Charlie and I didn't want to leave you in the doctor's office, so we brought you here where we could care for you better."

"Is Charlie here, too?"

"Yes, do you want me to get her?"

"I guess she'll come when she takes a notion."

Despite himself, Boone could not keep from trying to open his eyes. It seemed the natural thing to do, but every time he did, the double vision created havoc with his mind. He found, suddenly, that he was not as strong as he had thought. Desperately peering at Marie, he said, "Don't want to be trouble."

"How could you be that?" Marie put a hand over his lips. "Don't try to talk."

As Marie watched, she saw him begin to pass back into unconsciousness. She was frightened by the phenomenon of the double vision but did not know what to do. When he lay completely still, she leaned forward, kissed him lightly, and whispered, "Get well, Boone."

Suddenly the eyes opened, and Boone said clearly, "What's the kiss for?"

"I — I thought you were asleep."

"I was, but every time a beautiful woman kisses me, I wake up." Tired and dizzy, Boone wondered if he'd dreamed it. As he drifted back into the shadows, he said, "Glad you brought me here, Marie."

"He's going to be all right." Dr. Malone had arrived before noon to examine Boone carefully and discovered that the double vision was fading, now coming back only intermittently. "Not unusual," he said to the three women who gathered outside Boone's room to get the report. "It's something the brain does when it gets a pretty bad jolt. The eyes don't work right for a time, or the brain can't pick up what they're seeing. I don't know, but he tells me it's better." He smiled, saying, "He's got lots of good-looking nurses. I'd get sick myself if I could have you three wait on me."

Marianne and Marie were accustomed to Dr. Malone's teasing, but Charlie was not. She looked startled until she saw the twinkle in his eyes. Then she said, "We'll take good keer of him, Doctor."

"Don't let him get up. He'll be trying to, but he needs to lie down for several more days. A week would be better, but you'll never keep him in bed that long. But I want him to stay still. I've seen cases where people got better, then rushed it."

"I'll make him stay in that bed if I have to hog-tie him to it!" Charlie vowed. She lifted her head, determination in her dark blue eyes.

Malone grinned. "I expect you'd do it, Charlie. Well, I'll come back day after tomorrow. Nothing I can do that you three can't."

As Marianne left to see the doctor off, Marie said, "That's good news, isn't it, Charlie?"

"Yes, I was real worried."

"I was, too."

"Guess I'll go set beside him fer a spell," Charlie said.

"That's good. I'll see if I can cook something he can eat. Maybe just soup or something like that."

Marie left for the kitchen and spent the morning without seeing Boone. Charlie came in twice, once to get water and once to get some soup. "He says he's hungry," she said, her eyes bright.

"That's good, but just give him this soup. If he does all right with that, he can have something more solid tonight."

Late that afternoon, Charlie, who had left the house, looked up from her walk to see Austin riding up. She ran to meet him, and when he dismounted, her eyes were sparkling. She said at once, "Austin, he's much better."

"That's good." He reached out his hand, and she took it unthinkingly. "You look tired. I'll bet you've worn yourself out."

"No, I haven't done much. Just sat beside him. He's asleep now, though."

"Tell me about it while I unsaddle."

The two of them walked slowly to the barn, and Charlie spoke of Boone's condition as Austin put the saddle over a beam and turned the horse out into the pasture.

"Let's go down for a walk," Austin said. "I'll show you where I caught my first five-pound bass."

The two walked down around a copse of trees on the east side of the property where a large creek, still patched with bits of snow, gurgled among mossy stones. Reaching a pool twenty feet across, Austin said, "Right there. I still remember how my heart beat when I caught that big fish."

"How old were you?"

"Must have been about ten, I guess. Do you like to fish, Charlene?"

"Sure do. We caught a lot of trout up in

the mountains."

"No trout around here that I know of. Here, sit down. We'll watch the sunset." Crisscrossing his legs, Austin began to speak of his boyhood. "I must've come to this pond a thousand times. I still miss it."

As the faint rays of sun bathed Charlie's face, she shook her head, sending her black ringlets into motion. When she smiled at him, there was a restfulness in her face that caused him to remark, "You were pretty worried about Boone."

"I sure was. I don't know what I would have done if he had died, Austin."

Seeing the warm innocence in Charlie's expression, Austin asked suddenly, "What do you feel for Boone, Charlene?"

"Feel fer him?" Charlie looked down for a moment. "Why, I reckon I feel a lot fer him. If it wasn't fer him, I'd be all alone."

"No, you wouldn't, Charlene. You've got me, and Marie, and Mother," he said, longing to follow up the question, but not knowing how.

His words touched Charlie Peace. "I never knew there were folks as good as you, Austin, and your ma and your sister. We kind of lived alone, and all I knew was Ma and Pa. But you've taken me in, and I appreciate it." She wanted to say more but did not know what words to use. So instead she grasped his hand, then laughed. "I guess I'm pretty forward, holding hands with you."

"Don't mind a bit," Austin said, admiring her freshness and gently releasing her hand. Then, changing the subject, he said, "I've got to get out of that office, Charlene."

"You mean git out of the army?"

"No, I mean out of the office. It's driving me crazy."

"It sure would drive me crazy," Charlie said, "to be cooped up in a little place like that. What do you want to do, Austin?"

"I want to join the real army."

"You was wounded, wasn't you? When you were in the real army before?"

"That's all gone now. I'm fit enough."

Troubled, Charlie said, "I'd hate it if you had to leave."

"Would you, Charlene?"

"Why, sure I would! Don't you know that?"

Austin was amused. "I forgot how honest you are."

"Honest? What do you mean by that?"

"I mean many people aren't. They're always pretending to be something they're not."

"Why would they want to do that?"

"Why, I guess to catch a spouse."

"I'd want no man I'd have to catch!"

"Why, sure! You catch him, and he catches you!"

"Maybe it's so," Charlie said.

"So what about you and Boone?" Austin blurted out, unable to help himself.

"Oh, I don't know, Austin."

Austin thought she did know, but he said nothing. Finally, he rose and said, "It's getting dark. Let's go home."

When the two arrived back at Hartsworth, Austin was greeted by Marianne and Marie. While supper was being prepared, Austin visited with Boone. "You got it made, Boone. Just lie around and get waited on day and night. Some men have all the luck."

Boone smiled. "You're right about that. I'm a natural-born sponge. Take all the attention I can get. What's happening with you, Austin?"

Austin expressed his desire to be out of the office and into an active, fighting outfit. He ended by saying, "I'm going to get into this fight if I have to desert and enlist as a private."

"I wish I felt that strongly."

"It's different for you," Austin said. "I've been thinking about what you said about people in the far-off parts of this country,

394

way out in Colorado and Oregon. This must seem like another world, but for us it's everything."

Cautiously Boone asked, "Do you really think you can win this war, Austin?"

"I don't think there's a chance. But one of these days I'll have to explain to my sons what I did, and I don't want to have to tell them I shuffled paper in an office."

Austin stayed until suppertime then sat in the parlor afterward with Marie while Charlie was in with Boone.

Marie was unusually quiet, so Austin asked, "What's troubling you, Marie?"

"I've been going over the books, Austin, and I visited with Mr. Keith down at the bank. I don't see how we're going to make it."

"What did Keith say?" Keith had been their banker for years and had been kind, but times were hard, Austin knew. "Is he going to give us time to pay the bills?"

"He'd like to, but I could see he's getting pressure from others. We've got to get some money to pay at least the interest, Austin. Maybe sell some land."

"No! Not that!" Austin said quickly. Then gloom descended on him. "I've tried to put this all out of my mind, but we've got to face up to it, Marie."

"Maybe we could go to another bank in another place. Maybe in Charlotte."

"If our own bank won't lend us money, why should they lend us money in Charlotte?"

"I know. It was just a thought."

"It's going to take some faith," Austin said. "God will have to help us through this, sister."

"He never fails. He may not come always right when we want Him," she said, forcing a smile, "but He never forsakes those who trust Him."

"What do you think about Charlene and Boone?" Austin asked abruptly.

"I think she's in love with him."

"What about him?"

"I don't know. . . . Good night, Austin."

"Good night, Marie." Austin watched her go then went to his own room, thinking of the enormous debt that had gathered around Hartsworth. He wanted to get angry at his father, who was responsible for a goodly portion of it, but then he thought, *At least he's trying what he's never done before. I can't let myself get bitter. Something will turn up. God won't let us down!*

CHAPTER 20
"STRETCH FORTH THINE HAND"

In early April Boone sat in the rocker at Hartsworth, his feet planted firmly on the floor, listening as Marie, dressed in cobalt blue and ivory, read aloud. From outside the window came the sound of laughing voices, black and rich. Solomon and Alexander, who had helped carry Boone from the wagon in to his bed, were working in the flower garden, and with half his mind Boone was listening to Solomon tell about catching an enormous catfish on a trotline. He smiled at the exaggerated report: ". . . and I tell you that fish was as big as any *man* you ever seed, Alexander! Why, if I had 'nother 'un like that, we could feed this whole plantation for a month!"

"You find Solomon's fishing feats more interesting than this book, don't you, Boone?"

Looking up swiftly, Boone saw that Marie had closed the novel and was smiling at him quietly. "Well, I guess I'm not much for novels."

Marie laid the book down on the table beside her and examined Boone. "Your color's better. I think I'll change your bandage."

"It's all right. I don't need it."

"That's what *you* say. You just hate to be fussed with." Marie rose and carefully untied the bandage. It adhered a little to the raw wound, and he winced. "Sorry," she said, "I'm not a very good doctor." She looked down at the red scar and murmured, "I think it's finally healing up. I believe you're going to have a permanent scar, though." Boone reached up to touch it, and she slapped at his hand. "Don't meddle with that! I think we'll leave it open to the air for a while, and then I'll put some ointment on it and bandage it before you lie down again."

"It itches! I'd like to claw at it!" Boone protested.

"Well, that's all you need to open it again! Now leave it alone!"

Boone grinned at her, his eyes suddenly alive. "You're a hard taskmaster, Marie. When are you going to let me out of this room?"

"Dr. Malone said tomorrow, but you're not going far. Just for short walks."

Marie sat back down beside him, and they both listened to the voices of the men working in the garden. "They sound happy, don't they?" Boone said. "Do you ever talk to them about what it feels like to be a slave?"

Startled, Marie shook her head. Even dressed as simply as she was, Boone noticed she had the gift, as did Austin, of making the poorest of clothing look somehow graceful and right. Her hair was bound by only a single thong, for she had washed it and it was not quite dry. The rich chestnut color gave off glints of a reddish color as the sun struck it, and unconsciously she patted it as she thought about his question. "It's something we've always taken for granted here, up until the war — but we won't anymore. I don't think slavery will last even if the South wins. It's such a bad system."

Boone gave her a curious glance. "What does that mean?" he asked. "You'll just set them free?"

"That's what I'd like to do, and I know many others who feel the same way," she replied, continuing to talk about slavery. Boone, not being from the South, had not seen slavery first-hand. But he had read Harriet Beecher Stowe's *Uncle Tom's Cabin* and wondered if the mistreatment of slaves was as bad as the woman had presented it.

When he brought the matter up, Marie said, "It's very bad, to be honest, Boone. In some places, I mean. It all depends on the owner. None of our slaves have ever been mistreated that I know of. If we sold a slave now, we would be paid in Confederate money, which is worthless. And without selling a slave, we'd have no money to hire labor — which is what we'll have to do once this war is over anyway."

Boone said thoughtfully, "It looks like the South is in a no-win situation. Even if you win the war, slavery's not going to be in existence forever."

"I think that's right."

"Do you worry about the future, Marie?"

For one terrible moment, Marie thought Boone had become aware of the fact that she and Austin had talked about marrying for money. But when his hazel eyes were guileless, she realized he was simply asking out of interest. "Things are very bad, Boone. You can see the place going down. I wish you could have seen it before the war. We can't afford to fix anything now. Cotton's not worth raising, and there's no cash money if you raise other crops."

Although Boone had seen many dilapidated farms and plantations on his search and encountered the hopelessness that existed among many of the planters, he was still disturbed by Marie's attitude of failure. However, he hadn't known how bad it really was until now. Finally, he said slowly, "It's too bad. This is a fine plantation."

"It's been our life, I suppose you might say, Boone. My brothers — Paul and Austin — and I know every foot of it. Paul's now in Alabama, and Austin is in the army. So it's rather ghostly. A lot of memories bring back those days when we were all here and there was no war."

Wanting to change her mood, Boone asked, "Why don't you read some from the Bible?"

Immediately Marie pushed her thoughts away. "You like that better than novels?"

"I never read the Bible much. My people weren't religious."

"That's a shame. Some of my earliest memories," Marie said, "were listening to Mother read the Bible." She opened her Bible and riffled through the pages. "I always liked the story of Zacchaeus. Do you know it?"

"No," he said.

Marie began to read from the book of Luke, chapter 19, her love for the scriptures evident. That puzzled Boone, but at the same time he was drawn to it.

" 'And Jesus entered and passed through Jericho. And, behold, there was a man named Zacchaeus, which was the chief among the publicans, and he was rich. And he sought to see Jesus who he was; and could not for the press, because he was little of stature. And he ran before, and climbed up into a sycomore tree to see him: for he was to pass that way. And when Jesus came to the place, he looked up, and saw him, and said unto him, Zacchaeus, make haste, and come down; for to day I must abide at thy house. And he made haste, and came down, and received him joyfully. And when they saw it, they all murmured, saying, That he was gone to be guest with a man that is a sinner. And Zacchaeus stood, and said unto the Lord; Behold, Lord, the half of my goods I give to the poor; and if I have taken any thing from any man by false accusation, I restore him four-fold. And Jesus said unto him, This day is salvation come to this house forsomuch as he also is a son of Abraham. For the Son of man is come to seek and to save that which was lost.' "

When Marie stopped reading, Boone said thoughtfully, "That's a strange story. He was a short little fellow, wasn't he? Couldn't see over the heads of the people."

"Yes. I've always loved this story," Marie

murmured thoughtfully. "Perhaps because Zacchaeus stands for all the people who somehow get hungry for the Lord."

"I guess I've never had anything like that happen to me."

"I think," Marie said quietly, "that God calls every man and every woman at some point. I was only fourteen years old when I felt the Lord speaking to my heart."

"Were you in a church?"

"I'd been in church all my life, but it happened when I was out in the fields. I was gathering wildflowers and not thinking of God at all, and then suddenly I was thinking about God."

Boone, intently interested, leaned forward slightly. "What was it like, Marie?"

"Oh, it wasn't anything very dramatic. At first I thought it was just something in my mind. I thought of the sermon the pastor had preached a few weeks earlier about a woman who touched the robe of Jesus. She had been sick a long time, and when Jesus came by, she thought, *If I can just touch his robe, I'll be healed.*" Marie smiled and continued, "It came into my head, or my heart, or whatever part of us hears God, that I needed to touch Jesus, too."

"What did you do?"

"I sat down under a big chestnut tree, and

somehow I knew God was there — not just under the tree, but inside my heart. And as I began to think about Jesus dying for the sins of the world, I began to cry." Marie was silent, remembering. Then she said, "I began to pray and asked God to come into my heart somehow — and He did." Her eyes filled with tears, and she dashed them away. Looking rather shamefaced, she took a handkerchief out of her pocket. "Sorry, I didn't mean to subject you to all this."

"That's all right. I can see it was very real to you."

"It still is," Marie said. "From that day on I've been a Christian. That's why I like the story of Zacchaeus, I suppose. He got so hungry for something in his life that he made a fool out of himself by climbing up in a tree. Don't you suppose his friends must've laughed at him? After all, the Bible says he was a prominent man."

"A lawyer or something like that?"

"Probably a tax collector!" Marie laughed. "Can you see one of the government officials here climbing up a tree to see a preacher come to town? Not very likely! In any case, Zacchaeus must have had something happen to him up in that tree."

"I suppose so. You say he offered to pay back everybody he had cheated four times as much as he had gotten?"

"Yes, and that's not like a tax collector, is it? I think the Lord Jesus calls to everyone, but we don't all hear it the same way. Sometimes people are in church. I've been at camp meetings, Boone, when the Spirit of God moved, and I've seen people fall to the ground, struck with the power of God."

"I've heard about that. Dave, a friend of mine, said his great-grandfather was at one of George Whitefield's meetings, back about the time of the Revolution, I think. He told the story so many times, about how whole acres of people fell over. Dave never forgot it. I've wondered about that."

"I think it's far more common for people to just know that God is calling them, and then somehow or other they ask Him into their lives. . . . The last verse is one of my favorites. I think it was the first verse I ever memorized: 'For the Son of man is come to seek and to save that which was lost.' " She put her finger on the Bible and held it where he could see it. "Look, I've underlined what I think is the most important word."

Boone looked and then said with surprise, "You think the word 'that' is more important than the other words?"

"Yes, because I think God wants to save every part of us. Not just our soul, but our body and all that we are. *That* which was lost. Whatever we've lost, God's going to save it for us."

"That's pretty deep for me."

"Maybe I'm oversimplifying, but back in the book of Matthew, in the twelfth chapter," she said, riffling through her Bible to find the place, "there was a man in the synagogue who had a withered hand. The enemies of Jesus wanted to catch Him healing somebody on the Sabbath because that was against the Jewish law. Can you guess what He did?"

"From what I've heard about Jesus, I guess He healed him."

"That's right. In verse 13 He said to the young man, 'Stretch forth thine hand. And he stretched it forth; and it was restored whole, like as the other.' " Marie looked up. "I think God is saying that most of us have problems, and Jesus saw this man's problem as his crippled hand. So He told him to stretch forth the thing that needed fixing, and He healed it. Sometimes there are things in life that are a lot more troublesome than a bad hand."

"How do you figure that? It's pretty bad to have a crippled hand."

"Is it worse to have a crippled mind or a crippled heart, Boone?"

"I — I've never thought of it."

Seeing the astonishment on Boone's face, Marie said, "I've seen so much death since the war started. Our neighbors down the road lost their only two sons in the war, one at Shiloh and one at Fredericksburg. The father wasn't a Christian, and he grew very bitter. I wondered if he'd actually die of grief. But then he was able, with the help of a pastor and some good Christian friends, to hold that grief out to the Lord. Don't you see, Boone? It was as if God were saying, 'Stretch forth thy loss, and I will heal it.' "

"That's asking a lot even of God!"

"I think God's the only One who can heal us from things like that, Boone, and there are other things. Some men are lost in lust and others in drink; some get caught up in making money. Every one of us clings to something."

"You couldn't have had much sin in your life when you were fourteen years old."

"I had enough that I knew I needed a heart change. I was very envious, for one thing, of what other girls had, and I had to ask God to heal that in my own life. . . . Boone, I don't want to preach at you, but Jesus did come to seek and to save that which was lost. You almost lost your life, and I can't tell you how distraught I was thinking about your going out to meet God unprepared."

Boone looked down, unable to meet her eyes. "I had a bad time myself. All I could think of was, if Earl Dillon kills me, I'm lost forever."

"But you don't have to be lost forever, Boone."

"My life's a little more complicated than a fourteen-year-old girl's."

"You know better than that, Boone. Some people don't find God until they're in their sixties or seventies. We all need peace in our heart, and Jesus is the only peace there is."

As Boone listened, he felt a strange mixture of fear and hope. He saw the honesty and the love in Marie Bristol's eyes, heard the certainty in her voice, and knew that he lacked what she had.

"No one can force anyone to become a Christian, though," Marie said. "No one twisted Zacchaeus's arm. He was so hungry for God that he climbed a tree to find someone to help him. I don't know what kind of pain, or grief, or loss was in his life, but when he took Jesus home, a miracle happened inside his heart. And that same miracle — of Jesus coming into your heart — is what every man, woman, and young person needs."

"Jesus Christ is very real to you, isn't He, Marie?"

"He's more real to me, Boone," Marie said, "than this chair I'm sitting in. And that's why I want you to know the same peace."

Shocked at the feelings inside him, Boone knew he could not leave this behind him. The decision would only grow more and more demanding. "Thank you for talking to me, Marie, and for explaining this. I'll — I'll think on it."

"Would you do one thing for me, Boone?"

"Why, certainly, if I can."

"Would you let me pray for you?"

Boone was embarrassed, but he nodded. She began to pray very quietly, "Oh Lord, this is your wandering child, Boone Manwaring. You've known him even before he was born, when he was in his mother's womb, and now I'm asking You, Lord, to increase the hunger in his heart until he has to climb a tree, or stand up before the world, or whatever, in order to find his peace with You through the Lord Jesus Christ. Make this for him more important than anything in life, and I will thank You for it in the name of Jesus. Amen."

Boone opened his eyes and whispered

huskily, "You're some woman, Marie Bristol."

Marie shook her head impatiently. "I'm not much, but I have a great Savior. And one day you'll have that same Savior, Boone."

Austin looked up with surprise to see Charlie Peace, who had entered and stood over his desk. "Well," he said, "this is a welcome relief. What are you up to, Charlene?"

"I've come to go shoppin', and you're takin' me," she said, smiling, dressed prettily in a green dress with matching shawl. "Come along now."

Austin rose with alacrity. "Yes, sir! I mean, ma'am! Anything to get out of this office." He turned to the sergeant who was standing over to one side and said, "As you can see, I have urgent duty. If any of my superiors call, tell them I'm on urgent military business."

The sergeant grinned broadly. "Yes, sir! I can certainly do that!"

Charlie took Austin's arm as they left the War Department. The sun was shining, and she seemed happy. "I've finally decided," she said, "that I've got to do somethin' to pay my own way. I've been like a leech livin' off of you and your people."

410

"Don't be foolish, Charlene! You've been a guest."

"A nonpayin' guest, but I've got a purse full of gold coins, and we're goin' to load the wagon up with everythin' we kin find that will help back at Hartsworth. I talked to Solomon, and he gave me a list of things they need in the forge and some of the equipment that's got to be replaced. Then I want to git some groceries, whatever's to be had here in the way of staples."

Surprised but pleased with her generosity, Austin spent the next three hours escorting her up and down the streets of Richmond. She had driven the wagon in herself, and Austin moved it several times, loading it until the axles creaked.

"I don't think the wagon will hold any more, and you've spent a fortune!"

"Not enough. I want to buy somethin' nice for your mother and Marie." She tugged at his arm, and he laughed, accompanying her into Anderson's Dress Shop. "The first time I came in here," she said as they entered, "I was wearin' buckskins, and I chewed tobacco."

"You didn't!"

"Yes, I did! Just to make Boone and the store clerk, Mrs. Jones, mad. Hello, Mrs. Anderson," she said, smiling at the owner.

"Got to have somethin' very nice fer Mrs. Bristol and Miss Bristol."

Austin enjoyed the buying spree. He watched as Charlie picked out some things for the two women. As she paid for them, she said, "Now I guess we can go." Turning, she smiled graciously. "Thank you, Mrs. Anderson. You've been a great help." Austin could not help but think how much she had changed since the first time he had met her. Her grammar was still sometimes prone to go off course, and when she forgot, she would walk with the open stride of a mountain man. But no one looking at her now would have thought it was the same young woman he had met such a short time before. When they got outside, he said, "Why don't you stay over tonight? We'll go out and get something to eat."

"You know, I believe I will. Maybe," she said with a mischievous light in her eyes, "I kin git my old room at the Spotswood. I had my first all-over bath there, except fer the creek."

Austin laughed aloud, attracting the attention of several passersby. "You do say the most audacious things!"

"I guess a young woman ought not to talk 'bout bathin' to her escort."

"Well, it's not the most common conversation." He looked at her warmly. "You've changed a lot, Charlene."

"If I have, it's because of Marie and you and your mother. I know I still ain't a lady like those two —"

Austin took her hand and kissed it. "I think you're a lady," he said quietly.

Charlie stood there, shocked, for no one had ever kissed her hand before, and she did not know what to say or do. Seeing her confusion, Austin said, "Let's get your room."

It was a fine night for both of them. There was a minstrel show passing through, and Charlie had never seen one. She laughed until her sides hurt, and when they got back to the hotel, she said, "They shore kin play them banjos, cain't they? And how do they think of all them things to say?"

Austin was pleased Charlie had enjoyed her evening. They were now alone in the hallway outside her room. "I guess they say it over and over again," he quipped. "It was fun, wasn't it?"

"You reckon Boone ever went to a minstrel show?"

"I'm sure he has."

"I don't know," she reflected.

Austin plunged in. "I've been wondering about you and Boone, and so has Marie.

How do you feel about him? I don't mean to pry, but it's only natural we'd wonder."

"Well, I think a lot of him, Austin. I guess you see that."

"Do you love him?"

"I–I'm not rightly sure I know what love is. I didn't go in fer courtin' and such up in the mountains."

Her statement bothered Austin. "Does he love you?" he asked quietly.

"I — I don't know." Charlie turned her head away then said swiftly, "Good night, Austin. It was fun going to the show." She slipped inside the door, shut it, and then leaned back against it, thinking about what Austin had just said. *Does Boone really love me? Do I care for him?* She sat down at the desk, turned up the lamp, and, taking her quill, began to write rapidly:

Austin just asked me if Boone loved me, and I sed I didnt know. And then he asked me if I loved him, and I didnt know that either. Austin looked kind of funny when he asked the question, and I dont know what he thinks bout me. It sure is hard tryin to grow up and be a lady!

Malcolm Leighton had come to Hartsworth

with a set purpose, and now he faced Marie out in the scuppernong arbor. The two had come out, at his insistence, to where the spring breeze shook the tender vines, shutting off the view from the house. "I guess I'll get right to it, Marie," he said. "I want you to marry me."

Leighton's bluntness threw Marie off balance. Startled, she knew she could no longer put the matter off. "You've put up with a lot from me, haven't you, Malcolm?"

"It isn't that, but a man needs to know where he stands. I know you think I've been a woman chaser, and maybe I have, but that's all over. I want to get married and start a family." He looked around and said, "I know, Marie, that you've been worried about Hartsworth."

"It's common knowledge," Marie said in an acid tone. "Everybody knows everybody's business in Richmond."

"Your situation's not much different from others'," Leighton said, shrugging. "There's no money, and with this war on, there's not likely to be any. I know how much you love Hartsworth, and I could keep it. The ships have done well, and even if the South loses, I've got enough money to pay off the loans."

"How do you know how much they are?"

"I talked to Keith down at the bank. He

didn't give me the exact amount, of course, but roughly. He let slip what it would take to clear all the paper off this place."

Despondent, Marie knew that Malcolm Leighton had an affection, of sorts, for her, but this was not her idea of romance. So she said at once, "Malcolm, I don't love you as a woman should love a man whose bed she'll share the rest of her life."

Leighton blinked with surprise at her bluntness. "That's coming right out with it," he said. "I know you're an honest girl, Marie, but you've got to be practical. I've already told you I care for you. Maybe you don't love me now, but," he said, smiling and pulling her to him, "I can make you love me. After we're married you'll find out what it's like to be a wife. You'll love me then."

Marie wanted to protest, but he kissed her then. Something in her protested, but at the same time she was thinking, *Maybe he's right. Maybe I could learn to love him.* He was strong, and practically every unmarried young woman in Richmond would have loved to be in her position. But when he lifted his lips and said, "Marry me, Marie," she said, "I think there's more to marriage than a plantation." She thought this might discourage him, but he merely shook his head and insisted. Then finally she said, almost in desperation, "Give me a month."

"All right. One month it is. Are we engaged?"

"No, not even that. We have an *understanding.* In one month I'll give you my answer. I know this seems hard to you, but a woman can't make a mistake about things like this."

Leighton stared at her. "A man can't make a mistake either. I care for you, Marie, and you'll care for me, too. I promise you."

The next morning Boone came downstairs for breakfast, surprising Marie and Marianne, who were already seated. "I think I've been an invalid long enough," he said, taking a seat. "I'll be moving back into town today."

"Don't go yet, Boone," Marianne said. "It's too soon."

"I'm fine, Mrs. Bristol. You're a good nurse. You, Marie, and Charlie have been more than I deserve."

At that moment Charlie entered. "What are you doin' downstairs? I didn't tell you you could come down to breakfast! I was takin' it up to you!"

"I'm afraid I'm going to get spoiled," Boone said. He looked fit in spite of the bandage still around his head. He touched it lightly, saying, "This is all healed up pretty much. It's just so ugly I want to cover it, but I feel I've got to go to town."

All three women protested, but in the end Boone left. Charlie wanted to drive him, and he permitted that. When she dropped him off at the Spotswood, she said, "Why cain't I git me a room here, too, Boone?"

"You're much more comfortable at Hartsworth. I'll be looking around for a place."

"Don't you do too much," she warned.

"I won't."

He watched as she drove back out of town. Then he entered the Spotswood and again signed up for a room. It was a strange feeling, and soon he grew unhappy with the smallness of the room and left to walk the streets. He hadn't thought much of religion before his talk with Marie, but now he was aware of God's presence. He knew for a certainty he'd have to make a decision about what to do with Jesus. *A man has to face up to this matter of salvation sooner or later — and I think with me it's going to be sooner.*

He encountered Clay Rocklin as he walked. Pleased, the colonel said, "Well, you're up and around, Boone."

"Yes, Colonel, I am. I hope I don't meet

Earl Dillon."

"You haven't heard about Dillon?"

"I guess not."

"Well, you won't have to be worried about him. He joined the army. Some kind of a political appointment. He'll be serving in the western theater around Atlanta. He'll have his hands full there, and all the fighting he wants."

"I'm glad it turned out as it did. I'd hate to have his blood on my hands."

Clay studied Boone then said, "Things are happening. We're taking the army up to meet Grant."

"Didn't Marie say that your wife will be having her baby soon?"

Clay's eyes grew cloudy. "That's right," he said. "Although I don't have any choice, of course, this battle couldn't have come at a worse time for us."

After the men talked and Clay moved away, walking rapidly down the street, Boone thought of Austin Bristol. *I'd better go tell him I'm here. Maybe we can see each other.* When he reached the War Department, the sergeant informed him, "Why, he's not here anymore. Just transferred today."

"Transferred to where? To what?" Boone demanded.

"This mornin' he pitched a regular fit, the lieutenant did. Said he wasn't going to shuffle one more piece of paper. Got himself transferred immediately into the Stonewall Brigade. Guess he'll be serving under Colonel Rocklin. Got to be kind of a family affair. Colonel Rocklin, his boy, his uncle, and now his cousin."

"What about you, Sergeant?"

"Well, I'm goin', too. As a matter of fact, I think about every able-bodied man who can carry a gun's gonna go. It's gonna take that to stop Grant, from what I hear. Word is, he's got a hundred thousand men, and we don't have half of that. We'll stop 'em, though. The Lord will be with us."

Boone told the burly sergeant, "Wish I was a praying man. I'd pray for you all."

"Never too late to start," the sergeant replied.

Leaving the office, Boone noticed the excitement in the air. When he reached his hotel, he sat outside and watched the activity — wagons rumbled up and down the street carrying supplies, and men moved quickly. Somehow he felt left out, like a man without a purpose. Finally that night he went to bed, and early the next morning he saw the Army of Northern Virginia leave. He heard the trumpet and saw flags flying high as the troops began their march north-ward. The men, some of them in ragged uniforms but looking determined, formed a serpentine line that headed out from the camp. He saw Clay at the head of the brigade and looked for Austin, then finally caught sight of him walking alongside the troops.

"I wish I were going!" he whispered. "But it's none of my fight." He left town, riding restlessly as he struggled with his own heart. He'd heard Marie quote one of the fathers of the church once, saying, " 'Man has a hollow spot in his heart — and will never be content until it is filled with God Himself.' " Now as his horse's hooves pounded along the road, he said, head down and weary with life, "Guess I'll have to get that spot filled if I ever want any kind of peace."

When he went to bed that night, sleep would not come. Finally, he arose, feeling depressed, as if he had no hope or aspira-tions for the future.

Then just as dawn began to color the skies, he knelt beside the bed and cried out, "God — I'm not even fit to pray to You, but I've got to find some kind of peace!"

CHAPTER 21
SACRIFICE IN THE WILDERNESS

Ten miles west of Fredericksburg, Virginia, lies a region known as "the Wilderness." It had been called this long before the Civil War, and in the early eighteenth century German colonists had tried to tame this wild section of country and failed. They'd cut timber to shore up mine tunnels, planked roads, and chopped wood to fuel iron-smelting operations, then abandoned their endeavors. The forest grew back quickly, so by the time Ulysses S. Grant brought the Army of the Potomac out of Washington to face the Army of Northern Virginia, led by Robert E. Lee, the country was nothing but an impenetrable second-growth woodland.

Battles had been fought here before, for in May 1863 Lee and Stonewall Jackson had fought the battle of Chancellorsville, defeating General Joe Hooker in a savage and confused battle. At this spot Stonewall Jackson had been shot in the faint light of dusk by his own men and had died on May 10 from his wounds. Now, almost a year later, Robert E. Lee's army was drawn up near Orange Court House just west of the Wilderness. It straddled a broad turnpike that led to Fredericksburg, and it was on May 5 that these two rival armies marched into the heart of the Wilderness and began a fight that actually lasted to the end of the war, since it proceeded southward until Grant's army was knocking at the gates of Richmond.

The Army of Northern Virginia had 65,000 men, led by Generals Richard Elwell and James Longstreet. Grant's Army of the Potomac was 120,000 men, led by staunch commanders such as Hancock, Warren, and Sedgewick. Meade was ostensibly in command of this particular army, but Grant, knowing that Robert E. Lee and his Army of Northern Virginia were the real adversary, came personally. So in all truth the battle of the Wilderness, and those following in rapid succession, was fought by Grant against Lee.

Grant's advantage in numbers would count for much less in this theater, due to the impenetrable thickets. His artillery would be nullified, for few guns could be used over this terrain. Neither could masses of men be marched rapidly from one place to another through the undergrowth. As the two commanders eyed the spot that fate had chosen for the battle, both of them must have been apprehensive, for it would not be a classic battle. Here there would be no long lines of men neatly arranged in regiments and brigades, but small, struggling groups, broken up and fragmented, hidden from even their own lines by the thickets, vines, and saplings that clawed at their faces.

The collision point came promptly on May 5. Advancing Confederates were met by skirmishers of Grant's army on the turnpike, and from that point both Lee and Grant began to feed men into the furnace of war, much as men would feed wood into a stove to make the fire burn hotter. The battle was almost impossible to control. No man could see more than a few yards in any direction, and movements ahead of him might be his own fellow soldiers. In truth, many men were killed by those wearing the same uniform. Soon the rattle of musketry filled the Wilderness, and the roar of cannons added a solemn refrain as the men fought, almost blindfolded by the terrain. General Hancock said later, after the battle, that men who tried to make a charge could not tell where their enemies were until they ran full tilt into them. The generals knew where the battle lines were only by listening to the sounds of musketry, which was not very helpful, for musket fire made a staccato series of explosions throughout all the battlefield. Often whole divisions broke up into fragments, running into flanking fire. Gaps in the opposing line suddenly appeared but went unexploited because nobody could see them.

As the sun rose and fell, the battle was fierce. In many cases, men fought hand to hand, clubbing each other with muskets, stabbing with bayonets or even with pocketknives. The Battle of the Wilderness was, for all practical purposes, not one battle but hundreds or even thousands of battles where men stalked blindly and bled their lives out into the red clay. The wounded lay where they fell, for no medical assistance could be brought into the furnace of battle. As the night came on, many died alone, crying out for their mothers or to their God, and some simply and silently stepped across the threshold into death. Perhaps the most terrible part of the battle occurred when the dry leaves caught fire, sparked by musket fire, and a wall of flame began sweeping across the Wilderness. Men fled in panic, more frightened of being burned to death than of being shot down by their enemies.

But the wounded could not flee. Those who were too badly wounded to walk had to lie there, watching the flames licking the dry timber and knowing that their doom was sealed. After the war was over, many hardened soldiers would say, "I saw many hard things during the war, but nothing was harder than to hear the screams of wounded men as they were burned to death in the Battle of the Wilderness."

Clay Rocklin ducked behind a tree as the roar of musket fire shook the earth around him and yelled, "What's your report? I can't hear!"

The lean lieutenant, who had a bloody rag wrapped around his forehead, said, "It's General Longstreet, Colonel. He's been shot."

"Was he killed?" Clay asked rapidly.

"No — no, sir. Badly wounded, and by our own men."

"What else is happening?"

"General Ewell wants you to move your brigade over to the left. He thinks he sees an opening in the line there."

Clay's eyes swept the battlefield that was like no other he had ever seen, looking for

426

an opening in the dense woods. "Report back and tell him we'll move forward, but it will be slow work."

"Yes, Colonel."

As soon as the courier turned to make his way through the thickets, Clay turned to Major Tom Merrick, saying, "Orders from General Ewell, Major. He says go forward. Over to our left." Then he added, "General Longstreet's down. Not dead, but badly wounded."

Merrick's blue eyes fastened on the colonel. "We can't spare him, can we?"

"I suppose somebody will have to step in his place, but I don't know who it will be. How many men have we lost?"

"Hard to say, Colonel. We haven't got reports back from down the line, but it hasn't been cheap. When do you want to move forward?"

"You go down that side of the line, Major. I'll go down this one. We've got to move together as much as possible. You have a watch?"

"Yes, sir!" Merrick pulled out a large silver watch. "Belonged to my grandfather."

The two men compared times, and Clay said, "We move out in exactly thirty minutes. Tell the men to try to stay together."

"Yes, sir!"

Clay moved down the line as musket balls whined through the air, some of them ricocheting off trees and crying like a banshee, the most unnerving sound of all. Clay came upon the third company, where his son Denton crouched behind a log, looking over into the smoke-filled woods. "Dent, we move forward in thirty minutes!"

"Yes, sir!" Denton turned to look at his father. His face was already scarred from an earlier wound, but his eyes were bright with battle. "You're not going forward with the line, are you, sir?"

"You can't lead from behind," Clay said, grinning. "Keep your head down, son." He wanted to say more but knew that Dent understood. Moving on down the line, he spoke to the men, encouraging them. When he reached the edge of the regiment's line, he looked at his watch. "Still fifteen minutes to go." He traversed the line of battle again and moved the other way, running into Major Merrick. "Just checking, Tom. I'll say a word to the boys."

As he made his way along, speaking to as many of the men as he could, he ran into Claude Bristol.

"What are you doing here, Claude? I left you back at headquarters!"

His face blackened with powder, Bristol

said, "I thought I'd come and help the boys out a little bit."

"You don't need to be here, Claude."

"Don't send me back, Clay," Claude said quickly, looking down the line. "Austin's down there. I wanted to show him I'm good for something."

"You put me in a bad position, Claude. Marianne would hate me if you got yourself killed."

"No, she wouldn't." Claude Bristol's mouth tensed. "As long as we've been married, Marianne's been waiting for me to do one thing that was unselfish. I've gotten this far. Let me go the rest of the way."

Clay hesitated. He knew Claude was not in fighting condition, that he was soft from easy living, but then, so were many of the other men. But after studying Claude's face, he said, "You stay with me, Claude. We'll go along with the line together."

"Yes, sir!"

Clay moved down the line and found Austin, who was peering into the thick smoke. Turning around, Austin grinned. "A little different from my usual job, Colonel."

"You watch yourself."

"You, too, sir." He glanced down the line at his father, an odd expression in his eyes. "You're not letting him go, are you?"

"He'll be with me," Clay responded.

From down the line, Claude winked at his son. "A little warm work for an old man."

"You shouldn't be here, Father," Austin yelled down the line, then moved toward his father so he could hear his response.

Claude did not answer. "I wish you weren't going in, Austin. I haven't said this before, not as I should, but I've been very proud of you and Paul." He put his hand on his son's shoulder and squeezed it warmly. "I'm praying God will spare you in this battle and that you'll become a better man than I ever was."

Austin started to reply, but there was a lump in his throat. Then his father was gone, striding after Clay Rocklin. Austin turned back, tears in his eyes. He dashed them away, trying to focus his mind on the battle that was to come.

Clay studied the hands on his watch, and when the time came, he called out, "Charge! Stick together as close as you can!" This was the last command he was able to give to more than a handful of men. Then the brigade moved forward through the tangles into the very teeth of the enemy.

Clay had intended to stay back, but within ten minutes after the brigade moved forward, it was hard to tell where "back" was.

All around him the fury of battle surged. He saw men drop silently to the earth; others kicked and screamed. Clay fought blindly, but finally, as the sun began to go down, he was miraculously reached by a messenger with word to fall back. He lifted his voice, saying, "All to the rear! Everyone to the rear! Withdraw slowly!"

The withdrawal took some time, but only when they were back out of the immediate range of the guns of the enemy did Clay have time to check their losses. His heart bounded with relief when he saw Denton stride over, his face grim as he said, "We lost a lot of good men."

"Have you seen Austin?"

"No, he was on the other side of the line, wasn't he?"

"Yes. I'm going to pull the men together. You help Major Merrick."

For the next hour Clay searched vainly for Austin and Claude. Already he could hear the screams of the wounded as the fires, which had been reignited, swept over the battlefield. The sound grated on his nerves, and he was relieved when he came face-to-face with Claude.

"Have you seen Austin?" Claude asked. "Is he safe?"

"I can't find him. Come on. Get back to

the rear."

Claude hesitated. "You go on, Colonel. I think my boy's out there. I'm going to get him."

Clay snapped, "You can't do that, Claude — Claude, come back here!" He shouted this last, for Claude had plunged back into the Wilderness. Clay took two steps forward then realized he had the entire brigade as his responsibility. He called one more time to Claude then shook his head and turned back.

As the musket fire diminished, the blaze from the trees and dead leaves grew louder, and Clay could not keep from looking with agonizing anxiety toward the furnace into which Claude had disappeared.

"God help them! Bring them out!" he whispered then turned to his duty.

Austin had crawled as far as he could after being shot in the upper part of the leg. He did not know if the bone was broken or not, but he feared so. Standing was impossible. He had already fainted twice when he tried it, and crawling was no better. Casting his eyes back over toward the wall of fire that approached him, he gritted his teeth and, using his arm and his good leg, tried to drag himself along.

Five minutes later he passed out again. The world around him seemed to be nothing but heat, and the roar of the flames dimmed his senses. He knew he had no hope, and he began to pray that death would come quickly. A great sadness came to him as he realized there were so many things he would never do now. Then with startling abruptness, he saw Charlie's face. He was delirious and weak from loss of blood, but her face was as clear and sharp as a portrait in a gallery.

"Son — son, are you all right?"

Austin awoke to find himself staring up into his father's face.

"I've got to get you out of here. Can you sit up and get on my back?"

"Pa, what are you doing here?" Austin had not called his father "Pa" since he was a small boy, but now it came to him easily. "You can't do it! Leave me here!"

"Not likely! Come on. It isn't far, but we've got to get away from the fire."

Claude hauled Austin to a sitting position and then stooped before him. As best he could, Austin threw his arms around his father's neck.

"Hang on, son!" Claude Bristol said, plunging forward as the vines grabbed at his feet and slashed at his eyes. He shut

433

them and reeled on blindly, thanking God that He had led him to his boy. He gasped, "Hang on! Almost there!"

Austin was aware of very little. He felt the jolting as his father staggered across the tangled ground and held on as best he could. The sound of the fire muted, and then he heard the sound of musketry, for the battle was still going on in various parts of the Wilderness.

Finally, Claude, gasping for breath, looked up and said, "There's some of our men! We've made it, son!"

Austin heard his father's labored breathing, and then there was a sudden sound off to his left that sounded like a giant had exhaled his breath. He felt his father's body jerk and then fall to the ground. Agony shot through Austin as his leg struck the ground.

"Pa, are you hit?" Passing out from the pain in his leg, it was some time before Austin was aware of gray-uniformed men standing over him. Then he saw Clay Rocklin.

"Pa! He got shot — artillery shell!"

"I know." Clay helped Austin sit up. "It's pretty bad. He's still alive, but I don't think he can make it, Austin."

Austin turned his head and saw his father lying on his back. "Let me speak to him."

Clay nodded to Dent, who was there, too.

434

"Hold him up, will you, Dent?"

The two wounded men, father and son, were facing each other then, their legs out in opposite directions. Austin was supported by Clay while Dent Rocklin held Claude up. Reaching out, Austin touched his father. Seeing the blood that stained the left side of his uniform, he knew there was nothing to be done. "Pa!" he cried out, seeing Claude's eyes flutter then open.

"Son — you're all right." Claude Bristol's face was pale. "I'm glad — that you'll be the man God wants you to be."

"Pa, you saved me! I'd be burned alive if it hadn't been for you!"

Claude Bristol smiled then. It was a gentle smile, almost as if he were in a drawing room back home. He reached out his hands, and when Austin awkwardly embraced him, his arms went around his son. He whispered, "Tell your mother, at last I did something she can be proud of."

Austin held his father tightly. Tears of anguish ran down his cheeks, and he said huskily, "I love you, Pa!"

"That gives me great pleasure," Claude said, his eyelids starting to close. "Goodbye. Tell your mother I loved her — to the end." And Claude's arms fell lifelessly to his sides.

Clay watched as life passed away from Claude Bristol. His eyes met Dent's, and then Clay put his hand on Austin's shoulder. "He was a brave man, Austin. You must always be very proud of him."

Austin shut his eyes as Dent lowered his father to the ground. Then he said softly, "I will, Clay — and Mother will be, too!"

Chapter 22
A Soldier Comes Home

"I wonder who that can be." Marianne Bristol looked from her position at the dining table, and her eyes narrowed. "I don't believe I know that man."

Last light had come, that hour between daytime and darkness when the world begins to grow murky. The Bristols had postponed the evening meal until almost eight o'clock. "I don't know him either," Marie said. She got up and walked to the window, peering out into the gathering darkness. "He's an officer, but I don't remember him from the regiment."

Charlie and Boone sat beside each other to Marianne's left. As they waited for the visitor to be announced, Boone thought, *Charlie's changed so much.* Then, shifting his gaze, he looked over at Marie. The night before, as he and Marie had walked along the garden pathways, he'd asked her finally if she intended to marry Malcolm Leighton.

She had simply said, "Malcolm and I have an understanding." The words didn't satisfy him then or now, for he knew he loved Marie.

"A Lieutenant Bates be here," Ketura announced, waiting at the door for her instructions.

"Have him come in, Ketura."

"Yes, ma'am."

"I don't believe I remember any lieutenant. Maybe I did meet him. There were so many of them."

Marianne watched as the young lieutenant came in, his uniform dusty. "Lieutenant Bates, ma'am, of Colonel Rocklin's brigade," he said nervously.

"Good evening, Lieutenant," Marianne said. "You have a message from my husband or son?"

Lieutenant Bates shifted his feet then said, "Perhaps I could speak with you alone, Mrs. Bristol."

"Is it bad news, Lieutenant?" Marianne asked, rising to her feet. "Is it about my husband?"

"I'm afraid it is, ma'am."

Marianne straightened, and Marie came to stand beside her. "Has he been wounded — or is it worse, Lieutenant?"

Bates dropped his eyes. "I'm afraid," he

said, then lifted his gaze, compassion in his eyes, "your husband has been killed. I'm — I'm most sorry, ma'am."

Marie uttered a choking cry, and her mother took her in her arms. Marie's body shook, but Marianne Bristol was dry-eyed. She would keep her tears for later. She waited until Marie's sobbing had slowed, then said, "Thank you for coming, Lieutenant. It was kind of you."

"Well, ma'am, I have another message." Again Bates seemed embarrassed. "It's your son, Lieutenant Austin. He's been wounded."

"How bad is it?" Marie asked, turning to face Lieutenant Bates.

"I didn't get that word. The messenger just came in. We lost a lot of men, and the Yankees did, too. But General Lee is moving the army southward toward Richmond. It won't be good for the wounded."

Marie exclaimed, "We've got to know! Is that all the word you have, Lieutenant Bates?"

"I'm afraid it is, ma'am." Bates looked sorrowful. "It's going to be pretty bad. Grant came down with the biggest army, I guess, that's ever been in this country. When the Army of the Potomac got whipped before, they turned and ran back to Washington, but not this general! They're already calling him 'Butcher' Grant. He doesn't mind losing ten men to our one because his men can be replaced, and ours can't." Bitterness tinged his reply. "I've got to get back, ma'am. I'm very sorry."

"Where will my son be?" Marianne demanded.

"Hard to say. They'll be bringing some back in wagons, those too bad off to walk."

Marianne hesitated then asked, "Will you take some refreshments, Lieutenant Bates?"

"No, ma'am." Bates stopped at the door. "I'm sorry about your men," he said then wheeled and left. His boots echoed on the hardwood floor of the foyer; then the door slammed, and horse hooves began to clatter.

"We've got to do something, Mother!" Marie said, her voice weak and hands clasped together.

"There's nothing we can do, I'm afraid, except pray."

Then Charlie spoke, her dark eyes glowing and determination in her lips. "We'll go git him and bring him home."

"Why, you can't do that!" Marianne exclaimed.

"Yes, I kin! If I kin find my way 'round in the mountains with bears and panthers, I reckon I kin find one man."

"I think I might do it, Marianne," Boone said. Then, turning to Charlie, he added, "But you're not going."

"That's what you think!" Charlie snapped back. "I'm going with you or without you, Boone Manwaring! Now make up your mind!"

For a moment Boone considered running away and leaving her, but he knew Charlie Peace well. He understood that if he did leave without her, she would go alone. There was no use arguing against her deep streak of stubbornness. "All right," he said, "we'll leave tonight."

"Why, you can't travel in the dark!" Marie said, astonished that Boone had suggested such a thing. But her grieving heart warmed toward the young woman and Boone.

"I reckon we kin. Full moon tonight," Charlie said. "Come on, Boone, let's go!"

Marianne hugged Charlie, her heart filled with anxiety for her son and grief for her husband. "Charlene," she said, "I couldn't ask you to do this. But if you must go, God go with you," she said.

Charlie looked at the older woman with love. "Don't you worry. We'll bring 'em both back." Then she said abruptly, "I'm gonna shuck this here fancy dress."

"Wear anything you want," Boone said as Charlie ran out of the room and headed upstairs. "We'll do the best we can, Marianne. I'm sorry. I'd grown very fond of your husband. . . . I'll go out and see to the horses."

"You'd better take the wagon to bring Claude home, and you can make a bed for Austin, too."

"All right, I'll see to it."

Boone left the house. He rounded up Solomon and soon had the wagon hitched with two fine horses. Solomon, upon hearing the news, said sorrowfully, "Po' Mr. Claude! He done just found his way, and now he's gone to be with the Lord." He patted the horses on the rump. "These are the best hosses in the state of Virginia. You be careful now, Mr. Boone. Don't you be gettin' yourself shot — and take keer of Miss Charlie."

"I'll do that, Solomon. You watch out for things here."

Turning toward the house, he was surprised to see that Marie had stepped outside. When he went to meet her, he said, "Words don't mean much at a time like this, but I know a little about what you're feeling — since I've lost both my parents."

"Thank you, Boone." Marie had gained

some control, but she knew sorrow was beginning to form within her. "He was doing so well, and now we've lost him."

Boone said nothing. Aware of her trembling, on an impulse he put his arms around her. She surrendered to his embrace, tears streaming down her cheeks. "It's mighty tough," he murmured to her softly. "We'll find Austin and bring him back."

"I'll be praying for you, Boone."

Boone held her a moment longer then drew back. "I've got something to tell you, Marie. Two nights ago I got down on my knees and asked God to do whatever needed doing in my life." He related his experience then said, "I guess it was my time to find God, Marie. After you read the verse about Jesus telling the man with the withered hand to stretch out his hand," he continued, wonder touching his eyes, "something changed for me — like it did for you when you were fourteen."

Joy coursed through Marie as she touched his cheek. "I'm so happy for you, Boone —" And then Charlie's voice was heard, and he released Marie quickly.

Wearing a dark green traveling dress and carrying a suitcase, Charlie's eyes narrowed as she took in the fact that Boone and Marie were standing together. But she merely said, "Are we ready?"

"I guess so, Charlie." He went around, climbed into the wagon, and picked up the lines as Charlie jumped up to sit beside him. Turning back to Marie, he said, "I guess you can pray for all of us."

"I will," Marie murmured. She watched as the team stepped smartly out at Boone's command and then stood in the darkness. The sun had gone down completely now, and finally, as the wagon disappeared, she felt her mother's presence. She put her arm around her, and they made their way back to the house to begin their vigil of grief.

Boone drove the team without speaking for some time. Then he said, "About that place we looked at, Charlie — I haven't forgotten it."

"It don't matter now, Boone. I reckon if God wants us to have a place, why, He'll let us know."

"We'll look at it again after we get all this done."

"All right, Boone — if you say so."

Boone pulled the weary team to a halt in front of the white frame house. Both Boone and Charlie were exhausted, for the trip had been hard. They had changed horses at one point the day before to give the team a rest,

444

promising to exchange again when they made their way homeward. Charlie's shoulders were slumped, and he knew she had slept practically not at all during the rapid trip from Richmond. Now he said, "I'll go in and see if this is the Payton place." He stepped down from the wagon and stretched, then walked on stiff legs to the front door. It was two o'clock in the afternoon, and the sun was still high in the sky. As he approached the porch, an elderly woman dressed in black came out. "Mrs. Payton?" he asked.

"Indeed. I'm Mrs. Payton." The white-haired woman examined Boone. "Have you come to see about the lieutenant?"

"Yes. I'm Boone Manwaring, Mrs. Payton." He turned and said, "Charlie, this is it."

Mrs. Payton watched as Charlie slid off the wagon with one swift move and walked toward her, eyes expectant. "Is he here?" she asked.

"This is Charlie Peace. We've come to see about Lieutenant Bristol. We ran into a cavalry unit that said you had kept him here."

"Yes. I didn't think he could stand the jolting of those wagons they took the wounded off in." Her eyes clouded. "Poor boys!"

"Is he all right?" Charlie asked. She had done little but think of Austin on the journey, and the strength of her compassion had surprised her. She had thought over and over again of the times he had been with her, his kindness and wit, and especially of the time he had kissed her.

"He's doing very well. You didn't hear any details?"

"No. Only that he was wounded," Charlie said. "Is he hurt bad?"

"Not as bad as some," Mrs. Payton said. "I had three of 'em here, keepin' 'em, but two of 'em died already. I had my man bury 'em out there in the family cemetery."

"Can we see him?"

"Of course." Charlie and Boone followed Mrs. Payton inside the house then walked down a short hallway to an open door. Charlie stepped in, her eyes sweeping the room. It had a bed, nightstand, chifforobe, and several pictures of family members on the wall. Austin lay on the bed, eyes closed, a brightly colored quilt covering his lower body. Charlie moved toward his side and took his hand. "Austin, can you hear me?"

Austin Bristol's eyes fluttered then opened. He seemed confused for a moment and licked his lips before saying, "Charlene — ?"

"Yes, it's Charlene, and Boone's here with me."

Austin turned his head with some effort to see Boone, who had come to the other side of the bed. "Hello, Boone," he said, his voice raspy. "Didn't expect to see you two here."

"Manwaring and Peace Ambulance Service." Boone squeezed Austin's shoulder gently. "We've come to take you home."

Austin's eyes sought out Charlie. "Father's dead," he said, sadness in his feverish eyes.

"I know," Charlie said. "I'm right sorry. He was real nice to me."

"He died getting me out of a fire. The woods were on fire, and I was going to be burned up. He came in and carried me out of there. Just as he got me free, a shot caught him. He — almost made it." Austin shook his head feebly. "We'd just gotten to know each other, and now I've lost him."

"He ain't lost. He's with the Lord Jesus," Charlie said, smoothing his hair back from his forehead. "You're gonna be all right. We'll take you back to Hartsworth."

"We've got to take Father back, too. Mrs. Payton has been wonderful. She had her husband make a fine coffin. I've been trying to think of a way to get him home. He wanted to be buried at Hartsworth."

"We'll start in the morning at first light," Charlie said.

Boone asked Mrs. Payton, "How's the leg?"

"It's better now. There won't be any infection, I don't think, if you keep it clean. Can't tell if the bone was hurt. I don't think it was broken, though. At least that's what the doctor said. You going to move him tomorrow?"

"If we can," Boone said. "He'd feel better at home, and so would his mother and sister."

"I think if you go real slow, it will be all right, but don't bump him around." Mrs. Payton hesitated then added, "I lost a boy at Chickamauga. My only son. I thought if I could help with this one, it might save some mother the grief I've had."

"We're right grateful to you, Mrs. Payton," Charlie whispered. "I'm sorry 'bout your boy."

"I'll fix you a place to stay tonight and have my man take care of your team," Mrs. Payton said.

Aware that Austin was still clinging to her hand, Charlie squeezed it. "You'll feel better when you get back home." She saw, however, the grief on his face and knew he was thinking of his father. There was little

448

one could say at a time like this, but she was conscious of a tremendous lift in her own spirit. *He's alive,* she thought, *and he's gonna be all right.* Puzzled, she realized, *I didn't know I cared so much fer him. It woulda killed me if he had died!*

The next day Boone made a comfortable bed for Austin in the wagon, then thought, *He can't ride with the body of his father beside him.* When he mentioned this to Charlie, she said, "Oh no, Boone, that wouldn't be right! We'll have to get another wagon!"

Buying a wagon and another team presented no difficulty, for a neighboring farmer had one he was willing to sell, especially for gold coins. Boone placed Claude Bristol's coffin in it and covered it with a tarpaulin, and by ten o'clock they were ready. They gave their deepest thanks to Mrs. Payton, with Boone saying, "Mrs. Bristol will be writing to you. I can only give you my thanks, but you have done a great service for a fine family." Then Boone, driving the wagon bearing Claude Bristol's body, led out, followed by Charlie with Austin.

Boone took the easy route, traveling carefully so that Austin would not be jostled. When they stopped at noon for a quick meal, Boone said, "We can stop if it gets too bad, Austin."

"No," Austin said, "I'm fine." He was indeed looking better, with more color in his cheeks. He ate a little of the food Mrs. Payton had fixed for them, drank a great deal of water, and then went to sleep.

They drove steadily through the afternoon, pausing that night beside a stream. Boone fixed a fire, and Charlie cooked a hot meal. She made a dish called Hoppin' John out of rice, beans, and bacon, seasoned with salt and pepper, and also corn bread. Now she sat beside Austin in the wagon bed. As she helped him prop himself up, perspiration came to his forehead as the pain in his leg grew sharp. He made no protest, however, but ate hungrily.

"That's good for you. You got to keep your strength up," Charlie said, smiling. She was sitting across from him, her back braced against the wagon side as she ate her own food. "You look better."

Although he was light-headed, Austin was feeling better. "I'm lucky," he said briefly, glancing toward the wagon where his father's body rested. "So many of our fellows never made it out of the Wilderness." As darkness fell over the land, an owl drifted toward them in the still air, drawn perhaps by their activity. Austin took another drink of the water. "I can't tell you what it means, Charlene, your coming to get me like this. I thought I'd have to bury Father here in a strange land. Didn't look like there was any hope of getting him back home. How did you hear about us?"

Charlie related how Lieutenant Bates had come, and when she had finished, Austin asked curiously, "You were the one who decided to come after us, weren't you?"

Charlie flushed. "I reckon I was. Somebody had to do somethin'."

Austin smiled. "It's just the sort of thing you'd do. You're the only woman in the world, Charlene, who would come into the middle of a battle to get a friend who'd been hurt. I don't see how I can ever thank you enough for it."

"Why, you don't have to do that, Austin."

"I guess I do. When someone does something for us, we have to thank them, don't we? And I know Mother was worried about me."

"Yes, she was, but I don't think I could've got you if Boone hadn't been with me."

"Good man."

"He sure is. Never even hesitated 'bout comin' to git you. When he looked like he was gonna leave without me, we almost had

451

a fight. I told him I was comin' whether he went with me or not." She laughed. "I guess I'm a stubborn woman."

"Good thing for me you are," Austin said, knowing he felt something for her that he could not identify. "I guess I'd better lie down. I'm getting a bit feeble."

"Let me help you." Charlie maneuvered him back onto the mattress they had brought, and when he drew his breath in sharply once, she put her hand on his cheek. "I'm sorry. I didn't mean to hurt you, Austin."

"It's all right." Austin lay back, his head on a pillow. Charlie bent over him, trying to adjust him to a more comfortable position. Seeing the brightness of her eyes, even in the darkness, Austin suddenly reached up and without thinking gently touched her face. "I guess I'll have to tell you how much I admire you, Charlene." He pulled her head forward and waited, and then she lowered her face and kissed him softly on the lips.

"I guess any woman would have done it," she said, straightening up and pulling the coverlet over him. But the touch of his lips had stirred her. "I'll be up if you need anything."

"All right, Charlene. Good night — and

thanks for the kiss. Nobody's done that for me since I was a child. Mother used to come in every night to kiss me and say a prayer over me."

"I guess it was right forward of me." Kneeling beside him, she touched his cheek. "You're going to be all right, Austin. We'll get you home."

He said sleepily, "Sit by me awhile, Charlene."

Charlie hesitated for a moment then sat down, bracing her back against the wagon side. By the starlight she could see that his face was no longer tense but relaxed and young looking. Her lips broad and maternal, she stroked his hair. In the background she could hear the fire crackling and once glanced over to see Boone sitting in front of it, staring into the blaze. As she sat in the wagon with Austin, she silently compared the two men. Boone had come out of nowhere and had been her strength, and she felt a gratitude, an affection, an admiration for him for that. If it had not been for Boone, she would not have had a place to turn. She had thought herself in love with him, but now she realized she felt more at home with Austin. He knew how to make her laugh, and he had sensed her apprehensions and had gone out of his way to make her feel wanted and accepted. There was a goodness and a gentleness in him that she had not often seen in a man in her limited experience. As the silver light of the stars outlined his face, she knew she could no longer deny her love for this man.

Ketura came running in, crying out, "Miss Marianne, they's here!"

Marianne leaped up from the stool in the kitchen. She had been sitting there waiting for the bread to finish baking, but now she ran outside. When she saw the two wagons, her heart swelled with both joy and grief. She waited while the drivers stopped and Charlie met her, saying, "Austin's fine! He's gonna be all right, Marianne!"

"Thank God! Bring him into the house. I've got the bed all ready." She ran quickly over to the wagon and, discarding dignity, climbed up into the bed. She kneeled down beside Austin, who was watching her. "My boy," she whispered, "you're home."

"I'm sorry about Father. I'll have to tell you all about him. He saved my life, Mother."

Marianne glanced involuntarily at the other wagon. "I'm glad you're both home, son. I want to hear everything."

Solomon and two other servants carried

Austin in gently, as if he were a child. As they did, Marie came outside to stand beside Boone. "Did you have much trouble?" she asked. It was not what she wanted to say, for now that Austin and the remains of her father were actually home, she felt a great debt to this tall man and young woman who walked beside Austin as he was carried into the house. She wanted to speak what was in her heart, but somehow could not do it.

"Not too much. Austin was lucky. A lady took him in and cared for him."

"I — don't know how to thank you, Boone."

"No need for that." His hazel eyes searched hers. "It's been hard for you waiting and not knowing. We came as fast as Austin could take it."

"It has been hard," Marie said, feeling as if a great weight was lifted off her. When she saw how tired Boone was, she said, "I know you're exhausted. You need to go to bed."

Boone, however, was thinking of their trip. "That Charlie is some young woman. I don't think she slept five hours since we left here, especially on the way back. She's cared for Austin better than any nurse."

"She's a wonderful woman. I know you're

proud of her."

Her comment surprised Boone. "Why, I suppose I am. Not many young women could have done that."

The two stood there feeling ill at ease, both somehow thinking of Marie's "arrangement" with Malcolm Leighton. In the last few days, Marie had grown even more confused. In between the mixed feelings of elation that Austin was home safely and the grief that her father was dead, she had begun thinking of Boone Manwaring as a woman thinks of a man. She wanted to be comforted, and she thought, *If he just touched me, I think I'd collapse and fall into his arms — but he won't do that. He'll expect me to go to Malcolm with my grief, and I can't do that.*

Straightening, Marie said, "I'll go see what I can do for Austin."

As Boone watched her go, Solomon came to stand beside him. "You done fine, Mr. Boone. You and Miss Charlie done real good."

"Thanks, Solomon," Boone said, watching Marie as she left. "Find me a horse. I'm going back to town."

"You ain't gonna stay?"

"No," Boone said. "You take good care of Mr. Austin." Then he moved toward the

456

stable, wondering if the next day would bring some wisdom that he seemed to lack. Ten minutes later he rode out of Hartsworth, exhausted, weary, but strangely satisfied over the task he and Charlie had accomplished.

Claude Bristol's funeral was memorable, in spite of the many funerals that had already occurred during the war. The church was packed as Rev. Eli Samuelson delivered the sermon. An old friend of Claude Bristol's, Rev. Samuelson was honest in his evaluation. He spoke of the hope of the Resurrection and then finally on a personal note said in a ringing voice, "Claude Bristol, like all men, made his mistakes, but he died in a fashion that many of us would envy. He died saving the life of his son. The scripture says, 'Greater love hath no man than this, that a man lay down his life for his friends.' If we change the word 'friends' for 'son,' we have the crowning triumph of our brother's life." His eyes took in the family in the front pew. Insistent on attending, Austin was in the aisle with his wounded leg stretched out on a chair. Now his eyes glowed at the reverend's words. "As long as there are Bristols in the world, they will remember this man's sacrifice," the reverend finally concluded.

Afterward, when the family got back home, Austin was put to bed. The trip had not done him any good, and Charlie said to Marie, "He's got fever. I hope that leg don't git infected. We're gonna have to nurse him real good, Marie. I can't bear to think of anythin' happenin' to him."

Marie put her arm around the young woman. "You're good, Charlie," she said.

"No, I'm not good!" Charlie said with surprise. "It's just that — well, I'm right fond of Austin."

"And I think he's fond of you. He watches you all the time."

The remark confused Charlie, and she turned away, unable to answer. She went at once to Austin's room, picked up a basin, filled it with cool water, and began to bathe his face. "You done too much," she said quietly. "But you had to go; I know that."

"I'll never forget him, Charlene," Austin said softly. "He wasn't always the kind of father I admired, but he made up for it at the last."

Charlie nodded. "I reckon your pa and my pa are both with Jesus now. That's a good thought, ain't it, Austin?"

"Yes. Real fine." Austin moved restlessly. "I'm going to miss him. Just like you miss your father."

Charlie continued to mop his brow. "You lie quiet now. You're gonna take some real nursin' to git over this. I think you've got some fever, and we don't want infection in that leg."

But as his temperature shot up over the next few hours, Charlie grew fearful. She began to pray, *God, don't let nothin' happen to him now — not after all of this!*

CHAPTER 23
A TIME TO EMBRACE

The campaign that had begun on May 5, 1864, in the Wilderness transformed itself into a dance in which the two armies moved in almost minuet precision. General Lee had hoped that the Army of the Potomac might retreat at the end of such a hard-fought battle — which had been the pattern in the years gone by. But for the first time during the war, Grant's hard-bitten army that had suffered so many losses *advanced* instead of retreating to Washington. Their object was Richmond.

When Lee pulled his forces out of the Wilderness, one of his aides asked him where they were going. "To Spotsylvania," he replied. When asked by the officer, "Why there?" Lee responded, "Because General Grant will be there. It is the right thing to do militarily." Lee had a respect for Grant that he never had for the other generals he had faced, and now he moved his Army of

Northern Virginia toward Spotsylvania. On the night of May 7, General Grant also headed toward Spotsylvania, which was in the direction of Richmond, but when he arrived there he found General Lee's Army of Northern Virginia squarely across his path. Stubbornly, Grant threw his men against the emplaced Confederates and, during the next twelve days, mounted many assaults. The Union losses were horrendous. The Confederate losses were much less, but they had no replacements and so the lines grew thinner and thinner. There were too few men left in the South to refill the ranks.

Grant stopped at Spotsylvania as predicted, pulled out, and again launched a movement toward Richmond. Once again, at the North Anna River, he found Lee in front of him. Grant swung by his left flank, only to find Lee waiting for him again. At Totopotomoy Creek a frustrated Grant kept doggedly at the task. Richmond lay to the south only a few miles, and only the thin ranks of the Army of Northern Virginia lay between him and the trophy that could mean the end of the Civil War.

Charlie carried the tray into the room where Austin lay propped up in bed. He shook his head and said grumpily, "How long have I got to stay in this bed?"

"Until I tell you you kin git out!" Charlie said emphatically, putting the tray down. "Do you want to feed yourself, or shall I do it?"

"I'm no baby!" Austin growled. He flexed his leg upward, bending it, and made a slight grimace. The pain was not as severe, indeed had been growing less severe every day. But the two weeks that he had been cared for by Charlie had been hard ones. The wound had gotten infected, and his fever had risen. Day after day had passed, and always it seemed that when he awoke Charlie was there beside him. Sometimes, of course, it was his mother or Marie, but nearly always Charlie was there. As he cut up the meat on his plate, he asked, "Don't you ever get tired of waiting on me?"

"I never had a baby to take care of," Charlie responded, "and that's about what you've been."

Austin looked up quickly, a sharp retort on his lips, but then laughed. "I've been a lot of trouble to you, haven't I, Charlene?"

"I don't mind." Charlie sat down and watched him eat. "You know, I like it when you call me Charlene."

"Do you now?"

"Yes, it always makes me feel — I don't

know — more like a woman."

"Beautiful name."

Charlie thought of the days just passed when she'd been frightened that he might die. She had found out what it meant to live with praying people. Her mother had been a woman of prayer, but she, Marie, and Marianne had prayed not only individually but together, joining hands. Now as he sipped milk from a tall glass, she said impishly, "You got milk in your whiskers."

Austin grinned and picked up his napkin. "I never had whiskers before. I think I'll grow a beard all the way to my chest."

"No, don't do it. It wouldn't look right on you."

"How about a mustache? Would that be all right?"

Charlie smiled. "I suppose that would be all right. You already got a start on one. Maybe I ought to git my scissors and trim it."

"How big a mustache? One that droops down, or just a little one?"

"Not a droopy one. I'll take keer of it. I used to trim Pa's whiskers all the time. When he got sick once, I even shaved him a time or two."

When he finished eating, she removed the tray. "I think maybe you could git up out of that bed and sit in a chair for a while."

"Good. I'm sick of this bed!"

Pulling the rocker up close to the bed, Charlie helped him lift his leg over. She had changed the bandage earlier. "The wound's 'bout all healed up."

"You're a good nurse, Charlene." He put his weight on her, his arm falling over her shoulders. She was firm and strong beneath his grasp, and he groped with his free hand for the chair, then sat down in it with a sigh of relief. "That feels so good — just to sit on a hard chair!"

"You'll be walkin' soon, and before long we kin go ridin' again."

"Good. I won't feel like a man until I'm able to sit on a horse." He enjoyed the sensation of sitting up and finally commented, "You know, it's strange how little things can mean so much. When I was lying in that fire and it was coming toward me, I was pretty sure I wasn't going to make it."

"What did you think 'bout when you thought you was goin' to die?"

"I thought about you."

Charlie's eyes flew open. "No, you didn't!" she exclaimed.

"Well, I thought about Mother, and Marie, and about how I wished I'd made it up better with Father. But when it got closer, all of a sudden —" He stopped and looked at her. "Your face — your eyes and hair, all black and curly — came to my mind. Even when the fire was creeping up." He dropped his head and said, "You know, Charlene, I think one of my biggest regrets was that I wouldn't see you again."

"That's sweet of you, Austin," she said huskily. What he had said pleased her, made her feel warm.

"Nothing like that ever happened to me before. . . . You know, Charlene, you're the easiest young woman to be with."

"Me? Why would you say that?"

"Well, with some people there's always a reserve, especially between women and men. But with you, I'm always at ease." He looked up. "Why should that be, I wonder? I guess it's because," he said, answering his own question, "you're the most natural person I've ever known."

Charlie ducked her head. "I'm glad you feel that way, Austin. I've — I've grown right fond of you."

"Have you? That's good to hear." Feeling suddenly better than he had since his injury, he said, "Get the scissors. Let's trim this mustache; then you can let me beat you at another game of checkers."

■ ■ ■ ■

In late May Marie realized Malcolm Leighton was restless. He came to see her and fidgeted all through the visit. They went outside to where daisies, hyacinths, and roses dotted the garden with yellows, blue-purples, and reds and sat down on a bench.

"Something's wrong, Marie," he said bluntly. "You haven't been yourself lately."

"I suppose not. Since losing my father, I suppose, I haven't been in very good spirits. I'm not very good company for you, Malcolm."

"Have you been thinking about our engagement?"

"I hate to say so, but I really haven't. When Austin got so sick, it took most of my time, that and the loss of Father. I haven't thought of anything very much."

"Well, that's understandable. I'm sorry to intrude, and I don't want to pressure you." He rose abruptly. "I'll give you a little more time; then maybe you can give me your answer."

"Perhaps. Come back tomorrow, Malcolm."

After he left, she went back into the house and about her work. But she said so little that finally Marianne asked, "Marie, don't you feel well?"

"Oh yes. I feel very well."

"You're exhausted. I think all of us are." She sat down and folded her hands, then gave her daughter a more careful look. "Malcolm didn't stay long," she commented.

"He wants to announce our engagement."

"Oh! What did you tell him?"

"Nothing really. Just that I've been too upset over Father's death and Austin's sickness. . . . I feel so confused," she said finally.

"About Malcolm?"

"Yes. It seems so — so *businesslike*. It's not his fault. He's — well, he's not very romantic."

Then Marianne spoke what had been in her heart for a long time. "Be very careful. It's a dangerous time for you. You've had a great loss, and the burden of the plantation and financial pressures are terrible. I know you and Austin both have thought about losing this place. . . . Are you marrying Malcolm simply because he has money?"

"I'd hate to think I'm doing that, but it's a factor."

"Then I'd say don't commit yourself. There should be nothing at all like that between a man and a woman."

467

Relief broke free in Marie Bristol. "That's what I've been thinking," she said. "Malcolm's a charming man, fine looking, and so many young women have tried to catch his attention. I suppose I should be flattered that he wants me."

"He's all those things, but marriage is more than that. You know that, Marie. At least I hope you do."

Knowing she had a big decision to make, Marie got up. "I think I'll go for a ride." She left the house and rode the hills and paths of the surrounding countryside all afternoon. But even the beauties of the May season could not drive away the heaviness in her heart. Finally, she drew up on top of a ridge that overlooked Hartsworth. She caught her breath as her eyes took in the emerald lawn, the fine old house with its stately beauty, and the outbuildings. For a long time she stood there, on the precipice of her decision, as her horse chomped at the fresh grass. Finally, she shook her head in a gesture that was almost defiant. Looking down at her home, she spoke aloud. "I'll hate to have to leave this place, but a marriage is more than a plantation." Then, impetuously, she swung up on the horse and rode rapidly down the road that led toward her home. When she arrived, she dismounted and handed the reins to Solomon. Then she walked into the house and stood in the middle of the foyer, seeing it through different eyes. When she finally walked into the parlor where her mother was sitting, she said, "Mother, I have something to tell you. . . ."

"What's the news on the fighting, Marie?" Austin asked three days later. He was standing with the aid of a cane as his sister entered the house. She'd been talking to the man who delivered mail — at least whatever mail came through in these troubled times.

"He says there's been a terrible battle at Cold Harbor," she said. "Can you stand up like that? Does your leg hurt?"

"Cold Harbor? Why, that's just outside of Richmond!"

"I know. We're surrounded now. Grant lost five thousand men in one hour."

Austin took this in then said quietly, "It'll be over soon. It can't last long."

"I hope so. Oh, I hope so!" Marie said.

She turned to leave, but he detained her. "Marie?" When she looked at him with a questioning air, he asked, "What about Leighton?"

Marie hesitated. "I ended our agreement. It wasn't really an engagement," she said,

469

smiling wryly. "It was all wrong from the beginning. I hate to think I've been so uncertain."

"You've told him?"

"Yes, day before yesterday. He took it pretty well, I must say. Not at all like a man dying of love."

"Are you sure about this, Marie?"

"Yes. I feel like a load's been taken off my back. We might lose this place, but I couldn't marry just for money."

"I'm glad you did it, sis. I could tell you didn't care for him." Then he said shyly, "I've got news for you."

"What is it, Austin?"

"Would you think I was crazy if I said I'd fallen in love with Charlene?"

Marie kissed him, exclaiming joyfully, "I think it's wonderful, but what about Boone?"

"What about him?" Austin asked.

"I've always thought Charlie was in love with him. She's practically said so a couple of times. Have you said anything to her?"

"No, but I'm going to right now. I like Boone, but if he wants Charlene, he'll have to fight for her."

"He might do that," Marie said, a strange expression crossing her face. "I don't know what he feels."

She left the room with Austin staring after her, wondering what his sister was thinking. Then he hobbled into the kitchen, where he asked Blossom, "Where's Miss Charlene?"

"She's out there in the garden, Mr. Austin."

Austin limped out of the house to where Charlie was trimming the arbor. "Charlene," he said, "do you have to work all the time?"

"Not all the time." Charlie stepped down from the stool she was on, put down the shears, and gave him a critical look. "You're walkin' too much on that leg."

"Well, let me give it a rest. Come on and join me."

They sat down on a bench that had been painted white but now was peeling. "Needs paint," he said. "Maybe I'll do that tomorrow."

Charlene was wearing an older dress, and her hair was bound up with a green bandanna. She pulled it off now, tossing her hair and letting her curls fly free. Looking at him curiously, she said, "Did Marie tell you 'bout her and Malcolm Leighton?"

"I just asked her. I'm glad that's over."

"I am, too. She didn't care fer him. Do you know what I think? I think she's in love with Boone."

Startled, Austin was silent. Then he said, "I don't know how Boone feels."

"If you ask me, I think he keers fer her," Charlie responded. "Watch him sometime. He never takes his eyes off her."

Not knowing what to say, Austin let his hand drop to Charlie's shoulder. "I'm sorry, Charlene."

Astonished, Charlie turned to face him. "Sorry? Don't you like him? You wouldn't want him to be married to your sister?"

"Why, I wouldn't mind that, but — Marie and I both thought you cared for him — as a man, I mean."

Charlie could not meet his eyes for a moment. When she looked up, her voice was quiet. "I reckon I did keer for him like that at one time, or I thought I did. He was so good to me, bringin' me here and takin' keer of me after Pa died. I couldn't help but admire him for that."

"Do you love him, Charlene?"

"No — not like you mean." Charlie dropped her head again, for her heart was full. She had decided that Austin was the man she loved, but she didn't know how to tell him.

Suddenly Austin reached out his arm and pulled her toward him. He said abruptly, "Charlene, I've got to tell you something, and it's not going to be pleasant."

"What is it, Austin?" she asked, not taking her eyes off his face.

"A man does a lot of things he's ashamed of, and one of the things I'm most ashamed of is — well, at one time I thought about marrying for money."

"I know that, but you didn't. You never married Ida."

"Because she had sense enough and wisdom enough to see that it would never have worked. I can't say what I would have done otherwise, and that's not a thing a man likes to admit."

Aware of his arms holding her, Charlie said, "Austin?" But she found she could not ask the question.

"What is it, Charlene?"

"I don't know how to talk to men," she said haltingly. "I never learned how to court or nothin' like that, but I want to know somethin'. Will you tell me the truth?"

"Yes. What is it? Ask me anything."

Her lips soft and vulnerable, her eyes dark and intense, Charlie asked, "Do you love me, Austin?"

Stunned by the simple question and the courage it had taken for her to ask it, Austin said urgently, "Yes, I do. That's what I wanted to tell you, Charlene. You've got money and I don't, and that's galling to a man. But I have to tell you that I do love you. I'd love you if you didn't have a penny." Then he pulled her closer and kissed her.

As Charlie put her arms around Austin's neck, she felt peace, joy, and exhilaration. Drawing back after the lengthy kiss, she said, "Let's don't ever think 'bout money. It won't be mine or yours. Everythin' will be ours. Just love me, Austin. That's all I ask."

"I'll always do that, Charlene," he said, embracing her again. As they kissed again, he knew the exultation of finding what he'd been searching for all his life.

CHAPTER 24
"WHITHER THOU GOEST"

For Clay Rocklin the struggle to keep the Union army out of Richmond never ended. Each day he arose, mustered his men as best he could, buried the dead, tended the wounded, and then advanced to the line across which the Confederate army faced the Army of the Potomac.

The struggle that had begun at the Wilderness had not stopped for a single day. Skirmishes took place constantly, and Sheridan's Union cavalry was constantly in movement, countered by the Confederate cavalry. Always before, the Confederate cavalry had been superior, but now missing its great leader, Jeb Stuart, and worn down to a mere shadow of what it had been during its days of glory, the cavalry was almost paralyzed.

The worst day of fighting had come at the battle of Cold Harbor on June 3. Hoping to eliminate his adversary in one crushing blow, Grant sent his men forward against the Confederates, who were firmly entrenched. In one hour, six thousand men in blue were wiped out, and afterward Grant was to say, "The attack of Cold Harbor was the worst mistake of my military career." In the North men were shouting, "Relieve Butcher Grant!" But in the White House Abraham Lincoln hung on grimly. He knew the Confederacy was tottering, and though he walked the White House at night alone, a tragic figure mourning the death of so many young men, he refused to relieve Grant.

Over the South gloom was thick, and in the North men and women began to hope that the end of the terrible war would come. But all knew by now that there would be no real victory. Too many men were dead and wounded for there to be rejoicing.

Boone had come to Hartsworth often, mostly sitting with Austin. The two were both chess players and carried on some lively battles. So when Charlie met him the day after Austin had told her of his love for her, her eyes were shining.

"What are you so happy about?" he asked, handing his lines to Solomon. "You look like it's Christmas."

"I guess it is, for me anyway. Cain't you guess?"

Boone stood there baffled. "I don't guess I can. What is it?"

"It's Austin, Boone! He loves me!" She watched almost anxiously until his face broke into a broad smile; then she threw herself into his arms. "We're goin' to git married, Boone! It's goin' to be like Pa always wanted. We'll stay here at Hartsworth and use the money from the gold to pay the bank off."

Boone hugged Charlie then stepped back. "That's the best news I've had in a long time, Charlie. You're getting a mighty fine man, and he's getting a fine girl, too."

"Come on! He wants to talk to you!" She took his hand and tugged him into the house. Soon Boone was seated in the study, where Austin held hands with Charlie, both faces beaming with delight.

"I guess this catches you by surprise, Boone," Austin said, looking fondly at Charlie. "I can't believe it's really happening."

"I can," Charlie said, her face wreathed with smiles. She patted Austin's arm. "We're goin' to take the money Pa found and pay off all the bills, ain't we, Austin?"

Frowning slightly, Austin shrugged. "I

hate to be a beggar, but it's what Charlene wants."

"Of course it's what I want!" Charlie said indignantly. "This is goin' to be my home!"

"I think that's wonderful," Boone said. He listened as the two talked happily about the future, then asked, "Will you go back to the army when you get healed up?"

"I don't think there'll be any army left. It looks like the end, Boone," Austin said.

"The news is pretty bad. Have you heard from Clay?"

"No, but Dent came by on leave. He said all the Rocklins are fine. None of them got killed, but he was worn down. They're about fought out."

Boone shook his head. "What will happen, Austin?"

"Nobody knows. Lincoln is pretty well hated in the South, but he'll be the best friend the South ever had after the war ends. He's said many times 'with malice toward none.' He wants to put the country back together again."

"You know, I believe he might be able to do it," Boone said. "Everything I hear about that man is good."

Marie came in at that moment, and Boone rose to greet her. "Hello," he said. "How are you today, Marie?"

"I'm fine, Boone." Conscious of a certain stiffness between herself and Boone, Marie wondered if Boone was displeased with her for her semi-engagement to Malcolm Leighton. Both of them were quiet while Charlie and Austin did the talking. But from time to time Marie would glance at Boone, who was watching the happy pair. Finally, she rose and said, "You'll be staying for supper, Boone?"

"I guess I will, but this may be the last time."

"The last time?" Marie said. "What do you mean?"

"I guess my job's about done," Boone said, addressing Charlie. "You've got what your pa wanted, Charlie, and I can see he would have been very happy, he and your mother. I never was sure it would work. It's kind of like a fairy tale." He smiled then but seemed sad. "I'm glad for you, Charlie."

"But where are you goin', Boone?" Charlie asked plaintively. "Why cain't you stay here?"

"Guess I'll go back to the sea. Thought I might make a cruise to the South Seas. Never been to some of those islands. I hear they're pretty nice."

Marie suddenly left the room.

Watching her go, Charlie said quickly,

"Don't leave now, Boone."

"I think I'll have to, Charlie," Boone responded.

Austin asked, "When will you be pulling out?"

"Tomorrow, I think."

"I hate to see it. I'd hoped you would settle around here."

"Things come to an end, Austin," Boone said thoughtfully. "Never know what the next day will bring."

The rest of the day went badly for Boone. He felt out of place, and Marie scarcely looked at him during supper. *I've got to get away from here and try to forget her,* he thought. But he promised he would not leave before seeing them all again.

Later that night, after Boone left, Charlie went to Marie's room and knocked on the door. "Marie, are you awake?"

The door opened, and Marie said wearily, "Yes, I'm awake. What is it, Charlie?"

"I thought I'd come and talk to you 'bout Boone."

Marie bit her lip. "You'll be sorry to see him go. We all will."

"I don't think you ought to let him go," Charlie announced. She had stepped inside the room and shut the door and now turned to Marie with a determined look on her

480

face. "I guess you've taught me a few manners, but back in the mountains I got pretty much in the habit of sayin' whatever came to my mind, and now it comes to my mind that you're in love with Boone."

Marie shook her head quickly. "There's nothing to that."

But Marie's answer was too fast, so Charlie continued, "I don't think that's right. You're goin' to let him git away, and you'll be sorry the rest of your life."

"He doesn't care for me."

"I think he does. He watches you all the time. When you're not lookin', he keeps his eyes fixed on you. And when he talks 'bout you to me, I kin tell he feels somethin' for you."

"It's just friendship, Charlie. I know you mean well, but there's nothing to say. Boone's a fine man, and I admire him. I'll always be grateful for what you and he did for my father and for Austin, but that's all there is to it."

Charlie argued for a while then left, wondering if the situation was hopeless. As she moved down the stairs, she heard a knocking at the door and arrived there at the same time as Marianne.

Marianne took one look at the man outside and said, "Is there trouble, Eli?"

"Yes, ma'am, I guess, in a way." The tall slave shifted his feet nervously. "It's Miss Melora. Her time's done come, and she ain't doin' good. Mr. Clay ain't home, and Miss Melora sent me over to see if you would come and be with her while she has her baby."

"Of course! Tell her I'll be there as soon as I can get there, Eli."

"Yes, ma'am. I'll sure tell her."

"I'll go with you," Charlie said.

"No, you'd better stay here with Austin." She looked at Marie, who, hearing the commotion, had come down the stairs. "It's Melora," she said. "She's having her baby and it's not going well. We'd both better go."

"All right, Mother. I'll be ready in five minutes."

The two made record time to the Rocklin plantation, which was only a few miles away. When they arrived, they found that their doctor had come from Richmond. When he answered the Rocklins' door, he looked surprised. "Well, I didn't expect to see you ladies this time of the night!"

"How is Melora?"

"Why, she's fine," the doctor said, his eyes twinkling. "She fooled us, though. Sent Eli over to get you because it looked like a difficult delivery, but it wasn't."

"You mean the baby's already born?"

"That's right. Both of them."

"Twins!" Marie gasped.

"Yes, a boy and a girl. I don't know what she's named them. You can go see them if you want to."

The two women hurried into the bedroom, where they found Melora, her black hair framing her pale face. She was holding both babies, one in each arm, with an expression of love that Marie and Marianne would never be able to forget. Melora had loved children all her life, and now she had her own. "The Lord gave me a double blessing," she said, her voice clear but the lines of strain still on her face. "This is Jonathan, and this is Ruth."

Marianne and Marie went to either side of the bed, each taking one of the babies. Marie moved the blanket back and said, "She's beautiful!"

"Yes," Melora said, pride in her eyes. "I wish her father could be here."

Marianne traced the silky cheek of the other new arrival, Jonathan.

Melora watched as the two women held the babies, thinking of Clay. She knew he might be fighting for his life at this very moment, but she was a woman of tremendous faith. She felt that God had promised her Clay would be spared.

Melora soon drifted off and slept soundly the rest of the night. When she woke up just before dawn, Marie was sitting beside her holding Ruth in the crook of her arm. Jonathan, over in the cradle, was awakening, and soon the cries of both babies filled the room.

"I guess it's feeding time," Marie said, smiling. She brought both babies to Melora, thinking she'd never seen a more beautiful sight. "You're a happy woman, Melora. You've got two beautiful children and a fine husband."

"Yes. God has been good to me."

"It wasn't easy, was it? Did you love Clay all those years you waited for him?"

"I think I loved him," Melora murmured, "from the time I first saw him. I was just a child. He had been hurt in a hunting accident, and Jeremiah Irons had brought him to our house. I took care of him. I was just a little thing, but I bossed him terribly."

"It must've been hard all those years, knowing you might never have him."

"It was hard, but I believed God was going to do something. I didn't know what, of course." Melora looked up from the two infants. "I've been meaning to talk to you, Marie. I've been thinking so much about you these last few days, and I wanted to ask you how you feel about Boone."

Instantly Marie became evasive. "I — I thought I cared for him once, but he doesn't care for me."

"He hasn't told you that."

"Well, no. Of course not."

"Has he ever kissed you?"

"Yes." She had not forgotten the strength of Boone's arms nor the tumult in her heart, and now she couldn't face Melora's eyes. "I do care for him, but he doesn't care for me," she confessed. "Besides, he's going away."

"He came by here yesterday to say good-bye. We talked a long time. I think you're making a mistake, and so is he. He told me about how you led him to Jesus. When he speaks of you, there's something in his voice. And I can take one look at you, Marie, and tell you'll never forgive yourself if you let him get away."

"He's the one who decided to leave!"

"He thinks you don't care for him. I could tell from what he said." Melora lifted her voice. "Don't be a fool, Marie! Go to him! Tell him you love him!"

"Why, I can't do that!" Marie said, aghast.

"Why can't you do it? You do love him, don't you?"

"Yes," she said softly, humbly. "I love him."

"Then don't miss out on what God has for you. Go tell him."

Marie was as confused as she had ever been in her life. In truth she had thought more than once of telling Boone of her feelings, but she'd been raised to think a man should speak first about such things. She bit her lip. "You mean — right *now*?"

"I mean this morning!"

Realizing that if she missed this chance she'd never forgive herself, Marie said courageously, "All right. He'll probably laugh at me, but I'll do it."

"He won't laugh. Come back as soon as you talk to him."

"I will." She left Melora, but as soon as she was outside, she began to doubt the wisdom of what she had made up her mind to do. Then, shaking off her fear, she said, "Eli, hitch up my buggy. I'm going into Richmond!"

Boone had packed his few belongings and now stood looking out the window. He was unhappy, feeling somehow that he was making the biggest mistake of his life. He stared blankly outside, not really seeing the crowd below, but wondering where he would go.

The sea was always open, and he had tried to put a good front on it, but he had no desire to go to the South Seas nor to become a sailor again. The spell of the land was on him, and he had failed utterly to convince himself that going back to his old life would bring him peace.

A tap at the door interrupted him, and he sighed. As he opened the door, he said, "Marie!"

"Can I come in, Boone?"

"Why, of course." Stepping aside, he asked, "Is something wrong? Has Austin taken a turn for the worse?"

"No. Melora had her babies last night. Twins — a boy and a girl."

"Why, that's wonderful! Clay will be thrilled, I expect."

"Melora named them Jonathan and Ruth. They are beautiful babies, Boone."

"Sit down, Marie."

"No, I can't." Now that she was here, Marie wondered if she had the courage to go on. But his eyes were fixed on her, so she thought, *Well, I'll be a fool, then.* Aloud she said, "I can't let you go, Boone, without telling you something. You probably won't want to hear it, but I've got to say it anyhow."

"Why, I think I'd like to hear anything you have to say, Marie."

Taking a deep breath, Marie said, "Austin and I talked about marrying for money. Both of us thought it might work out. You knew that, didn't you?"

"I guess so. You couldn't do it, though. Neither could Austin. You have better judgment."

"Do you hold it against me, Boone?"

"Why, of course not!" Boone was astonished. "What would make you think that?"

"I thought so many things," Marie said, unable to meet his eyes. She walked to the window and felt him come up behind her. "I wanted so badly to hold Hartsworth for the family, and then I saw I was wrong about that. And I thought you cared for Charlie — that you were in love with her."

Boone turned her around, his hands clasping her shoulders. "There was never anything like that. She's a fine girl, and she and Austin are very much in love."

"I know that now. Oh, I've been such a fool! In the school I went to, young ladies were carefully prompted on how to speak to men, but I'll say what's in my heart. I — I love you, Boone."

Boone Manwaring had expected anything but this. He blinked with surprise as she looked up at him, eyes pleading. When he didn't answer, she said, "Never mind,

Boone. I didn't expect you to love me, but I think when a woman loves a man, he ought to know it." She tried to move away, but his hands tightened, and he began to smile. "Boone?" she whispered. "Is it with you as it is with me?"

Instead of answering, he gathered her in his arms, bent over, and kissed her. And Marie Bristol knew then, from the hunger in his lips and the pressure of his arms, that she had done the right thing.

When he lifted his head, Boone said, "I've loved you for a long time, Marie, but I was mixed up, too. I still am, I guess. I don't have a place, but I know one thing. Wherever I am, I want you to be there."

"Do you want to go back to sea?"

"No, I never really wanted that! What I'd like to do is stay here." He smiled then. "Maybe you can teach me how to raise pigs."

Amused, Marie caressed his cheek. "I think you and I can do more than raise pigs," she said, then grew serious. "It's going to be hard. The war will be over, but it won't really be. It'll take years for the South to recover."

Boone loved the smell of her perfume and the soothing touch of her hand on his cheek. As he pulled her even closer, he said,

"Whatever I do, as long as you're with me, it'll be fine." He leaned forward, and just before his lips kissed hers again, he said, "We're going to have a fine marriage and seven or eight children."

When Boone released her from his kiss, her eyes danced. "We'll have to talk about *that,* Boone Manwaring! Now how does it sound?"

"How does *what* sound?"

"Why, didn't you know women always experiment by putting their first name with the last name of the man they intend to marry?" She looked thoughtful and tapped her cheek in mock seriousness. "Marie Manwaring."

"It sounds wonderful to me," Boone said. Then he laughed aloud and, seizing her, swung her around. "Come along, woman; we're going to make our announcement to the world! The future Mr. and Mrs. Boone Manwaring are ready to be recognized!"